Prelude

JoAnn Durgin

ISBN: 978-0-9864076-0-4

All Scripture contained within is from the New American Standard Bible. Copyright © 1960, 1962, 1963, 1968, 1971, 1972, 1973, 1975, 1977, 1995 by The Lockman Foundation. Used by permission.

Text set in Garamond

Cover Design by Lynnette Bonner of Indie Cover Design
   (www.indiecoverdesign.com)

From the Author

~~♥~~

Dear Readers,

Prelude is the love story of Samuel J. Lewis and Sarah Jordan, the parents of Sam Lewis, Jr., the core character in The Lewis Legacy Series. If you've read the first book in the series, *Awakening*, you might recall that Sam and Sarah are featured near the end when their eldest son brings someone very special to meet them in their Houston home.

The events in *Prelude* begin when Air Force Captain Lewis returns home to small Rockbridge, Texas, in the spring of 1962 after an absence of eight years. Six years older than Sarah, Sam is surprised to discover the pigtailed neighbor he used to tease and call "Tomboy" has grown up into a lovely and fascinating woman who challenges him at every turn. Thus begins the enduring romance of the couple who establishes a lasting legacy of faith and love for the Lewis family.

This novel is unique in that my hero and heroine have known one another for years, and it is also my first attempt at writing what is now considered historical fiction (I prefer the term "modern historical"). *Prelude* has been a fun journey as I've revisited the styles, fashions, music, cars, popular catch phrases, as well as other aspects of the early 1960s, an exciting yet sometimes turbulent time in our nation's rich history.

While *Prelude* can be read as a standalone novel, it's my hope this story will be enlightening to readers of The Lewis Legacy Series. Sam and Sarah's story lends insights into the background, character traits, lives and career choices of four of their six children whose own love stories are told in the following books in the series: Sam, Jr. (*Awakening*, Book 1), Catherine (*Abide*, Book 7), Will (*Pursuit*,

Book 8) and Carson (***Assurance***, Book 11, the final book in The Lewis Legacy Series).

Rest assured, dear readers, I will never fully let go of my TeamWork crew. They are part of me, and I will always carry them in my heart. Many of the characters from this series will make fun appearances in my next series, The Wellspring Series. You never know when one or more of the original crew will show up! Set in Louisiana, this next series will introduce you to a new cast of characters in an offshoot ministry of TeamWork Missions.

I dedicate this novel to my lovely eldest daughter, Sarah, my "old soul" who fully appreciates the history and cultural aspects of the era in which this novel is set.

Many Blessings,

JoAnn Durgin
Matthew 5:16

Books currently available in The Lewis Legacy Series:

Prelude (A Prequel)

Awakening
Second Time Around
Twin Hearts
Daydreams
Moonbeams

More adventures to come!

Enchantment (coming in 2015)
Abide
Pursuit
Roundabout
Underground
Assurance

Theme Scripture Verses
in *Prelude*

Sam

Therefore I am content with weaknesses,
with insults, with distresses,
with persecutions, with difficulties,
for Christ's sake; for when I am weak,
then I am strong.
2 Corinthians 12:10
(NASB)

And we know that God causes all things
to work together for good to those
who love God, to those who are called
according to His purpose.
Romans 8:28
(NASB)

Sarah

Delight yourself in the Lord;
And He will give you the desires of your heart.
Commit your way to the lord,
Trust also in Him, and He will do it.
Psalm 37:4-5
(NASB)

Your word is a lamp to my feet
And a light to my path.
Psalm 119:105
(NASB)

Chapter 1

~~♥~~

On April 24, 1962, U.S. Air Force Captain Samuel Joseph Lewis came home to Rockbridge, Texas, reportedly to stay. What a pity.

The townspeople lined both sides of Main Street, awaiting the first glimpse of their returning military hero. Sarah Jordan smiled at the excitement rippling through the lively crowd.

"What a beautiful day for Sam's homecoming." Squinting in the bright sunlight, she shielded her eyes with one hand. A perfect spring day—clouds floated by in a pale blue sky and a light, warm breeze stirred the Crepe Myrtle trees soon to burst into glorious, multicolored bloom.

Standing beside her, Tess sniffled and nodded. Reaching into the pocket of her uniform, Sarah pulled out a tissue and handed it over.

"Thanks. I can't believe Sam's finally home. To stay, I mean. Never thought I'd see the day, but I'm so glad." Tess carefully dabbed the tissue beneath her eyes.

Slipping her arm around her slightly shorter sister, Sarah gave Tess a quick hug. Not to discount Sam's honorable service to his country, but why would a free-thinking man—one who'd seen the world and experienced all life has to offer—*purposely* choose to return to their little town?

Even at five foot ten, Sarah had to lift on her tiptoes in order to see over the heads of a group of high school boys standing on the sidewalk in front of them. Noting her dilemma, Donald Marcum motioned to her and stepped aside to make room.

"Thanks, Mr. Marcum." Sarah stepped to the edge of the curb with Tess beside her. She nodded to Jewell Marcum, Donald's pregnant daughter-in-law. "How are you, Jewell?"

The pretty mother of two young children appeared tired but otherwise healthy. "Ready."

"There's Captain Lewis! I see him!" A little boy jumped up and down, waving his arms. "The car just turned the corner!" Wild clapping, cheers and whistles erupted.

Moving one hand over her heart, her pulse racing, Sarah's breath caught with anticipation. Overcome with emotion, she wiped away a tear as she spied him. Sam sat on the back of his friend Charlie Sorrel's red Corvette convertible, waving and smiling. Judging by the ladies of all ages flocking around the car, his easy smile and blue eyes charmed them the same as they always had.

Sam. The ridiculously tall teenager who'd moved four houses down when she was ten and he was sixteen, two months older than Tess. Almost from the start, he'd teased Sarah as she imagined an older brother would do. A boy who'd tinkered with old airplane engines with his dad in their garage until all hours. The boy who collected every stray animal he found wandering around town, determined to find it a good home. The teenager who'd worked alongside his father, the president of Rockbridge Savings & Loan, learning the banking trade after school and on Saturday mornings— when he wasn't perfecting his finesse on the football field.

And now, Sam was a military veteran at the ripe old age of twenty-seven. Would he be the same fun, teasing guy as she'd known before? More cynical? Less optimistic? Stronger in his faith or sad and disillusioned? According to rumor, he'd served in covert military operations in the escalating conflict in French Indochina. Four years in active service to his country—active combat or not—was bound to change a man. Sam had seen the world while she'd rarely ventured outside of Rockbridge, much less outside of the Lone Star State.

Sam lifted his hat, waved it in the air, and then put it back in place as the car inched farther down the street. His hair was cut military short instead of its former curl-over-the-collar style. His shoulders were broader and they filled out his dark blue dress uniform quite well. Sam's parents, Catherine and Joseph Lewis, proudly beamed from the backseat of a second car driven by Mayor Silas Richards. They waved and acknowledged the well-wishers who called out their names.

The townsfolk had given Sam a similar send-off before he left to play football for the Longhorns at the University of Texas in Austin. He'd been the only graduate in his high school class to attend college. After two years at UT, Sam transferred to the Air Force Academy then based out of Lowry Air Force Base in Denver. A young man on the cusp of adulthood, he'd been full of ambition and dreams of flying jets. In 1959, Sam was one of first cadets graduated from the Academy following the school's official academic accreditation. By that time, he'd already completed his studies and been assigned overseas. In what capacity or where Sam served, no one knew, but there was plenty of speculation. The possibilities were mysterious and exciting, and Sarah wondered whether his parents were even privy to that top secret information.

A small brass and percussion band comprised of high school students and older townsfolk marched behind the cars playing "God Bless America" while more cheers arose from the spectators. Sheriff Tommy Farris, staunch and serious as ever, strutted down the middle of the street, ready to take charge if anyone threatened trouble. His new deputy—a more relaxed, congenial-looking young man—walked beside Tommy and occasionally darted off to shake hands with the kids. Local business owners lined both sides of the street, handing out cards and tossing candy. Sarah smiled when she caught sight of realtor Cora Blanton's outlandish new red, white and blue hat—no doubt made special for the occasion—featuring a bobbing airplane flanked by miniature American flags.

Bringing up the rear of the procession, the local firemen distributed badges and plastic red hats to the kids from their fire truck. Seeing Sarah, Fire Captain Randy Sweet saluted her with a wide grin.

"There's your Randy," Tess said, nudging her arm.

"He's not *my* Randy." Being mindful not to show too much enthusiasm, Sarah couldn't risk lending credence to Randy's "Sweet on Sarah" nickname. The fire captain didn't seem to mind the nickname, but *she* sure did, especially since she'd done nothing to encourage him. Last year, after she'd accepted Randy's offer to sit beside him at the town's Fourth of July ice cream social and band concert, he'd marched up the gazebo steps and announced his intention to marry her. Sarah had gone into a self-imposed exile until her father talked her into emerging from her cocoon the next day.

Goodness, if she ever agreed to an actual date with Randy, the Lord only knew what he might do. Best not to cross that line. He wasn't a bad guy, and she'd always been friendly—without being flirtatious—whenever he came into Perry's Diner where she worked. She just didn't feel anything for him in *that* way, at least the way she imagined she'd feel if she ever met the man of her dreams. A girl needed passion in her life, and Randy Sweet wasn't it.

Sarah's gaze traveled to where their returning military hero sat perched on the back of the car. A few men strolled beside the car, laughing and talking with him. Tanner Martin's two boys thrust a paper into Sam's hands. After reaching inside his jacket, he pulled out a pen and wrote something—an autograph?—on the paper before handing it back to the boisterous kids.

Tess waved her arms in an exaggerated manner as Charlie's car inched closer and stopped a few hundred yards away. Calling out Sam's name, Tess blew air kisses. As if she needed to resort to such theatrics. Her sister was the prettiest girl across several counties. Their shared bedroom boasted the trophies, tiaras, ribbons and banners to prove it. Granted, most of the awards were from a decade ago. From the time she was a teenager, all Tess had to do was smile at a man and he practically swooned at her feet.

Only one man had ever resisted Tess's charms—the Air Force veteran sitting on the back of the Corvette.

"Sam's more handsome than ever, don't you think?" Tess said. "He looks like one of those gorgeous movie stars. He wears his service to his country well although that might be an insensitive thing to say. Why, Sam's got more patches and pins on that uniform than a person can count in a month of Sundays."

Charlie stopped the convertible in front of Hartmann's Hardware, and Sam slid down from the back of the car. Magnanimous as a political candidate, he made his way down the row of townspeople, shaking hands, laughing and engaging in small talk. Sarah smiled when he pulled Lorraine Carmichael's baby girl into his arms and kissed her plump, rosy cheek. Sam had always been good with kids, and they seemed to naturally gravitate to him. In spite of all the attention focused on him, Sam appeared as approachable now as he'd always been.

"Is it possible he's grown even taller?" Tess said, her gaze never straying from Sam. He stood at least six foot three or four. The only man who came close in stature was Sam's father. "Mark my words, sis. I'm going to marry that man."

"Then no doubt you will," Sarah mumbled, unreasonably bothered as Sam climbed onto the back of the car again. In the last year alone, her sister had dated a handful of suitors, primarily those from neighboring towns since she'd finally exhausted the pool of eligible candidates in Rockbridge. Good looking, successful men, any one of whom would make a fine husband. Still, none of them had been good enough, and for ridiculous reasons. Excuses, really. Had Tess been biding her time all along, waiting for Sam's return? If nothing else, her sister always loved a challenge.

Unlike Tess, Sarah didn't date. She'd been asked out lots of times, and she was fully aware the boys in town considered her a challenge. None of them seemed very mature, including Fire Captain Sweet. Randy was a notorious practical joker and—other than physically— he didn't seem much older now than when he'd smeared glue in her hair in second grade, prompting her mother to chop off her long hair. That prank pretty much nixed any chance of a romantic future between them.

And you threw spitballs at the back of Sam's head in church. For all Sarah knew, Sam would still—and forever—view her as the plucky little girl from down the street. Maybe she should consider her own actions before being so quick to judge others.

Charlie stopped the car in front of Rockbridge Savings & Loan with its large banner stretched between two large stone columns proclaiming *Welcome Home, Captain Lewis!* An oversized American flag, brand new from the looks of it, flapped in the gentle breeze above the front entrance.

Tess nudged her arm again. "According to Susie Jacobs, Sam plans on stepping right in as the vice president of Rockbridge Savings & Loan. With his dad retiring in a few years, it makes perfect sense that he'll be groomed to take over. Susie says Sam's ready to find a wife, settle down and raise a family."

Sarah shot her sister a look, silently imploring her to lower her voice. Leaning close, she whispered, "How could she even know that? If that information came from Susie Jacobs, that's the first reason to discount it. Secondly, I can't imagine Sam ever saying such a thing." Would *any* man admit he was ready for marriage and babies?

Highly doubtful.

Tess's perfectly arched brows lifted. "Why not?"

"Because guys don't say things like that," Sarah said. "Talking about love, marriage and babies makes them all squirmy. Trust me. They discuss fishing, cars, sports, food or politics. Pretty much anything other than relationships and, heaven forbid"—she mock gasped—"love."

"I suppose you know a little something about how men think from working in the diner and overhearing their conversations," Tess said. "But maybe they talk about it among themselves when women aren't around." When Sam bounded up the front steps of the bank, Tess called out to him. "Sam! Over here!"

Mom always told them to always act like a lady and never, under any circumstances, to pursue a man. "Play hard to get, girls. That's the way to reel in a man and keep his interest. Lends an air of mystique." Based on her current behavior, Tess had forgotten that advice or else she'd chosen to blatantly disregard it.

Sarah placed a hand on Tess's arm, prepared to restrain her if she showed signs of running across the street and throwing herself in Sam's arms. After Tess called to him again, Sam quickly surveyed the area before his gaze settled on them from across the street. Smiling, he raised his arm and called out a greeting. Tess blew more silly air kisses while Sarah smiled and returned Sam's wave.

Tess was right about one thing. Sam was certainly handsome enough to cause a girl's heart to skip a few beats. But this was six-years-older Sam, closer-in-age to Tess—*that* Sam. The reminder did nothing to stop the fluttering in Sarah's stomach. Maybe it was the Air Force uniform. A heroic man, who selflessly served his country, willing to sacrifice life and limb, always choked her up with sentimentality.

"Speech! Speech!" Folks all around her chanted, prompting Sarah to clap and join in with their enthusiasm. If it had been a few years earlier, she would have jammed two fingers in her mouth and let out an ear-piercing whistle. Tempting, but not exactly appropriate, from a twenty-one year old. She laughed under her breath when a man across the street did that very thing. Guys could get away with so many things considered inappropriate for proper young ladies.

After a few moments, the crowd finally settled down. Removing his hat, Sam tucked it beneath his arm and stepped up to the festively decorated podium.

Once again, the man managed to steal her breath. Without saying a word.

Chapter 2

~~♥~~

Everyone quieted down quickly. Sarah waited, as they all did, to hear what their hometown hero would say. What kind of character-building, life-changing events had Sam experienced in the last few years? She'd heard how serving in the military could make or break a man.

Thank you, Lord, for bringing him safely home.

"My fellow citizens of Rockbridge, thank you for your warm welcome." *My, my.* Sam's voice was deeper, his native Texas drawl rich and authoritative.

"It was my great honor and privilege to serve my country. I stand before you today, a man incredibly blessed by the Lord's gracious watch care over me." When Sam's glance encompassed those assembled, his eyes appeared bright with emotion. "My friends, we live in a great nation, a blessed nation, an incomparable nation in many respects. Every morning, the first thing I did—after first downing some mighty strong coffee and breakfast"—he paused for the quiet laughter to subside—"was read my Bible and pray, not knowing where the course of each day would lead. Sometimes God's word was all we had to keep us going, but it was more than sufficient. Just as it always is."

He waited as many clapped and called out greetings or affirmations. "I served in the Air Force during a relatively calm period in our nation's history. However, recent events foreshadow escalating conflicts which should not be ignored. After the failed Bay of Pigs invasion last year, and the subsequent embargo ordered by President Kennedy on all imports from Cuba, new tensions are rumbling, especially in the Soviet Union. And what began as a military aid program by the U.S. to subdue communist rebels in French Indochina could conceivably develop into a full-scale war between North and South Vietnam."

Sam's words, combined with his tone of voice, held such conviction. Sarah moved one hand over her heart as she listened, impressed by his obvious depth of emotion and dedication to his country and community. What a strong, confident man he'd become.

"While I do not want to alarm you, we cannot deny—and must always be aware—of what's happening in the world, and always be in prayer. If our soldiers are once again called to serve in active combat, I'd ask that you keep Psalm 121:7 in mind: 'The Lord will protect you from all evil; He will keep your soul.' Evil undeniably exists, but we can never allow anyone or anything—no entity, whether foreign or domestic—to steal our joy in knowing that God is alive and continually at work in the world around us. No matter what may come, the Lord will be with those to whom He has called into service. Just as He always is."

Sam's voice sounded strained with that last statement. He bowed his head for a few moments before once again addressing the hushed group. "It thrills my soul to return home, but I would be remiss if I do not pay tribute to my comrades who have fallen in military conflicts. May they never be forgotten, and I ask that you especially keep in your prayers the families of those who gave their lives in service to our country. Those are the true heroes, the ones who willingly sacrificed their lives for the freedoms and liberties we often take for granted. But we can take heart in this verse: 'After you have suffered for a little while, the God of all grace, who called you to His eternal glory in Christ, will Himself perfect, confirm, strengthen and establish you. To Him be dominion forever and ever. Amen.'"

He waited until the enthusiastic applause died down, and Sarah heard a number of Amens! echoed from the crowd. Stepping forward, Joseph Lewis tossed Sam's signature black Stetson to his son, most likely the same one he'd worn around town throughout his teenage years. Laughing, Sam caught it and settled it squarely on his head. Wearing the familiar hat, he looked more like the neighbor boy that Sarah remembered. He smiled and waved again as the townspeople cheered.

"Thank you again for your warm welcome. I look forward to renewing my acquaintance with all of you. God bless America, God bless Texas, and God bless Rockbridge!"

"Meaningful and to the point," Donald Marcum said to the man standing beside him. "Sam will be a welcome addition to our Town Council."

"Can you believe he said all that without a cue card in sight?" Tess nodded approvingly.

"I was thinking the same thing," Sarah said. When he'd given the speech for his high graduating class, Sam had been articulate and well-spoken, and it seemed time had only improved those skills.

Mayor Richards stepped up to the podium and, after shaking hands with Captain Lewis, addressed those assembled. "'While the storm clouds gather far across the sea, let us swear allegiance to a land that's free, let us all be grateful for a land so fair, as we raise our voices in a solemn prayer.'"

On cue, the band started up again and everyone sang "God Bless America." Sam faced the flag and raised his hand in a salute before he joined in the singing. Still close to the microphone, his clear tenor rose above the others. Thank goodness the man could sing. Even if he couldn't, the townspeople wouldn't care. Her heart full, Sarah glanced around as young and old voices all rose together in song.

As the crowd started to disperse, the band launched into what she recognized as the Air Force song. While the band played, several of the men rushed forward to slap Sam on the back and shake his hand. Several children bounded up the bank's steps behind them.

Her family had prayed for Sam every night during their family devotions. Camped out in his favorite chair, Dad listened to the news on their small black and white television, and then he'd give them a running commentary on any news from South Vietnam. Air Force personnel had been in place there, headquartered in Saigon, since 1950. Not that any of them knew where Sam was stationed, but the mention of the Air Force always made Dad sit up straighter and pay close attention.

"I feel it in my gut that our boys are going to war again," he'd announce several times a week. "I'm afraid these conflicts are going to blow up in our faces soon enough, and off they'll march."

Sarah prayed the conflicts wouldn't result in a war, but after reading her Bible, she couldn't deny the truth. Before Christ's return, there would be wars, a mass uprising of nation against nation, man against man. As much as she wished otherwise, she couldn't ignore the prophecies of famines, pestilence, earthquakes, and other catastrophes.

Mom usually turned a deaf ear to Dad's predictions. "I don't want to hear such things, Bill. Thinking about a war that may or may not happen, and knowing some of those poor soldiers won't come home alive or in one piece, is simply heartbreaking."

"If and when war happens, we need to focus on those who *will* come home," Sarah had insisted. "They'll need our prayers as much as anyone." She'd reiterated the same statement when her father was wheeled into a Houston operating room for open heart surgery six months ago. Her mother had fallen apart emotionally while Tess paced the cold, sanitized floor. "God isn't done with Dad yet," Sarah told them, hauling both women into the chapel to pray. "He certainly doesn't need a bunch of weepy women falling apart around him." If she wasn't confident and optimistic, she'd get mired down in their gloom and doom, and that wouldn't be good for any of them, much less her father.

Snapping to attention, Sarah turned to Tess. "My break's almost over, and I need to get back to Perry's. I'm sure we'll get busy after the celebration. Why don't you come with me? I'll treat you to a piece of pie."

"Not right now." Tess sounded distracted. "Do you think I should give Sam my new private phone number?"

Sarah stared at her, unable to hide her shock. Was Tess that desperate to find a man? "That's a bold move, even for you. Why would you do such a thing?" She held up one hand. "Never mind." Tess planned on marrying Sam. Enough said.

Captain Lewis paused to speak with little Jeff Arnold, crouching down and ruffling the child's curly blond hair. When Sam raised his arms and pretended to soar like a bird or a plane, Sarah smiled. He never talked down to kids and treated them as equals. In the past, he sometimes seemed like an overgrown kid himself, but now he seemed so much more like. . .a grownup.

Tess tugged on her arm a few seconds later. "Sam's coming across the street. Oh, my lands, he's headed straight this way. Would you take a gander at those baby blues? I'd forgotten how pin-you-down beautiful they are. Like a deep ocean inviting me to take the plunge."

Her sister really needed to stop reading those Hollywood magazines. Tess jostled her arm as she rushed forward to embrace him, throwing her arms around his neck and kissing his cheek. Sarah tried not to frown at her sister's shameless behavior. Considering Sam's cheek sported a colorful collage of pinks and reds, Tess wasn't the only one who'd kissed the man.

"Sam, you're looking mighty handsome. Welcome home!" Tess's voice dripped with honey. "We sure have missed you around here. Prayed for you every day."

"Thanks, Tess. It's great to see you again. I felt the prayers of everyone in Rockbridge. They meant a lot."

Sam pulled back and Tess dropped her arms, her own cheeks flushed a pretty pink. Sarah almost laughed when Tess fluttered her eyelashes and gave Sam a coquettish glance. She could have sworn she'd seen Tess perfecting that move in the full-length mirror earlier that morning.

Clearing her throat, Sarah addressed Sam. "If you'd like to come down to Perry's after the parade, Captain Lewis, Myrna made a special peach pie in honor of your homecoming. She said to offer you a big slice. On the house. I'll toss in a cup of coffee, if you'd like."

Sam's appraising glance skimmed over her—in a respectful way— taking in her pale pink uniform, the same style the waitresses at Perry's Diner had worn for years. Something lit in his expression, almost as though he was seeing her for the first time. Didn't he recognize her? She hadn't changed that much. Had she?

"Sounds great, Sarah. I'll be there, thanks. Try not to actually toss the coffee at me, please. The uniform's expensive to dry clean." With a sparkle in his eyes, Sam stepped closer and tweaked her chin the same as he'd done before he'd left Rockbridge for college. She'd put on a brave front during the send-off celebration, but then she'd run all the way home and cried her heart out, muffling her sobs with her pillow, saddened that the most exciting boy in Rockbridge was leaving town. Suddenly, that night seemed more like yesterday.

With his touch, Sarah's pulse raced. His familiar, teasing smile emerged with a hint of those smile lines the girls used to drool over. "You didn't miss me at all, did you, Tomboy?"

"Not at all." A fresh wave of emotion swept through Sarah all over again. She would not cry. Just because he'd called her Tomboy? *Get hold of yourself, girl.* Sam had called her that nickname too many times to count in years past. He'd been the only one to use it, at least in her presence. Sarah didn't mind since she easily outdistanced all the other kids when they raced, and she could swing a bat with the best of the boys her own age. However, she'd long since outgrown the need to prove she could.

Partially to cover her muddled emotions, she reached into the pocket of her uniform for another tissue and beckoned Sam closer. Wearing a bemused expression, he complied while Sarah ignored Tess's stare. Angling his jaw away from her with a gentle touch, she attempted to remove the lipstick. Goodness, Sam's skin was smooth with a golden tan. His cheekbones were thinner, more refined, the smile lines more deeply etched to lend a certain maturity to his features. The effects of serving in the military and the added few years only enhanced his natural good looks and classic features. No wonder Tess wanted to marry him.

In spite of her best efforts, Sarah only succeeded in smearing the lipstick even more. Those blue eyes, as piercing as ever, held something—a sadness perhaps—she'd never glimpsed in their depths before. Based on his speech, Sam's faith was as steadfast as ever. For that, Sarah was grateful since she'd heard so many military men returned home disillusioned and broken.

Giving a slight shake of her head, Sarah pocketed the tissue. "I did the best I could, but you might want to give it your own final spit shine. After all, we can't have the local hero walking around town looking like a clown. Might spoil the image." She gave his arm a light pat, admiring his uniform and hoping she hadn't sounded too flippant or disrespectful. "I suppose some men might consider multiple lip prints on their cheek a unique brand of honor all on its own."

"I'll see what I can do," Sam said. "Thanks for trying to keep my image respectable."

Tess spoke up, interrupting the moment. "Make that two slices of that scrumptious peach pie, little sister, and I'll swing by Perry's, too." The batting of her eyelashes started again with increased fervor. "You don't mind if I join you, do you, Sam?"

"Not at all. The more the merrier."

Surely Tess wasn't naïve enough to believe the returning veteran wouldn't have a large group of admirers tagging along beside him who shared her same goal to spend quality time with the most famous person in Rockbridge. In the past year, Charlie Sorrel's younger brother, Howard, won a bit part in a New York stage production. That made front page news. Then again, so did the birth of a calf with five legs on Henry Newsome's ranch. Sam's triumphant homecoming would definitely be the biggest story of the spring season. Most likely, it'd be the best story of the entire year.

"I'll see you both in a bit." Sarah turned to go.

"Sarah?"

Her shoulders tensed as she slowly turned around to face Sam. "Yes?"

Stepping closer, Sam's gorgeous smile made her pulse race in a way it never had before. "Thanks for the poem. It was very special, and I want you to know it helped me get through some rough times."

Sarah's mouth gaped before she quickly recovered and closed it, unable to speak. He *knew*? How was that even possible? The ladies of the church met to assemble care packages on the third Saturday morning of every month. In a rare moment of frivolousness, Sarah had once slicked on pink lipstick then pressed her lips on an index card containing a poem she'd written. She'd tucked it inside the box marked special for Sam. Only God knew what had possessed her to do such a thing. Maybe all of Tess's love talk had finally seeped into her muddled brain. Or perhaps she wanted to remind Sam that someone was waiting for him back home, even if it was only the little girl from down the street that he'd teased and called Tomboy.

Standing behind Sam, Tess stared at her. Although he'd lowered his voice, she'd apparently heard every word. Her sister would recover, pester her with questions later, and maybe even accuse her of trying to hog the limelight.

Yes, the man was pretty much perfect. Except that Sam wanted to stay in Rockbridge. Settle in Rockbridge. Raise a brood of darling little Lewis offspring in Rockbridge. Not that those ideas were character flaws, but they *were* regrettable. Why Rockbridge? She'd never understand it.

Well, fine. That's exactly what made him ideal for Tess.

Time to get to work.

Chapter 3

~~♥~~

Could that beautiful girl really be Sarah Jordan? The little pigtailed girl from down the street who always had a dog trailing behind her and a softball in her hand? He'd stolen a quick glance at the name embroidered on her pink Perry's uniform. Sam didn't know of any other Sarah in Rockbridge. A lot of things probably hadn't changed in Rockbridge, but his neighbor sure had—in all the best ways, from what he could tell. What a knockout.

As he watched her walk in the opposite direction, Sam tried not to stare. In that moment, he regretted not sharing more than a passing conversation with Sarah in recent years. Before that, between his studies at the Academy, short-term mission trips and working at the bank during holidays and summers, he hadn't had much time for a social life other than a few dates here and there. Even so, the difference in their ages would have discouraged anything more than friendship.

But now? The six-year difference in their ages never seemed so insignificant. He'd certainly never seen a girl look as good as Sarah did in her Perry's Diner uniform. Gone were the chubby cheeks and stick-thin figure, replaced by lovely facial contours and womanly curves. Without a hint of makeup, Sarah's skin was lovely, and her brown eyes were clear, radiating a sweet innocence. Such a refreshing change from some of the women he'd met in the past four years who'd more freely offer themselves than a genuine smile to a man in uniform.

Her hair was a slightly deeper shade of blonde than he'd remembered, like spun honey, and she wore it gathered in a loose style at the back of her head. Wispy tendrils curled along the sides of her slightly flushed face in the warm temperatures. Soft. Pretty.

In a word, the grownup version of his neighbor was *stunning*.

Compared to the other girls hanging onto his every word at the moment—not to mention clinging to his arms—Sarah was a burst of fresh air. Air he wanted to breathe into his lungs and fully absorb. Judging by her reaction, his guess that she'd penned the poem had been spot-on. He'd love nothing more than to discuss that poem further with her. Without a doubt, the words she'd written had come from her heart with the purest of intentions. He'd thrown down the gauntlet, but he'd back off until she brought it up. *If* she brought it up, and he sure hoped she would.

On the chance he might get another glimpse of Sarah as she headed into Perry's, Sam glanced in the direction of the diner. Not seeing her, he chatted with more townsfolk, going through the rote motions—shaking hands, sharing small talk and catching up on the latest news. Hearing some of what was said and digesting very little. He was still recovering from jet lag, and it hadn't quite infiltrated his brain yet that he was actually stateside. *Home.* His mind was spinning. Everyone wanted to speak to him at the same time.

"So, did you find a sweetheart wherever you were in the world?" Tess tugged on his arm as if he hadn't heard her the first time. Perhaps he had missed a question or two while thinking about Sarah.

"No. I'm single as ever." Judging by Tess's coy smile, his answer was misguided and might only encourage her. As it was, Kathy Parker tightened her hold on his other arm. Wonderful.

Although Tess meant well, her behavior smacked of almost painful desperation. The tarnish must be showing on her beauty queen crowns. Through the years, he'd fended off the suggestions and innuendo concerning the two of them, but he'd never been interested. She'd always been very pretty, but as long as he'd known her, Tess had put too much emphasis on worldly things. To the point where he was surprised she was still in Rockbridge. Perhaps if Tess stopped trying so hard to find a husband, she'd allow a guy access to the woman beneath all the surface gloss.

Wow. He'd been home all of an hour and now he was making unfair judgments? Still, he detested how society made a woman feel

16

like she was washed-up with no prospects for marriage or babies if she was on the back side of twenty-five. Living in another country and serving in the armed forces had taught him a few things, among them the very real truth that life is fleeting and there are no guarantees. Contrary to what some believed, a person only got one go-around on this earth with no do-overs permitted. To the best of his ability, he needed to make his actions, his words, and especially his relationships, count.

One thing Sam understood: his personal feelings toward Tess Jordan would never change and she'd never be more to him than a good friend. All those years ago when she'd thrown herself at him in high school, he'd vowed to Charlie that he'd never kiss a Jordan girl. But now, after seeing the grownup version of Tess's little sister? Oh yeah, Sarah could make him seriously reconsider that teenage vow.

Sam's gaze strayed to Perry's Diner on the corner, now only a few hundred yards away. He smiled when he spied the same weathered, white clapboard storefront with its sign proclaiming the diner as "The Place to Meet and Greet Your Neighbor." That's exactly what he intended to do.

"Sam, honey, I asked you a question," Tess purred. "Poor man, you must be suffering from culture shock."

"I'm fine," he said, turning his smile on her. "Just a little jet lagged, a bit hungry and a lot overwhelmed. If it weren't for all the noise, you would have heard my stomach growling." He angled his head toward the diner. "Sarah's worked at Perry's a long time, hasn't she?"

Although Tess's smile stayed in place, her lips noticeably thinned. "Yes, since she was in high school, but not for much longer." Her grip on his upper arm tightened. This was getting old fast.

"Sam, why don't we skip Perry's today?" Kathy said. "You can go there any old time. This day calls for the best restaurant in town. Let me treat you to Quentin's. They have a live band starting at five. We can relax, kick up our heels and celebrate your homecoming in style. Have some real fun. What do you say?"

Kathy's tone dripped with innuendo. Seemed even small town girls could be world-class flirts, maybe even more so. He suppressed his sigh.

"I appreciate the offer, but a cup of coffee and a slice of Myrna's peach pie sound pretty great right now." He was careful not to meet

Kathy's gaze directly. Better not give her that leverage.

"You and your peaches." Kathy brushed a long strand of blonde hair away from her face, and her painted ruby lips upturned in a coy smile. "I do believe that's the magic word for you, isn't it?"

Charlie caught up to them after parking his car. "Hey, come on girls. Give the guy a break. Sam needs some breathing room here."

He shot Charlie a grin of thanks as Tess and Kathy released his arms. Straightening his shoulders, Sam shoved his hands into the pockets of his uniform slacks as he nodded to a few passersby. He began to whistle, hoping it would keep the chatter at bay until he finally reached Perry's. Why did it feel like he'd been headed to the diner for an hour instead of only a few minutes?

Left alone with his thoughts for the moment, Sam reflected on his memories of Sarah. A voracious reader, she'd often camped out on her front porch steps, lost in the pages of a book. She'd asked thought-provoking questions in the church Bible study. Her hair was often tousled and dirt streaked across her cheek or on her clothes was a common sight.

They shared a love of animals, and Sarah had eagerly volunteered to be his assistant whenever one of the mutts or cats he'd temporarily adopted gave birth to a new litter. He'd never forget the way she'd squealed with delight at the first glimpse of a newborn pup or how hard she'd cried when she'd once held a stillborn kitten. Sarah had insisted they hold a memorial service for that kitten, and she'd delivered an emotional speech that conveyed her deep compassion.

Playing a rousing game of softball with the boys was more Sarah's style than putting on a dress. Sam remembered how he'd heard she'd kicked more than one boy who'd tried to kiss her at school or on a playing field. A quick study, naturally athletic and taller than most girls, Sarah excelled at softball and had quickly grown into quite a contender. Early on, he'd coached her on how to perfect her pitch and the best stance for holding and swinging a bat. While he'd been away, his dad kept him up-to-speed on Sarah's high school victories. She'd led their tiny Rockbridge team to the state championship in girls' softball. They'd lost in the semi-finals to a much larger Dallas team, but they'd exceeded expectations. Nothing for which to be ashamed.

The thought of all the spitballs she'd sent flying to the back of his head in church made him smile. Sarah's personality had always been fun—honest, sassy, and warm. He'd teased her a lot, and she'd been good natured about it in spite of a few hearty punches to his arm. Always, her smile was without pretense.

He'd only known Sarah for two years before he'd gone off to college. Even so, they'd forged solid memories in that short time. After seeing Sarah, the flood of memories came rushing back to mind.

The grownup Sarah Jordan most likely shared many of the same qualities as the younger version, and he definitely wanted to get to know her all over again.

Sam hastened his steps. He resumed his whistling and couldn't stop his grin.

Chapter 4

~~♥~~

Sarah tried not to stare as Debbie Harrison pushed open the door to Perry's Diner, sending the bell jingling. Teased up the wazoo, her hair stuck out in all directions. Several customers snickered and whispered behind their menus as her friend threaded her way among the tables of the restaurant.

Giving Debbie an overly bright smile and a wave, Sarah prayed she could keep a straight face. What had Debbie been thinking this time? Goodness. She'd colored her hair a deeper shade of auburn and coated it with several coats of lacquer. Surely Debbie's boss at Wanda's House of Beauty would discourage her from experimenting with such a radical style. Debbie's boyfriend, Arnie, wouldn't be able to run his fingers through that hair. Then again, maybe Sarah knew way too much about everyone else's love life because she had none of her own. Not that she wanted one.

She hoped Debbie wouldn't ask for her opinion. She could never lie, and she'd hate to tell her friend how ridiculous she looked. People made fun of Debbie behind her back which riled Sarah since she knew beneath the sometimes outlandish exterior was one of the most genuine and loyal people she'd ever known. Whether they'd ever admit it or not, most people had to appreciate Debbie's lively personality and antics. They'd been fast friends since sharing a box of crayons in kindergarten and they'd reached for the purple one at the same time.

"Sarah, honey, could you please grab the ketchup for me?"

"Sure." Thankful for the distraction, Sarah grabbed the bottle from a nearby table. "Here you go, Millie," she said, handing it to her. After Jimmy called to her, Sarah darted into the kitchen and then delivered a tuna melt to Perry Sellers, the original owner of the diner who occupied his usual counter seat, same as he did every afternoon. During a regular shift at Perry's, she'd chat with a good number of the town's citizens. Unless they were out of town, sick or otherwise incapacitated, Perry's was the preferred gathering spot.

Debbie plopped down on one of the seats at the counter. "What a circus, huh? Still, I breathe a big sigh of relief every time one of our hometown boys comes home. Having Sam back will make things a lot more interesting around here, that's for sure. Hey, I was at Johnson's Market last night and overheard Tammy Simpson and Janet Marks laying odds on who he'll ask out first."

After retying her loose apron strings, Sarah retrieved a wet dishcloth and mopped up the coffee spill on the counter courtesy of her previous customer. "I invited Sam to come in after everything calms down. Myrna made a peach pie in honor of his return."

Debbie raised a penciled brow—last month's experiment. Sarah had been horrified when her friend had shaved off her eyebrows, believing it to be a hallmark of sophistication. Stupidity was more like it, but she loved Debbie too much to ever say such a thing. If she waited it out, Arnie would tell her or Debbie would figure it out for herself and grow them back.

"Sam's coming in here? Then all the more reason to stick around."

"What do you mean?" With a well-aimed shot, Sarah tossed the dishcloth in the sink.

"If Tess starts pawing him, between the two of us, we can run interference." Ah yes, Debbie knew her sister well. Not to mention Tess had jabbered about Sam's imminent return for weeks to anyone who'd listen.

Sarah gave a shake of her head. "I was referring to what you said about Sam and the whole dating thing. People are actually making bets?"

"Not real bets, no. At least I hope not. But people will talk, you know. Nothing like a handsome veteran coming home to get the rumor mill churning." With one elbow planted on the counter, Debbie drummed her fingers on her chin, bringing Sarah's attention to her deep red nail polish. She must have tried to match her hair color to her nail polish—or the other way around.

"I wonder how Sam's changed and just pray that he's okay. I mean, he's a man of the world now. He's bound to have seen and experienced all kinds of things. Serving in the military changes a man, wartime or not. That's what everybody says, anyway." She shrugged. "Sure, it might not be visible on the outside, but inside? How could it not change him in some way?" Debbie cracked a small smile. "Sam sure has matured quite nicely, I'll say that much. Wouldn't you agree?"

Sarah ignored that open-ended question although she secretly agreed. "Sam's also one of the most-leveled guys I've ever known. I'm sure his experiences, whatever they were, only reinforced what he's known all along."

Sarah greeted a middle-aged couple who claimed seats farther down the counter. After handing them menus, she returned to Debbie. "I used to wonder if Sam would become a pastor, but then his passion for flying jets took over. Like he said in his speech, there's evil in the world, but he knows there are more good people than bad. Bottom line? God is always in control."

"That's a profound statement if ever I've heard one," Debbie said. "True enough."

Sarah leaned closer so as not to be overheard. "Tess announced she's going to marry him."

"Oh, good heavens." Debbie drew back, her hazel eyes wide. "You mean to the entire town? What is it about you Jordan girls and public proclamations? First Randy Sweet announcing to the town that he's going to make you his bride, and now Tess—"

"No," Sarah said, shaking her head and unable to hide her smile. "Announced wasn't the right word choice. She only told me. For now, anyway. Maybe it's a good thing she didn't have a megaphone anywhere nearby or she might have actually trumpeted it to the entire town. As it was, she made a big show of waving to Sam and getting his attention before he made his speech. Afterwards, she made sure to mark him with her lip print. You know Tess. Once she sets her mind to something—"

Debbie waved a dismissive hand. "She's used to attention, but your sister's only interested until the next attractive man rides into town in his shiny new car. No way she'll settle for Sam, no matter that he's a veteran now and the most eligible bachelor in town her age. Everyone knows he's going to work with his dad at the bank. That's too boring for your sister. Tess wants glitz and glamor. Besides, Sam doesn't even own a car."

Sam Lewis was anything but boring. He'd never been boring, and based on his speech, he was intelligent and compassionate. She'd hug that thought close and watch all the other girls drool over the man. "He only got back to town an hour ago. Give him time. Don't forget Sam co-owns that vintage plane with his dad. A man with a plane can't be ignored. Besides, he's learned how to run a bank from the ground floor up by sweeping floors, emptying garbage cans and shadowing the tellers. You've got to admire that, and there's definitely something to be said for loyalty and tradition."

"Very nice speech," Debbie said. "You don't have to sell me on him. Sam will have a solid career and he'll make some woman a very happy, satisfied wife. I mean, look at the man! Other than my Arnie, Sam's the best looking man in Rockbridge. Before we know it, lots of little Lewis kiddos will be trotting in here—tall for their age, dark-haired and with stellar blue peepers—and plopping themselves into a corner booth."

"That might be the case, but I'll be long gone by then. Someone else will be taking their orders." *And birthing his children.* Where had that thought come from?

Sarah focused on Debbie. "Speaking of orders, do you want your usual?"

"Yes, but I've got a longer break today. Take care of whatever you need to do first."

Heeding Debbie's suggestion, Sarah stacked plates and dirty dishes from a few tables and then carried them into the kitchen. Eddie, the part-time busboy, was busy elsewhere with the added crowd from the homecoming parade. She called across the diner to Patti that she'd cover a couple of extra tables. After delivering a few sales tickets, she pulled her menu pad out of her apron pocket and jotted down the order from the new couple sitting at the counter.

"Are you new in town?" Sarah asked, handing their ticket to her boss as Myrna passed behind her, headed into the kitchen.

"I'm Jon Hastings, and this is my wife, Linda," the pleasant-faced, middle-aged man told her. His wife said nothing but gave her a polite head tilt. "I'm here to talk with Doc Meriweather about assuming his practice when he retires in a few months."

"Is that right?" That information shouldn't be surprising and was probably for the best, sad as it was. Doc had been less than reliable, if not missing in action, in recent months. According to Debbie's sources at the beauty parlor, the latest gossip held that Doc was spending a lot of his evenings—and in-between hours—curled up with a bottle of fine scotch. Not that Sarah paid attention to idle speculation, but Doc showing up blitzed at events around town a few times in recent months had done nothing to instill confidence in the town's medical services.

"It's very nice to meet you both," Sarah said. "Welcome to Rockbridge. Your order will be ready in a few minutes, but let me know if you need anything in the meantime."

They thanked her and then bowed their heads to pray. Yes, a praying doctor in town would be good. Not that Doc Meriweather wasn't a praying man. The elderly physician hadn't been the same since he'd lost his wife more than three years ago. Thank the good Lord that Doc had been sober after Sarah found her father sprawled on the kitchen floor within minutes of suffering a heart attack. According to Doc, her quick reaction saved her father's life.

"So, Tess was in the shop yesterday," Debbie said as Sarah headed to the shake machine. "She tells me you're still planning on going to nursing school. I haven't heard you talk about it as much lately, and I thought maybe you'd put it off or decided—"

Sarah placed a napkin and a spoon on the counter beside her friend. "Come on, Deb. You know me well enough to know I'm not about to give up on that dream. Nursing school is my ticket out of Rockbridge."

"Right. I just thought after your dad's heart attack—"

"Please don't remind me." Sarah didn't mean to snap at her, especially since she'd thought the very same thing not a minute before. The familiar stab of guilt resurfaced. "Dad's actually been more supportive than either Mom or Tess. He told me he doesn't want me to worry about him, and he encouraged me to follow through with my plan."

How long it would take to save another five thousand dollars was another matter. Even with taking on extra shifts at the diner each week, Sarah estimated it'd take another year. Sometimes nursing school seemed like a pipedream, but she'd persevere and make it a reality even if it took until she was thirty. If only she could make

Debbie understand it wasn't so much a desire to escape Rockbridge as it was to make an independent life of her own and be able to help others.

Debbie quirked a brow. "I hope you know Randy would marry you in a red-hot minute and you wouldn't need to bother with a career. Just imagine. You could open a bakery and call it Sarah Sweet's Treats." She giggled. "Or Sarah's Sweet Treats. Something like that. Sounds cute, don't you think?"

"Yes, it's very cute. Randy's a nice man, but contrary to what the fire captain says, we're not dating. Neither do I plan on starting anything with him." Sarah frowned. "Why give him false hope? I want to help people, but I need to leave Rockbridge in order to do that. Becoming a nurse isn't a 'bother' in any sense of the word. Medical training will give me the opportunity to change lives for the better. I can't imagine anything that would be more fulfilling than that."

Debbie's expression softened. "You'd also lose patients, honey. Could you accept that? Being a nurse takes a certain backbone. You're strong, Sarah, but beneath it all, you have one of the kindest, most tender hearts I've ever known. Death is a part of life we can't escape, no matter how much we might want to. I'm not sure you could withstand losing patients over and over again, and I hate the thought of you getting hurt."

Sarah swallowed the lump stuck in her throat. "I know, and I appreciate your concern for me. But I have to try, Deb. Don't you see? I don't want to be one of those people who, later in life, regrets what could have been and sits around bemoaning lost opportunities."

Debbie grabbed her hand, giving it a brief, warm squeeze. "That's the difference between you and the other girls in this town. You're thinking beyond Rockbridge. You have goals. If anyone can make it happen, it's you. Speaking for myself, my goal is to marry Arnie and have babies with him. He's my dream."

Relieved for the turn in conversation, Sarah smiled. "I know, and I'm sure you will. I'd better go make your milkshake before your break is over or else Myrna gets after me for dawdling."

"Thanks sweetie. Better make it with two small scoops this time." She patted her stomach. "I gained a few pounds last month."

After plopping the scoops of vanilla ice cream into the blender, Sarah went through the automatic motions of adding chocolate syrup, cocoa and milk before replacing the lid. As she absently listened to the loud whirring of the blender, she pondered how different her goals were from Debbie's. Her friend came into Perry's every single weekday afternoon on her break from the beauty shop. Although she frequently experimented with different hairstyles, she'd worn the same perfume the past four years. Debbie always ordered a chocolate shake, usually with three scoops of ice cream. She'd dated Arnold Franklin exclusively for five years. When Arnie eventually proposed, they'd marry and start a family. Safe. Familiar. Predictable.

Stopping the blender, Sarah removed the lid and then poured the thick shake into a tall parfait glass. Grabbing the can of whipped cream, she swirled it over the shake and then spooned chocolate shavings on top. She tried not to breathe in the tempting aroma of the rich chocolate. Every time her friend complained about her weight, Sarah turned a deaf ear. If she didn't have height on her side, she'd be sunk. With her height and the larger bone structure of her dad's side of the family, she'd never be considered dainty, and she'd worked hard to lose the extra twenty pounds she'd gained in the past couple of years. Another reason to miss playing softball, but swimming laps at Thornton's Creek helped her stay slender.

"Here you go." Sarah placed the milkshake on the counter. Debbie was working a crossword puzzle, but she smiled and thanked her.

As she delivered more lunch platters and took orders, Sarah's thoughts strayed to Sam again, wondering how he could have known she'd written that poem. She hadn't considered it very good, but maybe it hadn't been so silly after all. Who knew it'd actually reach him all the way across the globe? Then to think he'd read it and, based on his comment, taken it to heart—even received a blessing from it? Without knowing it, Sam had given her encouragement and a return blessing.

You always have these things under your control, don't you, Lord?

"I'm leaving my money on the counter, sweetie." Grabbing her purse and crossword puzzle book, Debbie gave her a quick wave and headed to the door. "See you tomorrow."

"Bye, Deb. Have a great day."

The relative quiet of the diner was dispelled a few minutes later when the front door swung open, sending that bell jingling. Captain Lewis had finally arrived with his boisterous entourage to the tune of

Elvis Presley crooning "Can't Help Falling in Love" from the jukebox.

Somehow, that seemed very fitting.

Chapter 5

~~♥~~

Sarah couldn't keep count of the people streaming in through the door behind Sam. Everyone seemed to be chattering at the same time, increasing the level of noise and filling the diner with excitement. Talking with Charlie, Sam removed his Stetson and led the group as he slid into the big corner booth. As many people as possible, both men and women, squeezed in with him. A couple of guys pulled up chairs, crowding the already narrow space between tables. If it were anyone but Sam, taskmaster Myrna would hustle out of the kitchen and demand they not block the aisles.

"Scoot on over there and get their orders," Myrna said from behind her. "Be sure and suggest the sandwich platters with fries. And malts or shakes. Whatever Sam wants is on the house."

"Yes, ma'am." Pulling her menu pad from the pocket of her apron, Sarah approached the table with a smile. Tess sat next to Sam and the way she fawned over him was shameless. If one more person joined the party, she'd practically be on his lap. Sarah hoped Sam would have more propriety than to allow such a thing from happening. When it came to her sister, she'd seen several guys act the part of a fool. She wouldn't put it past Tess to toy with the affections of a returning serviceman.

The next few minutes passed quickly as Sarah explained the day's specials to various members of the group. Instead of listening to her, the girls hung on Sam's every word and then had to ask her to repeat the rundown again.

"Stop staring at Sam and write down my order."

Sarah's cheeks flared with warmth at Kathy Parker's barked command. "I'm sorry," she said, trying not to show how the other girl's harsh comment flustered her. She hoped her nerves didn't betray her as she poised the order pad in her hand. "What would you like?"

"I imagine Sarah's thinking about how she'd like to scrub the lipstick off my cheek," Sam said. "I'm sure I look like a clown." When he gave her a slight nod, Sarah shot him a grateful glance.

"More like Sarah wants to add her own lip print to your cheek, Sam. Pity, though. She doesn't wear lipstick. Never does." Kathy tossed her a dismissive glance. "Once a tomboy, always a tomboy." Her blue eyes fixated on her. "Right, Sarah?"

Sarah steeled herself not to lash back in anger. Her father always advised her to smile and wish an antagonist a "great day." Even on the softball field after a game, the hallmark of good sportsmanship was to shake the hand of the opponent, win or lose.

Sorry, Dad. Lord help me, but I can't bypass this opportunity.

"That might be so, Miss Parker, but I'd prefer going swimming or fishing down at Thornton's Creek any day than shopping for a ridiculously expensive party dress I'll wear once and then throw away."

Kathy stared at her, aghast, and Tess barely disguised her shock. Sam leaned close to hear whatever Charlie whispered, but they both appeared amused. Sarah didn't want to know what might be said about her after that most unbecoming outburst, and her cheeks burned with shame.

What am I doing? Sarah wished she could sink into the floor. So what if everyone in town knew Kathy was spoiled and bought an expensive new dress for every occasion? More than one of her fancy frocks had been found in the trash bin behind Tucker's General Store the next day. Couldn't the girl or her family donate them to the Salvation Army or some other deserving charity? Still, in spite of Kathy's rude remarks, she was her customer. She'd paste on a smile and give her the best service possible if it killed her.

Catching Myrna's stern glance from across the diner, Sarah inhaled a quick breath. "I'm sorry. That comment was inexcusable, and I hope you'll accept my apology. Now, if I can please get the rest of your orders, we'll start preparing everything."

Never one to back down, Kathy gave her a tight-lipped smile. "Be a good little girl and bring me a strawberry shake. Lots of whipped cream and a cherry on top. Plumpest one you can find."

"I'll do my best." At least Sarah could still speak through gritted teeth. The one good thing to result from her lack of civility was that everyone at the table was now quiet and focused. In a matter of another two minutes, she'd taken the rest of their orders. Aware that Captain Lewis studied her with curiosity, she avoided him.

"What was that all about?" Jimmy said as Sarah fled into the kitchen. "I could feel the shock waves all the way in here." The aroma of burgers and onions on the grill greeted her, normally something she liked and found oddly comforting. Now, with everything combined, she didn't feel so good.

Draping one arm across her middle, Sarah groaned and leaned against the sink. "I think I might be sick. Kathy Parker said something I didn't like, but my pitiful attempt to kill her with kindness didn't exactly work. Failed miserably, in fact. Oh, Jimmy, my big mouth gets me in such trouble sometimes."

"Take a couple of deep breaths and you'll be fine. You don't have a big mouth, but you're honest and forthright. From where I'm standin', that's a real good thing. I don't know what she said, but that girl's jealous of you. Gettin' in her digs makes her feel better about herself. Don't you pay her any mind."

Sarah lifted her head. "Jealous of me? How do you figure that?" Doing as Jimmy suggested, she breathed in and out a few times before moving over to the steel table in the middle of the kitchen. She spread out the menu tickets, quickly separating them. She'd worked at Perry's so long, she could go through the motions in her sleep. Keeping busy now was the best thing.

"You got better grades all through school, for starters. That's one thing her daddy's money couldn't buy. Not to mention you could swing that softball bat like nobody's business."

"Yes, but Kathy's attending college while I'm still here." Sarah caught herself before she used the word *stuck*. Like most of the citizens in Rockbridge, Jimmy was a native and probably never considered leaving. Been married forever and raised four children, all of whom still lived in town with their families. In one way or another, half the townspeople were related to one another.

"All in good time." Jimmy's dark eyes were kind. "I've always said you're gonna do great things, Jelly Bean. You wait and see."

"Thanks for the vote of support, Jimmy." She kissed his cheek. The man was like a favorite uncle who'd slip her a bag of cherry jelly beans—her all-time favorite—when Dad brought her into Perry's most Saturdays for lunch. "I'll go make the milkshakes, get the coffee, and slice the pie if you can start on the rest."

"Sure thing, boss." After giving her a salute with his spatula, Jimmy tossed more beef patties onto the grill.

Her stomach and spirits soothed, Sarah lifted her chin and pushed open the swinging door leading to the dining room. Passing her on the way, Myrna nudged Sarah's shoulder, her customary gesture of reassurance. "Don't let that blonde bomber bother you none, honey. She's a bigger fan of herself than anyone else out there is." With the encouragement from Jimmy and now Myrna, their support went a long way toward assuaging her frazzled nerves. These people were part of her, like family.

Three minutes later, in the middle of mixing more milkshakes, Sarah turned off the blender.

"Very impressive."

No mistaking that deep voice.

Her heart racing, Sarah slowly turned around to face Sam. He'd hung up his uniform coat, removed his tie, and the top button of his starched white dress shirt was unfastened. If that wasn't distracting enough, his sleeves were rolled to reveal tanned, muscular forearms. She couldn't ignore how Sam's broad, straight shoulders tapered to his trim waist. He'd always been athletic, but now his physique was more filled-out and masculine. Military men certainly knew how to impress a girl by virtue of being so precise and neat. Among other things.

She grinned. "I'm sure even an esteemed Air Force pilot can learn to make a milkshake in one or two easy lessons."

"Another day, perhaps. I'm referring to the way you stood up to Kathy. Not that you didn't stand up for yourself when you were a kid." Sam crossed his arms on the counter and surveyed her. "You've grown up, Sarah."

Clearing her throat, she returned to her task. "Well, I'm not sure insulting the daughter of one of the town's most prominent citizens is worthy of praise or in any way advisable, but thank you. I think." She darted another quick glance at him before returning to her task.

"You, of all people, should understand that tact can sometimes be a stumbling block for me."

"It's not an insult if it's true. You made your point convincingly."

She poured the strawberry shake for Kathy into a glass and began to add the whipped cream. "That might be so, but I was unbelievably rude and should have held my tongue. I don't intentionally set out to cause trouble, you know. Thoughts roll from my mind and come tumbling out of my mouth apparently without any forethought or sensitivity."

Sam chuckled. "I wouldn't call you trouble. You've always been spirited and, as such, you sometimes find yourself in situations, for lack of a better word."

Enough about her shortcomings. Time to change the subject. "So, you've got the entire town abuzz today. Your parents must be very proud of you. Rightly so."

He waved his hand. "Today being the key word. Tomorrow morning, I'll be yesterday's news and nothing more than the new guy behind a desk at Rockbridge Savings & Loan."

Was he serious? "You'll never just be *that* guy, Sam." She nodded to the table behind him. "Your entourage is waiting. Don't let me keep you."

"I needed to escape for a few minutes. Find some sanity. Catch up with an old friend. All of the above." Sam nodded to the counter behind her, his gaze moving down to the lower shelf. "Is the book yours?"

"Yes, in a manner of speaking. I've borrowed it so many times from the library that it might as well be mine." With a glance to make sure Myrna was busy elsewhere in the diner, Sarah pulled it out and held up the copy of *To Kill A Mockingbird*.

"You always did spend a lot of time in the library. I've heard this book's excellent. May I see it?"

She held onto it for a few seconds and they enjoyed a playful tug-of-war. The same as they'd done years ago, something she'd nearly forgotten.

"I did say please." He used to say that, too. Sam's familiar, teasing smile lines surfaced, doing strange things to her stomach as he tugged harder on the book. Something pinched her insides at the same time but not in a bad way. Sarah allowed the book to slip from her fingers. At least Sam would actually read *To Kill A Mockingbird*. Most people in Rockbridge would be more concerned about the price of milk at Johnson's Market or the weather forecast than reading a powerful story of racism and the good and evil warring within the souls of men.

He eyed the cover. "This book won the Pulitzer, right?"

"Last year. For a first-time author, that's quite an accomplishment."

"I need to catch up on my reading," he said. "I'll see if I can get a copy and we can compare notes." Sam ran his finger over the author's name. "Harper Lee."

"Sounds like a man's name, but it's a woman." Sarah leaned her elbows on the counter. "The book's fabulous, and very thought-provoking. There's going to be a movie, too, and it's supposed to be out by the end of this year. I only hope it does justice to the novel."

He thumbed through the book for a few seconds before handing it back to her.

Dropping a pitiful looking cherry on top of the shake, Sarah plucked it out with a frown and then tossed it in the trash can.

"Nice shot. You play ball?" That comment brought back full-force the first time they'd met almost eleven years ago.

"Thanks. Not so much anymore." She stabbed a straw down into the shake.

"Why not?"

Sarah met Sam's gaze head-on. "Because I've grown up." Selecting the fattest, juiciest cherry she could find in the jar, she plopped it on top of the strawberry shake. "If you want to make yourself useful, would you kindly deliver this strawberry confection to Miss Parker? I'd be most obliged. Maybe it'll help smooth things over if the resident hero brings it to her."

"Will do. I hope I'll see you again soon." Taking the spoon she handed to him, Sam gave her a wink and headed back to his table. *Oh, my.* He used to wink at her a lot, too, but it was different now. Or maybe she was imagining things.

You've grown up, too, Mr. Lewis.

Chapter 6

~~♥~~

Two Nights Later

Cleaning the tables at Perry's Diner shortly before closing time, Sarah's thoughts strayed to that long ago, humid August day when she'd first met Sam. Side by side with Tess, she'd marched down their street to the Lewis house, a modest but well-maintained, one-story ranch. She'd carried a homemade pie while Tess prattled on endlessly about her expectations for the new boy in town.

After ringing the doorbell, they waited on the front steps. The oven mitts were almost threadbare and the heat from the dish started to sting Sarah's hands. "Please open the door sooner than later," she muttered, tempted to put the pie on the ground.

As if on command, the front door swung open and Sarah raised her chin to meet the eyes of a very tall teenage boy with the bluest eyes she'd ever seen. Her favorite color of blue, reminding her of a robin's egg. Wearing a San Antonio Missions T-shirt and shorts, he sported a mop of longish, dark curls.

"Wow," Tess murmured under her breath.

Whatever. At least he didn't have hideous acne and seemed cleaner than most boys. Uppermost in Sarah's mind was getting back home to her puppy. "Hi. Welcome to the neighborhood." Shifting the pie in her arms, Sarah stuck out one hand. "I'm Sarah Jordan and this is my old—old*er* sister, Teresa. We live four doors down. Can I please put this pie down somewhere?"

"Here, let me take it."

"Watch out," Sarah said as he took the dish from her, along with the oven mitts. "The dish is hot—"

"Yowza! You're not kidding." Darting into the kitchen, he called over his shoulder for them to follow. "Can you open that drawer and pull out a towel?" He used his foot to indicate which drawer. After Sarah yanked out a dishtowel and quickly spread it on the counter, Sam dropped the dish on it and yanked the mitts from his hands. "At least I know what to get you for Christmas."

"Sorry about that. You can get some for our mom, but I don't bake. I hope you didn't get burned." Without a second thought, she reached for his hands, inspecting them for any signs of burns. How embarrassing. *Welcome to the neighborhood. Sorry for almost burning your hands off.* Thankfully, other than being a pinky red color, his fingers apparently hadn't suffered any permanent harm.

"I think I'll survive. I'm Sam, by the way. Thanks for the pie. Is it peach?" Pulling out of her grasp, he handed the oven mitts back to her.

Tess brushed Sarah's arm with more force than necessary as she reached for Sam's hand. "It's apple, actually, and I go by Tess. *Not* Teresa. Really nice to make your acquaintance." She pumped his hand up and down.

"You too, Tess."

Spying a trash can in the corner of the kitchen, Sarah aimed and tossed the oven mitts inside.

"Nice shot. Great eye-to-hand coordination. Ever play ball?"

"Thanks," Sarah said. "Softball." She nodded to his T-shirt. "My sympathies."

At first, he seemed confused, but then he laughed. "Yeah, the Missions are destined for obscurity. I can't believe you're a girl and know about baseball."

She smirked. "Right on both counts. Don't look so surprised. Listen, we heard you had a little sister who died. I'm really sorry about that, too. What happened?" A sharp stab of self-remorse threatened to overwhelm her when Sam's smile evaporated, replaced by a pained expression.

Tess gasped. "Sarah! I can't believe you said such a thing. That's no way to welcome our new neighbor. You must forgive her, Sam. My sister's only ten."

"It's okay." Looking Sarah straight in the eye, in an equally matter-of-fact manner, Sam told them their station wagon had been struck from behind by a drunk driver in San Antonio the year before. His younger sister, Rachel, had been thrown from the car and killed instantly. "At least she didn't linger and suffer. As weird as it might sound, that was God's biggest blessing."

"Well," Sarah said, "at least you have the comfort of knowing she's with Jesus, right?" He'd mentioned God, after all. What boy actually talked about the Almighty if he didn't have faith? She could already tell Sam was different from the other boys in Rockbridge. In a good way.

"Right." Sam nodded. "That was the Lord's greatest blessing for my family."

"Enough of this sad talk," Tess said. "Can we please talk about something else?"

"I'm sorry." Feeling awkward, Sarah turned to go. "I need to get back to Hershey now." Thank goodness Sam hadn't shed any tears when he'd told her about his dead sister. That would have been horrible, and would have made her feel worse than she already did. The story was tragic enough, but she'd never liked cry baby boys. Sam took his loss like a man, and that impressed her.

"Hershey, huh? You must be a chocolate lover." Sam trailed behind them through the house and back into the front room. Thankfully, their new neighbor didn't seem to hold her lack of tact against her.

Tess laughed. "Sarah's a dog lover. Hershey's the name of her newest pet because his coat's smooth and rich as dark chocolate."

"Great name. I love animals, too," Sam said. "Maybe you'll introduce us sometime."

"Sure. He's a Labrador Retriever, four months old. I walk him every night. You're welcome to join us." From the corner of her eye, Sarah caught Tess's glare as she waved and headed out the front door. Walking away from Sam's house, she heard her sister telling him about school and offering to help him get acquainted.

Of course, Sam was all Tess could talk about for days afterward. "Sam Lewis is the most beautiful boy I've ever seen," she'd gushed. "He looks like one of those Greek gods come to life."

Sam had joined her on many nights as she'd walked Hershey. Sometimes he'd bring along the newest stray dog he'd temporarily adopted. They'd talk about school and sports mostly. Sometimes they'd discuss books, but he preferred crime and war dramas while she devoured the classics.

"I can't believe you've read some of those books," he'd told her once, "much less understand them. I thought only old people read them unless it's required reading for school. Are you sure you're not really thirty years old?" She'd given him a good punch in the arm for that remark. "Hey, it's a compliment when you think about it," he'd protested with his customary grin.

As long as Sarah had known him, Sam had been straightforward without exhibiting any self-consciousness when he talked about God, as if the Almighty was his close, personal friend. That boldness was the way it should be, but it was more than Sarah could say for most people. Other than some of the older female prayer warriors, deacons and elders in their church, she'd never known anyone else—male or female—who could talk about the Lord and make it sound natural instead of forced.

Hearing a shuffling noise and a grunt, Sarah snapped back to the present. She'd really zoned out, but at least it was quiet in the diner, giving her time to indulge in her memories. In the middle of stacking chairs upside down on the tabletops, she paused. Merle Smithers, son of the now-deceased legendary town drunk and seemingly destined to follow in his dad's footsteps, rose from his table and lumbered toward her. For the past forty minutes, he'd sat quietly in a corner booth, the only customer.

"Gotta go outside since I can't smoke in this joint," he mumbled. "What's wrong with you people? A little smoke never hurt nobody."

"I disagree." Sarah stood her ground, hoping he'd turn around and go back to his table. "I'm sure you know Myrna's husband died last year from lung problems. The doctors said it was caused by all those cancer sticks he inhaled on a daily basis."

"Spoken just like a nurse." Holding onto the back of a booth, Merle swayed.

"His lungs were black, Merle. They did an autopsy. Ask Doc Meriweather."

He waved his hand. "Ah, come on, Nurse Sarah. How about some mouth to mouth? Put that pretty mouth to better use than criticizing my vices." When he stumbled forward, Sarah spied the top of a liquor bottle sticking out of his pants pocket. Usually he kept his bottles—and his inebriation—to himself.

"Oh, Merle." What a sad figure he painted. Why did people seek solace in alcohol? Addiction was a foreign concept to her, but she'd heard from others how it could be all-consuming, fueled by anything from loneliness and heartbreak to a sense of hopelessness. Still, she'd probably never fully understand the reasons if she lived to be a hundred years old. Not that her heart didn't break for those suffering from such addictions. She'd hoped his father's death from alcoholism might have sobered up Merle once and for all.

"Just one little kiss. Be nice to old Merle. I'm not that bad lookin', am I? Ain't that old either. I still got all my working parts."

Clutching the back of a chair, Sarah positioned it between her and Merle, her cheeks burning with embarrassment. Why did it have to be one of those rare nights when Myrna hadn't been feeling well and had headed home early? Considering she'd worked at the diner forever, Sarah knew the owner trusted her to clean up and lock the diner for the night. But how could either of them know that Merle would get drunk and act like this?

Jimmy was in the kitchen washing dishes, so she wasn't completely alone. At thirty minutes before closing, she didn't expect any more customers. Tonight, she wouldn't mind if a group of kids decided to come in late for malts and fries.

"You're the best lookin' woman in Rockbridge," Merle said. "Some of the guys might think that sister of yours is the fox, but that chick's a-a big te-tease. You're the special one, Sar-Sarah." He moved closer and started to reach for her hair. "So pretty with all your blonde hair. Gorgeous"—his eyes scanned her figure—"everywhere. I bet you'd look—"

She had no intention of hearing the rest of that sentence. "That's enough out of you, Merle. Sit down, and I'll go pour you an extremely strong cup of black coffee. You have no business going out on the roads in this condition."

"I'm fi—fine." His gaze rested on her. "So are you."

Sarah aimed a nervous glance in the direction of the kitchen. If she called out to Jimmy for any reason, he'd come running as best as his bum leg would allow. Not that she was afraid of Merle. She could handle him, but she'd never seen him so drunk that he'd slurred his words and made advances toward her. Although his words and insinuations made her uncomfortable, she didn't believe Merle would ever touch her inappropriately. The man was all talk. Still, best not to tempt anything.

"Sit down. Now." She infused her voice with as much authority as she could muster.

"Whoa," he said, stumbling backwards. "Now you sound like my mama, God rest her soul. Don't need you tellin' me what to do, too. I'm the man, you hear me?" Merle's voice had risen, and he glared at her.

Sarah's eyes widened. Hearing the bell on the door as it closed, she glanced up to see Sam. Not that she needed a hero, but he'd shown up at a mighty opportune moment.

Sam's tall frame swallowed the space as he stood just inside the door. How much had he heard? She breathed a silent prayer of thanks and hoped her glance conveyed her gratitude. Why he'd be near the diner at this hour of the night, she couldn't imagine. With his black Stetson, worn jeans, boots, and a short-sleeved red shirt that revealed well-developed upper arm muscles, Sam made her heart race. Much more so than even the twenty-year-old version of Sam she'd adored as a fanciful teenager.

Moving to stand between her and Merle, Sam slid his hands down to his hips. "Merle, you've had too much to drink. Time to go home."

"Lookee he-here. It's the bi-big hero man, S-Sam Le-Lew-wis." Merle snarled the comment.

His features creased with concern, but Sam didn't flinch. When he darted a glance Sarah's way, brows raised, she nodded.

"Why'd you come back to this Podunk town, anyway? The only thing worth it would be this little lady." Merle pointed to her and then his gaze traveled back to Sam. "Hey, you got something goin' on with our beautiful Sarah? She's quite the looker, ain't she? Take a number, buddy. Half the men in this town—"

"I came back to Rockbridge because this is my home," Sam said, thankfully interrupting Merle. "Home is where you're going right now. Come on. Let's go." When Sam reached for him, Merle shrugged him off.

"Nah, man. Leave"—he burped loudly and stumbled a bit, slumping down into the closest booth—"me alone." Merle hung his head and let out a loud, obnoxious belch.

"Would you prefer I call the sheriff? On duty or not, I'm sure Tommy will come collect you and give you a nice jail cell for the night. Your choice." Sam's voice was as firm and commanding as Sarah had ever heard it. She liked it.

Walking behind the counter, she glanced over her shoulder and then grabbed a mug. After pouring steaming black coffee into it, she carried the mug to Merle along with a napkin. "Here, Merle. Drink up."

Sam shot her a grateful glance.

"That's mighty hospitable." Tugging the mug closer, Merle lifted it to his lips with shaky fingers. A stream of the dark liquid spilled over the top and onto the table, but he seemed oblivious.

"Careful there." She moved the napkin closer to him.

"I'll be fine. You can go on now." Merle slurped a longer sip of the coffee. "Always said you made the best coffee in town, Sarah."

"Want a piece of blueberry pie to go with your coffee? It's on the house."

"Sounds like a plan." Sam slid into the booth on the seat across from Merle. "I'll take a slice, too, and you can give me the tab."

"Of course. I'll bring you some coffee, too."

"Thank you, Sarah." Sam's appreciative gaze made it worth the events of the past few minutes. Not that she'd care to relive them.

As she cleaned tables and helped Jimmy in the kitchen, Sarah stole a peek at Sam and Merle every now and again.

"They're gettin' along pretty well out there," Jimmy said, scrubbing the last pan by hand. "Sam's a good man. Always has been. He could have a swelled head with his background, but he's a fine man, like his dad. His mama raised him right, and he respects women. Not like old Merle out there."

Sarah was aware she was blushing but had no idea why. It wasn't like she could take credit for Sam's accomplishments, but she was proud of him nonetheless. "Merle's lost his way, and I wish I could help him. Other than pray, I mean. From what I know, he doesn't have any family to speak of since his father died, and he can't seem to hold down a job."

"It's a double-edged sword for some people. The alcohol." Jimmy put the pan upside down on the counter to air dry. "Keep praying for him, honey. Maybe Jesus will get hold of him and kick some sense into him."

"I'm not sure Jesus works that way, Jimmy."

Jimmy gave her a look. "And who's to say He doesn't? At least

Sam's talkin' with him and treatin' Merle like a human being which is more than I can say for a lot of people in town. I think it's the sins of the father stigma. His dad bein' the town drunk for years and all. Maybe Merle thinks he needs to keep up the reputation."

"I certainly hope not." Untying her apron and hanging it on the hook by the back door, Sarah checked the time on the wall clock. "It's late. If you want to go ahead and leave, I can lock up."

"I'll agree to that plan, but only because I asked Sam to make sure both you and Merle get home safe tonight."

Sarah raised a skeptical brow. "When did you do that?"

Jimmy pulled his soiled, damp apron over his head and balled it beneath one arm. "You were moppin' the floor at the time and doin' some mighty serious thinkin' from the looks of it."

"I walk home on my own almost every night, and I've always been fine."

Jimmy gave her a wink. "Now that Captain Lewis is home, I think some things are gonna change around here. I'll see you tomorrow, Jelly Bean. Good night."

Before switching off the kitchen lights, on a whim, Sarah reached for her apron hanging on the hook.

Pulling out a little bag from the pocket, she smiled. Cherry jelly beans.

"Night, Jimmy."

Chapter 7

~~♥~~

"That was a really nice thing you did for Merle tonight. Thank you."

Sam appreciated the sentiment, especially coming from Sarah. "You're welcome. I'm glad my mom needed me to take something over to her friend tonight. It's so nice out, I decided to walk." He laughed under his breath. "I'm not sure Myrna would have been as charitable as you in giving Merle a stiff cup of coffee, and especially the slice of pie. Even if she did, Myrna would probably force it down his throat and then push him out the door."

As they walked through the quiet, moonlit streets, it took everything in Sam not to stare at Sarah. Her profile was lovely. In his eyes, she was much prettier than Tess, beautiful without question but in a very different way than her older sister. Physically, they looked nothing at all alike. Tess was shorter, dark-haired, petite, and more flamboyant in the way she dressed and acted. By contrast, Sarah was leggy, blonde, dressed more modestly, and lived her faith. He didn't know why, but he was having difficulty wrapping his mind around the idea that this was the same girl from his past.

"Myrna can be tough, but she might have taken a different approach since he was inebriated. Merle didn't know what he was saying, but it was nice of you to step in and defend my honor. Is that something they teach cadets in the Air Force Academy?" Sarah didn't wear lipstick the way the other girls did. The irony was that lipstick was worn to attract a man, entice a man, and yet he was drawn to her because of how natural she was.

"Defending a woman's honor is a matter of principle for a man, especially a Texan."

"I have a confession," she said.

He glanced at her in mock surprise. "Are you sure you want to confess your secrets to me? I've only been home a few days."

"You seem trustworthy, and I'm not just talking about the military uniform. Truth is"—Sarah darted a glance his way before lowering her gaze—"I'm really glad you came into the diner tonight. And imagine Sheriff Tommy coming in right at closing time to get a last cup of coffee. Wasn't that something?"

"I figure it was God's timing. Like most things in our lives." Sam pulled aside a low-hanging oak branch from the tree in front of the Anderson house. Harry had neglected his yard lately. Maybe he should offer to help with some yard work. He missed the physical labor and training of the last few years. From what his dad told him, the older man had been despondent and neglectful of things since his wife, Delores, died earlier in the year. They'd been married over fifty years. What must it be like to share a love that spanned the generations? Pretty great, he imagined. He'd always hoped to find love, but he'd better get moving if he had a prayer of living long enough to celebrate his own golden anniversary.

"Was it God's timing for you to come home to Rockbridge?"

Sarah's question, as well as her drawl—sweet and deeper now, no longer the voice of a little girl—shook Sam out of his daydreaming. No other girl in the world could entrance him with her native accent like a girl from Texas. Especially the girl walking beside him now.

"I think so, yes."

"Why?" Her tone conveyed nothing more than curiosity.

"For one thing, Dad's counting on me to step in at the bank. I start on Monday."

"Yes, I caught wind of that. I know you've trained for it from the time you first moved here." The corners of her mouth upturned. "You can expect all the single girls in town to apply for an account early next week. Maybe even some of the married women."

Sam chuckled, amused by her sense of humor. Not knowing what Sarah would say at any given moment was fun. "Does that include you?"

Avoiding his gaze, she dipped her head. "I already have an

account at Rockbridge Savings & Loan, but I might come in to make a deposit."

They walked in silence for a few minutes. Even when they were kids, Sarah seemed to understand him in ways others didn't. Since he'd returned to Rockbridge, he'd harbored no illusions about the way the other girls touched him, flirted with him, and tried to get his attention. Sarah made it incredibly easy to like her, to want to get to know her better, to want to spend time with her.

"When I was talking with Merle, he referred to you as Nurse Sarah. Unless it was the liquor talking, I take it you want to be a nurse?"

"That's the plan, yes. I'm headed to study nursing in Austin."

"University of Texas?"

"None other. The same university you attended until the illustrious Air Force and the lure of flying jets called to you."

He smiled, pleased that she'd apparently kept track of him through the years.

"They started offering courses at UT in Austin a couple of years ago after transferring some of the medical faculty from the Medical Branch of UT in Galveston. I'm hoping it'll eventually develop into a four-year program in Austin, but I might need to transfer to Galveston. Whatever it takes to get the credentials I need."

"You're planning on attending UT for the fall semester?"

A frown flickered over her lovely face. "I've received my acceptance and everything's in place. Now, I need to save another five thousand dollars. By the time that happens, I might need to reapply." She shrugged. "Like I said, whatever it takes."

So much about Sarah impressed him. "That's an admirable goal, and you seem determined. Not to be too personal, but is five thousand dollars the amount you need to get your degree?"

"I mentioned it, so no, it's not too personal. Not that I go around telling everyone." She darted a quick glance his way. "In answer to your question, it should be enough money, given any unforeseen circumstances. I've saved enough otherwise. I'd rather not split my loyalties by working while I'm in school, though. That way, I can concentrate on my studies."

Maybe he should let the matter drop and steer their conversation to other matters, but Sam couldn't let it go. "I take it that's why you're working extra shifts at the diner?"

"How did you know about that?"

"I didn't. I just assumed since you were at Perry's earlier this afternoon and then had to work so late tonight. I hope you don't do it too often."

"Actually, I do. Unless you know how to make money grow on trees, it's realistically going to take another year." Sam heard her deep sigh as they turned the corner onto their street. "My parents have spent all their spare funds on the senior living expenses and care for my grandparents, in case you're wondering."

The thought hadn't crossed his mind, but he appreciated Sarah's candor.

"I thought about leaving the diner and finding another job," she said, "but I've worked at Perry's since I was sixteen. Myrna treats me well, and she was always willing to work around my afterschool schedule with the softball games and tournaments. She adds a little extra in my paycheck when she can, and she gives me a holiday bonus and regular raises. Not to mention more shifts if I ask. She's the best employer I could have, all things considered."

"I meant more in terms of your social life. Don't you date?"

His question appeared to surprise her. "No. I don't want to be the kind of girl to lead anyone on when I have no intention of sticking around Rockbridge. That wouldn't be fair to them or me."

Those words unsettled him. While he respected her consideration for a potential date's feelings, she sounded so adamant about leaving town. On the one hand, he was thrilled to hear she'd be in Rockbridge at least another year, but then he was disgruntled when she mentioned leaving town.

Nothing made much sense. Everything about Sarah appealed to him as a man and as her friend. She was comfortable and easy to be with, and she didn't seem to expect anything from him other than friendship. Here it was, the first night they'd spent any time together since his return home, and yet they shared the same familiar give-and-take as they'd done all those years ago. As if they'd just spent time together the day before, although the dynamic he shared with Sarah was different now, in a very good way. Of all the girls in Rockbridge, she appealed to him the most. However, she probably considered him too old. Washed up at twenty-seven? Nah.

"Well, this is me." Sarah stopped in front of the Jordan home. Lost in thought, Sam hadn't noticed they'd already canvassed the short distance.

"So it is." Sam tried to keep disappointment from surfacing in his voice, not sure he succeeded. The way he felt in this moment, he could walk beside Sarah a lot longer and it wouldn't be long enough.

The Jordan home hadn't changed much from what he remembered. A fresh coat of white paint on the shutters and the front door perhaps. His gaze moved upward. Looked like a new roof. He nodded to the covered porch. "I see you've added a swing. Mom asked Dad to install one this summer. Now I think I know where she got the idea."

"Our mothers have grown closer since you've been away," she said. "They've been doing some volunteer work together, and they're on a committee or two at the church."

"That's nice. Since you've been away," Sam repeated. The air between them was charged with something he hadn't experienced in too long to remember. An invisible but incredibly strong pull toward this girl who was no longer a girl. Sarah Jordan was very much a woman now. A woman who attracted him on many levels.

Sarah glanced at him over one shoulder as she walked toward the house. "I did, you know."

"Hold up just a minute." Sam waited for her to turn back around. When she did, her lovely smile grew, making his pulse jump in an unprecedented way.

"I missed you. Welcome home, Captain Lewis."

Chapter 8

~~♥~~

Tuesday Night—May 1, 1962

Selecting a smooth, flat rock, Sarah sent it soaring over Thornton's Creek. She watched as it skimmed the surface, leaving ripples in its wake. After stretching her legs, she dipped her toes in the water, wiggling them. The creek temperature was ideal, cool and refreshing, but not too cold. The Spicy Plum nail polish Tess had loaned her looked good on her toenails—rich and classy, although probably better for the fall season instead of almost summer. Painting the nails on her toes had been whimsical, a fun change.

Her thoughts strayed to Sam, as they'd done quite a bit in the week since his return. What she'd told him was true—she'd missed him. More than she'd realized. In the past few years, her studies, working at Perry's Diner, teaching the girls in Sunday school, and helping her mother with household chores occupied nearly every hour of her day. Most nights, she fell into bed exhausted.

In high school, Sam had never seemed motivated by the need to be the best at everything, but he was highly proficient at most things. Although he wasn't the top student in his class, he'd been asked to make the graduation speech because his classmates voted him the best public speaker. Football practice had gobbled up a lot of his study time. He was well-liked and managed to find a good balance between his academic and social life. "A well-rounded fellow" as her grandmother would have said.

From what Sarah knew, Sam had only gotten in trouble once—

skinny-dipping with his buddies at the creek one hot summer night—but that incident was nothing more than speculation. She hated rumors, but working at Perry's, she heard most all of them. Boring, straitlaced boys—especially upstanding Christian boys—didn't skinny dip. Sarah secretly hoped the rumor was true and suspected it was.

Maybe she couldn't help thinking about Sam because she'd always considered him her first love, if she could even call it that. Well, her *only* love, and he didn't even know it. A one-sided love. How pitiful was she? At fourteen, when she'd awakened to the fact that not all boys were complete toads, she'd developed a massive crush on him when he'd returned to Rockbridge for Christmas break. Sam's eyes *were* the most gorgeous shade of blue, alive with excitement and energy. What a travesty that all of his thick hair was cut so short, but hair could always grow hair back.

On Christmas Eve, she'd run into him at Johnson's Market in the produce section. They'd both been sent by their mothers to pick up some missing ingredient for their holiday meal. He'd hugged her and taken the time to share an actual conversation. No other boy had ever made her feel so special without even knowing it.

Her girlish daydreams had been soundly squelched when Mom chastised her for staring at Sam in church, of all places. Mooning over boys was frowned upon as a matter of principle but especially when worshipping in the house of the Lord. Throwing spitballs hadn't been much better, but mooning was apparently the bigger sin.

"God helped make Sam Lewis, and I'm admiring His wonderful creation," she remembered telling her mother. Serious and pragmatic as a general rule, Mom failed to appreciate her humor and had not been amused.

Two days ago, on Sunday morning, Sam sat three rows in front of her at Rockbridge Community Church, sitting with his family on their customary pew. Seriously tempted to throw spitballs at the back of his head for old time's sake, she'd refrained. She didn't wish to spoil his illusion that she'd actually grown up.

Something short-circuited inside her, and Sarah's nerves went haywire whenever Sam was near. Which was nearly every day when he stopped in at Perry's. A couple of times, he'd asked her to share her break with him. After Myrna encouraged her, she'd joined him. They discussed world events, books and other things most people her age could care less about since they'd prefer to talk about the newest dance craze or Hollywood couple. She'd talked with Sam until Patti tapped her on the shoulder and told her she needed to get back to work. Embarrassed, Sarah had excused herself, but not once did she regret spending time with him.

"Mind if I join you?"

Sarah startled and brought her hand to her chest. *Sam.* What was he doing here? Not that she minded the least little bit. "Not at all. Please do." She tried to calm her pulse, but it was a lost cause.

"Sorry if I scared you. I tried to crunch a few twigs to tip you off, but you seemed lost in your own little world. It's a good thing I come in peace."

Sam's humor always made her smile and put her at ease. She patted the moss-covered ground beside her. "Have a seat."

"Don't think I've ever seen you here before."

"I was about to say the same thing to you. If I didn't know better, I'd say that's a really bad pick-up line."

He looked at her askance. "Since when did you grow up enough to know what a pick-up line is?"

"While you were away. Remember?"

She heard his soft chuckle. "Seems to be a running theme with you. You've discovered my favorite place in the world to sit and think." After kicking off his tennis shoes, Sam settled beside her. Sarah liked seeing him in his denim shorts and burnt orange University of Texas T-shirt emblazoned with the Longhorns logo.

"Mine, too." Birds chirped on either side of the creek, bubbles from fish skimmed along the surface of the water, and a light breeze ruffled the leaves in the trees directly behind them. They sat in silence, but it wasn't awkward. Just two friends enjoying the quiet. "Everyone needs a special place to ponder, and to be honest, the company is nice."

Leaning forward, she pulled a stray blade of grass from between her toes. She tossed it and watched it flutter down to the surface of the water, carried away by the gentle current. "It's so peaceful here, and sometimes I feel like I'm the only person in the world. I also feel God's presence here more than anywhere else." Raising her knees, Sarah wrapped her arms around them.

"And, in those moments, you understand you're not alone at all."

"Exactly. Sam, do you remember when we used to fish here? We caught a lot, as I recall."

"We did. Small mouth bass, spotted bass, catfish." He laughed. "I remember you standing on my doorstep on my seventeenth birthday, grinning from ear to ear with a black crappie dangling from your hand. You pretty much threw it at me, wished me happy birthday, and then ran off down the street."

She grinned. "I'm surprised you even remember."

"Kind of hard to forget a fish being thrown in my face. It was one of the more unique birthday gifts I've ever received. 'Here, have a happy crappie birthday.'"

Sarah wrinkled her nose even as she enjoyed the rich sound of his laughter. "I always liked catching and reeling them in, but not gutting and preparing them." She mock shuddered.

"Admit it. In the case of my birthday fish, you just liked saying crappie."

That made her laugh. "Maybe. My dad used to say the crappie was a little fish with a big heart."

"Interesting theory. It tasted good, anyway. And you sure were cute."

She smirked. "Back then, you didn't think two seconds about whether or not I was cute."

"Well, looking back on it now, I do."

Unsure how to answer that one, she needed to keep the conversation moving forward. "You know, there's something I find interesting."

Sam waited for her to speak again, patient but wearing a curious expression.

"As boring as I find our little town at times, this little creek is quiet, but it's not boring at all."

"Ah, so what you're really saying is the *people* of Rockbridge are boring."

"I guess I am. Does that make me a terrible person?"

"No, of course not," he said. "I don't think Rockbridge is boring. I happen to believe that boring is what you make it."

She shook her head. "I don't follow."

He reclined, stretching out to his full length, crossing his arms behind his head. "For one thing, I'll take life in Rockbridge any day over the places I've lived in the last few years. They were beautiful countries, but I'm talking more in terms of basic liberties we often take for granted."

Sarah's cheeks warmed. "Sorry. I didn't mean to sound insensitive." She cared what Sam thought of her and hated to think she might have offended him.

"No worries. You didn't. Just making an observation." Shifting onto his side, Sam faced her, supporting his weight on one elbow. The action seemed natural yet intimate. She liked how comfortable he apparently felt in her presence. The give-and-take. The teasing. The closeness. This was Sam, her friend. Not Sam the military man. Not Sam the vice president of Rockbridge Savings & Loan. Not Sam her regular customer at Perry's Diner, although he always seemed more relaxed there.

"The way I see it, it's the people in your life that make it interesting, more fulfilling," he said. "Your job and the joy you find in it also make a big difference. I know you love working at the diner, but you've yet to enjoy that satisfaction in a career you love. It'll happen soon enough."

"I hope you're right. Sometimes I feel like I'm stuck in a time warp. I mean, how have I changed since high school? I've been out of school for three years, but what do I really have to show for it?" Stealing a glimpse at her companion and meeting his eyes, Sarah marveled at their intensity before returning her focus to the creek.

"Trust me, Sarah. You've changed quite a bit."

His statement sounded like a compliment. Or maybe she was imagining too much. "You think so? It was meant more as a rhetorical question, but now you've intrigued me. Name one way."

His lips upturned. "For one thing, you're much taller now."

"Not really. I reached my full height at fifteen. Name another one."

He scrunched his features into a comical frown. "You're not as much of a tomboy."

That observation made her laugh. "Stick around."

"Notice I said *not as much of.* Very important qualifier. Okay, here's another way. You also seem more articulate."

She glanced at him in surprise. "No fair. Now you're mocking me? You know that's definitely not true. You witnessed my social gaffe with Kathy Parker in the diner. We shared a conversation about it, as I recall."

"Notice I said you're *more* articulate."

"As opposed to falling-over-my-tongue tactless? You and your qualifiers. Where I come from, those comments could be considered backhanded compliments." She blew out a sigh.

"As a general rule, you're agreeable and don't let others provoke you to speak your mind."

Smirking, she tossed a small pebble at him.

He caught it one-handed and winked. "Kathy Parker is enough to make anyone lose their cool."

"Tell me something. Do they also teach cadets how to wink at girls in the military or do you have some kind of weird twitch?"

"A twitch. Nothing more. Except when I'm sitting beside a pretty girl. Then all bets are off."

She mock gasped. "You're a betting man now? For shame." *He thinks I'm pretty?* At the thought, a shiver of pleasure coursed through her, all the way down to her Spicy Plum painted toes.

"Figure of speech. That's all. And what's with the misperceptions of the Air Force Academy? Our national security doesn't depend on military officers knowing how to flirt."

Feeling silly, she giggled. "Sorry. Sam, do you remember that day when we first met?" Stretching her legs, Sarah dipped her feet into the water again. "I still can't believe what I said to you. I went into semi-seclusion after that, you know."

"That explains why I didn't see you around for a while. I figured your parents had you carted off to a private school."

"Watch it." Grabbing another pebble, Sarah tossed it at him and then stretched out beside him.

"Or else you were playing with your dog morning, noon and night."

"Well, that much would be true," she said. "Here's another confession, and I can't believe I'm going to tell you."

"No one's forcing you." Humor laced Sam's words. "You seem to like confessing things to me, so who am I to stop you?"

She shrugged. "I don't know why, but maybe the Holy Spirit's prompting me or something. The thing is, I used to pretend you were my big brother. Mostly because of the way you teased me. But there were times when you stood up for me, too. Kind of like you did on a small scale with Kathy Parker and her insults, and then in a much bigger way with Merle at the diner."

Sarah made sure she had his eye contact. "What I'm trying to say is that I liked it, especially because it was you. Then *and* now." She tilted her head. "Thank you."

Sam's eyes softened as they met hers. "It was my honor."

Good answer, Captain Lewis.

Chapter 9

~~♥~~

The Next Afternoon

"Fletcher? You in there?" Not hearing a response, Sarah knocked on the door again. If she didn't get an answer, she'd leave the container of chicken soup on the front doorstep and depart. Wouldn't be the first time, and she only hoped he'd open the door and retrieve it before the unleashed dog next door got into it.

"Keep your cool! Hang on! I'm coming." A minute later the door swung open. Fletcher Monroe gave her a lopsided smile. As usual, he leaned heavily on his crutches, his left pant leg swinging in the breeze created by a large floor fan in the middle of his living room. "Hey, Sarah. Whatever you got there sure smells good."

"Some of Jimmy's homemade chicken soup and Myrna made a fresh batch of her blueberry muffins, so I brought you some of those."

"You're an angel. Come on in." Opening the door wider, he limped aside to allow her to enter the small dwelling. Sarah walked into the kitchen and set the containers on the counter. "Do you want the soup in the fridge or should I just leave it here?"

"I lost a leg, sweetheart. I'm not incapable of making decisions or putting soup away."

She was used to the disabled truck driver saying such things, but Sarah wished he'd get out in the community more. Maybe it'd lessen his bitterness and make the man more agreeable. Help him see that people in town genuinely liked him and didn't look at him as a cripple.

"I see you're as crusty as ever today. Be sure and eat those muffins. A touch of sweetness might help that disposition of yours." When he laughed, Sarah nodded. "Much better. How are you feeling?"

"About the same, I guess. My cold's a little better. How are things with you and those big plans to go to nursing school?" He scratched his grizzled chin and dropped onto a nearby chair. "Have a seat."

Leaving the soup on the counter, Sarah took the chair opposite him. "I can only stay a minute. Everything's in place except for the remaining funds I need. I'm thinking now—with all the extra shifts I'm picking up at Perry's—I might be able to enroll for the second term this coming year."

He nodded, and his brown eyes met hers. His sandy blond hair was on the longish side and he could use a shave, but the dark circles under his eyes weren't as pronounced as they'd been last week. "I know you're happy about that. The way you come out here to bring me soup and things, you'll make a great nurse."

"Thanks, Fletch. I appreciate that. Do you need anything else?" She snapped her fingers. "I picked up a new bed pillow for you on sale at Tucker's the other day. The kind with real goose feathers that you told me you like, but I forgot it at the house. Sorry. I'll be sure and bring it by in the next few days."

"What do I owe you?" He started to dig into his back pocket.

She waved her hand. "Nothing. You should know that by now."

"You're never gonna get to that school if you keep doing things for everybody else and don't take any payment, girl. I got bread. I got a good settlement from the trucking company, and I'm no charity case." A familiar sadness shadowed his features. "Least not in the monetary sense."

"I wish you'd let me talk with Doc Meriweather about measuring you for a prosthetic leg—"

"I already told you I don't want no artificial leg." He frowned. "That's not about the money either."

Sarah swallowed hard. Stubborn old coot. "I heard you the first time, and the second, and the fifteenth." What could she say that might persuade him? A snippet of conversation she'd overheard at Johnson's Market flittered through her mind. "I don't know how you're going to dance with Sally Barksdale at Quentin's otherwise."

She cast a glance at the crutches resting on the side of his chair. "Kind of hard to sway to music on those things, I imagine."

He scoffed. "You think Sally has any interest in me? Come on, Sarah. A girl like that wouldn't have any interest in a washed-up guy like me. You're charitable, but you're not blind."

"No, I'm not. Want to know what I see when I look at you?"

Fletcher's smile faded. "Not sure. Knowing you, you're gonna tell me anyhow."

"You're a very nice looking man under all that stubble on your face. You could stand a haircut, too. Not to mention that perpetual scowl. Fletch, you're only crippled because you're allowing yourself to act the part." She drew in a quick breath, saying a silent prayer for guidance. She wanted to encourage this man, not wound him more by unintentionally hurtful comments.

"A leg doesn't represent who you are inside. I remember you used to be one of the fastest runners in school. I'm sure that desire to run is still inside you, and you *can* run again, so don't go thinking you won't. Just not as fast, but you know what? That's okay. We all slow down a little once we hit our twenties. You *will* run again, if I have anything to say about it."

"I like your confidence, girl." Fletcher scratched his chin again. Why did men, especially those with beards, always do that? Probably for the same reason she sometimes twirled a lock of hair around her finger. Gave her something to do while she pondered someone's words. That was probably a good reason she usually chose to wear her hair up most of the time, even when she wasn't working. Silence settled between them for a few seconds, broken only by the soft whirring sound from the floor fan.

"So, do you know something about Sally?" When his gaze settled on her again—filled with what looked like renewed hope—Sarah bit her lower lip.

"I overheard something at Johnson's Market the other day," she said. "I wasn't eavesdropping, mind you. A couple of ladies happened to mention Sally thinks you're a handsome man underneath all of your rubble and stubble. Their words, not mine. They said that Sally, um"—Sarah lowered her gaze—"thinks you could be a stud if you weren't so determined to be a hermit."

He snorted and looked the other way. She waited, and a second later, Fletcher nodded. "Go ahead. You got my attention now. Are

56

you sure 'stud' was the word you heard?"

"Positive since I don't normally use that word. There might even have been a 'groovy' in there somewhere." Sarah's smile faded. "If you don't want to try the prosthetic leg, I wish you'd call one of your friends and have them bring you to church sometime. Or bring you to the diner." She wiped away a tear and hoped he wouldn't tease her for the show of emotion. "I'd offer to treat you at Perry's, but I know how you feel about that. Do you understand what I'm trying to say?"

He nodded slowly. "I think you've made yourself pretty clear. You want me to stop feeling sorry for myself. Want me to get off my sorry duff and get out among the townsfolk again."

"You're finally getting it. I remember how popular you were in high school. You hung out with Tess and her group and wouldn't deign to socialize with the likes of me."

"That's not true, Sarah. Tell you one thing. There's no one I'd rather socialize with right now than you." He broke into a smile. "Except maybe Sally Barksdale. Don't you go giving me false hope now."

She laughed. "Wouldn't think of it. Think about what I said. The invitation's open if you decide to get out and about in Rockbridge society again." After lifting out of the chair, Sarah helped Fletcher adjust his crutches. Was it her imagination or did he already seem to have a little more spirit in him?

"Thanks for coming by."

"Welcome. You'd better eat that soup soon or it's going to get cold. And don't forget to eat a blueberry muffin."

"Yeah, yeah. To sweeten me up. I'll be sure and do that."

"Bye, Fletch." She put her hand on his arm, giving it a light squeeze. The muscle tone in his arms was still well-developed. Those crutches were good for something.

"Peace, sweetheart. You're welcome to come by and boss me around anytime."

"Count on it."

~~♥~~

That Evening

"So, tell me why you want to be a nurse," Sam said. After prayer meeting at the church, he sat on the creek bank beside her. "Last I'd heard, you wanted to be a space explorer."

Sarah heard his quiet chuckle. "Do you find that funny?"

He nudged her shoulder. "Yes, but not for the reason you think. I was thinking the space program could use a few more prayer warriors like you. The way you prayed for Merle tonight in prayer meeting was cherry."

"Cherry?"

"What? You've never heard that term?"

"No," she said, nudging him back. "Must be something you kids are saying these days."

"It's all good, I assure you. Cherry means outstanding, excellent."

She grinned. "I never considered you to be the type to use current slang."

"You found me out." Sam hung his head and stuck out his lower lip in an exaggerated manner. "I'm trying to fit in around here. Talk the lingo. Be hip."

"I thought you were more hip without doing those things. Stick with the man you are. He's impressive enough on his own."

Sam cocked a brow. "You think so? I appreciate the vote of confidence."

"You're welcome. To answer your question, I seriously doubt NASA's ready for a female in their ranks yet since the program's only four years old. When the Soviets launched Sputnik 1, it created the whole Pearl Harbor effect, and then the race was on."

"Pearl Harbor effect?"

She couldn't believe an Air Force man with a mechanical engineering degree wasn't familiar with the term. "Heaven forbid any other nation should be more technologically advanced than the United States. I'm sure you heard about President Kennedy's Apollo Project announcement, right? It was in late May, about a year ago."

He frowned a little. "I haven't been completely out of touch with the rest of the world, you know. As I recall, President Kennedy announced plans to send a man to the moon. An exciting pursuit if ever there was one."

"Right, and then bring him home again to earth. That last part's very important. An important qualifier, as you might say." Sarah nudged him again and they shared a smile. "Proving our scientific and technological superiority over other nations. We're on our way with Alan Shepard completing the Mercury space flight and John

Glenn orbiting the earth. All steps to move us forward in space travel. We live in exciting times, my friend."

Sam watched her but said nothing. "What?" His scrutiny unsettled her, but not in a bad way. "You're staring at me."

"Sorry. You surprise me, that's all. I love your enthusiasm. Your eyes light up whenever you're talking about something that excites you. Everyone should have a passion like that for something—or someone—in their life."

"Agreed." She nodded. "Whether it's your job, faith, kids or whatever, everyone should have a reason to get up and face the day."

"Yep, but the sad fact of the matter is, a lot of people don't." Sam tweaked her chin. "Count yourself among the blessed."

"Oh, I do. Trust me."

He stretched out on his back. "You sure you don't want to apply for a position at NASA?"

She released an unladylike grunt. "Not likely. First, I need to complete my education. And, let's face it, at the rate I'm going, that could be a while down the road. But who knows?" She shrugged. "I think an Air Force pilot would be a perfect candidate for the NASA astronaut program."

Sam's smile sobered. "Not this Air Force pilot, if that's what you're implying."

"Okay, then. It just seems like you'd already have one foot in the space capsule door, in a manner of speaking. I mean, you understand complicated controls, know how to pilot a craft"—she raised her hand in the air—"and we have liftoff." Sarah slowly lowered her hand. From the way Sam's jaws flexed, she could tell she'd touched a raw nerve.

She stretched out beside him. In some ways, Sam was quickly becoming her best friend. Debbie was always with Arnie, Tess with her friends, and most of the other girls in town either looked down on her for working at the diner or were busy planning their next social outing.

"If I ever get married, maybe I'll have a son or daughter who becomes an astronaut and goes to the moon," she said. "That'd be even more exciting. . .and a whole more frightening, I imagine."

At least that sentiment made Sam smile again. "Yeah. That would be pretty awesome."

She'd like to ask Sam about his passions, but the time wasn't right.

Side by side, stretched out on the bank of the creek, they were both quiet again until a small pebble hit Sarah in the middle of her stomach, making her jump.

"Dollar for your thoughts."

She grinned. "Coming from a financier, it's now a dollar instead of a penny, huh?"

"Fooled you. I'm no financier. I'm just a guy who tries his best to use the brain God gave me. I can tinker around with airplane engines and make them work, and I can also manage money."

"Sometimes you sound like Pastor McDonald." At least he didn't sound irritated with her, and for that, she was relieved. "I used to think you might go into the ministry."

"Really?" He sounded surprised. "My faith's a big part of who I am, but ministry wasn't anything I ever considered. Not to change the subject, but you still haven't told me why you want to be a nurse."

She didn't need to think about her answer to that question. "I want to give my patients hope. Let them know—even if I'm not allowed to say the actual words—that I care, and that I'm praying for them. Of course, I want to do everything in my power to help my patients get well. Especially if I'm the last person someone sees before they die, I want my words to count for something." She had Sam's full attention now. "I want them to know they meant something to someone else. And, if they have no one else, I want to hold their hand so they're not afraid."

Sarah focused on the creek, watching as a squirrel scampered nearby. "I hope that doesn't sound like too much to ask or self-important on my part."

"Not at all. It's very selfless and admirable." His tone was quiet, respectful.

"I just can't imagine what it feels like to know the life is slowly draining out of your body. But I sure as anything know it's got to be a whole lot easier when you know where you'll be spending eternity. How do people live without that assurance?"

He blew out a breath. "I met guys like that all the time. As difficult as you might find it to believe, some people have never heard about Jesus. Then you have the ones who've heard the gospel message at one point or another, but they've rejected it. That's the toughest thing of all to accept. And the saddest."

Surprising her, Sam reached for her hand. "What you said about why you want to be a nurse sounds like what I imagine a missionary nurse might say."

"It's a possibility." Sarah slowly pulled her hand away from his. Not that she was uncomfortable, but more because she liked it. "I'd love to travel the world. I've never even been in a plane, but I know you've probably flown hundreds of missions. What's it like to fly?"

"The most unbelievable feeling in the world." His voice took on a faraway tone. "If you want the truth, I'm thankful we weren't involved in active combat. As much as I love to fly, I couldn't knowingly destroy innocent lives. Just so you know, my role overseas was more of an advisory capacity, but I flew relief and medical aid missions. Wherever they needed me, I'd go."

His words reminded her of what she'd told him about nursing school. Whatever it takes. "In other words, you put your faith in action."

Sam locked gazes with her. "Yes, you could say that. I tried, anyway."

"That's all any of us can do. I'm sure you did your best. From what I've seen, you always do." Sarah tossed another pebble his way. "Your turn. Tell me why you like banking."

Again, his chuckle stirred something inside her. "Call me weird, but I really like numbers. I like how they operate independently and how they fit together."

"You're right," Sarah scoffed. "That *is* weird."

"It's more than numbers. I'm sure your beloved astronauts know a thing or two about numbers. They couldn't go into space without a working knowledge of how to read those complicated controls and instruments or how to make scientific calculations."

"I know that. I'm only teasing you." She tossed a tuft of grass at him, a totally ineffective move.

"Take my interactions with our bank customers," he said. "They're not just account numbers. Charlotte Simms, for example. Did you know she trained for the Olympics in ice skating?"

Sarah almost choked on her incredulity. The woman was getting up in years and was nearly as round as she was tall. "She *what?*"

Sam yanked a few blades of grass from the ground and she watched as they filtered through his fingers. "Charlotte grew up in Minneapolis and trained six hours a day from the age of six. She passed the first few qualifying rounds but then fell off a horse and broke her ankle. End of Olympic dreams."

"That's sad." Sarah crossed her arms beneath her head. This was nice, spending time with Sam. No pressures, no time constraints. Sharing their thoughts and ideas.

"In a way, yes," Sam said. "But here's where it gets good. She ended up marrying the doctor who set her broken ankle."

Sarah gaped at him. "No kidding?"

"True story. She was sixteen when they met, he was twenty-two, and they married when she was of legal age in Minnesota."

Six years between them, same as the age difference between her and Sam. "So, Charlotte freely volunteered this information to you?" Sarah shook her head. "I've known her my whole life and didn't even know that. And don't you dare say *you didn't ask*. You can be very smug sometimes, you know."

"Hey, cut me a break. I didn't say a word." He raised both hands in a gesture of innocence and those smile lines surfaced again. They could quickly become addictive, and she felt the irrational urge to trace them with her fingers. Sam was close enough for her to do that very thing, but it would be highly inappropriate.

You're just friends. Sam doesn't look at you that way.

Jumping to her feet, Sarah brushed the pebbles and grass off her shorts and sleeveless blouse. "It's getting late, and I need to get home."

"Let me walk with you."

Sarah hesitated. "Maybe it's best if you don't. People might talk." At first she suspected he might challenge her, but then he nodded.

"You're one of the most independent, confident girls I know. Besides the fact that you were born and raised in Rockbridge and everyone here adores you, do you honestly care what people might say?"

She raised her chin. "You think you have me all figured out, do you?"

"I'm not sure anyone could ever completely figure you out, Sarah, but I'm willing to try. Like it or not, I'll be fifty yards behind you. All the way home."

"Fair enough, but it makes a girl a bit uncomfortable knowing a man's. . ." Sarah bit her lip and lowered her gaze. Could she dig the hole for herself any deeper? "Never mind." Talk about inarticulate.

Her backside wasn't her best view, and she hated knowing he'd be right behind her. Why was she even thinking this way? Why should it matter?

Sam leaned close. "Strictly for protection if that makes you feel any better."

She grunted. "Fine. Whatever you do, don't pat my head like I'm a little girl. I hardly think the Big Bad Wolf is lurking around Thornton's Creek today. I'm sure it's safe enough."

"Suit yourself, Squirt." When he reached out his hand, she ducked. She'd led herself right into that one.

"Want me to go first?" Crouching down like a runner about to begin the race, Sam prepared to launch.

"Oh, come on." Getting a head start, Sarah sprinted as fast as she could with the rich sound of Sam's laughter following her all the way home. She couldn't help but smile.

I could get used to this.

Chapter 10

~~♥~~

Two Weeks Later

"Mr. Lewis, can you please come over here?"

Sam glanced up from where he stood beside Merle. Since his dad was in a meeting, he knew his assistant's call was meant for him. With a nod, he raised his hand to indicate he'd be with her momentarily. Looking across the bank lobby to where Gina talked with an older gentleman, his gaze met the wounded eyes of Martin Benson.

Sam turned back to Merle. "Merle, if you could finish washing the windows and then take a look at the fan in my dad's office, that should do it for today."

"I appreciate you giving me a job, Captain Lewis." Merle shuffled his feet. "Means a lot that you'd show that kind of faith in me. I didn't ever properly thank you, and I'm going to do a good job for you."

Sam nodded. "You're welcome. Let me know if you have any questions or need anything." Merle nodded and turned back to his work.

"Mr. Benson." Sam strode across the bank lobby and extended his hand to the other man. "How are you today, sir?"

"Captain Lewis." Removing his hat, he clasped it against his chest and shook Sam's hand with his free hand. "I've come on a personal business matter, and"—he nodded to Gina—"the receptionist said you'd be the one I need to see."

"Of course. Miss Armstrong, if Larry Grainger calls or comes by, tell him I can meet with him in an hour."

"Certainly, Mr. Lewis."

Sam motioned to Mr. Benson. "Why don't you come into my office? We can talk privately there." He stepped aside and waited as Martin walked into the office. "What brings you here today?"

"First off," Martin said, taking the chair opposite the desk, "I feel a little strange with the awkwardness between us." He lowered his gaze and shifted in the chair.

"It doesn't need to be awkward, Mr. Benson. I'm glad you've come to us for whatever you need to discuss." Sensing he should say something more, Sam tried to capture the man's direct eye contact. "Marty was a good man, and I'm very sorry for your loss." Why hadn't he ever said those words to this man or his wife face-to-face? Fresh regret sliced through him.

A full-time fireman, Marty had perished while rescuing an older man from his burning home a couple of years ago. Mr. Benson's only child—his son and namesake—had been in Sam's graduating class, all twenty of them, at Rockbridge High. Their families attended the same church, and he'd played football with Marty. Martin, Sr. and Doris were good, God-fearing people who'd been dealt perhaps the worst blow parents could ever endure. Marty had been a bit of a rebel, but he'd loved the Lord. No parents should ever bury their child, but Sam hoped this man and his wife took comfort in knowing their son was with the Lord.

"Marty was as brave of a man as I've ever known. He died a hero," Sam said. "You have every reason to be very proud of him. Your son brought great honor to your family and this town."

Moisture glistened in Martin's dark eyes. "Those are kind words, son. I don't think Audrey will ever get over the loss. Our boy was everything to her. When he died, her dream of becoming a grandma died, too. She'd hoped and prayed for grandbabies to spoil someday."

Sam hesitated, at a momentary loss for words. He hadn't thought of that angle, but the possibility of never having grandbabies to spoil and love would be a huge loss to his own mother.

Lord, give me your words.

"I don't know if you're aware, but we lost my younger sister, Rachel, in a car accident. Shortly before we moved to Rockbridge from San Antonio. My parents and I can understand your deep pain, Mr. Benson." He made a mental note to mention this conversation to his father later.

Martin held his gaze as he slowly nodded. "I'd heard something about that. I'm sorry."

Sam nodded. "Rachel was killed within a mile of our home, and the site where she died proved too much for my mom to see every day. Dad felt she needed a change of scenery to help her heal. Living in Rockbridge has been good for us in many ways."

His throat clogged as Sam recalled Rachel's pretty face. She'd been such a sweet, loving kid. The mental image of his little sister made Sam smile, a reminder of how God in His mercy also brought blessings and joy to replace the once overwhelming sadness. "I remember Marty as a guy who helped anyone who needed it. I saw him walking around town a lot with Harold Raines."

Martin sat up straighter and visibly brightened. "They walked every day so Harold could get out of the house and exercise. His bad hip was always acting up and walking was good to help ease out the kinks. Marty made Harold laugh, and vice versa. They shared a love of old movies and could talk for hours over a chess game."

Sam's smile grew wider, thankful he could remind the other man of fond memories. "As I recall, Marty's the person who introduced Harold to Betty." He'd seen the lovebirds around town, holding hands and sharing food across a table at Perry's Diner. Both in their late sixties, Harold and Betty had married the year before his return to Rockbridge.

Martin raised his chin. "You're a good man like your father. When you first came back, I wasn't at the parade. To make it worse, I haven't said anything to you since. I should have taken the opportunity to thank you for your service to our country, Captain Lewis. That's why I thought it might be awkward between us. Don't get me wrong. It's not that I didn't support you. I'm glad you're home safe, and I know your mama and dad are proud of you, but I couldn't bring myself to stand and cheer. Don't take it personal. Like it was for your mother going by the place where your sister died, I imagine. I didn't know if I could take seeing you because it reminded me of. . ."—he hesitated—"well, it reminded me all over again of what—of the boy—I'd lost."

What a humbling yet admirable admission. The pain in the older man's eyes, the lines etched around his eyes and mouth, made Sam's stomach clench. Coming to the bank was intimidating to a lot of people, especially in a town the size of Rockbridge where everyone seemed to know their neighbors' business.

"I understand." Sam cleared his throat. "Now, why don't you tell me how I can help you?"

Sam sat back in his chair, prepared to listen. If financially feasible, he intended to help this man.

~~♥~~

"You'll never guess who's working at Rockbridge Savings & Loan."

Sarah quirked a brow as she put Debbie's chocolate shake on the counter. "I have no idea." She held her breath, hoping she wouldn't hear the name Kathy Parker, Sylvie Foster or any number of pretty girls vying for Sam's attention. She wasn't blind, and she'd noticed the way the girls made fools of themselves around him. You'd think they'd never seen a handsome man up close and personal before. Okay, so maybe she was jealous.

"Try Merle Smithers and you'd be right." Debbie circled the pink striped straw in her shake a few times. "You ask me, your friend Sam had a lot of to do with Merle getting the job."

Sarah's brows rose. "Really? That's wonderful. What's he doing at the bank, do you know?"

"Maintenance and odd jobs, I think. I was in the bank making a deposit the other day and saw him. Merle's not half bad-looking when he's cleaned up. I mean, he had on some kind of ugly dark jumpsuit or uniform, but his hair was combed and he seemed to be in full possession of his faculties."

"Meaning he was sober," Sarah said. She glanced at the front door when she heard the bell. A young colored couple—she estimated both to be no older than their early-to-mid twenties—stood inside the front door. Conversations ceased and the clink of dishes and silverware halted with an almost shocking abruptness. They didn't see many minorities in Rockbridge apart from a few Hispanic couples who'd settled on the outskirts of town.

Without a second thought, Sarah stepped forward with a welcoming smile. She hoped everyone would behave, resume eating, and mind their own business.

"Please come in and have a seat," she said. "Would you like a booth or a table?"

"A table by the window, if that's okay." The man had removed his hat and now held it between his hands. The woman gave Sarah a tremulous smile but avoided meeting her gaze. Sarah noted their plain, narrow wedding bands.

"Of course." She ushered them to a table halfway down the aisle next to the window. "Is this okay?"

"It will be fine. Thank you, miss," he said.

"I'm Sarah. I'll go get your menus. Would you like something to drink?"

"Coffee for me, please." He looked across the table. "You too, honey?" The woman—not more than a girl, really—silently nodded. Poor girl appeared intimidated and sat ramrod straight in her chair, holding onto her purse like it was an anchor, probably wishing she could disappear. Sarah sensed the stares from other patrons boring into her back. She wished she could give them all a tongue lashing like the grade school principal, Mrs. Darden, used to do whenever the kids were disrespectful or unruly.

"Sanka or regular?"

"Regular is fine," the man said.

"I'll get it right away. The sugar shaker is on the table if you need it," Sarah said, giving the woman what she hoped was a reassuring smile. "Would you like cream for your coffee?"

"That's not necessary, thank you." Again, it was the man who'd spoken.

As she walked away from their table, Sarah made casual comments to some of the other customers to generate conversation. Making her way back to the counter, she mentally willed a couple of potential troublemakers to be on good behavior and not cause trouble.

"Well, if it ain't Rosa Parks and Martin Luther King. Come here to spread equality in Rockbridge." That growled comment came from old Wally Simms from a counter seat behind her as Sarah poured coffee into mugs for the couple.

Lord, help me. Why did the color of someone's skin have to be such a big deal?

Turning, Sarah narrowed her gaze. "What did you say, Wally? You'd better speak a little louder because I don't think everyone in the diner heard you."

Wally ran a hand over his unruly beard and eyed her with

suspicion. Opening his mouth to speak, he then closed it. She bore her gaze into him, silently daring him. He remained silent. A momentary reprieve, most likely.

After delivering the coffee and menus to the couple, Sarah paused behind Wally, speaking for his ears only. "I'm going into the kitchen to get an order. If I hear anything unkind come out of your mouth, you will be asked to leave."

Wally swung around on the counter seat to face her. "Who died and made you the boss, girl? Perry Sellers and I have known each other for years. You ain't gonna tell me what to believe. Like it or not, it's a free country. I got the right to think or say whatever I want, and I'm sayin' their kind ain't got no right to be in here."

Moving between the counter seats, thankful no one was sitting close to Wally, Sarah leaned close. "Perry hasn't owned the diner for years. Myrna does, and I know I speak for her. That young couple has every right to be in here, same as you, because it *is* a free country, and I intend to serve them the same as you, Perry, Harold and Betty, my parents, Donald Marcum, Joseph Lewis, Cora Blanton or anyone else who comes in here for a good meal."

"They got the wrong color skin, or are you color blind?" Wally hissed. "They'll cause trouble."

Sarah bit back a sigh of frustration and sent up a silent prayer for words that wouldn't come across as unkind but would convey how judgmental Wally was acting. The older man wasn't all bad, but like now, he never hesitated to speak his mind.

"You know what, Wally?" She made sure to keep her voice low. "God doesn't look at the outside of us as much as what's on the inside. Maybe you should take a peek at what color *you* are inside. I'd venture to guess it might be a whole lot darker than the color of their skin." Pulling out her order pad, she tore off Wally's ticket, slapped it on the counter and pushed it toward him.

Myrna eyed her with a quirked brow after Sarah shoved the swinging door and walked into the kitchen. She raised her hand. "I know. Please don't say anything." Myrna had been nearby during the exchange with Wally. Hopefully, she wouldn't be fired. Heaven knows, through the years, she'd given Myrna a few reasons to sack her, usually something to do with shooting off her mouth. Although she believed in defending those who wouldn't—or couldn't—defend themselves, she'd yet to learn the lesson that she couldn't singlehandedly save the world. But she'd do her part if she died trying.

"Relax. I was just going to say good job," Myrna said. The lines around her eyes crinkled, and she blew a strand of gray hair away from her face. "Wally's an old coot. About time someone put him in his place. I've never known anyone—much less a lady—as fearless as you, Sarah. Well done."

"Yep. If anyone can do it, it's our Jelly Bean." Jimmy nodded to her from the grill. "I've been wantin' to tell Simms off for a couple of decades myself." He placed a grilled cheese on one platter, a tuna melt on the other, and handed them both to Myrna.

Myrna laughed. "Maybe you should leave the kitchen every five years, Jimmy. And you," she said to Sarah as she added fries, "have the face of an angel but the fierce conviction of one of those lawyers. You're smart as a whip, state your case, and people listen." Myrna handed the plates to Sarah. "No wonder you like that Atticus Finch character so much."

She'd never thought about her fascination with the fictional lawyer in *To Kill A Mockingbird* from that angle before. Spearing pickles from the large jar on the counter, Sarah added three each to the platters. The Morrisons liked their pickles and considered them a food group all their own.

Jimmy nodded to the dining room. "Awful quiet out there. Too quiet, if you ask me."

"Goodness, I pray that sweet young couple hasn't left because of all the stares and whispers." Sarah wiped her hands on a dishtowel, hoping she wouldn't hear the bell on the outer door until she could get back to the dining room. "What's wrong with people?"

"You can't stop them from staring." Myrna shook her head. "It's human nature to stare at something or someone we don't see much of around here." Seeing Sarah open her mouth, Myrna spoke again, most likely trying to preempt her. "I'm not saying it's right, honey. It's just the way it is."

"Here." After digging into his pants pocket, Jimmy tossed a coin her way.

Sarah caught it one handed. "What's this for?"

"What's one thing that always makes people happy if they're sportin' a frown as deep as old Perry's well?"

"Besides your food?" Myrna said, laughing.

Jimmy angled his head toward the dining room. With a grin, he moved his hips, hummed a quiet tune and shuffled his feet.

After puzzling over his meaning for a few seconds, Sarah dropped the coin into her apron pocket. "Gotcha." Sliding the platters off the table, she gave Jimmy a wink. "I think it's Wah Watusi time."

Chapter 11

~~♥~~

Sam's steps slowed as he approached Perry's. Loud music could be heard from inside the diner, and he tried not to stare as he paused in front of the large, plate glass window. Half the customers were dancing or gyrating to a tune blaring from the jukebox. "The Loco-Motion" from the sound of it.

Unable to hide his smile as he stepped inside the door, Sam caught sight of Sarah dancing in the middle of the diner with Debbie and Arnie. A young colored couple danced beside them. Laughing together, they all seemed be having a grand time. Even Harold and Betty were dancing, and was that Perry Sellers swaying to the music with Ella Hardesty? That was something he'd never thought he'd see. His intuition told him Sarah had something to do with this impromptu dance party.

Charlie waved to him from his table. Excusing himself as he made his way through the onlookers clapping and watching the dancers, Sam slid into a seat a few seconds later. Putting his green folder on the table, he nodded in Sarah's direction.

"Just look at her, would you?" She'd ditched her shoes and her smile mesmerized him. Her hair looked about to tumble out of the confines of her hairnet. "She's so. . .effervescent." That's the word that came to mind, but it was only one of many adjectives to describe Sarah. Tearing his gaze away from her with reluctance, Sam focused on Charlie. "What's the story?"

Charlie finished his roast beef sandwich and swiped his napkin over his mouth. "That couple came in here about a half-hour ago. You know these people. Stopped eating and gave them the stink eye." He took a long swig of his soda. "Half of them acted like they'd seen a ghost, which is kind of ironic when you think about it. Anyway, Sarah got them settled at a table, then got their food and— before long—she put a coin in the jukebox and got everybody up and dancing. Good to see old Perry out there shaking a leg, too." He winked. "Sarah's not bad, either."

Sam sat back in the booth to watch. Patti approached a couple of minutes later. "Want some iced tea, Sam?"

"Sure. Thanks, Patti."

The young, dark-haired mother of two toddlers looked tired. Nothing new about that. He knew she was run ragged at the diner and again when she went home every night. Her husband, Tony, helped out as much as he could, but neither one had family nearby. Maybe he'd mention it to his mother and see if she could round up some ladies willing to babysit so Patti and Tony could enjoy a well-deserved date night.

"You've got it bad for her, don't you, buddy?"

Sam stared at Charlie. "Patti? Nah." He laughed when Charlie shook his head. "Afraid so, but as smart as she is, I don't think Sarah has a clue. She's going away to nursing school, and I have no plans to leave Rockbridge. At least in her eyes, that's probably an insurmountable obstacle."

His friend sat back in the booth and crossed his arms. "So, that's it? Since when did you base your actions on probability?" When Sam gave him a look, Charlie frowned. "Come on, Sam. You're a numbers man. You like everything finite and measurable. Sometimes life isn't that way. You ask me, you should pursue the idea and see what could happen between you and the lovely Miss Jordan. I'd venture to say something already has."

"We're friends, that's all." Not that he didn't want more. "I don't see any future between us." It was Sam's turn to frown. "Look, I've had my time away from Rockbridge. I pursued my dream, and by the grace of God, I achieved it. Now, it's Sarah's turn. I can't deny her that time to find her own dreams." He sat back in the booth and crossed his arms, mirroring Charlie. "As much as I hate the thought that she'll be leaving Rockbridge, her happiness trumps my selfish desires."

Charlie straightened his shoulders in a move indicative that he wasn't giving up until he'd stated his case. Oh no, his friend was only getting started. "I gotta love your sense of martyrdom. Now that you've done what you wanted in life, you've come home dragging your proverbial tail between your legs? Is that it? You make it sound like you're old and ready to lie down and die."

Sam snorted. "I don't think so. I'm six years older, you realize. Sarah might not even look at me as dating material. Matter of fact, she told me she used to pretend I was her older brother."

"Oh." Charlie's brows drew together. "That's not so bad, I guess, as long as she doesn't look at you as a sibling now. Do me a favor. Since you can't seem to stop staring at her, I want you to look at Sarah right now and tell me what you see. Be completely honest." Charlie chuckled under his breath. "Something other than the fact that she's effervescent. Whatever that means."

"You're on." What could it hurt? Following Charlie's advice, Sam returned his gaze to Sarah. She was still talking with the new couple and now sat at their table. Considering Myrna and Jimmy weren't in sight, Sarah must not be in trouble. Patti was waiting on the customers, and they appeared happy and content.

"She's full of life, energy, and she radiates joy from the inside out," Sam said. "There's an honesty, a purity of spirit in her. I like her fire, her generosity, her intelligence. Pretty much everything about her. I don't know any girl who would dance with a couple of color much less in the place where she works and with her hair half-falling down." He loved her hair, and with her face flushed, those golden blonde waves in disarray, she'd never looked more beautiful. He wouldn't even have guessed she could dance since the church didn't exactly encourage such things. He'd danced a few times in high school and then when he was overseas. Not much, but enough to know he enjoyed it. Unlike some people, he didn't believe dancing was inherently sinful, if kept respectable. The thought of dancing with Sarah appealed to him more than ever. Especially a slow number.

When he hesitated, stuck on that last thought, Charlie gestured for him to continue his observations. "Go on."

"I don't know many girls who'd be willing to get dirty and sweaty on a softball field by choice, either. I used to tease her and called her Tomboy when we were kids. She was more than willing to get covered in slime when all those puppies and kittens were born in our garage. Sarah was beside me every step of the way. I got queasy and upchucked a whole lot more than she ever did. She's smart, and she's tough." Forcing his attention away from where she still talked with the couple, Sam focused on Charlie. "Sarah's funny, and she challenges me. Then as now, she has a strong, fearless spirit. I've always admired her for that."

"That's what I thought." The smirk on Charlie's face smacked of *I told you so* smug satisfaction. "So, the next question has to be, *when* are you going to ask her out?"

That question brought a quick frown to Sam's face. After thanking Patti when she brought his iced tea, Sam traced a pattern in the sweat already forming on the outside of the glass. "Not that I don't want to ask her, but like I said, I don't see much point."

Charlie slid out of the booth and rose to his feet with his lunch ticket in hand. "From what I hear, Sarah's not planning on leaving until she gets enough money saved to go to nursing school. That might take another year." He lowered his hand to Sam's shoulder. "That's a lot of time. Don't let Sarah go without letting her know how you feel. For one thing, you don't have a girl like that come into your life very often. Besides, I don't want to hear your bellyaching after she's left Rockbridge, lamenting about how you missed your chance with her. You've got your chance now, buddy. Take it." He patted his shoulder again and turned to go.

For whatever reason, Charlie's comment sparked something inside Sam. "Right back at you."

Charlie paused and turned around to face him, brows lifted. "What's that supposed to mean?"

Sam motioned for him to sit back down. When he did, Sam leaned close and lowered his voice. "Don't think I haven't seen the way you look at Tess. As far as I know, she plans on sticking around Rockbridge permanently, a fact I find somewhat surprising. None of the other guys around here have apparently worked out for her. So, you tell me, when are you going to get around to asking Tess out on a date?"

"I don't know, man." Charlie avoided his gaze. Sam knew he'd struck a chord, and his friend's reaction confirmed his suspicion. On several occasions, he'd caught Charlie stealing glances at Sarah's older sister. "Tess is way out of my league."

Sam grunted. "That's crazy talk. You're a good looking guy, you've got a great car, you're one of the few single men in town who owns a house—not in the same neighborhood as your parents—and you've got a solid, reliable job." He rapped the tabletop with his knuckles. "You ask me, it's time for you to show Tess Jordan what she's been missing."

Charlie appeared to ponder his words for a few moments before a grin slowly spread across his face. "Maybe there's something to what you say, Sam. I'll think about it."

"Let me know how I can help."

"Ditto." Charlie tapped his shoulder again as he rose to his feet. "I'll see you later."

"Count on it, Charles." After he departed, Sam pulled out his green folder. He set to work while keeping one eye on Sarah. She bid the young couple goodbye and then disappeared, returning a few minutes later with her hair once again pinned back and neat. Her cheeks were still flushed the prettiest shade of pink, almost as pink as her uniform, and her eyes were bright.

Sam watched as Sarah served Perry Sellers his usual late lunch. The man was like clockwork in coming into the diner every day at two o'clock. He ordered one of three different platters, always with fries and black coffee to drink. A few seconds later, she planted a kiss on old Perry's cheek. Even sweeter was the way the elderly gentleman blushed. Sam closed his folder and drained his glass, wondering what Perry had said or done to warrant that kiss.

"Hi Sam," Sarah said, approaching his table. "Do you need anything?"

Good one, Lord. That was a loaded question, especially now. He lifted his empty glass and gave Sarah his best smile. "I could use a refill on the iced tea." He'd intended to leave, but he could spare a few more minutes before his next appointment at the bank.

"Coming right up. I'll bring you some lemon slices, too." Sarah always remembered the details. Had she also noticed how he'd been coming into the diner every weekday afternoon, sitting in the same booth, hoping for a word with her? A few times, she'd joined him during her break. Without fail, sharing even a short conversation with this girl considerably brightened his day.

"Who was the couple?" he said a minute later when Sarah put his iced tea on the table.

"Passing through town on their honeymoon. Isn't that the sweetest thing?"

"Yes, it is, although I can't imagine anyone just passing through Rockbridge. We're not exactly a hub of activity."

Sarah's brown eyes widened. "Oh, you must not have seen the new billboard. It's out on the highway, headed south, right before the Rockbridge exit."

"Billboard? No." Matter of fact, he hadn't been outside of town since he'd returned. He'd had no reason since everything he needed—and then some—was within the town limits. "I'm surprised I haven't heard about it."

"Well, it's only been up a couple of days, and to be honest, I haven't even seen it myself. Drive by when you get a chance and let me know what you think."

He cocked a brow. "Does the billboard have a photo of the Perry's Diner staff? If so, I'm sure you'll be getting a whole new clientele coming in here."

She laughed, and her beautiful eyes lit even more. "No, but I'll take that as a compliment."

"I meant it as a compliment." All over again, Sam appreciated this girl's enthusiasm for life, for people, and how it showed in everything she said and did, unconsciously or not. Maybe there was something to what Charlie said, and he should definitely try to get to know Sarah again before she left for nursing school. She'd be in Texas, after all, so it wasn't like she'd be clear across the country.

"Sam?"

He snapped his gaze back to hers. "Sorry." When Sam felt his eyes straying to her lips, he focused on Perry sitting at the counter over her right shoulder. "What did you say?"

A slow smile curved her mouth. "I was telling you the billboard is an artist's rendering of the inside of the diner. He did a very good job based on the photo Myrna showed me. Then I asked if you wanted anything else?"

He held her gaze. "I'm good, thanks."

Pausing in his work again a few minutes later, Sam tapped the pencil on the table, content to watch Sarah move among the customers in the diner. She was very efficient in serving her customers, making them feel special and valued. When the high school kids came in after school, she joked and talked with them the same as she did the older folks. That took a unique brand of talent. Shaking his head, he smiled.

"Sam?"

Sarah walked toward him as he prepared to leave the diner. "Want to meet Saturday afternoon at the creek? Say three o'clock or thereabouts?"

He nodded slowly. "I have to help my dad with something, but it sounds like a plan. I'll be there as soon after three as I can." Who was he kidding? Nothing short of a family emergency would stop him from meeting Sarah. Why did he suddenly feel like a kid again who wanted to punch his fist in the air after a football victory? As much as he loved the thrill of lifting off the ground in a jet, it paled in comparison to what he was feeling in this moment.

She's asking as a friend. Nothing more.

Without a doubt, Charlie wasn't the only Rockbridge citizen who'd noticed his fascination with the younger Jordan sister. He'd sensed the speculation. Some of the older ladies, in particular, didn't bother hiding their curiosity about his love life. They'd come into the bank and—while filling out a deposit slip or passing by him in the lobby—they'd hint around or suggest the names of eligible young ladies. He'd run into Myrtle Newcomb at Johnson's Market, and she'd offered to arrange a meeting with her niece or her hairdresser's oldest daughter. He'd smiled and politely declined. And for what reason? Because he'd rather sit in a diner pining away for the one girl who couldn't wait to get out of Rockbridge.

He needed to remember that, but as Sarah walked over to a table of new customers, Sam couldn't help but hope she might soon start to see him as more than a friend. As more than a man who came into Perry's Diner every day and stared at her like a besotted idiot.

Charlie was right. Yeah, he had it bad.

Chapter 12

~~♥~~

The Next Monday Night

"What was being overseas like, Sam? *Really* like?" Sarah stole a glance at where he sat beside her, both dangling their feet in the creek. Same as they'd done on Saturday afternoon and then again on Sunday evening. Meeting Sam was becoming a very nice habit, and something she looked forward to after a long day at the diner. He was easy to talk to, and he listened with interest as she made random observations of life. She liked hearing about Sam's work. Not so much about his actual job as the deep satisfaction he found in getting to know the townspeople.

"Fascinating, challenging, and then there were the days we experienced the kind of sadness I'll carry with me the rest of my days." Dipping his feet in the water, Sam flexed his ankles and sent a spray of water shooting into the air and across the creek.

"At times I'd wonder why our forces were over there at all. Then I'd question why specific decisions were made. Why certain actions weren't taken." He stared straight ahead. "But then I'd remind myself it's where God planted me and what I'd trained to do. In Taipei, Chiayi, Vietnam, to name a few."

She was surprised he'd revealed that much to her. "Do you think serving in the military strengthened your faith, or the opposite?"

He appeared to consider his words before answering. "You ask the tough questions, but the good ones. As a matter of fact, I'd never felt more compelled to share my faith than when I was in the service.

Telling others about the Lord and how He's worked in my life somehow felt more natural than ever. Like I couldn't *not* say something to give those guys hope. It's ironic that it takes something like the threat of a potential war to do what I should have been doing all along."

Sam blew out a breath and closed his eyes before reopening them a few seconds later. "A lot of the guys suffered from depression, loneliness, and some waged a battle with the bottle or other drugs. It's a big world out there, Sarah. Full of people warring with inner demons, family members, or fighting something or someone else that has nothing to do with the threat against our national security."

"I know. Those kinds of battles are probably the hardest to fight," Sarah said. "I'm sure it changes your perspective, too, right? To be honest, I can't imagine what it's like."

When he met her gaze, the light in Sam's eyes faded somewhat. On instinct, Sarah reached for him. Glancing down at their joined hands, Sam laced his fingers through hers, holding on tight.

"I was at Taipei Air Station in 1959 and part of a tactical reconnaissance squadron. We lost a few of our guys, but not from anything related to our mission. A couple died from disease. Two in car accidents. One got in a street fight, was stabbed through the heart and gone like that." He snapped his fingers. His voice had grown quiet, thick with emotion. "Men with sweethearts, wives, kids. Even though I know God is always in control, sometimes it didn't seem fair. None of it."

She frowned. "They knew the risks going in, just the same as you did. At least they knew they were loved. Their families and sweethearts will cherish their memories." Turning to face him, Sarah made sure she had his complete attention. "Lots of people here in Rockbridge waited on your homecoming, you know."

The tiniest hint of a grin teased the corners of his lips. "Is that your way of saying you waited for me to come home?"

"Not at all." She dipped her head to hide her smile.

Disengaging his hand from hers, Sam splashed her lower legs as she dangled them in the water. She splashed him back.

"Enough serious talk." Jumping to his feet, Sam tugged his T-shirt over his head and tossed it on top of his tennis shoes. Before she could recover from the sight of seeing him shirtless, Sarah gasped as he tugged on her arm and jumped into the water, pulling her in with him. She fell against his strong, firm chest, and cold water rushed over her, enveloping her from all sides.

"Oh! You stinker!" She feigned offense, but she knew Sam wasn't buying the act for a single second. Struggling out of his arms, Sarah splashed him full in the face.

Sam laughed and used his palms to smooth his hair back from his face, an action that highlighted the strong, distinctive planes and those great cheekbones. "I guess I deserved that."

"You sure did." The water was even colder near the bottom of the creek bank, and she bobbed up and down, shifting from foot to foot beneath the water. Shivering, she rubbed her hands up and down her arms. "It's almost summer. Why is it so cold in here?"

"That's why I like it. Wakes you up, and it's refreshing. There's only one way to get rid of the shivers. Come on." Grabbing her by the hand, Sam pulled her farther into the water. "Full immersion."

"Oh, no, you don't!" When she tugged on his hand, he surprisingly released her without a fight. "Tell me something else, Hero."

His eyes sparkled. "Ask away, Tomboy."

"I'm no longer a tomboy, remember?"

"And I'm not really a hero unless the act of coming home qualifies me for that distinction. Air Force guys are called by any number of nicknames, and the ones that aren't completely derogatory are things like propeller heads, prop tops, wing nuts, fly boys, zoomies." He raised his hands. "How about it? Any one of those strike your fancy?"

"I still think Hero qualifies by virtue of your willingness to serve your country overseas, but fine. I'll call you Captain, then, since you earned that title legitimately. Better?" Without waiting for Sam's answer, she kept going. "Tell me something, *Captain.* Is it true you were caught skinny dipping in this very creek once upon a time?"

"Guilty as charged." Sam laughed and raised his face to the sky. A moment later, he lowered his head and leveled that blue-eyed gaze on her. "For the record, I wasn't in mixed company. It was me and a few guys trying to cool off on a hot summer night. Playing around and acting stupid. Lest you think the worst of me."

"I didn't ask who kept you company." She gave him an impish grin and her pulse skipped a few beats when his smile widened.

Slowly moving backward—still facing her—Sam waded into the

middle of the creek. "Sarah Jordan, are you asking me to skinny dip?" The evidence of his intense physical training for the Air Force—the strength of those broad shoulders, the trim waist, rock-hard chest, the well-developed muscles—was in full view. Oh, it was glorious.

"Never." The cold water felt good since she was feeling a bit heated now.

"I'm surprised you don't wear a swimsuit when it's this hot outside. Don't you swim?"

She could feel her cheeks flooding with warmth. "I normally do, yes."

"Fully clothed?"

Sarah snapped her gaze to his. "Since you've been coming here lately, I didn't want you to. . ." She huffed. "I didn't want you to see. . ." She raised her hands in the air. "None of your business."

"You're beautiful, Sarah." The admiration in his eyes stole her breath.

Oh, Lord, what am I supposed to do with that statement? Her cheeks grew even warmer.

Knowing Sam, it probably didn't enter his mind that she might consider him physically distracting to the point where she found it difficult to tear her gaze away from him. Jumping on him from behind might not be the best idea either. Riding piggyback as he waded through the rushing waters of the creek wouldn't be good as much as she'd love to do that very thing. No, that would be much too close, too intimate.

She wanted to have fun with him at the creek, just as she always had, but any physical contact left her wanting more. Sam was just being himself. Considerate. Kind. Nice. But she wasn't ten anymore, and he wasn't sixteen.

Needing a distraction, Sarah prepared to dive. "Let's swim."

"Race you to the rocks." With sure strokes, Sam splashed water in her face as he passed her. Although he'd allowed her to win their little footrace before, this time he seemed intent on being victorious. Fine, she'd give this one to him. Adopting a slower pace, she followed behind him, content to let him forge ahead.

Later, they rested once again on the bank of the creek, basking in the warmth of the early evening. A gentle breeze stirred the trees and she trained her gaze straight ahead. She'd teased Sam and they'd played around in the water, but she'd been careful to keep her distance. If she wasn't mistaken, he'd done the same. Good, although her traitorous feelings threatened to betray her when he'd grabbed her around the waist at one point. She'd moved her hands around his neck and they'd stared at one another for a few seconds before he'd gently lowered her back into the water.

She couldn't shake his words from her mind.

You're beautiful, Sarah.

He'd never said those words to her before. Sure, he'd told her she'd grown up. Told her he thought she'd been cute as a kid. She'd glimpsed admiration in his eyes. He'd praised her, complimented her. Laughed at her bad jokes. Teased her like she imagined he'd teased his kid sister.

No, Sarah, he doesn't treat you the same as a kid sister.

As it was, she was self-conscious enough in her thin shorts and with her cotton top clinging to her. In some ways, she felt exposed although she was modestly covered in something more than a one-piece swimsuit. Besides, she needn't worry about Sam. He was a gentleman. Then why did she suddenly *want* him to treat her as more than a younger friend?

Be honest, Sarah. You want Sam to notice you as a woman. Not flat-as-a-board, ten-year-old Sarah. The twenty-one-year old Sarah with curves and perhaps a tiny ounce of that sex appeal everyone else seemed to talk about incessantly.

Forgive me, Lord, if these are sinful thoughts.

Seeing that Sam's eyes were closed, she studied him. Smooth, tanned skin, sculpted high cheekbones. Classically handsome features. What would it be like to feel Sam's lips on hers? She'd only kissed one boy—Kenny Meyers after senior prom—and wished she hadn't. Not that it was bad, but there wasn't even the tiniest spark of that elusive thing called passion.

Moving her gaze away from Sam, Sarah lifted her face to the sky and closed her eyes. More than any man she'd ever met, Sam made her believe passion could exist. The way she felt in this moment, she figured it was fairly close to that type of passion. *Am I crazy?*

"Martin Benson came into the bank the other day," Sam said a minute later, breaking into her reverie.

Sarah propped herself on her elbows and glanced over at him. "How's he doing? I guess it's been well over a year now since Marty died."

"As well as can be expected, I suppose. When I was talking with him, it was one of those times when I wish I could have traded places with Marty."

Sarah frowned. "I really wish you'd stop saying things like that."

"Like what?"

"How you wish you'd died in someone else's place. People die all the time, Sam. Accept it and get over it."

"Well, that's blunt."

She narrowed her eyes. "Maybe so, but it's the truth. I've said it before, and I'll say it again. I'm sorry about your sister's death, but you seem to have some kind of misplaced martyr complex. It makes me worry about you, if you want the truth."

"Oh? How's that?" His frown deepened. "And this isn't about Rachel. I've accepted that, but it doesn't mean I don't get sad and miss her sometimes."

"That's only human. Of course, you miss her. I miss my grandparents now that they're gone, too." She paused, wishing she hadn't made it sound like a personal attack. "I'm talking about what you said about wishing you could take Marty's place. That's like saying you wish God would take you in their place and bring them back. Wish all you want, but that's never going to happen."

"You got all that from what I said?" After staring at her for a few seconds, Sam turned toward her, elbows on his raised knees, those incredible blue eyes boring into her. Gone was the fun, carefree mood of a short time ago.

A warm breeze ruffled her hair, blowing damp strands across her face. She pushed them aside with a sigh of impatience. "Well, for one thing, if you go back for another term of service, tour of duty or whatever it's called, I'd be afraid you might do something. . .ill-advised." A nice way of saying stupid, but surely the man understood her implied meaning. Sam wasn't stupid, by any means.

"It's not like I'd volunteer for a suicide mission, Sarah. Give me some credit." Now he sounded peeved. Honestly, she couldn't blame him.

"There *is* a strong likelihood you'll be called for another term, right, especially if any one of these conflicts escalates?"

Something indefinable flickered in Sam's gaze as he faced the creek and then closed his eyes. "No." A simple word, but spoken so quietly and with such a measure of regret, Sarah recognized she'd touched a raw nerve again. When she said nothing further, Sam opened his eyes and turned his head to look at her again. "Go ahead. You can ask me if you want."

"Not if it's hurtful."

He ran his hand through his hair. "I'm not going back. I was discharged. Honorably, in case you're wondering."

"I'd never have doubted that for a second."

"Number one, I'm getting older as we speak."

"Since when is twenty—"

"Sarah, for once in your life, please listen for a minute and let me speak. Hear me out on this."

Sufficiently chastised, she nodded and gestured for Sam to continue.

"I started suffering from vertigo in the last year. I'd get dizzy and sick because of sudden pressure in my ear and temporary hearing loss." Sam exhaled a prolonged sigh. "By the grace of God, I was able to finish all my missions without mishap or incident. Always with an air sickness bag nearby. Trust me, vertigo's not a good thing when you're piloting a plane."

"May I speak?"

His lips lifted slightly. "Go ahead."

"I'm thankful it didn't negatively impede any of your missions."

"Thanks. The thing is, if it hadn't happened, I would still be over there, serving until ordered to come home. I was prescribed medication, but I didn't want to take the chance something might happen. The doctors ran a litany of tests: hearing, balance, medical history interview, physical examination. They finally diagnosed Ménière's Disease." Sam motioned to his left ear and his shoulders slumped. "It's a disorder of the inner ear, sensory in my case. I haven't told anyone else besides my parents. Not even Charlie."

In his tone, Sarah heard resignation, and she couldn't believe it. "Wait just a red-hot minute. Don't even tell me you feel like a failure in some way, Sam Lewis. Because if you do, then that's just plain wrong."

The muscles in his jaws flexed. "How can I not feel like I've let down the Air Force, my country, my parents, the people in Rockbridge? The entire time of the homecoming hoopla—while everyone was cheering for me—I felt like a fraud." His voice had become raspy.

"How can you even say that?" Sarah inhaled a quick breath, tamping down her sudden rise of anger.

"You know, would it hurt to get a little sympathy instead of you lashing out at me? Forgive me for thinking I might get a little compassion by sharing something so personal with you." Sam rose to his feet. Grabbing his T-shirt from the ground, he tugged it down over his head and then shoved his feet into his tennis shoes. With a grunt of exasperation, he dropped to one knee to tie the laces.

Sarah jumped up, standing over him. "If you want a pity party, Captain, you can apparently do that perfectly well all by yourself without any help from me. Furthermore, if you think anyone in this town would think any less of you because of what happened, then you're not giving them enough credit. The most important thing? War or no war, you were willing to serve your country—willing to die for your country—and you came home in one piece. And for that, my friend, we're all thankful."

Especially me.

Overwhelmed with a rush of emotion, Sarah gulped and tried to catch her breath. Tears slipped down her cheeks before she could stop them. To her chagrin, they plopped on Sam's hand as he finished looping the laces of the second shoe. Good heavens. She couldn't even cry daintily. What a mess she was.

Sam slowly rose to his feet. "That's just it, Sarah." His irritation of a moment ago seemed to have dissipated. Using the pads of his thumbs, he swept them over her cheeks as he cradled her face with a light, gentle hold. "In some ways, I don't feel like I'm intact. I left part of my pride over there, part of my honor. Those things are every bit as important as an arm or a leg. And even though I received an honorable discharge, and served out my time in the Air Force, I still feel like I somehow failed."

Wiping away another tear, she lifted her gaze to his and glimpsed such profound sadness that it stole her breath. "You didn't fail in any sense of the word, and not to disregard your feelings, but you might have lost a few brain cells somewhere along the way." She regretted those words the second they escaped.

Sam didn't flinch although he released his hold on her and moved his hands down to his hips.

"Do you need some kind of medal to prove your worth?" she said. "Matter of fact, you're plenty decorated. I've seen the badges, pins and patches all over your uniform, Sam. If you'd lost a limb or even your life, would that somehow prove your service counted more?"

Sarah lowered her gaze and shook her head, trying but failing to comprehend his reasoning. "I'm sure you know the scripture verses about pride as well as I do. If anything, your willingness to fight for your country means you're much *more* of a man. At least to me, if that counts for anything. You just said that if you hadn't been diagnosed with"—she waved her hand—"that disease, you'd still be over there today. I can't begin to understand why you'd feel this way, but I guess there's nothing else I can say. Except that," she sputtered, swallowing hard, "God's not done with you yet, Captain. He brought you back home safely, and I know in my heart He's got something very special planned for you."

She turned to go.

"Are you done?"

When she faced him again, they stared at one another for a long moment. Blinking hard, she nodded. "Yes, I think so." She lowered her gaze to the ground. "I'm sorry about my little rant. I hope you can forgive me." With a shrug of her shoulders, she tried to smile. "You know me. I get passionate about something, and I can't seem to help myself. Rest assured, God's working on me."

Stepping forward, Sam moved his strong arms around her, pulled her close and leaned his head against hers. "Your feelings count for a lot, Sarah. Thank you." His lips were warm against her hair. In his arms, she felt comforted, protected, and she never wanted to leave.

"It's nice to know someone other than my parents believes in me," he whispered. "I wasn't just representing my country over there or trying to prove the United States is superior to any other nation. More than anything else, I was there for my family. My neighbors. My town. For the people that I love most in the world."

"Sam." Her voice was muffled against him. "You're crushing me. You didn't lose any strength in your arms, that's for sure."

She felt a quiet, deep chuckle rumbling in his chest. "You're good for me and won't let me get away with much, will you?"

"Not if I can help it. I need to get home, and you"—she patted his chest and stepped back again—"seriously need to get over yourself. You coming?"

"I think I'll stay here a while longer. Do some thinking."

"Promise me no pity parties, and please don't think too hard. You might strain something important."

"Sarah?" he called to her when she was about fifty yards away.

This was getting to be a nice habit. She glanced at him over one shoulder. "Yes, Captain?"

"Thank you. And I've changed my mind. I'm coming with you."

"For protection?"

"You got it. For my own as much as yours."

She nodded and turned, waving one hand over her head. "Fine. Stop dawdling then."

"Coming." He was beside her within seconds.

Lord, he's all yours. Please give him your peace.

Chapter 13

~~♥~~

The Next Afternoon

"Do you need help finding anything, dear?"

Engrossed in her search, Sarah shook her head. "No. Thanks all the same, Betty. I'm sure I'll find what I need. Just doing a little research." She returned her attention to the row of books. Maybe if she didn't encourage conversation, Mom's librarian friend would move on to another patron. It wasn't like she was a stranger in the library and didn't know how or where to search. Many in town joked that the library was Sarah's second home and that they'd set up a permanent cot for her in the staff lounge.

"Did you enjoy *To Kill A Mockingbird*?"

Sarah turned back to where Betty stood behind her. "Yes, I loved it. It's a powerful book and makes me think. That's the best kind of book, wouldn't you agree?"

"Indeed." That word seemed to be Betty's favorite, and she'd heard it often.

Not that she was trying to be secretive, but neither did Sarah want Betty Raines telling Mom that her youngest daughter was seeking a book in the medical section. Especially since she knew her mother regularly met Betty for coffee at Perry's. Mom had panicked enough over Dad's heart attack. Goodness, given this information, she'd probably jump to any number of false assumptions and think she had a potentially debilitating or fatal disease.

"I've had a request for the book," Betty said. "I thought perhaps if you were done, then. . ."

Didn't the library have multiple copies? She'd checked it out several times already, so perhaps she was being selfish and shouldn't hold onto it and deprive someone else of the joy of reading her new favorite novel.

Sarah nodded. "Certainly. I'll bring it back tomorrow."

"Thank you, Sarah. I appreciate your understanding. I'm sure we'll have another copy returned soon, so please feel free to check it out again."

She waited until Betty walked away before tugging out a medical dictionary. What was the name of the disease Sam said he had? Mad at herself for not writing it down immediately after she'd returned home, Sarah closed her eyes. *Think.* Opening the book, she scanned down the list, but it only confused her more. The letter M came to mind. That was the first letter. *Men* something, as she recalled. Menyers? Minyards? Quickly flipping to the index in the back, she moved her finger down the list. She paused at one or two before pausing on Ménière's Disease. Yes! That was it.

Pulling a stepstool closer, Sarah settled on it to read, never taking her eyes from the book.

Ménière's Disease results when a change occurs in the fluid volume of the labyrinth, a part of the inner ear. *Interesting.* Several million people suffer from the condition in the United States. The symptoms of Ménière's Disease can occur suddenly and arise daily or as infrequently as once a year. *So, it is unpredictable.* Usually affects adults in their thirties—Sam was close to that—or middle-aged adults but it can also occur in childhood. Possible causes include ear infection and head injury.

Sam hadn't mentioned either of those things.

Accurate measurement and characterization of hearing loss are of critical importance in the diagnosis. Vertigo is the most debilitating symptom of the disease and vertigo attacks can lead to severe nausea, vomiting and sweating. *He'd mentioned vertigo and being sick.* Attacks often start with tinnitus—a loss of hearing—or full pressure in the affected ear. *The left ear, in Sam's case.* Some sufferers could experience intense, uncontrollable tinnitus while sleeping. Others might notice hearing loss or feel unbalanced for prolonged periods. Occasional symptoms include headaches, abdominal discomfort and diarrhea. A person's hearing tends to recover between attacks but over time becomes worse.

Sarah paused and inhaled a quick breath when she read the next words.

There is no cure.

So, it wasn't like it was a death sentence. Not like it was a horrible thing, except she knew how much Sam loved to fly—it was more than a hobby. For four years, flying had been more than his occupation. Flying jets had been his passion, his livelihood, his life. He said he was on medication. The worst that could happen might be eventual hearing loss.

She could better understand his not wanting to fly in any kind of conflict because of the uncertainty of his condition. What she hated most was how this disease seemed to make Sam somehow feel like less of a man. That notion was ridiculous, but how could she convince him of that? Men could be so stubborn.

Returning her focus to the book, Sarah continued to read. Through the use of hearing tests, physicians characterized hearing loss as sensory, arising from the inner ear, or neural, arising from the hearing nerve. *Didn't Sam say his was sensory?* A change of diet can help control symptoms. Eliminating caffeine, alcohol, tobacco and salt may relieve the frequency and intensity of attacks in some people. Reducing stress levels may lessen the severity of the symptoms. Medications that either control allergies, reduce fluid retention or improve blood circulation in the inner ear could also prove beneficial.

She paused, an idea forming in her mind. Sam didn't drink alcohol, and he didn't chew or smoke tobacco, but she might be able to help him reduce his caffeine and salt intake.

"My my, who have we here? And what could you be studying so intently?"

Startled, Sarah clasped the book to her chest, breathing heavily. That action only served to make it easier for Tess to see the title of the bulky volume. "You startled me. I didn't hear you."

"Obviously." Tess tilted her head and read the name of the book out loud. "Why are you reading this book?" A frown creased her forehead. "You're not sick—"

"No, I'm not sick. Thanks for your concern." Sarah bit her tongue, determined not to say more and fuel the fire.

"Then why do you have your head stuck in this medical dictionary?" Her sister's blue eyes widened. "Are you afraid Dad's going to have another attack? Has something happened? Or is it Mom? Tell me now. Are you worried about her? What's going on?"

Sarah shook her head. "Tess, please calm down, and don't jump to hasty conclusions. I'm trying to read up on something to help a friend. That's all. Really." Avoidance wasn't lying the last time she checked. She was under no obligation to answer her sister's nosy questions.

"Well, that's good, but why can't you at least share the name of your friend's malady? Must be serious." When Tess stepped closer, Sarah snapped the book closed. Dust rose from its pages, making her sneeze—a very loud, distinctly unladylike sneeze. She wiped the back of her hand over her eyes and then fumbled for her handbag. Tugging out a tissue from the front pocket, she coughed a few times to clear her clogged throat. Tess watched, appearing embarrassed at the intrusive, loud sound in the otherwise hushed library.

"I've read enough for today." Rising to her feet, Sarah took great pains to pick up the stepstool and move it out of the way. "It's time for me to get back to Perry's, anyway." She reshelved the medical dictionary and grabbed her purse. At least she'd read enough to give her some insight into the disease that brought Sam home.

"Right." Tess glanced at her watch. "I was hoping to get to the bank earlier this morning and invite Sam to join us for dinner tonight at the house. He's already been home a few weeks, and we need to be more neighborly. We had a new case come up at the office this morning, and unfortunately, I couldn't get away for ten minutes to run over and see him."

"Oh, are you cooking?" Sarah bit her lip, but she didn't regret the question. Her sister had a habit of inviting others for dinner while fully expecting Mom to do all the work. Not that Mom minded, but advance notice would be nice. She wouldn't tell Tess she'd made a chicken casserole the night before and Mom had already planned on putting it in the oven at five o'clock.

Tess frowned. "Mom lives for this kind of thing. Besides, she loves Sam."

"Why don't you go see Sam tomorrow and ask him to come for dinner later in the week? Invite his parents, too," Sarah said as they exited the library together and walked down the front steps.

"I have a better idea." Tess practically bounced down the remaining stairs to the sidewalk, reminding Sarah of an enthusiastic child. "Hello there, Mr. Lewis."

Walking past the library, hands in his pockets and whistling, Sam appeared deep in thought. "Hi, Tess. How are you?" His gaze moved past Tess to where Sarah stood on the steps. "Sarah."

She nodded. "Hi, Sam."

"What's got that handsome forehead of yours all scrunched up in a big old frown?"

Sarah watched, appalled, as Tess traced the lines on Sam's forehead with her finger. Speaking of pride, did her sister have any left in that petite frame of hers? That disgustingly thin, perfect figure? *Down, girl. Be gracious. She's your sister. You love her.*

"You look like a man in need of a good meal and conversation. No doubt, you're working too hard. I want you to come to dinner at our house tonight."

Sam looked up at her as she walked down the last few steps to the sidewalk. "What do you think, Sarah? Do you agree with Tess's assessment?"

"I'm sure I don't know." Sarah hoped her smile belied her words, and she prayed Tess wouldn't feel the need to mention where she'd found her in the library and especially the book she'd been studying. Judging by Tess's current demeanor, it was the furthest thing from her mind as she flirted with abandon.

"Tell me what time and what to bring." Sam kept his gaze trained on her, not Tess.

"Just bring yourself," Tess said. "That's all we need to dress up our table."

Sarah exchanged amused glances with Sam. It was either that or groan. How was it possible she'd come from the same gene pool as Tess?

"You could bring dessert, if you'd like," Sarah said.

"Count on it."

Sarah nodded. "Sounds good. Dinner will be served at six. Please invite your parents, too. We'd love to have them join us."

"I'll be there, but my folks have another engagement tonight. If you'd rather do it another night—"

"Don't be silly, Sam." Tess playfully swatted his arm and her hand lingered a little long for Sarah's liking. "We can always do it again, and your parents can join us then."

"Very good. If you'll excuse me, ladies, I have a luncheon at

Quentin's, or I'd offer to escort you wherever you're going."

"Another time," Tess called after Sam as he departed.

Mom lowered the bowl of steaming mashed potatoes on the table. Then she stopped and stared at something behind Sarah. "Teresa Elaine Jordan, you march right back into your room this instant, young lady. Take off that shameful outfit, put on an appropriate dress, and go scrub that hideous gook off your face."

Turning from where she was setting the table with the fine English bone china, Sarah moved one hand over her mouth. Standing in the hallway, Tess wore the shortest skirt imaginable and enough blush for a clown. And what was that strange iridescent blue color on her eyelids? Her eyelashes looked longer than the ones on Emmett Blanton's cow, and they were the longest in the county. If her sister had any idea of how silly she looked, Tess wouldn't show herself to anything other than her full-length bedroom mirror. Was her sister really that gullible?

"Don't you think I look sophisticated?" Tess slowly turned in a full circle, modeling her outfit. As if that would convince anyone. "I'll have you know this look is all the rage in Paris, my darlings. This is the mini-skirt. Mary Quant features it in her shop in London."

Mom frowned. "I don't know or care who this Mary person is, but it's nothing more than someone taking a pair of scissors and whacking away on the length of a skirt to make it indecent."

"You liked my pillbox hat inspired by Jackie Kennedy." Tess stuck out her lower lip in a pout.

"Completely different," Mom said, pulling a serving spoon from the tray of fine silver in the breakfront. The silver reserved for only the most important dinner guests. Shaking her head, Mom returned to the kitchen.

"Come on, sis." Tess turned big eyes on Sarah. "What do you think?"

Sarah glanced at her watch. Sam should arrive momentarily. Tess should know better than to ask her about fashion choices. "I think if Paris designers put a woman in a plain brown potato sack and paraded her down the Champs Élysées, they'd convince gullible buyers worldwide that it was the height of fashion. Sophistication isn't something you wear. The key is understatement, not something you parade in someone's face." Maybe that was too harsh. "Sweetie, you definitely have the legs and figure to wear a skirt that short, but the point is, you—"

"Don't sweetie me," Tess huffed. "Maybe you don't know how to recognize sophistication. You don't read the fashion magazines the way I do or keep up with what they're wearing in New York and Europe." She gave her a disparaging glance. "You actually look pretty good tonight, but normally you look rather. . .well, frumpy."

"Frumpy?" Sarah silently counted to five under her breath. *Lord, hold my tongue.*

"Maybe you should try a potato sack like Sarah mentioned." Mom came back into the room and gave Tess a pointed glance. "At least it would cover you up more. Show a little respect for yourself, Teresa. I don't care what they do anywhere but right here in Rockbridge. In this town, you'd be held up to ridicule if you dared show yourself in public dressed like"—she waved her hand up and down—"this. And quite possibly, you'd be taken to task by the church elders, which would be extremely embarrassing for your father. I know one thing. You're not going to sit here at the dinner table looking like you do now, especially with Captain Lewis expected any moment."

Get a clue, Mom! That's why she dressed like this in the first place.

"Your mother's right." Coming around the corner, Dad lowered his glasses and peered at Tess. "No daughter of mine is going to show herself off like that. The kind of attention you'd get from wearing that skirt isn't what you'd want, even from a gentleman like Sam Lewis. Go change." With a grunt, he hiked up his pants by the belt buckle and headed for his chair at the table.

Sarah continued setting the table, lost in thought. Surely Sam wouldn't be attracted to a girl simply because she had a good figure? Tess was two inches shorter, twenty pounds thinner and better proportioned, so she could pull off more clothing styles than she could. She'd inherited their mother's fine bone structure and petite features whereas Sarah took more after Dad's bigger-boned side of the family. All over again, Tess's barbs chipped away at her self-confidence by pointing out the differences in their physical size.

Still, she'd caught Sam stealing glimpses of her at Perry's a few days ago. He seemed to like her appearance and he certainly hadn't run away screaming when he'd seen her in all her soaking wet glory at

Thornton's Creek. If that hadn't sent him running, she couldn't imagine what would. A small smile tipped Sarah's lips at the thought of the special moments they'd shared, both lighthearted and serious. She wouldn't trade those memories for the world.

"I hope you're not laughing at me."

Surprised by the anger in Tess's tone, Sarah's jaw gaped. More surprising were the tears shimmering in her sister's eyes.

"Not at all, Tess. Of course not. I was just thinking—"

"Oh, give it up, Sarah! I know you were thinking about *him*. That lovesick look on your face gives you away every time. Which seems to be happening a lot lately. You really should try to be a little less obvious." Tess's voice assumed a defiant tone. "I suppose you have another little rendezvous planned with him?" She raised a brow and waited, her arms crossed as she tapped one foot.

Sarah's cheeks burned and she tamped down the quick rise of anger. She'd never known Tess to be so vindictive. "No, I do not." How could Tess know? Had she been spying on her? Sure, Sam had a habit of showing up at the creek, but it certainly wasn't anything they'd prearranged or planned. Other than when she'd asked him to meet her there on Saturday afternoon.

"Care to explain?" her father's voice boomed from behind her.

"Seems our little Sarah is infatuated with Captain Lewis," Tess said with a deep pout, an expression she'd perfected.

"Well, he's a fine man, and I'm sure that statement applies to a lot of the women in Rockbridge, but what's this about a rendezvous?" Her mother gave her a curious look as she pulled the fine crystal glassware from the hutch. Captain Lewis was getting the very best they had to offer tonight.

"It's a private, clandestine meeting—"

"I *know* what the word means, Tess." Mom's tone was firm.

"Mom, stop treating me like a child. I'm a grown woman!"

"That might be so, but at the moment, you're acting like you're six and a spoiled, petulant child. Need I remind you that you still live under our roof? I'm not going to tell you again or you're not coming to dinner at all. Now, go change and then scoot back out here to the dinner table. We're almost ready to eat as soon as our guest arrives, and I want you here for the prayer. I believe you could benefit from it."

Tess hesitated in the doorway, no doubt dying to hear her

inevitable interrogation.

"Now!" Dad bellowed.

"Yes, sir." Uncrossing her arms, Tess stomped around the corner and down the hallway.

Rarely did her father raise his voice to that level. Sarah only prayed Tess's behavior—or hers—wouldn't give him heart palpitations. Tonight, they'd failed miserably in keeping everything in the home calm, as Doc Meriweather had advised. She hoped Sam hadn't been walking toward the front door to overhear their heated discussion. Through the open window, that would be a strong likelihood. If he'd heard anything, Sarah wouldn't blame him if he'd decided against coming into the house of contention and promptly marched home.

Sarah waited until she heard the bedroom door close before she faced her parents. Their expressions were stern, but they didn't appear unduly alarmed. She kept her voice calm and low. "Sam sometimes joins me at the creek. We're good friends. You know he's always treated me like a kid sister." She shrugged. "We talk and swim, have fun together."

"You're a few years younger than Sam," Mom said. "I wouldn't entertain any romantic ideas about him, honey." Of course not. She was the younger, plainer, taller, bigger-boned Jordan sister. The one destined for the crumbs beneath Tess's table.

Mom put the salad and basket of homemade rolls on the table. "However, come to think of it, Sam did seem to flirt a bit with you at the church, and I've heard some whispers around town. I know he comes into Perry's every day and sits in your section."

"Tess has her sights on him, anyway," Sarah muttered. Now who sounded like a pouty child? Yet another reason to leave Rockbridge. She didn't want to be around if Sam decided to court her older sister. "End of story." Hopefully, she'd infused her tone with sufficient finality to end the discussion. She could find a man all on her own without resorting to one of Tess's leftovers. Not that she'd ever consider Sam Lewis a leftover in any sense of the word.

Staring at the swirled pattern of the pale gold linen tablecloth, Sarah resolved not to reveal even the smallest hint of her mixed emotions. Inside, her stomach was unsettled. Mom and Dad knew as well as she did that once Tess set her mind on something, she wouldn't stop until she accomplished her goal.

When Mom walked back into the kitchen, Dad reached for her

hand. "Trust in the Lord with all your heart. . ."

"And do not lean on your own understanding," Sarah murmured.

"In all your ways acknowledge Him, and He will make your paths straight."

Tears stung her eyes and she squeezed her father's warm hand. "Love you, Dad."

"Love you, too, Sarah. Give it to the Lord. Let Him figure it out."

She nodded. "I know."

"Sam Lewis is a discerning man. He's also smart enough to see when he's got a jewel right under his nose."

Her eyes widened, causing him to chuckle.

Hearing footsteps on the front walk, Sarah's pulse quickened as the doorbell rang.

Chapter 14

~~♥~~

From his perspective, Sam thought the evening was progressing quite well. Tess seemed subdued, a fact which somewhat enhanced her disposition. He'd hoped she wouldn't flirt so audaciously with him when her parents were present in the same room. After Bill Jordan asked the blessing, Sam answered their polite questions about living in another country and how he was adapting to civilian life again.

When he complimented Nadine on the delicious chicken, rice and broccoli casserole, she informed him that Sarah had prepared it the night before. "Always helps to marinate it overnight in the fridge."

"You cook? Or marinate?" Sam shot a quick glance at Sarah with the belated realization he shouldn't have blurted out that question. "I mean," he said, trying to backpedal, "I recall you once said you don't cook. I'm just surprised."

Sarah lowered her glass of milk to the table. She'd always loved milk and drank more of it than any girl he'd ever known. "Yes, well, I *was* ten years old at the time." She hesitated, as though measuring her words, and the corners of her lips twitched in a telltale way. "In case you haven't noticed, I've aged a bit since then."

No kidding. Sarah had aged extremely well. Tonight, she wore her hair down, and it fell past her shoulders in soft, loose waves. Sam hid his smile behind his napkin and gave her a wink when her parents and Tess weren't watching. A slight flush of color began at the base of her neck and crept into her cheeks. Hopefully she wouldn't believe he went around winking at all the girls in town, and definitely not in his position at the bank. He reserved his winks for Sarah, but he should cool it. Somewhere along the way they'd transitioned from teasing to flirting, and he didn't know when it happened. He liked flirting with her, but Sarah might not appreciate it.

"This strawberry cheesecake is to die for," Tess said a short time later, speaking up after being silent for most of the meal. "Thanks for bringing it, and please give your mother our compliments."

"Mom didn't make it this time, believe it or not."

"Oh? Did you get it from Myrna?" Nadine said.

"No, I didn't get it from Myrna. I don't want to cause any of you good people to faint, but you're looking at him. Cheesecake maker." He pointed both thumbs at himself.

Seated beside him, Sam heard Sarah cough. "*You* cook?"

Nadine put her fork on her empty dessert plate. "Captain Lewis, I must say, that's wonderful. It's also surprising, but. . ." She shot a glance full of meaning—of what, he didn't want to know—at her eldest daughter.

"Cheesecake is the only thing I can make at this point, but I figure it's a start. Once Sarah and Tess invited me to dinner, I called Mom and she pulled one out of the freezer to thaw." He frowned. Hopefully, that statement didn't detract from his masculinity. Maybe he should mention he was going to rope cattle at his cousin's ranch next weekend.

"You surprise me, Captain Lewis." Sarah took a quick sip of her after-dinner coffee and then poured him another cup. He didn't need more coffee, but he wasn't about to refuse if she wanted to pour it for him. Did Sarah even have to think about it as she passed the sugar bowl and pitcher of cream to him? She did the same for her father, and Sam tried not to stare as she quietly served Bill. Even with such a simple action, her movements were graceful. Sarah genuinely enjoyed serving. Sam's gaze automatically moved to Tess, who sat pouting and fiddling with her empty glass. Maybe the comparisons weren't fair, but they couldn't be denied.

"Why is that?" Sam said, snapping to attention and directing the question to Sarah. "Do you believe a man should stay out of the kitchen?" From the corner of his eye, Sam caught the look exchanged between Nadine and Bill. Yes, maybe he should watch it, but he couldn't seem to help himself. Something about Sarah brought out the teasing side of his nature, and he loved to egg her on.

More than any other girl, she challenged him, and he'd miss the give-and-take of their relationship when she moved to Austin. That thought sent a pang of disappointment shooting through him.

Sarah shrugged. "Not at all. I think it's sweet in more ways than one and very. . ."—she appeared to search for the right words—"original." When Sarah finally met his eyes, something inside him shifted.

"Why not peach pie?" Tess said next.

Sam forced his attention away from Sarah. "Never fear. That's next on the list."

He offered to help with the dishes but was waved off by the women. Didn't women love it when a guy rolled up his sleeves and pitched in to help in the kitchen? He'd helped his mom with after-dinner cleanup for years, but in this case, his motivation was completely different. Doing anything with Sarah would be fun.

"Let the ladies handle the dishes. Come with me. Let's chat." Bill ushered him into the living room and offered him a seat on the sofa before sitting in his recliner. As long as Sam had come to the Jordan home, Bill always sat in that chair. From all appearances, it was finally starting to fray around the edges. Sarah's dad had spent many hours with his father over the years rebuilding old airplane engines and chewing the fat about politics, economics, you name it. Bill listened with great interest, asking questions every now and then, as Sam told him about the Convair F-106 Delta Dart he'd piloted on relief and test missions and the Lockheed A-12 Blackbird he'd test flown earlier in the year, shortly before his discharge.

Sam liked Bill, but he wondered how he'd react if he told him he was interested in dating his younger daughter. He'd heard some of the guys talk, and he was aware a number of them had dated Tess at one time or another. While she was reportedly a "good" girl, she could sometimes push the limit in her teasing and temptations.

"What's on your mind now, sugar?" Tess plopped down on the sofa uncomfortably close to him. Now she was calling him sugar? After one dinner shared with her parents and sister in their home? Perhaps seeing Nadine's stern glance directed her way, Tess inched away, putting more distance between them. Not much, but enough. Sarah and her mother took matching chairs across from the sofa. Sarah didn't look at him but sat demurely in the chair, ankles crossed and hands in her lap, like a shy schoolgirl.

Wait a minute. Was this evening a set-up to get him to ask Tess out on a date? Sam's frown grew deeper. Four members of the Jordan family stared at him, awaiting his response. What could he say that wouldn't have Bill showing him the door, perhaps asking him never to return? Being politically correct was a skill he'd learned in the Air Force after being interviewed countless times for stateside newspapers. But that was business, more or less. His personal life was an entirely different matter, and one he didn't wish to discuss, especially now.

"I was thinking about something Martin Benson and I discussed recently." He wouldn't tell them he'd been approached by Martin at the bank. As it was, it would be a privacy violation if he revealed Martin's request for a loan. After he'd filled out a loan application, Sam told Martin they'd review it and get back to him. His gut told him to seek another way to gather the funds instead of the man going into debt simply because he wanted to remember his son in a tangible way. His instincts prompted him to broach the subject with this family. Plus, it would help cover his awkwardness with the current *what to do about Tess?* situation.

"What's that?" Bill said.

"Martin wants to erect a headstone out at Rockbridge Haven Cemetery in Marty's honor. But that's not all. He also wants to set up a fund for future memorials, whether for public servants like Marty, or for servicemen and women killed in the line of duty."

"That's a good idea, and very nice of Martin." Bill nodded his approval and Nadine echoed her agreement.

Sam glanced at Sarah, wondering if she remembered that he'd brought up Martin Benson out at the creek. Right before his whole ridiculous *I feel like less of a man* speech. Before she'd soundly chastised him. Rightly so, as much as he hated to acknowledge the truth.

Her suggestion that he'd lost a few brain cells hadn't set well with him. That had been a low blow. He hadn't been able to sleep last night after returning home from their time at the creek, and he'd never had a problem sleeping. Tossing and turning, he'd been unable to shake the vision of Sarah's gorgeous blonde hair, her beautiful face and smile. However blunt, she was funny, compassionate, and she cared enough to give him "what for" as his mother would call it. In the midst of her tongue lashing, Sarah's eyes had sparked with fire.

Unforgettable, those beautiful brown eyes, so wide and brimming with emotion. This girl spoke her mind, but she was full of life and energy.

"How can we help with the cause?" Sarah said.

Sam cleared his throat, corralling his thoughts as he shot her a grateful glance. "I'm thinking we might put some collection containers around town, that sort of thing. Get a number of Rockbridge's citizens involved to help." He raised his fist as he used to do with his teammates at a football rally.

"Oh, yes," Nadine said, sitting up straighter. "That sounds like a wonderful idea. I'll be happy to talk with Betty about putting several donation boxes or cans at the library. Same with LuAnn at Johnson's Market. Maybe we can plan a couple of fundraisers."

"I'd be happy to help drum up donations at Perry's and donate a portion of my tips," Sarah said. "I'm sure I could talk Patti into doing the same, and maybe Eddie."

Sam nodded. "Thanks. Those are great suggestions. Sheriff Tommy said they could collect for the cause, and I'm hoping a small portion of the school's summer carnival proceeds could be donated, too, in honor of Marty. I realize it's short notice, but—"

"Aren't you and your dad both on the school board?"

Ah, Sarah. She wouldn't allow him to get away with anything. "Yes, as a matter of fact." He gave her another wink without a second thought, no matter that they were in the presence of her family. If he wasn't mistaken, he sensed Tess stiffen from where she sat a few inches away.

"Working in the court system like I do, I'm sure I can get some of the attorneys and Judge Larson to empty their pockets." Tess's words sounded measured, her smile tight. "With all the money those men drop on their fancy lunches at Quentin's every week, I'm sure I could get them to pony up some donations."

"Thank you, Tess. Anything you can do." Sam gave her an appreciative smile.

"I'll volunteer to make the donation cans." Sarah seemed quite enthused with the idea, and he couldn't be more pleased. "We can use coffee or vegetable cans. You'll help me, won't you, Tess?"

"Yes," Sam said. "Use all the frilly lace and ribbons you want."

That statement was perhaps ill-advised and an inadvertent jab when he noticed that Tess frowned and Sarah looked the other way, chewing on her lower lip. She'd told him that Tess's contribution for the soldiers was always a pretty bookmark she'd made with ribbons and lace. According to Sarah, she'd suggested to her sister that no self-respecting soldier in his right mind would ever use such a frilly bookmark, although the female medical personnel and the nurses would certainly appreciate them. As usual, Sarah was right.

After discussing a few more ideas, Sam rose to his feet. "I'd better get home. Thanks for the great meal and the fellowship. I had a wonderful time." His gaze zeroed in on Bill. "Do you mind if I borrow Sarah for a few more minutes? I need to discuss more plans about the donation cans."

"Of course, we don't mind," Nadine said quickly before Bill could speak.

Moving his gaze to Sarah, Bill nodded. "Go right ahead, son. I enjoyed our chat, and I'll look forward to hearing more sometime."

"Yes, sir. Mrs. Jordan, thank you again." He gave Tess his best smile. "Thanks for the special dinner invitation."

"Don't mention it." Tess barely nodded to him before leaving the room.

"I'm sorry about Tess," Sarah said once she closed the front door behind them. "She's a little out of sorts tonight."

"I could see that. I hope it wasn't something I said or did." When she didn't answer, Sam motioned to the swing. Discussing Tess wasn't in his best interest right now. He waited until Sarah took her place and then dropped down beside her.

"Sam, I need to ask your forgiveness. I shouldn't have said some of those things at the creek last night. I couldn't sleep, and I stewed over what I'd said to you and how I'd said it. I was surprised and shocked by what you told me, but as usual, I should have exhibited more tact. I hope you can forgive my insensitivity."

Her apology surprised him, but he needed to reassure her. "Of course, you're forgiven. Not that an apology is necessary. Know one of the things I like most about you?"

"Haven't a clue."

"You're a deep thinker. You keep me sharp, and I never know what you're going to say."

Sarah's lips twisted. "Those are mighty heady words. Funny, I wouldn't have pegged you as an idle flatterer."

Raising his hands as if in surrender, he laughed. "Yeah, that's what they call me."

"You wanted to talk about the donation cans?"

He locked his gaze with hers. "No. I don't want to talk about donation cans."

"But you said. . ."

She really couldn't see where he was headed with this discussion? That it was an excuse to spend some private time with her? "My turn to ask your forgiveness, if it's needed. I wanted to spend some time alone with you."

Her smile grew into a thing of pure beauty. "We spend time at the creek all the time, and we're alone there."

Sam swallowed his sigh. Was she teasing him? She certainly wasn't making this any easier, not that he expected she would. "Here's an idea. Want to go change and meet for a midnight swim at the creek?"

"Don't tempt me." She sounded intrigued, and that's all the encouragement he needed.

"It's very pretty with the moonlight shimmering on the water. Romantic." His voice had grown husky, and he wondered if she understood what that huskiness meant. When Sarah turned her head, he noticed the small mole on her neck. Unless he was losing his mind, it formed the shape of a heart. His gaze traveled upward to the small scar above her left eyebrow. That happened when she was in grade school, caused by a random collision with a softball.

"Maybe you should write a poem." Her tone teased him.

"I could try, but you're a lot better at it than me." Using his foot, Sam set the swing in motion.

"Sam, how *did* you know I'd written that poem? The one—"

"I know which one. 'He soars with the clouds, seeing in their transparency the unending majesty of God,'" he said. "'Knowing He is watching. Recognizing the miniscule role he plays in the universe yet wrapped in the eternal arms of His Savior. Understanding how the heavenly Father will prevail, no matter what triumph or calamity may arise. In all things, giving Him the glory, for now and always.'"

"You know it by heart?" Sarah's surprise was obvious.

He tipped his head. "I meant it when I said that poem got me through some rough times. Here's a confession for you." Stopping the swing, he angled his body toward her, their knees touching. "Believe it or not—and I hope this doesn't make me sound like a teenage girl—I kept your poem beneath my pillow until the ink started to fade. I couldn't risk not being able to read it, so—even though I'd memorized it—I finally tucked it away in order to preserve it. But I imprinted it in my mind. I'll never forget those words from my favorite deep thinker."

"You're much too kind," Sarah said. "It's really not that good, and it certainly doesn't rhyme."

"I beg to differ, and the poem came from your heart. That's the most important thing."

"But it still doesn't explain how you knew I was the one who wrote it."

"First of all, because of the penmanship, I could tell it was written by a woman. And," he said slowly, his eyes skimming over her lovely face, "I knew it was someone with a deep soul. Someone who loved the Lord as much as I do. Someone who cared about me." He placed his hand beneath her chin. "You do, don't you, sweet Sarah?"

She stared at him for a long moment. "You know I do, Sam. You've found your dreams, lived your dreams. You want to settle in Rockbridge. But leaving town is the first step in finding *my* dreams." Her lower lip trembled, tempting him to still it with a kiss. "That's why you need to date Tess. Or anyone else but me."

Sam sat back in the swing. Whoa. Not what he wanted to hear, and he felt like he'd been slapped.

"It couldn't work between us in the long run, so why start something?"

"My turn to say hold on a red-hot minute." He raised one hand. "You make me sound like I'm an old man at the end of my life. I figure I still have a few good years left in me. The thing is, I don't want to date anyone else. You can't tell me I'm the only one who knows we have something special between us, Sarah. Something that could develop into much more. Why aren't you willing to explore these feelings and allow the Lord to work? From where I stand, it's called faith."

Her eyes widened and moisture filled them. "I don't want to start something with you, Sam Lewis, because you're the one man who holds the power to break my heart."

"What are you saying?" Fear whittled its way into his heart and twisted him inside, squeezing and pressing hard. On the flip side, her statement—subconsciously or not—revealed her deep affection for him. He had no intention of breaking her heart. If anything, the opposite was true.

Sarah blew out a breath. "I'm saying you shouldn't meet me at Thornton's Creek anymore. Don't come into Perry's every day. Just. . .don't." Jumping up from the swing, she headed to the front door and grabbed the handle. When she hesitated, it gave him renewed hope. "I'll help with the project for Mr. Benson, but please don't ask me for anything more. That's all I can give you."

"Sarah—"

"Good night." Said with the finality of a forever good-bye as she opened the screen door and stepped into the house. With everything in him, he couldn't allow that to happen.

"No." He'd kept his voice low but forceful, not wanting her parents, Tess, or any of their neighbors to overhear. Rising from the swing, Sam crossed the porch in seconds. Stepping back out on the front porch, she closed the screen door behind her.

Thankful she hadn't slammed the door and shut him out, Sam grabbed both her hands and held on tight. "We've always been friends, first and foremost. I've enjoyed our talks by the creek, and I thought you had, too."

She lowered her gaze. "Of course, I have. Very much."

"Then don't take that away from us."

"Don't you see?" Her voice wavered with emotion and her eyes glistened in the dim light. "The more time I spend with you, the more difficult it will be to say good-bye when the time eventually comes. And it will come."

"Okay, this is what we're going to do." *Lord, give me your words. Help her to understand.*

The corners of Sarah's mouth lifted slightly. "You always have a plan, don't you?"

"I try. We're going to make a pact—right here, right now—that no matter what happens in the future, we will never say good-bye."

Sarah moistened her lower lip with her tongue and appeared to ponder his words. "I'm not sure—"

"Since I've been back, you've become a very important person in my life, Sarah Jordan. No matter how hard you try to push me away, now or in the future, I'm not about to let that happen." He brushed the pad of his thumb over her cheek, loving the softness of her skin, the scent of her. "If all you want from me is friendship, then so be it. Just know I'm offering more." With that statement, he'd said it all.

Best to leave with his dignity somewhat intact.

Releasing her hands, Sam pivoted and walked down the steps to the sidewalk without looking back. Since he hadn't heard the screen door close again, he figured Sarah stood on the porch.

In the end, this evening had gone nothing at all like he'd planned.

Chapter 15

~~♥~~

Wednesday Afternoon

A single guy his age shouldn't be going home to his mother and father's house every night. Sam made a mental note to call Cora about available rental properties. He could live there while he searched for a home to buy. He'd spent very little of the money he'd earned the past four years, so he'd have more than enough for a substantial downpayment. Maybe even enough to buy a small home outright.

Charlie slid into the booth opposite him. "Watch it. Your disgruntlement is showing."

Sam chuckled under his breath. "Join me, why don't you? I didn't see you come in, and I have no idea what you're talking about." His words came out more like a grumble. Yeah, maybe he was disgruntled. Finished with his sandwich, he shoved his plate aside.

"Sure you do." Charlie gave him a grin guaranteed to irritate him further.

"Am I that obvious?"

"'Fraid so, buddy. You still haven't asked her out yet, huh?"

"I tried, but she pretty much spelled it out that she wants me to date someone else. I more or less told her I was still planning to meet her at Thornton's Creek. She can't take that away from us." When Charlie raised a brow, Sam figured he'd better explain. Heaven forbid old Mrs. Saunders with her selective hearing, sitting in the booth behind them, heard that remark. No matter what, he would not instigate any rumors slandering Sarah's good name.

"We meet there sometimes to talk. We discuss life, swim, toss around ideas."

Charlie's brows lifted higher. "Uh huh. Sounds completely innocent to me."

"You know as well as I do that Sarah doesn't date."

"Don't think half the guys in town haven't tried."

Sam grunted. "That's supposed to make me feel better?"

His friend laughed. "You're the guy meeting her at the creek, buddy. So, tell me, do these little creek meetings, or whatever you're calling them, involve any serious flirtations?"

He smirked. "I've always joked around with Sarah. She's a lot like Rachel. She teases me back, and we have a lot of fun together." Sam could tell Charlie wasn't buying it. He shrugged. "Okay, fine. Don't believe me. Before you came in to harass me, I was sitting here trying to figure out how to change her mind."

Charlie chuckled. "Only one way to find out. Time to ask her, my friend."

Sam rubbed a hand over his brow and darted a glance Sarah's way. "Shh. She's coming."

"Hi, Charlie. How are things in the hardware business?" Sarah put a napkin and silverware on the table beside Charlie and glanced at Sam's half-empty glass. If nothing else, the woman was very good at her job.

"Great. Hey, Sarah, are you going to the Saturday night dance over at Harbison Hall?"

What was Charlie thinking? Sam had half a mind to kick his friend under the table. He poised his foot, ready and waiting. He slanted his gaze to Sarah, unable to ignore his racing pulse.

"No. I hadn't planned on it."

"Well, my buddy Sam here—" Charlie flinched when he gave him a targeted, swift kick to his left shin— "is planning on being available to drive anyone home who's had too much to drink."

Sarah turned her gaze on him. If he wasn't mistaken, admiration shone in those lovely brown eyes. "Is that so? That's very noble, Sam."

Sam leveled his gaze on Charlie, silently imploring him to let it go.

"Here's a thought," Charlie said. "Why don't you help him? Keeping watch over the troops. Hopefully, no one will get soused so he actually has to drive them home." He shot Sam a grin. "I'll vouch that he's decent company. I'm sure he's got some good stories in his back pocket. Guaranteed to keep you entertained. Nothing too graphic for a young lady's sensibilities, of course."

"I'm sure. Would you like something to eat, Charlie?" Avoiding Sam's gaze, Sarah shifted from one foot to the other. That was a change. She rarely acted nervous. Her behavior now indicated she might be a little rattled at the thought of being forced to sit beside him in a social situation. Quite different from their heartfelt conversations at the creek.

"Myrna made a fresh batch of carrot cake muffins. Real cream cheese frosting."

Charlie released a low groan. "No fair. You know that's my ultimate temptation. All right, bring me one. I can't pass that up."

Taking Sam's empty plate, Sarah headed back toward the kitchen.

"What do you think you're doing?" Sam hissed as soon as Sarah was out of earshot.

"Relax." Charlie leaned back in the booth. "Just trying to get you a date, my friend."

"I can get my own dates, thanks."

"Can you? From what I've seen, you're sitting over here in this booth day after day, staring at her, and getting your eyes full. You can drool over her efferves—whatever you called it, all you want, but that's not getting your lips locked with hers now, is it? Say, here's a thought. Maybe you should take some of that romantic pining and put it to good use."

"Watch it, Charlie."

His friend held up one hand. "I meant no disrespect. Man, you're in a great mood. How long's it been since you've had a date? Held a woman? Kissed a woman?"

"That's getting a little personal. Maybe you should answer that question for yourself and leave me alone."

With a chuckle, Charlie shook his head. "Don't you worry. I'll take care of me."

Sam shook his head and drained his glass. He'd float out of Perry's at the rate he was going. Either that or make an embarrassing number of trips to the men's room if anyone was keeping count. One of the hazards of living in a small town was that people always seemed to be watching.

"Come on, Sam. You've only had eyes for Sarah Jordan since you slid off the back of my convertible after the homecoming parade. You had two beautiful girls hanging onto you—one on each arm—and yet you needed me to rescue you. Admit it. You had a one-track mind bent on heading over here to Perry's as fast as you could. Why else would you leave our table and waltz over to the counter to talk with Sarah?"

"Maybe because I felt a little claustrophobic. The table was overcrowded." He frowned. "And I don't waltz. That sounds girly."

Charlie laughed. "You might not admit it to me, but be man enough to admit it to yourself. Turn off that engineer's mind of yours for once, stop thinking logically, and discover your emotional side. Try it. You might find it freeing. Kind of like flying around in that wide blue yonder you love so much."

"Now you're really talking crazy." The reminder of flying sliced through Sam, but that was a place he didn't want to go.

Sarah returned to their table with the carrot cake muffin for Charlie and another fresh glass of iced tea with lemon. Sam mumbled his thanks, and it was hard to ignore the way Sarah avoided looking at him. He didn't like it, but he'd try to repair the damage the next time they met at the creek.

"So, what do you say, Sarah? Want to go to Harbison's on Saturday night with our man Sam?"

Sam wanted to slide under the table. He thought Charlie would drop it, but now he was proving him the fool. He'd kill him later.

"I'll think about it." She darted a nervous glance in the general direction of the kitchen. "I, um, might have to work an extra shift on Saturday."

"If it helps, I can pick you up for our *non*-date"—Sam shot a withering glance at Charlie—"either here or at your house." Above all, he couldn't have Sarah leave the table thinking he couldn't ask for his own dates. That would be the ultimate humiliation. A guy had his pride, after all.

Staring at him for a long moment, Sarah finally opened her mouth to speak then closed it again. She started to walk away before turning back around. "Like I said, I'll think about it."

Charlie nudged him under the table. Yeah, he'd definitely have to kill him.

That Evening

Like some kind of stalker, Sam stared out the front window. In terms of a schedule, Sarah was pretty much a creature of habit. Hopefully, that would work in his favor tonight. If she followed her customary pattern, she'd head out to Thornton's Creek any minute. Like a heathen, he'd skipped prayer meeting, but Sarah had arrived back home at the same time his parents pulled into the driveway. Which meant in twenty minutes, she'd be heading to the creek.

Sure enough, he spied her soon after. The dirt path leading to the creek necessitated that she cross the street behind the Barton house. She'd changed into denim shorts that showed off her long, tanned legs and a white, sleeveless cotton top that highlighted her slender, toned arms. Gorgeous.

Throwing down the newspaper he'd been pretending to read, Sam startled his mother. Catherine sat on the sofa, working on a quilt. One of her favorite hobbies, she spent a portion of each evening with her newest project. He usually didn't say much to her when she had her head bent over one of her quilts, knowing she was either deep in thought or talking with the Lord.

"Going somewhere?"

Sam stopped with one hand on the doorknob. "Just thought I'd go to the creek for a while."

"You've always liked going there." Using her scissors, she snipped off a hanging thread. "Your dad and I had a favorite meeting place in San Antonio."

"I didn't know that." However, now wasn't the best time to talk about it. "You'll have to tell me about it sometime." Thankfully, she didn't chastise him for skipping out on church. The Lord knew he was so agitated he couldn't pray although he knew good and well that's the one thing he *should* be doing.

His mother lowered her needlework to her lap and gave him one of those motherly looks she'd perfected. "Go, son. Give Sarah my regards. Try not to be too obvious."

She could read him so well. Mothers always could.

"A little late for that." With a quick salute and a smile, Sam dashed out the front door like the kid he'd once been. Like a consuming passion, he needed to speak with Sarah.

Chapter 16

~~♥~~

"You might not believe this, but I've always admired you." As usual, Sam sat beside her on the edge of Thornton's Creek, their feet dangling in the water.

"You're right. I can't believe it."

So much for asking him *not* to come to the creek anymore. Sam's impassioned plea that they not give up their times together here had been so heartfelt and sweet. How could she refuse him? He'd become her best friend in a short time, and they'd shared so much. He'd told her things about himself no one else knew, and she'd done the same for him. She'd need to figure out how to be with him and resist him. That could be a problem, but she'd pray about it and get on with her life.

"Too many people hide behind their feelings." Sam's voice was quiet. "For instance, I liked the way you kissed Perry Sellers on the cheek the other day. Unabashed affection, that's what it was. Genuine and real."

"Perry turned seventy-five. It was a special day for him, a milestone. Do you notice everything?"

"Not always. I am a guy, after all."

Oh, how well she knew. Sarah wished she could ignore that fact, but it was impossible, especially with him sitting beside her.

Her next mistake was glancing at him. Those smile lines deepened, causing her pulse to shoot to the heavens.

"At least with you, I always know where I stand," he said. "Good thing for you I like a person who's forthright and honest. Someone whose actions are motivated by a pure heart."

Sarah shifted her position and nudged his thigh with hers, hoping it wasn't inappropriate, trying to ignore the strength and muscle tone in his legs. She focused her attention on the slow moving water in the creek.

"You're not like any other girl I've ever met. You're different in all the best ways."

She dipped her head, confused. While she adored compliments from Sam, she wasn't sure what to say in response. "I thought you'd agreed not to talk about things like this."

"I'm only complimenting you. Is that a crime?"

"No, it's not, but you're befuddling me. I'm surprised you didn't find a bride overseas and bring her home to Rockbridge. An exotic beauty with dark hair, beautiful eyes, and a lovely, lilting accent."

"Why would you think that?"

Lifting her shoulders, she didn't trust herself to look at him. "I don't know. Maybe something about the finality, the intensity, and the threat of war, I suppose. You told me some of your fellow soldiers died. We never know when our time on this earth is up, right? The whole life and death thing. Being in a foreign country and realizing you might not ever have the opportunity. . .to love again."

"Is there a question in there somewhere?" Sam's tone had grown serious and the color of his eyes deepened as she dared to meet his gaze. "If you want to know something, just ask."

Now he was irritated with her. Great. She blew out a sigh. "Let's please forget I ever brought it up. This conversation is getting dangerously close to trespassing the 'just friends' limits." Why had she believed for one second that she could spend time with Sam and not be attracted to him, not want more?

"No, let's not forget it," he said. "You started it, so please finish your thought. I want to know what's on your mind. It's pretty clear something's bothering you where my love life is concerned. Other than the fact you don't want to be a part of it." He raked a hand through his hair and blew out a breath. "What makes you think you know what my type of woman is, anyway?" Now he sounded this side of testy.

"I have no idea. Heaven knows, you dated all types of girls before you left for the Air Force Academy."

"You noticed what girls I dated? For the record, there weren't that many." A look of male satisfaction creased his lips, disgruntling her.

"I never said I didn't approve. That's none of my business." Catching herself twirling a long lock of hair around her finger, she impatiently tucked her hair behind her ears. Then she reached into the pocket of her shorts, pulled out a hairband, and fastened it around her hair in a high ponytail.

"Speak your mind, Sarah. It's what you do so well, after all. Be as inarticulate as you want."

The man asked for it, so she was going to give it to him. "Okay, fine. I think we have a situation here." She waved her hand between the two of them. She rued the way her voice had risen and come out more like a squeak.

A glint of surprise surfaced in his eyes as he turned to face her. "What do you mean?"

"I think we should get it all out in the open. Get it over once and for all, and then we can move on. As friends."

"I'm game," he said, his brow furrowed. "Let's get whatever it is—as you put it—on the table."

Sarah took in a quick breath as a way to bolster her nerves. "Unless I'm incredibly naïve, when we talked on my porch, you implied you'd like a relationship. With me. Between the two of us. As in—"

"Right. As in boyfriend and girlfriend. Dating. Holding hands. Kissing on the doorstep." He nodded to the creek. "Moonlight swims. I don't think I could be any clearer about what I want, Sarah."

"I know what dating is," she said, holding up one hand. "I might not have done much of it, but that's my point. Argument number one, you're much older than me, and a man of the world—"

Sam released a groan of frustration. "Six years isn't all that much. It's true what they say. The older you get, the less important age becomes. Trust me, I'm no man of the world, at least not in the way I think you mean. That description implies certain things that have nothing whatsoever to do with me or my lifestyle. Yes, I've dated. Plenty. I find girls fascinating and—especially when it concerns the one sitting next to me now—beyond frustrating on occasion. Sure, I might know how to pilot a jet, and I've lived across the world in another country for a few years while defending my country. But, deep down, I'm still the same guy from Rockbridge, Texas. No more, no less."

"I didn't mean to imply anything bad." Sarah dropped her gaze, embarrassed. "But I've heard things about men in the service. The types of women—"

"You can rest assured I'm not that kind of guy, so to speak."

"You mean you've never—"

"No, I haven't." Sam's voice was firm and edged with irritation. "I thought you knew me—understood me—better than that. Frankly, I can't believe we're having this discussion."

She dared to glance at him again, needing to lighten the mood. "You couldn't possibly know what I was going to say. Maybe I was going to ask if you've ever played the trumpet, or gone to bed without brushing your teeth."

They stared at one another for a few seconds before the corners of his lips twitched, relaxing his features. Much better. She hated to think she'd made him uncomfortable or mad. She wished his shirt wasn't buttoned wrong and crooked, but no way would she fix those buttons. Put her hands on him. No, it definitely wouldn't be a good idea.

"No to the first, and yes to the second," he said finally, breaking the silence. "And I should append my statement by saying I wouldn't until I'm in a committed, God-honoring marriage. Then? Oh yeah. Most definitely."

Oh, my. No fair saying something like that, Captain.

"That settles it," she said. "I could certainly never ponder the possibility of a situation with a man who doesn't practice sound dental hygiene."

"Well, then, I guess that settles the issue. If you ever decide you could be in a situation with a man with questionable dental hygiene, promise me I'll be the first to know."

With that, Sam hopped to his feet, dusted himself off, and headed in the opposite direction.

What was that all about? Sarah stared at him, his long strides carrying him quickly away from the creek.

"Sam?"

He raised his hand in the air. "Not now. I'm going home to brush my teeth."

Chapter 17

~~♥~~

Feeling like a fool about the way he'd abruptly left Sarah at the creek the night before, Sam sat beside her again the next evening. No matter what happened—or didn't happen—between them, he enjoyed her company. In recent days, he'd found himself checking the clock throughout the day and looking forward to lunch or his afternoon break. But it was these quiet times, after dinner when they sat by the creek sharing their thoughts, lives, dreams and the events of their day, that he loved most. When they didn't meet at the creek, he missed her.

"I'm sorry I took off on you last night, Sarah."

"Not a problem. Are you okay?"

"I'm fine."

"Well, that's a blanket answer that doesn't necessarily mean you're okay."

He shot her a grin. "I mean it. Really. My teeth are clean, just so you know. I brushed them before I walked over here." Sprinted was more like it. Like a lovesick fool. Maybe he was.

"Fair enough," she said, laughing quietly before her grin faded. "Listen, I want to talk with you about Mr. Benson and the donations."

Not sure whether to be relieved she'd changed the subject or not, Sam nodded. Maybe it was for the best. "Sure. What about it?"

"Am I to assume Mr. Benson came to the bank and applied for a loan?"

Sam snapped his gaze to hers. "How could you possibly know that? And yes, but please don't say a word to anyone since it's confidential bank business."

"I wouldn't dream of discussing it with anyone else." She shrugged. "Call it intuition. Headstones can be expensive, and I don't think the Bensons have much extra money, even for something as important as a permanent marker for their son's grave."

What was she saying? "Are you reconsidering your offer to make the donation cans?"

"No, not at all. I've already made them. Mom and Tess helped, but I haven't distributed them yet." Smoothing her fingers over a patch of velvety-smooth, emerald green moss, Sarah appeared deep in thought. "I'd like to suggest that you think about something first. I know how prideful men can be about money. Before I distribute the donation cans to businesses all over town, I think you should discuss your idea with Mr. Benson."

Contemplating her words, Sam nodded slowly. "Go on."

"Think about it. He came to you, in private, to discuss a very personal issue. He might not appreciate everyone donating to the cause, as wonderful an idea as it is. Your motives are good, and I know Mr. Benson would understand that in time, but I'd just ask that you try to look at it from his viewpoint before we take that next step. Not to sound flippant, but Marty's been gone for a while now, so I don't believe there's a rush to collect the money or to give him a loan."

"I still need to give him an answer." Sam had passed on the loan application to the proper officer at the bank, but he hadn't heard yet whether it had been approved. He needed to get on that right away. Sarah was right, and he should have thought of that angle before.

"All I'm saying is, maybe you should propose your idea to him and see how he feels about it before we carry out the plan." She sat up straighter and gave him a small smile. Sarah's smile worked its way into his affections—admittedly, his *heart*—each time they were together, whether in private or in public. "You could tell him you know the townspeople would be glad to donate for such a worthy cause, tell him about the idea for the donation cans, and then suggest that you see how much is collected within a certain period of time. If it's not quite enough for what he wants to do, and if he qualifies, then the bank can give him a loan."

"But it wouldn't be for nearly as large an amount." He planted a kiss on her forehead. "You are brilliant."

Sarah appeared surprised by the kiss, but she didn't pull away from his show of affection. "Thank you." Avoiding his gaze, she selected a rock and tossed it across the creek.

"That the best you've got?" Choosing a larger rock on the ground beside him, he handed it to her. "Skim it."

"I accept your challenge." Jumping to her feet, Sarah wound up and sailed it across the creek.

"Much better. That's the star softball player I remember."

She sat back down beside him again. Another benefit of spending so much time with her was being able to read her emotions a bit better, as much as that was possible. Sarah was a very expressive, passionate girl. She didn't play games, she didn't say things to try and test him in any way. Neither did she set out to tempt him, but she managed to accomplish that quite well. And now, Sam knew something weighed on Sarah's mind. He'd wait it out, knowing she'd broach the subject when she was ready.

It didn't take long. When she shifted to face him, he watched her, prepared to listen.

"Sam, what was that conversation in the diner all about?"

He could play dumb and act like he didn't know which one she meant, but Sarah deserved better than a vague response or for him to play it off as if it was nothing.

"Charlie has appointed himself as my dating consultant. He thinks it's time I choose a candidate." That hadn't come out right, and he ran his hand through his hair. "Not that it's any kind of contest or competition."

"That's what I figured. No offense, but you've been pretty cranky lately. A date might help improve your disposition." She gave him a grin which he didn't return. "So, have you thought about which girl you'd like to ask out?"

Turning his head sharply, Sam stared at the creek. Clearing his throat, he kept his gaze trained straight ahead since he didn't trust himself to look at her while discussing his non-existent love life. Especially with the one girl he most wanted to date.

"Are you still thinking? Because if you have to think that hard about it, I can make some suggestions."

The muscles in his jaws flexed. "I'm not actively seeking a girl to date, Sarah. You, of all people, should know that."

"I want to see you happy." Sarah leveled her beautiful brown eyes on him. Flecks of warm honey danced in those eyes. If she started spouting the *let's be really good friends* speech, Sam wasn't sure what he'd do. Talk about a frustrating female. From the set of her chin, and the spark in her eyes, Sarah was about to share her opinion. Talk about a creature of habit. Oh, what he wouldn't give to kiss her. Talk about consuming need.

"I *am* happy, but you don't seem to get that." Fine, he'd humor her. This conversation could prove enlightening in spite of his misgivings. "Go right ahead."

"Not to make you uncomfortable, but candidate number one. My sister."

He blew out a breath. "If I had any interest in dating Tess, I would have asked her out a long time ago. End of story, as you would say."

"But she's your age, skinny, the prettiest girl in the region with the tiaras to prove it—"

"Is that all you think I care about?" Did she know him at all? He had to wonder. "Physical looks?"

"Well, no. Of course not. I didn't mean to imply that, but if you want to talk fact, you're a very handsome man, Sam. Brave, strong, a military veteran." Her voice had grown quiet, and her cheeks blossomed with a sweet pink flush. "Do I need to keep going?"

"You think I'm handsome?" He said it a teasing manner, intending to play it off if she was only trying to placate him. Her compliments massaged his bruised ego, but he needed to get over himself, see what she had in mind, and then figure out his next plan of action.

Sarah rolled her eyes. "Don't let it swell your head. How about Janet Marks?"

"Nope. She's fixated on Deputy Ron."

"Tommy's newest sidekick? She is? Hmm. I didn't know that. How is it you've only been home for such a short time and yet you know this?"

"Watch them when they're both in the diner at the same time. Plain as day."

"I'll do that. Now you're making me wonder what else I've missed. Maybe I need to reevaluate my powers of observation. I'm impressed by yours, I have to say. Any other couples you know about? Let's get them out of the way now so we can rule out any other potential dating candidates."

He swallowed his mounting frustration. "You're busy in the diner and can't see everything. Okay, here's another one. Tammy Simpson likes Randy Sweet."

She sat up straighter at that comment, just as he suspected. Fair or not, he'd thrown that one out there to gauge her reaction. Nothing like putting out the bait to see if she'd bite. He'd heard all the rumors pairing Randy with Sarah. Charlie told him what Fire Captain Sweet had announced to half the town at the Fourth of July picnic last summer. He'd laughed it off, but that niggling question in Sam's mind wouldn't leave him alone.

Randy Sweet had apparently caught wind of the fact that he'd been coming to the diner on a regular basis. He'd strutted into the diner earlier in the week, coinciding with his usual afternoon break. After a courteous nod in his direction, Randy parked himself on a counter seat where he'd monopolized Sarah's attention for an indecent length of time. No one could tell him that was coincidence, not that he believed in such a thing.

"Is that right?" Was it his imagination, or did she squirm? Could she hold some tiny bit of affection for Randy, after all?

"And does Randy like Tammy?"

"Not from what I can see. He has his eye on someone else in town."

That statement caused the corners of her mouth to downturn. "If you're talking about me, then you can forget it right now. Randy knows I have no intention of dating him, and besides, I'm—"

"You're leaving Rockbridge as soon as you can. Right." Stretching out his legs, Sam couldn't keep the exasperation from his voice. "Tell me something else the entire town doesn't know." That came out sharper than he'd intended. If he didn't watch it, he'd push Sarah so far away he'd never have a chance.

Sam heard her quick intake of breath. "Sounds like Kathy Parker might be more your type than I'd thought."

"Bite your tongue." He met her gaze. "Never."

"Cindy Gray?"

"Too involved in all that feminist stuff. And don't start a debate with me on that one. You know I have all the respect in the world for women, and I like to believe my views on those subjects are modern and progressive...to a point."

"Cheryl Simms?" At least she hadn't pushed the women's liberation issue.

"Too short. Sorry, and call me lazy, but I don't want to get a permanent crick in the neck by having to sit down or perch a girl on a step to kiss her."

Sarah giggled, and the sound of her laughter relaxed him a little. "If she were your type, I'm sure you'd make an exception. Pity the girl if she wanted to kiss you or she'd strain *her* neck. Okay, how about Marsha Barton? Now, she's a cute girl. Don't you agree?"

Would her list of potential girls to date never end? "Nope. As superficial as this probably makes me sound, she always has spit in the corners of her mouth when she talks."

"Excuse me? Really?" He could tell she was trying her best not to laugh.

"Take a close look at her sometime. Right here." He pointed to one corner of his mouth. "Spittle. Isn't that what it's called? Sad, but true."

"I'll take your word for it. How about Tina Hardesty?"

"Nope. Tina wears too much makeup. She wears so much stuff on her lips that a guy would slide right off her mouth if he tried to kiss her."

That ridiculous comment made her laugh. "Candy Wright?"

Shaking his head, Sam made a tsk tsk sound. "I refuse to date a woman named Candy. If you ask me, she should consider marrying Randy Sweet."

"Candy Sweet? Wait! Candy and Randy Sweet? That's perfect! You should suggest it to him." Sarah threw her head back, laughing even harder. Her long hair slipped from its ponytail holder and tumbled around her shoulders. She was distracting enough with her hair back, highlighting the beauty of her face, but with it down, she was breathtaking. Yeah, he'd definitely be thinking of this image for a long time. Those gorgeous blonde waves—combined with all the rest of Sarah Jordan—could give even a devout monk serious reason to rethink his vows.

"I know!" She snapped the fingers of one hand. "Sylvie Foster. What's not to like? She's tall, very pretty with all that dark hair, has a normal name, doesn't have an excess saliva problem as far as I know, and she's not a feminist from all appearances. Yes, I think Sylvie's absolutely perfect for you. What do you think?"

Sam closed his eyes, counting to ten under his breath. "Does this mean you won't come to the dance on Saturday night?"

Surprising him, Sarah groaned and fell on her back, covering her face with her arm.

"It's a simple question. Yes or no will suffice."

She moved her arm and glanced up at him. If Charlie had dared him, in that moment, he would have leaned over and kissed her until she was breathless and begged for more. He should do it, anyway, but she wasn't ready. Would she ever be ready? With Sarah beside him now, so pretty and tempting, his mind was going in all kinds of directions.

Lord, forgive me and help keep my thoughts honorable.

"No, I'm not going," she said. "You're going to ask Sylvie. End of story."

That comment cut him down to size.

Lord, this is torture. I need to change her mind.

"There you are!" They both turned. Within seconds, Tess appeared, gasping and panting. "Mom's looking for you, Sarah, and needs you to come home. I figured you were probably here." Tess didn't bother to disguise her surprise at seeing them together. "What I didn't expect was seeing you here, too, Sam. Imagine that." She moved her gaze to Sarah with a raised brow.

"Hey, Tess." Although he nodded, Sam was perturbed at the interruption and didn't bother disguising his irritation.

Sarah quickly rose to her feet and slipped into her shoes. "Sam, I'll see you again soon and we can talk more, if you want."

"I'll try to stop by the diner for lunch tomorrow." He didn't make a move to leave and sat watching them. What a dumb thing to say. He went to the diner every day like clockwork the same as Perry Sellers always did. And every day, he sat in Sarah's section. Then he'd leave her a ridiculously large tip which she'd finally given up trying to protest.

"Sure. I'll see if I can take a break. Bye."

Sam forced a smile, recognizing that telltale gleam in Tess's eyes. Sarah was going to be on the receiving end of chastisement or questioning worthy of a law enforcement official. Or both. Coming from Tess, he wouldn't wish that on anyone. Another thing he knew:

he wouldn't be discussing his love life further with Sarah. She could toss out all the names on the planet, but he had to do what he could to convince the stubborn woman that *she* was the only one he wanted to date.

Rising to his feet, Sam dusted off his shorts and started off behind them. He'd keep his distance, but close enough to step in if Sarah needed him. Not that she couldn't hold her own against Tess. Matter of fact, she was used to handling her older sister, so she'd be just fine without him.

That didn't stop him.

Just keep on walking.

~~♥~~

"Are you going to tell me or do I have to drag it out of you?" Tess demanded as soon as they were a reasonable distance away. The glances she'd darted her way had been borderline accusatory. "Why was Sam there?"

"He comes sometimes." Sarah shrugged. "We talk. I thought you already knew that."

Stopping, Tess moved her hands down to her hips and stared at her. "Tell me the truth, little sister. Are you dating Sam?"

Sarah laughed, but the sound rang hollow. "Hardly. Come on, Tess. You know we're just friends, the same as always. We talk about all kinds of things. As a matter of fact, when you interrupted, I was suggesting names of girls for him to consider dating. I'm glad he feels comfortable enough to confide in me."

"My name wasn't among the ones you suggested, I imagine." It wasn't a question.

"Well. . ."

Tess blew out a breath. "Admit it, Sarah. You don't want me to date Sam because then *you* won't have a chance with him. Don't think I couldn't feel all the sparks flying around the room the other night when he was at our house. I almost called Randy to come over with his fire hose to spray you and Sam down."

Mirroring her, Sarah moved her hands to her hips. "Tess, look. It's time to face the facts. Sorry to be blunt, but if Sam had an interest in dating you, don't you think he would have asked you out years ago? I know he likes you, but he's had numerous opportunities through the years."

Tess's blue eyes grew wide. "Did Sam tell you that or are you making it up?"

"Do you really want me to answer that?"

They stared at one another for a long moment. "Lie to me if you want, little sister, but don't lie to yourself. I've seen the way you look at Sam." She moved her gaze away and dropped her hands to her sides. "The problem is, I've seen the way he looks at you, too."

When Tess resumed walking, Sarah fell into step beside her. She wasn't ready to have this discussion. Sometimes her sister possessed a remarkable clarity of vision.

I'm falling in love with Sam, yes, but is it possible he could feel something for me?

"Why'd you come find me, Tess? What's the big emergency?"

"Mom's trying to find their airline tickets. She's having a hissy fit because she can't put her hands on them. She thought you might know where they are, and she also needs our help to get all the laundry done. I've never seen her so out of sorts." Tess's words were matter of fact, her tone devoid of emotion.

Thankful for the change in topic, Sarah knew Tess had made it up as an excuse to seek her out since Mom and Dad weren't leaving tomorrow. More likely than not, she'd wanted to find them together at the creek for her own reasons.

Sarah smiled. "I know Mom's excited about their trip, and I can't blame her."

"You're probably right," Tess said, "especially considering she's never flown before."

"Can you imagine what it's like, Tess?" Sarah raised her arms and twirled in a circle as she walked. "I've asked Sam what it's like to fly, and he says that's when he feels closest to God. It must be so exhilarating. Just up there, zooming around, soaring among the clouds. Like you can reach out and touch them. So white, fluffy, pretty. Doesn't it sound wonderful?"

Tess smirked. "You and your fascination with flying. Why don't you ask your creek companion to take you up in that vintage plane of his sometime? I'm sure he'd love the opportunity."

Sarah quirked a brow as they reached the line of trees by the main road and headed for home. "Please don't tell me you're jealous, Tess. If that's the case, there's no reason." Even as she said the words, a little niggling started in her mind.

"I'm not jealous. I would be, but I can tell that Sam's not interested in me." Tess smiled a little. "I think he and his plane will get along just fine soaring through life together."

"I'm sure Sam will settle down eventually." Even as Sarah said the words, the tug inside her grew more insistent.

"Right." Tess kicked a stray pebble, sending it skittering across the road. "In spite of his best intentions, Captain Lewis will most likely tire of this little town soon enough and fly off into the sunset."

Chapter 18

~~♥~~

May 26, 1962

Wiping down a table at Perry's on Saturday night, Sarah glanced up when the bell jingled. Her traitorous heart lurched when she spied Sam standing in the doorway. She covered her mouth in an attempt not to laugh. What was he wearing? Thankfully, the only other patrons of the diner were Harold and Betty, and they were holding hands and staring into one another's eyes. Like always. Predictable, yes, but in the best way imaginable. Those two lovebirds put all the younger couples in town to shame.

As if on cue, they stood and waved after leaving a few bills on the table for the check and her tip. Harold exchanged a few words with Sam, and then the older gentleman escorted Betty out the door.

"Find something amusing?" Sam quirked a brow as if challenging her.

Wow. Someone was in a cantankerous mood. Intuition warned her that this exchange could get interesting, if not heated. She'd never had an out-and-out argument with Sam, and she didn't wish to start one now. He hadn't come to the diner at all yesterday, the first day she could remember that he'd missed since he'd been home in Rockbridge. She'd wondered why, but she wasn't about to ask the man.

Lord, please help both of us hold our tempers.

"No, not really," she said. "I have to ask. What is that jacket— and I use that term loosely—you're wearing? Or should I say it's

128

wearing you?"

Sam pivoted like a male model. Even in his silliness, the man was so very attractive. "It's called a Nehru jacket. Why? You don't like it? I think it's cool. Groovy." He shrugged. "Whatever you kids are calling it these days."

She'd already insulted him and now she needed to be nice. "It's a very good color on you."

"It's black, Sarah. The color is black. Actually, I'm not even sure it's a color."

"Sure it is," she said. "Just like white."

"Is that what everything is to you? Black and white?" Raising his hand, Sam started to rake his fingers through his hair. Apparently thinking better of it, he smoothed down a few strands on the top of his head. Of course, the action only drew attention to the fact that the ends of his hair curled over the top of his silly jacket.

She swallowed, focusing on Sam but feeling unsettled with the direction this conversation seemed to be headed. At the same time— knowing she'd regret it later but spurred on by some irrational need to aggravate him further—Sarah couldn't hold her tongue. "No, I see things in color, too. But, tell me why would you even want to wear a jacket named after the prime minister of India?"

"Why not?" Sam's eyes flashed as he leveled his gaze on her.

Sarah raised her chin. "For one thing, it's got like a hundred tiny buttons. I should think that'd get annoying real quick."

He stepped closer, standing in front of her. "Do you think it somehow makes me less of a Christian if I wear it? Tell me the truth."

She stared at him. Why would he think, much less say, something like that? "That's quite possibly the most ludicrous thing you've ever said."

"Don't judge me."

"I'm not judging anyone, Sam, but it sounds to me like you're trying to pick a fight." Turning away from him, Sarah began cleaning another table. If she didn't have to cover Patti's shift, she wouldn't be working tonight. Why was he even here?

She counted to three below her breath before speaking. "I've always considered you one of the strongest Christian men I've ever known. Current behavior excepted."

"I'm sorry." He followed behind her. She bit her tongue not to call him Hershey. He definitely wouldn't take kindly to being called by that nickname right now.

"Here's a fun bit of trivia," he said. "Want to know what the collar on this jacket is called?"

What an odd question. Shaking her head, she scooped up the money Harold left on the table. She walked to the register and quickly deposited the bills, dropping the change into the Benson Fund collection can on the counter. At least Martin Benson had agreed to their plan, and the donations were already mounting.

"Aren't you going to pocket your tip?"

"Nope," she said. "We were low on donations today."

When she glanced at Sam, something in his expression softened. Moving over to Table 9, she scrubbed it with more energy than was warranted. "I'm sure I don't know what the name of your collar is called." What a silly thing to discuss. "I assume you have a date for the dance, after all?" What made her ask *that* question? Would she never learn? She glanced at the clock on the wall. "It's almost seven o'clock, and I'm sure somewhere in Rockbridge, a young lady is waiting for Captain Lewis to arrive and sweep her off her feet."

"Now you're mocking me?" If the situation weren't so tense, she'd laugh. Sam's eyes were a little wild, and he was clearly not amused.

"No, I'm not. I absolutely meant it." Sarah returned to her work. "Any girl would be crazy not to want to go out with you."

Sam blew out a breath. "Right. Which means you're calling yourself crazy?"

She shrugged. "Maybe I am." He made a valid point. More than anything on earth, she'd love to go out with Sam. Being near him set her pulse flying out the door and she hated the thought of him taking another girl on a date.

"I thought you'd be thrilled that I finally took your advice."

Sarah stopped cleaning and met his gaze. "I am. Did you change your mind and ask out my sister? I'm sure Tess can easily answer your little trivia question. Although why it matters I have no idea," she muttered under her breath.

Stop being so sarcastic.

"No," he said. She was irritating him, which could be both a good and bad thing.

"I'm going out with Sylvie tonight. Out of all your potential dating candidates for me, she was the one voted most likely. Okay, that didn't sound right, but you know what I mean." Moving one hand to his hip, Sam shot her a glance simmering with barely contained aggravation. "According to the salesperson—and this is the only reason I know it—this collar is a"—he faltered, snapping his fingers—"what's the name of those little orange slices in a can?"

Sarah stared at him. What was he talking about now? This entire conversation was increasingly inane. "Mandarins?"

"That's it!" After he snapped his fingers, she caught a whiff of his cologne. Oh, but it was nice. Heady and overwhelmingly masculine. Sarah steeled herself not to sway. She'd never known a man could smell so wonderful.

"It's called a mandarin collar."

Focus. "Interesting way to remember it," she said. "I have to wonder why you keep bringing up the collar. You must have left town to go shopping for your big night out. For one thing, you must have bought a bottle of very expensive cologne. And here I thought you hadn't escaped Rockbridge since you'd returned home." Wrong thing to say. Now she sounded jealous. And ridiculous. Moving to another table, Sarah began scrubbing it with renewed vigor.

Sam stepped even closer, making it impossible to ignore him. "I left town to get a few things, if you must know. And yes, I saw the Perry's Diner billboard. It's very nice." His eyes bore into hers. "Do you like my cologne? Think Sylvie might like it?"

She gritted her teeth. "It's very. . .nice. I'm sure she won't be able to resist you."

He stared at her for another few seconds, exasperation written in his creased brow, in the tiny little lines forming around the corners of his eyes, and on either side of his mouth. "One of these days, I'm hoping you'll open those big brown eyes of yours and see what's easily within your reach, Sarah. Under your nose, as it were. You just have to *want* it."

Inside, she was quaking as her eyes settled on his chin. She couldn't bring herself to look him directly in the eye. "I. . ." She gulped. "I. . ." The words wouldn't come. "It's not that I don't want it, Sam. You must understand that. And it's not to say I won't ever want it. But maybe. . .at this point in time"—she heaved a sigh—"I want something else. I'm sorry if that hurts you, but I'm asking you to try and understand."

A fleeting expression of confusion mixed with hurt flittered across his distractingly handsome features. He stepped so close the toes of his shoes touched hers. "You can't have both at the same time? Because I think you can."

She heaved a huge sigh. "Tell me how that's even possible."

"At least I'm not afraid to try new things." His gaze traveled down to her feet. "And I don't wear rubber-soled shoes intended for senior citizens."

Okay, that comment pushed her to the brink. Seemed when the man's feelings were hurt, Sam shot back with biting comments. Inside, Sarah seethed. "Why not go ahead and insult my hairnet and get that out of your system, too? Have at it. I'll have you know these shoes are a necessity since I'm on my feet for hours every day here at Perry's."

"I know that."

Tossing the rag on the table, she lowered one hand to her hip. "You try working eight hours on your feet. Wiping up spit and snot, serving sometimes surly and rude customers, and then keeping a smile pasted on your face and calling out 'Thank you for your patronage' when someone walks out the door without leaving a tip."

Sarah bit her lower lip. That last part was uncalled for since Sam had singlehandedly given her nearly a hundred dollars in extra tips in the last couple of weeks alone. Ridiculous amounts, really, but she'd given up trying to return any of it. She'd tried at first, but he'd adamantly refused. Before she burst out and said something they'd both regret—or weep in his presence—one of them needed to leave. Considering she was in her place of work, Sam had to go.

"You should leave."

"I agree." He pulled at his silly collar named after miniature orange slices in a can and stalked toward the door. Pausing, he spun around. "Look, I know you do a great job here at Perry's, and I'm sorry if some of your customers don't appreciate you. But you're one of the most stubborn women I've ever known."

Sarah swallowed the huge lump in her throat. "Have a wonderful evening."

Sam tugged on the handle of the door, sending the bell jingling and making her want to yank off that bell. "Same to you." He lifted his head to the ceiling and closed his eyes—sure looked like he was counting under his breath—before walking back over to her with his purposeful stride. "You could stop me with one little word, Sarah. One. Word." Fire sparked in his blue eyes and the muscles in his jaws visibly tightened.

"I'll give you five. Thank you for your patronage." She didn't flinch although his gaze bore straight into her soul. "I'll see you at church tomorrow morning if you can manage to get all the buttons of your jacket undone by then."

With a disgusted grunt, Sam jerked open the door, sending that bell jingling, and left without another word. She watched as he passed in front of the plate glass window, not looking back.

Sinking onto the red vinyl seat of the closest booth, Sarah rested her head on her arms, crossed on the tabletop. "What do I do now, Lord? Laugh or cry?"

You pray, Sarah.

Chapter 19

~~♥~~

"Hey, Sarah. Want a ride home?"

Sarah recognized the voice as Merle's. She gave him a grateful smile. Pausing on the sidewalk, she debated her options while he pulled his car to the curb. He waited, the car idling. After working a double shift, she was exhausted and the offer was too tempting to resist. Besides, it was only a few blocks.

"Thanks. I appreciate it." Opening the passenger car door, she climbed inside.

"Been working longer hours today at the diner?" he said as she slid onto the front seat and closed the passenger door.

"Yes. One of Patti's kids is sick, so I covered her shift tonight. The diner was a mess, so I stayed late to help clean up." She covered her yawn with one hand.

Merle nodded and pulled back onto the street. Within a block, Sarah recognized the signs that he'd been drinking.

Don't panic. It's only three more blocks. It'll be fine.

"You know what? I need to do some reading tonight. The fresh air will be invigorating and help revive me. Why don't you pull over? I'll just hop out and walk the rest of the way."

"Ah, Sa-Sarah." Merle darted a glance her way and chuckled. "You're n-not afraid of me, are you?"

"Of course not, Merle. I've known you my entire life. But I think you've—" She bit her lower lip, unsure of what to say. Knowing if she mentioned her suspicion that he'd been drinking, it'd probably prompt a negative reaction.

Without a word, Merle gunned the accelerator and the old Chevy jerked forward at an alarming rate of speed. Leaving Sarah's sense of security in the middle of the street a block behind them.

"Please slow down, Merle. There's no hurry."

Loud honking behind them prompted Sarah to look over her shoulder. She breathed a sigh of relief when she spied Sam's dad's truck.

"Oh, great. The Lewis patrol. I'll show them."

"Merle, don't be foolish," Sarah said, starting to put her hand on his arm before thinking better of it and withdrawing. "Pull over." Her nerves threatened to take over.

Lord, please watch over us.

In a daring move, the Lewis truck—with Sam behind the wheel—passed them on the left, spun around sideways in the street and halted a few hundred yards ahead of Merle's car. Slamming on the brakes, Merle cursed. Sarah screamed and held onto the arm of the passenger door for all she was worth.

The car skidded a few frightening seconds before screeching to a stop inches from the truck. Breathing hard, Sarah put her arm over her stomach, willing it to behave. Her head pounded, but other than a few broken fingernails, she was otherwise unharmed.

Within seconds, Sam was on her side of the car. Opening the door, he crouched down beside her. "Are you okay, baby?" When she nodded, momentarily unable to speak, Sam glared at Merle. "What do you think you're doing, driving crazy like that in the middle of a residential street?"

Merle snarled. "All the kiddos should be tucked safely in their beds by now. Just havin' a little fun. No harm done. Go take a wiz in somebody else's yard and leave me alone."

Sarah stared at Merle in horror. Why hadn't she recognized the signs that he'd been drinking before accepting the ride? She moved her hand over her forehead, embarrassed and humiliated at how foolish she'd been to get in the car with a known drunk, supposedly recovering or not.

"Sarah, you wait in the truck. I'll drive Merle home and then run back."

"That's not necessary," she said. "I'm close enough to walk home."

"No, I'm taking you. Wait in the truck." Sam's voice was commanding. Not sure she liked being ordered by him, Sarah still couldn't help but admire his protectiveness.

"The military hero speaks." Merle smirked at Sam. "Look, Sam, I appreciate you givin' me a job and all, but that doesn't give you the right to interfere with my courting Sarah."

"Your *what*?" That's all she needed to hear. Sarah started to climb out of the car and allowed Sam to assist her. "I'll wait in the truck."

Sam nodded. "Thanks." Closing the passenger door, he started toward Merle's car. Sarah turned to look when she heard more screeching tires. She gasped as she saw Sam jump out of the way as Merle backed up his car. Swerving around the truck, he sped off into the night.

"Lord, help him get home safely," she murmured.

Sam slid in the truck beside her. "I share that sentiment. Merle's behavior is disappointing, to say the least." He gripped the wheel, and bowed his head. A few seconds later, he turned to her. "Are you okay? Really?"

"I think so. A little shaky from my own stupidity, but otherwise I'm fine. Thank the Lord for your quick reflexes. Merle could have mowed you down!" Sarah moved her arms over her middle.

When she glanced at him, Sam turned his head, meeting her eyes. "Are you saying you care about me, Sarah Jordan?"

Closing her eyes, she leaned back against the headrest. "Always. You called me baby."

"Let's go home. And yeah, I did."

"Are you going to fire him?"

Sam didn't say anything for a long moment. "Not sure. Probably not. I'll see if he shows up for work first. Then we'll talk."

They rode in silence for the short ride. When Sam pulled into her driveway, Sarah paused with one hand on the door handle. "Thanks for paying attention, Sam. Again. I owe you one."

He nodded but didn't look her way. "You're welcome. Glad I was there, but you owe me nothing."

"I hope you know I normally wouldn't accept a ride from a man I don't know well."

"Good to hear." His voice sounded tight, his words clipped. Was he mad? Although she was very curious about his date with Sylvie, she wasn't about to bring up the subject. The timing certainly didn't seem right. She couldn't help but notice he'd ditched the ridiculous Nehru jacket and now wore a regular shirt. Red, the color she loved most on him since it brought out the brilliance of his blue eyes. Who was she kidding? Sam looked great in anything.

"Since Merle's been working at the bank, I thought maybe he'd cut back on the drinking." For some unknown reason, she felt a need to explain herself, not sure Sam would listen.

"I hoped the same thing, but it's the weekend, so he's on his own time now." When Sam turned to face her, she glimpsed the firmness in his jaw.

"You've done what you can for him, Sam. More than most people would have done."

"Look, I know it's not my right to tell you not to ever get in a car with another man, but please do us both a favor and don't get in another car with Merle."

"Agreed. Good night."

"Good night."

A sense of sadness threatened to overwhelm her, but Sarah had no idea why. After closing the passenger door, she started up the walkway, aware he waited. She liked that, too, even though he lived four doors down.

"Sarah?"

She turned, her stomach doing a little flip. "Yes?"

"I'll see you tomorrow morning."

Sam sat in the truck in his driveway, replaying the events of the evening in his mind. He'd been unsettled after his date with Sylvie, but for reasons he didn't want to think about now. If he was honest with himself, he'd been unsettled before the date. Because of his discussion with Sarah. Why had she accepted the ride with Merle? She'd given him her answer, but he wasn't buying it. In his heart, he knew.

Because she really is that innocent, that trusting. She'd also been really tired after working a double shift at the diner, bless her heart.

He'd been surprised by the force of his anger as he'd noticed Merle's car weaving on the road. But was it anger at Merle for drinking again or more anger that Sarah was in the car with him? Not that he was angry with her. Sam couldn't imagine ever being angry—gut angry—at Sarah, but he'd wanted to punch out Merle. Pound some sense into him for putting Sarah in potential danger.

He should take Merle to lunch, sit him down and have a heart-to-heart talk. Find out what demons, if any, lurked in the man's soul. Why he felt compelled to find solace in a bottle of alcohol instead of in a healthier, more soul-satisfying way. Some men found their worth, their security, in a good job. From what his dad told him, Merle had never held down a decent job for more than a year at most.

Some men found their solace in the arms of a good woman. Merle wasn't a bad looking man, a little paunchy around the middle but nothing regular exercise couldn't help whittle away. A few years older than Sam, Merle had never married, never had children as far as he knew. Maybe loneliness was the issue?

After rolling up the side window—rain was expected in the night—Sam grabbed the silly jacket and climbed out of the truck. Even his bones were weary. It'd been a long night and he looked forward to getting to bed. Hopefully, tomorrow would be better.

His dad sat in his pajamas, glasses perched on his nose, reading the newspaper in the kitchen when he entered the house through the side door. Slammed into the house was more like it, using more force than he should have as he shoved the door behind him.

"Take it a little easier on the door, son."

"Sorry, Dad. I didn't realize you were up."

"I couldn't sleep. There's more warm milk in the pan on the stove. Pour yourself a cup and have a seat, if you want. Didn't you have a date with Sylvie tonight?"

"Yep." After pouring a mug of the milk, Sam pulled out the chair across from his dad and dropped into it. "The first date, and I think it might have been the last date."

His dad didn't appear surprised as he folded the paper. "Want to talk about it?"

Yes. No. Not really. Sam heaved a sigh. "She's a nice girl, but after one—*one*—date, mind you, Sylvie's already pushing me to have dinner with her parents."

"And you're not sure that's what you want?"

Sam raked a hand through his hair, thankful it had grown out to the length he liked. He'd never liked it cut short for the military even though it kept his neck cooler in the hot temperatures and was easier to maintain.

"It seems like such an important step. Like she wants to be serious. I haven't even kissed her."

With his brow furrowed, his dad sipped his milk. "I don't know her parents well since they've only been in town a short time. Sylvie seems like a nice girl. Pretty, too." He met Sam's gaze over the top rim of his mug. "Not that being pretty is any reason to date, or kiss, a girl."

His father's words hung heavy with what he didn't say. Sylvie was pretty, all right. She was good company, but she hung on his every word. That drove him nuts, and not in a good way. Sylvie agreed with every single thing he said instead of speaking her own mind. No one could agree with all of his opinions. He had half a mind to say something completely unfounded just to see if she'd concur. Sarah, on the other hand, challenged him at every turn. While she agreed with some of his statements, she'd argue her point against him just as often. In many ways, it kept him sharp and also attracted him to Sarah more than ever before. Nothing like a good sparring session to get the old hormones flying all over the place.

Lost in thought, Sam took a long drink, draining half the mug. How many years had it been since he'd had warm milk? So long he couldn't recall. "Seems half the town expected me to take up with Tess Jordan," he said finally, aware his father watched. "We've been neighbors and friends with her family for years, so I guess it's a natural assumption. Tell me, Dad, are you one of them?"

"No, I'm not part of some big conspiracy to get you married to Tess or anyone else, if that's what you're thinking." His dad's words were tinged with humor.

"Sorry." Unconsciously, he'd made his question sound like an accusation. Sam tapped his fingers on the table in a slow march. "Flying a plane in the Air Force was easier than trying to figure out a woman."

Joseph chuckled. "I know what people expected, Sam, but you don't always do what people expect. That's a good thing. You have plenty of time to court a girl and get married. Don't let all the overeager mothers and daughters in Rockbridge put pressure on you. Do it in God's time, and you'll be just fine."

Sam shared a grin with his dad. He'd heard the story a few times about how his parents met and married. They'd been friends a long time and then one day—when they were both in their late teens—it clicked. Sam rarely heard them disagree, and they'd been married almost thirty years. Coming in from work just last week, he'd found a box on the doorstep, addressed to his mother, from one of those slinky lingerie places. Not knowing what to do with the box, he'd stared at it as he walked inside the door. His dad, seeing him with the box, had taken it from him. "You'll understand one day when you're married, son." Wow. That had been an eye-opener.

Joseph cleared his throat, startling him. "I know Tess has dated a lot of the single men in Rockbridge."

"What are you saying?" Crossing his arms, Sam leaned back in his chair.

"Mind you, I'm not criticizing Tess," Joseph said. "But there's a part of me that has to wonder why she's dated so much and doesn't stay with one fellow for more than a few dates." Pushing away from the table, he walked to the sink. Rinsing out his mug, he placed it upside down in the drainer. He leaned back against the counter, arms crossed, and surveyed him.

"Could be because she hasn't found the right guy yet and doesn't want to waste their time." That was to Tess's credit. She might be flighty sometimes and put too much emphasis on the wrong things, but deep down, he knew she had a good heart. Swallowing the last of his now lukewarm milk, Sam followed his dad's lead and moved to the sink to rinse his empty mug.

"On the opposite end of the spectrum, you've got her younger sister, Sarah, who apparently doesn't date much at all. Any theories on that one?"

Sam considered it for a moment. "I'd have to give you the same answer."

"Exactly, except to say I know a certain young waitress from Perry's Diner who's spent an awful lot of quality time with a bank officer in recent weeks. And you've been walking around town with a goofy grin on your face lately that I don't think Sylvie Foster's put there."

With a quick squeeze of his hand on Sam's shoulder, Joseph gave him a smile. "Get some sleep, son. I'll see you in the morning."

Chapter 20
~~♥~~
The Next Morning

Sarah startled when Sam dropped onto the pew beside her. She scooted over, making more room for him. From the other side of Mom and Dad, Tess peered at her with narrowed eyes. She could already imagine the whispers behind her. Why did people gossip in church? Pastor McDonald had preached any number of sermons on that very topic, at least one per year, but that particular message must have fallen on some deaf ears in his congregation.

Sam laid his hand on her arm. "I'm sorry about those things I said to you in the diner last night. I was a real jerk and said things I didn't mean. I hope you can forgive me."

Her eyes filled with unwanted tears and Sarah squeezed them tight for a moment, willing them not to spill over onto her cheeks. That would be humiliating.

"Shhh." Sam departed and came back within a minute, pushing a tissue into her hand.

"I'm not crying over you. I have something in my eye."

"You're a terrible liar. Always have been," he said, his voice low as Juanita Rivers began playing the opening hymn. "If it makes you feel any better, that little voice inside me—otherwise known as the Holy Spirit—wouldn't let me rest last night."

She glanced over at him. "Sam, you were my hero last night in getting me out of Merle's car. I can handle a few insults about my choice of footwear." She managed a small smile. "You can rest easy during your Sunday afternoon nap. You're forgiven."

A moment later, she heard his light chuckle. Daring to glance his way, she dabbed at the corners of her eyes, praying the skin around her eyes didn't appear blotchy. Tess was the pretty crier in the family. Tess was the prettiest at everything she did. She might as well give it up and blubber like an idiot. When she peeked at him again, he was smiling.

"Care to share what you find so amusing?" When Sam angled his head at her feet, she adjusted her position on the pew and swung her feet out of sight.

"Nice shoes." Placing his hand beneath her elbow, they both rose for the first verse of "Great Is Thy Faithfulness."

She'd borrowed a pair of Tess's sandals, the highest heels Sarah had ever worn. Walking in them without falling flat on her face was the trick, but if it brought that gleam in a certain man's eyes, she'd gladly risk it. She certainly hadn't planned on wearing the shoes, but as she'd reached for her own low-heeled shoes in the closet, she'd spied them. Black sandals with straps—respectful enough for church without being considered inappropriate except to a few of the more conservative older ladies perhaps. Ironic how she and Tess shared the same shoe size.

Lord, why am I thinking such things? In your house, of all places. With new resolve, Sarah concentrated on the lyrics of one of her favorite hymns. Hearing a commotion behind them a minute later, she turned. Sam took her hand in his, giving it a quick squeeze. He nodded to the opposite side of the church. Following his nod, she almost cried aloud as she spied Merle coming in with Jimmy. As she watched, the row of Jimmy's family moved down on the pew, making room for him.

The wooden pew creaked when Sam leaned close, his warm lips next to her ear. "It's a great day in the house of the Lord."

"Amen." After last night's events, it was a miracle Merle was even up for church. She had a feeling Sam might have had something to do with it. In any case, his nearness was doing all sorts of things to her. Things of which Mrs. Bittenbottom, her former Sunday school teacher, would definitely not approve.

Tiny shivers ran through Sarah. Not a good thing while sitting in church. Ranked right up there with mooning over a man.

~~♥~~

A Few Days Later

Sarah delivered a third glass of ice water to Sam along with a small bowl of lemons. "Maybe you should eat something to soak up all this liquid."

"Good idea," he said. "I could eat a mid-afternoon grilled cheese since I skipped lunch today. Can you come and sit with me on your break?"

"Yes, but not for another ten minutes."

He nodded. "I'll wait. I don't have an appointment at the bank for another hour."

"Not a problem. Is everything okay?"

"I'd just like to talk something over with you. Get your opinion."

"Sure. Do you need anything else in the meantime?"

"No, I'm good. Thanks for the water. And the lemons."

"Welcome. I'll be back soon with your grilled cheese."

"Something up with Sam?" Debbie said a few minutes later when she plopped down on a counter seat. "I could see his frown in that corner booth the minute I walked in here. That pout's deep enough to sink a ship." A rush of relief ran through Sarah to see her friend's hair was back to its normal dark brown with reddish highlights. And, if she wasn't mistaken, Deb was growing out her eyebrows again. Maybe Arnie had finally convinced her.

"He asked me to sit with him during my break. Said he wants my opinion on something."

"Don't you do that on a regular basis these days?"

"When I can, yes. Depends on how busy we are when he comes in, of course."

Debbie gave her a coy grin. "You can't see it, can you?"

As she gathered the ingredients for Debbie's chocolate shake, Sarah shook her head. "I guess I don't. Two scoops of ice cream or three today?" She nodded at Myrna as she walked by her with Sam's grilled cheese in hand.

"Better make it two. Okay, here's the thing. Sam comes in here every day. He's fascinated by you. Those piercing blue eyes follow you around when he thinks you're not looking. I don't think he even realizes he's doing it. From where I'm sitting, I'd say he's got it pretty bad." Debbie winked. "I'm not just talking puppy love either."

Sarah shook her head as she added the chocolate and powder to the blender. "I think you're fishing, and I'm not taking the bait."

"Fine. Act like you don't know he's watching you right now."

The whirring of the blender drowned out any more conversation, granting her a grace period of a minute. She took a quick survey of the customers in the diner, immensely thankful Sam wasn't watching her at the moment. As usual, his head was bent over something inside that green file folder. One of these days, she'd ask him what was inside that folder if he didn't first offer to show her. Mentioning it to Debbie would only bring another round of theories, so keeping it to herself was best. Then again, her friend's speculation might prove entertaining.

A minute later, Sarah dropped a cherry on the top of the shake and set it front of Debbie.

"Looks great, as always. Thank you."

"Welcome." She grabbed a spoon and a straw and placed them on the counter. As she started to turn away, Debbie held up her left hand and wiggled her fingers.

With a small squeal, Sarah grabbed her hand. "You're engaged! You stinker. You sat there this whole time without saying a word! Arnie finally proposed?"

Debbie laughed. "No, Sheriff Tommy did. Yes, my Arnie finally asked me to marry him!" She stared at her diamond ring with a huge smile.

Within a few seconds, Sarah skirted around the end of the counter and enveloped Debbie in a tight hug. "I'm so thrilled for you, Deb. Congratulations!" Grabbing her hand, she admired the heart-shaped diamond and gave her another hug. "What a gorgeous ring! So, tell me all about it."

"He asked me after dinner last night. We were walking around the park, and he got down on one knee and everything. Now that he's finally asked, we decided why wait? We're having the Justice of the Peace marry us at City Hall. I'd like you to stand up with me and be my maid of honor. And, well, you know who Arnie's best friend is." Debbie lowered her gaze.

"I'm fine with Randy," Sarah said quickly to reassure her. "I haven't seen him much lately, and it'll be good to catch up with him."

Debbie giggled. "You're not afraid he'll grab the Justice and ask him to marry you two while you're both in City Hall? He might see it as mighty convenient."

Sarah laughed. "Just tell me what you want me to wear, the date and time, and whatever else you need me to do."

"Friday, June 15th at three o'clock. I'll have your bouquet as well as mine. Why don't you wear that pretty light blue dress you bought for Easter last year? You look beautiful in it, and it highlights your brown eyes. Just meet us outside on the front steps about fifteen minutes beforehand. We're going to hop in the car and start our honeymoon immediately after. You know how I've always wanted to visit the Grand Canyon, and Arnie wants to take me there."

"That sounds fabulous, sweetie." Sarah put a hand on Debbie's shoulder and squeezed. The happiness radiating from her friend's face swelled her heart.

"Just promise me you won't wear your hairnet." Debbie giggled. "I want to see all of that gorgeous blonde hair down around your shoulders for a change."

"Promise. My break's starting now, so I'm going to talk with Sam. Congratulations again. Holler if you need anything."

As usual, Sam closed the green folder as soon as she headed his way. She was tempted to lift the cover and peek inside if he excused himself for even a minute. Problem was, he'd no doubt tuck that file folder under his arm and take it with him. Must be private bank business, so she needed to respect the privacy of both Sam and his account holders. She admired his dedication and integrity. For some reason, she couldn't believe he'd bring his bank business into the diner on his break. Sure, Sam was dedicated to his work, but neither was he a slave to it.

"Arnie finally popped the question to Debbie." Sarah slid into the corner booth opposite him.

"I heard. I couldn't be more thrilled for them." He smiled wide enough for those fascinating lines on either side of his mouth to appear. Not dimples, but they made the man even more attractive. More and more, she felt drawn to tracing them with her finger. She needed to shake that thought from her mind.

"When is this momentous occasion?"

"June 15th, but they're not doing it in the church. City Hall at three o'clock." She shrugged. "Since Debbie's parents are both gone now, and Arnie's more or less estranged from his folks, I guess they figure it's the easiest thing." She blew out a sigh. "They're both

Christians even though they're not always in church."

"How do you feel about that?" Sam cocked his head to one side, surveying her.

"What?" Sarah shook her head, confused. "That they're not always in church? I guess I need to understand their relationship with the Lord is their own business, not mine."

"Sorry. I mean, would you be willing to do a City Hall marriage ceremony?"

His question surprised her. "Why?"

"Just curious. The fact that you felt the need to point out they're not getting married in the church tipped me off."

"I'd prefer a church wedding with the pastor officiating. Makes it more official, I suppose. I'd definitely want scripture and a hymn or two in addition to the usual parts of a traditional wedding ceremony. Those are givens. You?"

"I like your scenario better than City Hall, that's for sure."

"Sam, why are we talking about weddings?"

He stared out the front window before settling his gaze on her. "Since Debbie brought up the subject, more or less, I figured I might as well ask. The female species is a puzzle to me."

"Well, right back at you with the male species. Since we're talking about weddings, how do you feel about the whole cleaving thing?"

Sam had just taken a drink of his iced tea. At her question, he clamped a hand over his mouth and gulped down the rest. She leaned closer. Was it possible she'd made Sam blush? He coughed and cupped his fist over his mouth. "What on earth made you ask that?" He glanced out the window again, tapped his fingers on the tabletop, and appeared to be formulating his answer.

She followed his gaze. "What's so interesting? Is someone out there cleaving?"

Stop it, Sarah. She bit the inside of her cheek not to laugh.

Sam shook his head, but she could tell he was also trying not to laugh. "What exactly do you want to know about the whole cleaving thing? I happen to think cleaving sounds pretty great, and I look forward to it. You?" His eyes bore into her and he held her gaze. If he thought she'd squirm, she was determined not to give him the satisfaction. With him looking at her like that, the idea of sticking like glue to Sam didn't sound so bad.

"I got curious about the whole concept of cleaving a few years ago," she said. The lesson was part of the whole series at church taught by Mrs. Bittenbottom in a coed class about the birds and the bees. "Funny thing about cleaving. Did you know the word cleave actually has two distinct meanings? It's true," she insisted, not giving him the opportunity to answer. "It can mean sticking like glue to something—or someone, of course, like in the scriptures—or it can mean to split or cut something apart with a sharp instrument. Don't you find that interesting?"

"Quite the dichotomy," Sam said with a wry grin. "I prefer the newer translation in a verse from the Book of Mark. Instead of the word cleave, it says a man shall *leave* his father and mother and be united to, joined to, or hold fast to, his wife." He lifted his glass in a toast before taking another long drink.

"Thank you for not saying anything else before I swallowed," he said as he put his glass back on the table. "Listen, before your break's over, I wanted to run something by you."

"I'm listening, Captain Lewis," Sarah said, assuming a professional tone. "Talk to me, please." Her pulse raced, and a sense of foreboding swept through her.

"I feel like I'm back in high school even talking about this." Sam shifted on the seat. "Here's the thing. Sylvie invited me to meet her parents. But then she said, 'Only if you want. Absolutely no rush and no pressure from me.'"

Sarah was rendered momentarily speechless. Tears stung her eyes. How his words disappointed her. All she wanted was to run away and hide and ponder the reasons why later. For now, she needed to keep talking or she'd burst out in tears. Then she'd be the one acting like she was in high school. When Sam drummed his fingers on the tabletop again, she put her hand over his, stilling them.

This is what you encouraged him to do, you silly girl. You tossed out the name of every eligible woman in town and told him he should be dating. What did you expect?

"Meeting the parents is a big step," she managed to say. Needing something to do with her hands, she grabbed a napkin from the dispenser on the table and smoothed her fingers over the edges. "Sounds like you two are getting serious."

"That's the thing." Sam's tone sounded agitated. "We only had that one date for the dance at Harbison's. I picked her up, we talked a little, ate a little, danced a little, and then I drove her home. End of story, as you'd say. Unless things have changed on the dating scene since I've been away, I think that's moving way too fast." He sat back in the booth, shaking his head. "What happened to old-fashioned courting?"

"No kiss on the doorstep?" She couldn't look at him and didn't know where she'd garnered the nerve to ask the question.

"What if I say yes?"

Sarah stopped fingering the edges of the napkin and resisted the urge to ball it in her hand and throw it at him.

"I've always heard a girl doesn't invite a guy to meet her parents unless she thinks the relationship is going somewhere," he said. "Why would Sylvie push for something like that so soon? And no, I didn't kiss her. Didn't even come close. Thanks for caring. I figured you could help me out here and lend the female perspective."

"One date or not, it sounds to me like Sylvie wants the two of you to be exclusive," she said slowly, her mind racing. "Her invitation confirms that. But this is the key as I see it: Sylvie doesn't want you to think she's being pushy or demanding." Sarah ran her finger over the edge of the napkin, back and forth several times. Reaching for her, Sam covered her fingers until she stopped and put the napkin on the table.

They sat in silence as Sam appeared to consider her words. "Let me see if I've got this straight. You're saying Sylvie wants to be serious, but she's also giving me an 'out' of the relationship?" He shook his head. "It's crazy to even call it a relationship. So, no matter what happens, she's going to make it seem like it's *my* idea?"

"You're not as dense as you might believe, Captain Lewis. I didn't think you paid attention to such things. However"—she smoothed the napkin on the table top, ruing how her voice wavered—"it would seem you actually catch on pretty quick." The guy could fly a jet, but he couldn't understand women. To be fair, he'd admitted as much. Well, they were even since she couldn't understand men.

"I, um, need to get back to work now." Tucking the napkin in her pocket, Sarah rose to her feet with as much dignity as she could muster. Why did Sam's words bother her so much?

Because you don't want Sam dating Sylvie or anyone else, you fickle girl.

"Oh, be quiet," she mumbled under her breath, hoping he hadn't heard. Wonderful. Now she was talking to herself. Out loud.

"Sarah?"

She halted. What now? Turning around slowly, she pasted a smile on her face.

Sam rose to his feet and pulled out a piece of paper from the green folder. Her eyes widened as he handed it to her. "This is for you."

"What is it?" She dared not look at what she held until he'd left the diner.

He stepped abreast of her and lightly rested his warm hand on her forearm. His touch electrified her, and she could barely breathe.

Leaning close, his lips next to her temple, he whispered for her ears only. "Something to show you that I pay attention." With a quick tweak to her chin, Sam turned and strolled toward the front door without another word.

Frozen in place, Sarah couldn't move until she heard the bell jingle. She waited until he walked past the front window before glancing at the paper. She stared at a drawing of her with Perry Sellers in the diner. Rendered in pencil, the likenesses were amazingly lifelike. The definition in the lines on the elderly man's face, the shading of her hair, and the nuances in her facial features were exquisite.

Had Sam drawn this? He'd even added the heart-shaped mole on her neck. Her hand moved to her neck and, lost in thought, Sarah absently ran her finger over it. Even the faint scar over her left eyebrow—courtesy of a wayward softball many years ago—was visible in the drawing. She brought it even closer, inspecting it. In the right bottom corner were the initials, SJL. Yes, Sam must be the artist.

As if in a daze, Sarah collected Sam's money from the table. She shook her head when she saw the large tip he'd left. More than his usual excess. This time, it was positively obscene.

Debbie had already left the diner, and Sarah walked slowly toward the front counter. Leaning against it, she studied the drawing some more. She couldn't seem to stop staring at it but knew she needed to store it somewhere safe, away from food, steam, liquid and anything else that could possibly stain or hurt it. Maybe she should have asked Sam for the folder to protect it. At least this solved the mystery of that green folder. Never would she have guessed this was what Sam had been working on while he watched her.

A few minutes later, Tess slid onto a counter seat. "What do you have there?" When she stretched out her hand, Sarah handed it over. She was somewhat in shock, not sure what to think about the beautiful drawing. Without a doubt, she'd treasure it.

"My, my. This is really good. Who's the talented artist?"

Sarah met her sister's eyes. "Sam."

Tess visibly blanched. "Sam Lewis?"

When she gave her a look, Tess lowered the drawing onto the countertop. "Come to think of it, he did take art classes in school. I just don't remember ever seeing his work before, though." She shrugged and gave her a half-smile. "Seems Sam has some hidden talents, huh? Who knew?"

Sarah certainly hadn't known. Guilt stung her conscience. Was she supposed to read something into the reasons he'd made this drawing? Sam's words came back to her. *To show you that I pay attention.* Maybe he'd made a drawing of Tess, too. Or any number of girls in town.

No, Sarah, he probably hasn't.

She snapped to attention when the bell on the front door rang and some of the high school kids walked inside the diner. A glance at the clock confirmed it was already three o'clock. Where had the day gone? "Want a chocolate shake?"

"No more shakes." Tess shook her head. "I need to shed a few pounds. Just give me a cup of black coffee, if it's fresh."

"It is. Myrna made it ten minutes ago." She pulled a mug from the rack on the wall and poured the steaming brew before carefully placing the cup in front of Tess. After storing the drawing carefully beneath the counter, Sarah turned back around, not bothering to hide her frown. "Tess, I think Sam's mad at me."

"Why would that be?" Tess lifted her coffee cup and took a tentative sip.

"I have no idea."

Tess shrugged. "Maybe he had a disagreement with Sylvie or something."

"Or something," Sarah murmured.

Tess leveled her gaze on Sarah as she took a longer sip of her coffee. "Like I said before, military service changes a man. We can't know what he's done, what he's seen."

Sarah swallowed. "What are you saying?"

Tess lowered her cup. "I'm not saying anything."

"Do you know something?" Sarah parked one hand on her hip.

"No, no." Tess said, waving her hand. "Nothing like that."

"Sam's one of the strongest Christians I know." Sarah leaned across the counter so as not to be overheard by any big ears around them. "We've never heard rumors about him the way we have about other boys in town."

"True enough, Sarah, but Sam Lewis is quite obviously. . .no longer a boy." Tess arched a brow, and her expression was full of meaning. "Men have passions, desires. Even strong Christian men."

Sarah's spine stiffened. "If that's the case, then he needs to get married, sooner rather than later." Do some cleaving of his own. That thought shot straight to her heart.

Tess smiled and her gaze lingered on the drawing. "Oh, I think he's working toward that end, little sister."

Chapter 21

~~♥~~

Wednesday Afternoon—May 30, 1962

The moment he walked into Perry's, Sam sensed something was wrong with Sarah. At the very least, she was bothered. If it wasn't her creased forehead or the way she moved as if in a trance, the way she asked him to repeat his lunch order was a dead giveaway. The spark wasn't in those lovely brown eyes, and he missed it. She didn't call out greetings to the customers the way she always did when she moved among tables. Even old Perry Sellers followed her with his eyes, his shoulders slumped.

Sam caught her hand as Sarah finally worked her way back to his table. "What's wrong?"

She stared at their joined hands for a moment before slowly withdrawing from his grasp. "Nothing." Sarah wasn't the type of person to say that particular word. *Nothing* was a non-answer if ever he'd heard one.

"I don't believe you."

She visibly tensed. "Fine. Then don't believe me. What would you like to order today?" After nodding when he gave her his order of a cup of white chili and a chicken fried steak sandwich, Sarah departed, leaving him to stare after her. The remainder of his meal, she only came near his table when necessary—to refill his iced tea, to ask if he wanted a slice of pie, to give him his ticket. Pushing the issue wouldn't help. He'd have to wait it out. He only hoped she understood he wanted to help her if he could.

When Debbie Harrison came into the bank late in the afternoon, Sam spied her from his office. Tired of poring over charts and reports, he tossed down his pencil and rose to his feet. Strolling into the bank lobby, he walked over to the teller windows with the pretense of making sure they were preparing to close their stations and completing the necessary daily reports.

"Hi, Sam."

He turned, pleased that Debbie called to him first. "Debbie. How are you?" As he walked across the lobby toward her, he schooled his features into a neutral expression. The light streaming through the windows highlighted the faint red highlights in her now natural hair color. He's seen it all since his return to Rockbridge—deep blue streaks in her hair and that crazy red, shellacked hairdo she'd sported when he first moved back home. Arnie must be relieved. Ditto her normal looking eyebrows that had suddenly reappeared. He'd ignore the miniskirt she wore that could use a few more inches in length. He wouldn't mind seeing Sarah in one of them, although she probably wouldn't think of wearing one. Even if she did, her mother would bar the door and prevent her from leaving the house.

Focus, man.

"I'm just peachy," Debbie said, recapturing his attention. "Did Sarah tell you my news?" She held out her left hand adorned with a fairly large diamond engagement ring, wiggling her fingers in front of his face. He had to love this girl's enthusiasm.

"Yes, and I'm very happy for you both. Arnie's a blessed man." Genuinely pleased, Sam gave her a quick hug. "So, when's the big day?" He knew better than to say anything about how long she'd waited for Arnie to pop the question. Neither would he let on that Sarah had already given him the basic details of the wedding. Never one to stand on ceremony, Debbie might have been the one to fall on her knees and do the proposing. Wouldn't surprise him a bit.

"We're not having a big wedding. Just a private ceremony at City Hall with the Justice of the Peace. Friday the 15th at three o'clock." She shrugged. "We're putting our money into a honeymoon trip to the Grand Canyon, and then we'll have a reception here in town later on."

"I see. If you need to open joint bank accounts, we'll be glad to open those up for you."

"Thanks. Arnie's taking care of the financial stuff, so I'll tell him. I only came to deposit my paycheck. Well, I guess I'll see you later." She turned to go.

"Debbie, have you seen Sarah today?" This girl was one of Sarah's closest friends. If anyone knew what was wrong, Debbie should.

"Earlier when I stopped in at Perry's for my break, like always."

"Did she seem out of sorts to you?"

Debbie lowered her gaze. When she chewed on her lower lip, it was a dead giveaway.

"I care about her and want to help her, but she won't tell me anything. She wasn't herself when I went in for lunch." Sam pinned her with what he hoped was his most earnest gaze.

Jerking her gaze away from his, Debbie glanced around the bank—everywhere but at him—before stepping closer. "Can we go somewhere private to talk?"

"Sure. Let's go into my office." He motioned for her to go first and then followed her inside.

She didn't sit in the chair opposite his desk but fidgeted beside it, holding onto her handbag. "Sarah will kill me if she finds out I told you."

"I'm not asking you to divulge any secrets. If it's something you don't think I should know, then you have every right not to tell me."

Debbie gave him a small grin. "You're so proper. Formal without being stuffy. You're a lot like that Atticus Finch character in the book she likes so much."

Pleased by that comment, Sam smiled and indicated the chair. "Please. Have a seat. For the record, I don't close my office door when I have a woman of any age, married or not, in here with me."

"As it should be, and that only reinforces my point. You're a true gentleman, Sam. Don't mind if I do." Debbie dropped into the chair, settling the handbag on her lap. "First off, you should know that Randy Sweet is Arnie's best man. I've asked Sarah to stand up with me, and Randy will be there for Arnie. They've been friends forever, since they were little boys."

Sam nodded, wondering why Debbie felt the need to divulge this information. "I know Sarah and Randy are friends." He took the chair across from her.

"I think Randy still believes something might happen with Sarah. He's held out hope for her for years. Poor man can't seem to get it through his thick skull that she's not interested. Although. . ."

Chewing on her lower lip again, Debbie dropped her gaze to her lap.

"Although?" he prompted.

"Things might be changing with Sarah. That's why she's upset. Not that it would change how she feels about Randy."

Sam shifted in his chair, tempted to blurt out his question again. He liked straight talk, not skirting around the truth. Another reason he didn't like Sarah's "nothing" non-answer. Especially when that word came from a woman—in response to a man asking what was wrong—guaranteed, things were *not* okay.

Debbie's shoulders lifted and then lowered as she drew in a deep breath. "Sarah was supposed to get scholarship money from the nursing school, but they're going to withdraw the offer if she can't enroll by the end of June. She got a letter. The school needs to award the money to other students if she's not enrolled for the fall semester."

Sam's eyes widened. Sarah hadn't told him about scholarship money, but that made perfect sense. "She can reapply again in the future, right?"

"As far as I know."

Leaning forward, Sam rested his arms on his thighs. "Do you know the amount of the scholarship?"

"I'm not sure, but apparently enough to make her feel like she'll never get to go. She was depending on that money." Debbie's hazel eyes met his. "You know Sarah. She'll bounce back from this, but right now she believes she'll be here in Rockbridge forever."

Sam nodded. "I appreciate your confidence in telling me."

Debbie rose from the chair. "Sam, if Sarah has to stay in Rockbridge, I don't think it's the death sentence she used to think it'd be. In the past few weeks—more specifically since the twenty-fourth of April, I'd say she's pretty much had the time of her life."

Seemed his mother wasn't the only woman who'd perfected that knowing look. The same look Debbie gave him now. "So have I, Debbie." He walked her to the door. "Thanks for being such a good friend to Sarah, and congratulations again on your upcoming marriage. Like I said, Arnie's a blessed man."

"Thank you." Quickly lifting on her toes, Debbie planted a quick kiss on his cheek before patting his arm. "Now it's your turn, Atticus. Time to put your brilliant defense into action." She giggled. "You two are next, you know."

Chuckling as she departed, Sam rubbed a hand over his chin. No wonder Sarah liked this woman so much.

Not two minutes later, he heard female voices engaged in a spirited debate. Sam walked to the door of his office and almost collided with Kathy Parker as she came around the corner. Oh joy. He had the feeling his day was about to go south fast. Dressed to kill, the girl must have bathed in enough perfume to suck the oxygen from, and asphyxiate, a person.

"Hello, Miss Parker. Do we have an appointment?"

Her blue eyes narrowed. "No, but I'd like a word with you, Captain Lewis."

This woman suffered from a sense of inflated entitlement and always had. Perhaps he should tell her he had an appointment, but that wouldn't be true. He might as well hear her out now. Hopefully, she'd have her say and that'd be the end of it.

"Of course. Come into my office."

"Sam, why are you paying attention to that little waitress from Perry's?"

He flinched since she'd raised her voice. Kathy had been the head cheerleader in high school and, as such, had learned how to project her voice. She couldn't wait until they went inside for some privacy?

"As I said, let's come inside my office so we can discuss this without an audience." Several bank customers eyed them and the tellers tried to appear busy, but they weren't fooling him. Stepping aside, Sam motioned for her to go into the office.

"I'm coming, too." Debbie gave him a conspiratorial wink as she marched behind Kathy. That might be a good thing. Debbie would be a good ally, if needed, to defend Sarah. What a strange thought, but when it came to Kathy, nothing was outside the realm of possibility.

"Care to sit down?"

"No, thank you," Kathy said. "This won't take long." She patently ignored Debbie even though she was standing right beside him.

"First of all, her name is Sarah, and calling her names won't help your cause." Sam crossed his arms. "Whatever that cause happens to be."

Kathy lifted her chin. "Congratulations. You're the talk of the town with your shameless flirtations all over town with that Jordan girl, including in the church, of all places. I'd have thought you'd have more reverence for God's holy place."

"Thanks, and funny you should mention church since I haven't seen you darken the doors since I've been back in Rockbridge."

Debbie grunted and then coughed.

Tossing her long blonde hair behind one shoulder, Kathy gave him a smile no doubt intended to mollify him. With a come-hither look, she stepped closer and tugged on his silk tie. When she attempted to pull him closer—in essence, to reel him in—Sam stood his ground.

"Sam, you're a handsome, accomplished military man with a bright future here at the bank. You'd make any woman a fine husband. Surely you're aware that Sarah Jordan's not planning on sticking around town. I don't want you to get your heart broken when she leaves town."

Sam smoothed his hand down the length of his tie, dislodging Kathy's grasp in a not-so-gentle way. "Thanks for your concern, but my heart will be just fine." He moved toward the door, hoping she'd take the hint. Kathy didn't budge but neither did Debbie. Of all things, he couldn't have a showdown between two sometimes hot-headed, stubborn women in the middle of his office. He willed his dad to walk in right about now.

"Kathy, answer a question for me." Debbie's voice was low and controlled.

Kathy glanced at Debbie as if seeing her for the first time. "Why is this any of your concern? Don't you need to be off somewhere planning your wedding?"

"I'd like to know why you're treating Sarah like she's the dirt beneath your feet," Debbie said. "You've been vindictive and nasty to her since eighth grade. Tell me what Sarah's ever done to you other than treat you with kindness?"

Kathy moved both hands to her hips, settling them there, her handbag dangling from one arm. "How can you even ask me that? Did you hear what that little twit said to me in the diner the day of Sam's homecoming? She was positively rude and insulting. The only reason I didn't insist that Myrna fire her on the spot was because I didn't want to cause a scene on such a happy occasion."

Debbie snorted. "What a crock! Who died and made you queen of Rockbridge? Sarah Jordan's got more class in her little finger than you'll have in a lifetime—"

"Why, you impertinent little snit!" Both women faced off and glared at one another.

Oh, Lord, this can't be good. Sam considered pushing the panic button beneath his desk to summon the security officer, but doing so would only make him a laughingstock.

"Kathy." He used his commanding officer tone. "It's best if you leave now."

"I know what it is!" Debbie snapped her fingers and stared at Kathy.

"What *what* is?" Kathy's frown deepened.

"Sarah beat you out for the biggest award in school at the end of eighth grade. She got a write-up in the newspaper and they honored her at an assembly in front of the entire student body." Debbie's eyes widened. "Then somebody started that nasty rumor about how Sarah cheated on an English test and didn't deserve the award." She advanced toward Kathy, one slow step at a time. "Something tells me you were *directly* involved."

Sam figured he might as well pull up a chair and watch the unfolding drama. To his surprise, Kathy appeared to be backing down in the face of Debbie's anger. He moved his gaze from one woman to the other.

"You don't know what you're talking about," Kathy spouted.

"Oh, yes I do. Know what gave you away, Miss Parker?"

"Like I said, you don't know what—"

"Travel back with me a few years," Debbie said. "Let me paint you a little picture. Maybe it'll jog your convenient memory loss."

Sam raised a brow, curious as to where Debbie was leading with that statement. This whole scenario was starting to get a little fun in a weird way.

"I was in the ladies room right after that assembly honoring my friend. I was in a stall and overheard two girls talking." Debbie shot him an apologetic glance. "Sorry Sam."

He held up one hand. "Trust me, not a problem."

"They were hatching a plan to smear Sarah's reputation. One of those two girls said she'd get Sarah back for stealing *her* award. Then she called Sarah an impertinent little twit. Snit. Whatever." Debbie took another step closer to Kathy, her sensible work shoes toe-to-toe with the other woman's fancy high heels. "Now, you tell me, what kind of eighth grade girl uses words like that? No one else I knew, that's for sure."

In a huff, Kathy stomped out of his office without another word.

Debbie shrugged. "Now that I've called her bluff, hopefully she'll leave our girl alone."

Sam wrapped his arms around her in a quick hug. "Thanks, Deb. Who needs Atticus when I've got you? You're my hero."

Chapter 22

~~♥~~

Thursday Afternoon

Sarah glanced at the front door of Perry's Diner as the bell sounded. "I don't believe it. Fletcher Monroe." With Sam beside him.

"No one's seen him in a few weeks. He's been holed up in that little house of his, playing the hermit." Debbie took another drink of her chocolate shake. "What makes you think of him now?"

Sarah nodded to the front door. "Take a look."

Twisting on the counter seat, Debbie spied the two men and then spun back around, her face beaming. "I should have known!" She slapped one hand on the counter. "Good for Fletch! Seeing how Sam's with him, he must have made it his mission to get him into town again."

Arnie chuckled. "Sweetums, I think Sarah's talking about the fact that Fletch is walking on his own speed. Hallelujah to that!" He lifted his glass of soda in a salute.

Debbie swiveled around again. "Wow. You're right," she said a few seconds later, her eyes wide. "He's got himself a prosthetic leg now. Half a leg. Whatever. Isn't that something else?" She giggled. "Sally Barksdale around? She'll want to see this."

Sam caught her eye across the diner as he and Fletcher made their way to Sam's table. Sarah's heart swelled when she noted how Sam walked beside the other man. He wasn't touching Fletcher, or supporting him in any way, other than with his presence. But if Fletch needed him, Sam would be there. Although his efforts were slow, Fletch was walking on his own speed.

First Merle in church, and now Fletch walking without crutches? *Thank you, Jesus.*

Arnie pushed his empty plate across the counter when Sarah asked if he was finished with his meal. "Tell Jimmy he outdid himself. Best burger yet. That barbecue sauce and onion ring on top made it extra special."

"I'll tell him. He'll be glad to hear it."

Approaching Sam and Fletcher a couple of minutes later, Sarah gave them both a bright smile. "Hi, Fletch. We've missed you around here. Good to see you. Would you like your usual?"

Fletcher gave her his lopsided smile and pushed a shock of hair away from his eyes. Although it was still long, he'd shaved his beard and appeared rested and more at peace with himself than she'd seen him. "You remember my usual?"

"It's been less than a year since you were here. Not a lifetime."

Fletcher's brown eyes clouded and he dipped his head.

Would she never learn? "I'm sorry." Sarah glanced at Sam, silently imploring him to help.

"I think we need to mark this occasion with one of Jimmy's specialty burgers." Sam handed the other man a menu and opened his on the table. "What's your pleasure?"

"Jimmy has a fabulous new dressing with bleu cheese crumbles in it," Sarah said. "I remember how you like bleu cheese." She found bleu cheese an acquired taste, albeit bitter, but she was grasping for whatever might work to make Fletcher more comfortable. "While you're looking over the menu, I'll bring you a root beer."

"Go ahead and bring me the bleu cheese burger. It sounds like a winner." Fletcher's smile encouraged her. "You're a real good waitress, Sarah. You care about your customers. Like I told you last time you were out at the house, you're gonna make a great nurse, too."

Releasing the breath she'd been holding, Sarah's apprehensions dissipated. She caught Sam's expression of surprise but ignored it for the moment. "Thanks. As long as I think before I speak, I should be fine."

"Same burger for me," Sam said, returning their menus to the slotted rack on the table. "With iced tea. Thanks."

"With lemon. You've got it." After asking if they both wanted fries, Sarah jotted down their order. "Coming right up, guys."

"So, Sam managed to drag Fletcher out of his cave," Jimmy said as soon as the kitchen door closed behind her. "Good for him. I wondered what it would take to get that man out again." Oblivious to their conversation, Myrna worked on putting together lunch platters at the large prep table in the middle of the kitchen.

"Fletch has a prosthetic leg now." Sarah handed him the order.

Jimmy raised a brow but didn't stop his work as he dropped two large beef patties on the grill. "Even better." The burgers sizzled and Jimmy turned his attention to the chicken and burgers in various stages of readiness.

"You see so much even though you rarely venture out of this kitchen, my friend. How do you manage that?"

Jimmy's kind smile crinkled his eyes. How she loved this man's smile. "Sometimes you don't need eyes to see, Jelly Bean."

She laughed. "I'm convinced you've also been blessed with supersonic hearing."

"For one thing," he said, not missing a beat as he flipped burgers and reached for the hamburger buns, "I can pretty much guarantee Captain Lewis is sitting out there wondering how he can stop you from going to Austin."

Her smile faded, and Sarah's pulse picked up speed. "What?"

"As sure as you're staring at me right now, your eyes bugging out of that pretty face of yours, that boy's fallen hard. Yep"—sliding the spatula beneath a hamburger patty, Jimmy transferred it to a bun—"he's in love with my Jelly Bean." Jimmy shot her a quick glance. "I'd bet my life on it."

"Well, don't do that. You're too important to me, and I don't want to lose you." She moved one hand down to her hip, determined not to ask him the next logical question. Shaking her head to clear her mind, Sarah pushed through the door and entered the dining area again to get the drinks for Sam and Fletch.

Sure enough, Sam's gaze met hers. What she saw in the depths of those blue eyes thrilled her. Scared her. Intrigued her. As usual, her favorite burger flipper might be right. He usually was.

Oh, Lord. What do I do now?

~~ ♥ ~~

That Evening

The water was warm but still cool enough to be invigorating. After swimming across the width of the creek several times, Sarah finally stopped. Panting, she stood in the shallow water and smoothed back her wet hair. In years past, whenever something weighed on her mind—good or bad—she'd slam softballs and run around a field. Now, the physical release to be found in swimming was the best way to stay focused on something other than her personal life.

Is that what Sam was, an issue? A problem of some kind?

Raising her face to the early evening sun, drinking in the rays filtering between the overhanging branches of the trees, Sarah released a deep sigh. She plopped back in the water, making a small splash, and then she floated on her back.

"Come here often?"

She screamed and jumped upright in the water. "You scared the living daylights out of me, you bad, bad man!" Seeing the amusement on Sam's face, she began her attack, splashing him as hard and fast as she could. She laughed the entire time, felt his smile everywhere. While she wished Jimmy hadn't planted the idea in her mind that Sam might be falling in love with her, she was secretly thrilled.

I'm wearing my swimsuit. Oh, no. This could not be good. Ducking beneath the water line, Sarah glanced longingly at her towel on the creek bank. How could she distract Sam long enough to swim back, grab the towel, and then wrap herself like a mummy?

Surprisingly, Sam didn't splash her back. In times past, he'd always retaliated. This time, he stood, arms crossed over his chest—that broad, muscular chest—and smiled, which only made the situation worse. And wonderful, all at the same time.

"You believe in making a big entrance, don't you? Show off!" Not knowing what to do, she splashed him again. "Shouldn't you be courting Sylvie tonight? Sipping iced tea with lemon on her front porch?"

Sam smirked. "I'd much rather be here with you, thanks. How often have you been out to Fletcher's house?"

Her eyes widened. "I have no idea. A few times. I don't keep count." When he cocked his head and raised a brow, she shrugged. "I go out there about once a week on average, sometimes more. I didn't want him to become a hermit. Seems you had the same idea. He's a great guy, but he lost a lot of confidence along with. . ." She took in a quick breath. "Along with his leg." She tilted her head as understanding dawned. "That's what you were trying to tell me, wasn't it?"

"Now you've lost me." Sam dropped down into the water, mirroring her, so that only his head and shoulders were visible above the water line.

"When you were telling me about Ménière's Disease."

"I'm impressed you remember the name. I can barely remember it myself."

They faced one another, both lightly treading water. "I looked it up in a medical dictionary at the library."

"Even more impressive. Learn anything interesting?"

"A few things, yes," she said. "Whether it's the loss of a limb or one of your senses, it's still a part of you. In your case, in terms of flying jets, I can better understand how the temporary—and potential long-term loss—has affected you."

Sam studied her for a long moment. When he waded closer, her pulse pounded into overdrive. "You read up on it, you say?"

Sarah nodded slowly. "Yes. I wanted to understand it a bit more." She dropped her gaze from the intensity of his gorgeous eyes. "I wanted to be able to help you, if I could."

He surprised her when he chuckled. "That explains some things."

"I beg your pardon?"

"Sarah Jordan, have you—or have you not—purposely removed the salt shaker from my table at Perry's?"

Sarah stared past Sam's shoulder, not daring to meet his eyes. She'd been found out.

"And that awful coffee you've been giving me isn't really coffee, is it?"

She grinned. "It's Sanka, actually. Decaffeinated coffee."

Laughing, he gave a thumbs-down gesture. "Surely there's a better way. I think I'll abstain." He waded even closer. "Want to know what I find really heartwarming?"

His nearness was making her dizzy. After dipping her hands in the water, she smoothed her palms over her wet hair. "What's that?"

"You cared enough about me to look it up."

Sarah held his gaze. "That's what friends do. Tell me something."

"Sure, but let's float for a bit. What do you say, friend?" Sam dove backward, splashing her, and then floated on his back a few feet away. "What's your question?"

"Have you been up in your vintage plane since you've returned home?" She paddled a bit so that she was abreast of him.

He didn't answer right away. "No, as a matter of fact."

"Why not?"

Pulling ahead of her, he still floated on his back. "You ask the tough questions, you know that?" When she smirked, also flat on her back beside him, Sam laughed. "Don't tell me. That's also what friends do for one another. Right?"

"You've got it," she said. "And it's a friend's inherent responsibility to answer the question."

"What happened to my prerogative? That's not exclusively reserved for women, is it?"

"No, but you're treading some very chauvinistic waters with that statement. Really, Sam." Sarah rose up in the water, not caring anymore that he saw her in her swimsuit. They were friends, and for better or worse, this was the way she looked. Might as well get it over now since the opportunity had presented itself. She was well aware he glanced at her before turning his gaze to the opposite side of the creek. Hopefully, Sam wasn't in some way embarrassed, or heaven forbid—repulsed—by seeing her figure. She felt her cheeks flood with warmth.

"If you'd ever like to take your plane up in the air again, and wouldn't mind a passenger, I'd love to go." When her voice wavered, Sarah despised how her nerves betrayed her. "I've never been in an airplane, you know."

"That surprises me, especially with your interest in NASA." Sam returned his gaze to her, prompting her to dip back beneath the creek's water line.

"Think about it," she said. "I've been working every shift I can at Perry's in order to save enough money to go to nursing school. It's not like I've had the money to fly anywhere. Besides, where would I go?" She frowned. "Sometimes I really hate money."

"I know people who have a lot of it, and they aren't so fond of it either. It can be a double-edged sword."

Sarah nodded. "I wouldn't mind trying it from their perspective for a couple of days, but I'm sure being wealthy has its own unique set of problems. Not to sound ungrateful. I realize how blessed I am." Working with financial matters was this man's livelihood and ambition, but she couldn't imagine wanting to be around money as a full-time career. Not that it wasn't an important position, and she respected Sam's strong work ethic.

"You haven't been far outside of Rockbridge, and it's understandable you'd feel that way. Take a look at this beautiful creek, for instance." Turning in a slow circle, Sam waved his hand at their surroundings. "The trees, the fish, the rocks, the mossy bank. God's richest blessings are right here. In Rockbridge, Texas. This town is nothing more than a tiny speck on the map of the world. But whether in Rockbridge, Houston, New York, Rome or anywhere else, God's people are the same. They're precious to Him."

Sarah considered his words. "Yes," she said. "Even with all our many frailties."

"That's one of the greatest things about God, I think. He accepts and loves us, especially when others don't. No matter what color we are, or how good or bad we are, if we trust Him with our lives, He won't let us go. Ever." Sam's smile seared through her. "I guess my point is that He knows your heart, Sarah. The Lord will honor your desires, and at this point, only He knows where you'll go, what you'll do, who you'll meet. But He's got it all under His control. I hope you take comfort in that knowledge."

"I do." She gave him a bright smile. How Sarah loved their talks here—beside the creek, in the creek, walking home from the creek. As much as anything else, this man opened up to her like no one else. And she did the same for him.

His eyes fixed on her. "When I'm flying, it makes me realize all over again how small I am in the universe. Like your poem said, and that's another reason it impacted me so much. Flying humbles me, but it also makes me feel free. And very thankful."

"Thankful for the knowledge and ability to fly a plane, you mean?"

When he rose out of the water, she did the same, and they faced one another. Sarah held his gaze. What she saw in this man's eyes gave her confidence, empowered her like never before.

"Yes," he said, nodding. "I'm also thankful for the liberties I have as a citizen of a free nation. Thankful for being able to honor my family and my country in order to maintain those liberties. Most importantly, I'm thankful to be called a child of the one true King."

"I understand that, but it still doesn't explain why you haven't been up in your plane since you've been home." Something urged her on although she should probably let the matter drop. "Are you afraid for some reason, Sam? Do you feel the plane isn't air-worthy, or are you concerned you might get dizzy while you're up in the air? If you are, it's okay. I want to help you—"

"I'm not afraid, Sarah." He gazed into the distance, but his jaw visibly tightened. "I'm just not ready yet. That's all."

"I didn't mean to pry or push you, Sam."

"I know. Thank you for caring."

She nodded. "Always. Well, I'd better be going home. Walk with me?"

Sam angled his head to the creek bank. "You go on ahead. I think I'll swim a little. Holler when you're ready, and then we'll walk back together."

Sarah watched as he dove into the water and began swimming with long, sure strokes. The fact that he'd admitted he wasn't ready to fly again was admirable in its own way, and she needed to respect his feelings.

As she dried off and pulled her T-Shirt and shorts over her swimsuit, she watched Sam still swimming farther down the creek. Although she couldn't be sure, she felt reasonably certain he was swimming not so much for the benefit of exercise as to spare her feelings and awkwardness. And maybe, just maybe, to work through the questions she'd posed to him.

He's such a good man, Lord. Help him to fly again. In your time.

Chapter 23

Tuesday Morning—June 5, 1962

A knock sounded on the bedroom door as Sarah prepared for work.

"Come on in!" Tucking a long strand of hair into her loose bun, Sarah anchored it with a bobby pin. The door opened and her mother stood in the doorway. "Hi, Mom."

"Honey, I started out for the market a few minutes ago and found this envelope tucked halfway beneath the front door. Someone must have hand delivered it, and it has your name on it."

"Really?" Turning, Sarah took it from her. Her name was typed in all capital letters on the outside of a business-size white envelope. No return address. Nothing else. "Wonder what this could be?" She slipped her finger beneath the sealed flap and carefully slid it across the envelope. Nadine watched as she pulled out a cashier's check from Rockbridge Savings & Loan. Noting the large amount of the check, Sarah covered her mouth with one hand to stifle her cry.

Her Mom leaned over her shoulder. "Sarah Jane, do my eyes deceive me or are there five figures in that amount?"

Speechless, Sarah could only nod. She handed the green paper check to her mother. Moving one hand over her heart, she deep breathed a few times. "I can't believe this. Who signed the check?"

"Joseph Lewis as the bank president. Countersigned by Sam."

Taking the check from her mother again, she stared at it. Her hands shook to the point where the check almost fell from her hands and onto the carpeted floor. "So, there's no way of knowing who funded the check? The only notation in the memo line is some kind of account number." Crossing the room, Sarah sat down on her bed. "Do you think I should pay Sam a visit and ask him? Not that he'd tell me anything, but I guess it wouldn't hurt to try."

"I would. If nothing else, see if he can give you any information." Nadine's gaze met hers. "My guess is that this is a gift to pay for nursing school. I should think the amount is certainly more than enough." She frowned and chewed on her bottom lip. "Someone is being extremely generous, but your father might not like this. You know how men can be if their pride is offended." Her mother sat down beside her on the bed. "You don't know how he's hated that we couldn't pay your way to college."

"I don't want anyone to feel guilty." Sarah blew out a sigh, "I'm not sure I can accept it. The donor—is that the right word?— obviously wants to remain anonymous. If I can't find out anything from Sam or his dad, there's not much else I can do. I mean, it's a legitimate check made payable to me. If I want the money, I'll need to cash it, right? Or, I can return it to the bank. That's another option. It *is* a very large sum of money." She shook her head. "Who in Rockbridge could even afford to give me this much money, Mom? I guess the more important question is: *why* would they do this for me?"

Her mother squeezed her shoulder and gave her a gentle smile. "Someone who loves you would be my guess. Someone who wants to see you fulfill your dream of becoming a nurse." She rose to her feet and headed for the door, pausing in the doorway. "Go see your friend Sam and see what you can find out. That's the first step, and then you can better determine what to do next."

Walking into the bank a short time later, Sarah headed toward Gina Armstrong seated behind the reception desk in the middle of Rockbridge Savings & Loan.

"Hi, Sarah. Don't you look like a vision today?" Gina gave her a bright smile. "Do you need some help?"

"I need to speak with Sam if he's available. Privately."

"Of course. Let me check." Gina picked up her telephone receiver and pushed the intercom button. She drummed her fingernails on the top of her desk while she waited. "Mr. Lewis? Sarah Jordan is here to see you if you have a moment. Of course. Thank you."

Replacing the receiver, Gina angled her head toward Sam's office. "He said he could see you now. Go on in."

"Thanks, Gina. I appreciate it." Smoothing one hand over the front of her uniform, Sarah swallowed her nerves and lifted her shoulders. Hopefully, Sam wouldn't be able to tell how nervous she was. Since she'd applied fresh lipstick—something she rarely wore—she ran her tongue over her teeth. Nothing was worse than discovering she'd been carrying on a conversation, especially with a man, with lipstick on her teeth. That's why she usually stayed far away from lipstick. What had she been thinking?

He's Sam. Your friend. Talk with him the same as you always do.

She raised her hand to knock on the frosted glass door boasting Sam's name and title, but the door opened from the inside. "Good morning, Sarah. Nice to see you, as always. Come on in." Standing aside, Sam ushered her into the office.

"Hi, Sam. I have to start my shift at Perry's soon, but I need to ask you about something."

"If you can spare a few minutes, have a seat so we can talk about it." Waving his hand at the chairs in front of his desk, Sam waited until she seated herself and then took the opposite chair. She noted he left the office door open. Ah, yes, this was Professional Sam. Banker Sam. Sarah drank in the sight of him. Finding it impossible to ignore how handsome he looked in his dark suit with the starched white shirt, she lowered her gaze. But not before noting his ridiculously wide, colorful tie. Although it was the popular style, she found it completely absurd. Was this another way Sam was trying to fit in with popular culture?

"Nice office," she said, noting the framed diplomas, awards and certificates on the walls.

"My dad insisted I display them all, more for my Mom's benefit than mine, I assure you."

Sarah's jaw gaped. "How could you possibly know what I'm thinking?"

He chuckled. "I don't always. Tell me what's on your mind."

Fine. He wanted to stick to business. She could do that. No problem.

"Mom found an envelope containing a cashier's check under our front door this morning. Drawn on funds from Rockbridge Savings & Loan, with my name as the payee, and for quite a large sum of money."

Sam's brows lifted. "Is that a problem?"

"No, not really. I mean, of course not. It's a very generous gift, but I don't know that I can accept it."

A slight frown downturned his lips. "Not many people come into my office complaining they've received a check for too much money."

"Neither do I know many people in Rockbridge who have that kind of money to throw around in the first place." Inhaling a quick breath, Sarah willed her pulse to slow down. She didn't want to come across as accusatory, but she was as confused as she'd ever been in her life. This whole situation made no sense. Sam had to know the identity of her benefactor since he'd signed the check. Or was it possible his dad took care of it and only asked him to countersign? Of course, he'd trust his dad, if that was the case, and he wouldn't think twice about signing the check.

"Even if they did have the money," she said, choosing her words carefully, "I can't imagine anyone who'd anonymously gift me with such a large amount without expecting something in return."

"You must have a low opinion of the townspeople in Rockbridge."

"Of course, I don't," she snapped. "Please don't put words in my mouth. I'm just being honest, between us. I could live in any other town in Texas, and I'd probably say the same thing. People are people, Sam. You and I both know—even in the church—members don't usually donate a large sum of money without expecting their name on a pew or a stained glass window. Or printed in a hymnal. Something." She stole a glance at him, irritated further by his look of amusement. "You know what I mean. It's basic human nature. As a rule, people want to be recognized for their generosity, and a public acknowledgment of some form or another is. . .well, it's more or less expected. No matter how much they might deny it."

Sam leaned forward, resting his elbows on his thighs and regarded her with a look of compassion that went a long way toward softening her frustration. "I appreciate your honesty, as always, but the way I look at it, there are plenty of people in Rockbridge who give money for various causes without expecting anything in return. Take the donations for the Benson Fund, for instance. We've already gathered more than we need for Marty's headstone. I seriously doubt any of the people who've donated money—including you, since I've seen the tip money you drop into the donation can at Perry's—would expect to be publicly recognized for their generosity."

Sarah frowned. "You can be insufferably honorable sometimes, Sam Lewis. I might as well go since you're obviously not going to tell me anything." Maybe she wasn't playing fair, but the glimmer of amusement flickering in those blue eyes both infuriated her and attracted her.

"I can tell you plenty of things, but they're not what I think you want to hear, Sarah. Thanks for the questionable compliment. Never been called insufferably honorable before. At least not to my face."

"Stick around." When she glimpsed the broadening grin on his face, she rose from her chair. Perhaps it'd been a mistake to come so soon after she'd received the cashier's check. She should have reasoned through it some more.

"I plan on it." Sam lifted out of his chair. "Let me give you another example. Suppose you donated the money for a stained glass window in the church. You can't tell me you'd need a plaque emblazoned with your name, proclaiming to the world, 'Sarah Jane Jordan donated the funds for this beautiful, expensive stained glass window'—"

"Do you have any idea how much those are? As much as I'd want to, I couldn't afford to give that much. . ." She turned away from him. "I dare you to ask how I even know how much those windows cost."

"I didn't know you ever played softball near the church."

She managed a small smile. Again, the man could read her so well. "I never did again, I'll tell you that much."

Lightly taking hold of her arms, Sam scanned her face with such affection that she felt lightheaded. "Sarah, baby, the evidence of your giving is everywhere in the church. It's in the faces of the teenage girls you teach on Sunday mornings."

"Once a month," she said. "It's a rotation."

Sam raised her chin with a gentle touch of his hand. "Please try to calm down and listen for a minute, okay? My point is, the girls admire you and they look to you as a role model. Mrs. Eldercroft lights up like a light bulb whenever you enter the church. You're so good with helping her distribute blankets to the residents of the nursing center over in Springhaven. You have to know everyone in town is aware of your plans to attend nursing school." Releasing her, he took in a deep breath and blew it out. "As much as we all hate it that you won't be here with us every day, working at Perry's and walking among us"—a look of sadness surfaced in his expression—"we all want you to fulfill your dream of becoming a nurse."

"Thanks for making me sound like the dearly departed."

He returned his gaze to hers. "Accept the gift, Sarah. Say thank you, deposit it, and use it to find your dreams. I assure you it was given with the purest of intentions with no expectations of anything in return other than your personal happiness."

Sarah blinked hard and nodded. "Thank you, Sam. May I make a suggestion?"

"What's that?"

"You might want to rethink that tie."

Lifting his tie, Sam gave her a curious glance. "What's wrong with my tie? It's colorful and fun, and it livens up an otherwise boring suit."

"Your suit's not boring. It's very. . .well-tailored. And the jacket doesn't have a bunch of little annoying buttons." Sam must not have learned the lesson that the man made the suit, not the other way around. Tess was right about one thing: men could be clueless, especially when it came to clothing. Still, had she actually said those words aloud? Based on the look of male satisfaction that crossed Sam's face, she had.

"Thank you for noticing my attire." His gaze settled on her lips. "Nice lipstick, by the way."

What was it about this man that made her tongue-tied at times? "Thank you for your time. I can show myself out." She needed to escape was more like it, and she headed for the door. From behind her, she could hear Sam mutter something under his breath a second before he touched her arm.

"You know I'd tell you if I could."

She faced him again. "I know. You're bound by professional ethics or whatever. I appreciate that. I really do. I certainly don't want to cause you any trouble. I'd just like to thank the generous person who gave me this unexpected, lovely gift." Maybe that statement would convince him. No sooner had the words come from her mouth than she glimpsed the determination in the firm set of Sam's jaw.

"I can thank them for you, although again, it's not necessary."

She lifted her chin. "You're not going to tell me, are you?"

"I don't plan on it, no." Another grin teased the corners of his mouth. Sarah stood her ground and then startled, realizing she was staring at the man's lips, wondering what it would be like to feel them on hers.

What am I thinking?

"Like I said. Insufferably honorable," she mumbled under her breath as she exited his office.

Chapter 24

~~♥~~

Sunday June 10, 1962

"Good morning, Miss Jordan."

Sarah's pulse skipped a few beats, a familiar scenario whenever Sam was around. "Mr. Lewis."

"Fancy meeting you here. Come here often?"

"You need some new lines, old man, but you have a nice singing voice, and you are a fervent prayer warrior if ever I've heard one, so I'll forgive you for stale pick-up lines."

"That was one of the longest sentences I've ever heard you say. Complimentary and insulting all at the same time. Fascinating." Sam stepped aside to allow Sarah to exit the pew ahead of him. "Even so, we're in the house of the Lord now. Watch yourself."

"Not to be flippant, but the good Lord and I are on good terms. We have an understanding." She tossed her hair over one shoulder as she passed by him. Goodness, that was a move she'd never made before, but she'd seen Tess and other girls do it when they were flirting.

"Is that right?" He crossed his arms. "Meaning He understands you can't help yourself."

"Yes," Sarah said, moving to the center of the church. Dropping her purse on a pew, she began to move down the row, collecting empty communion cups. "I think I'm going to nickname you Hershey."

"Because of my puppy dog eyes that melt you with one glance?"

She laughed and then slapped her hand over her mouth to muffle the sound. "I meant, are you going to follow me around like a puppy or will you help me?" She frowned after she picked up a cup smeared with bright red lipstick. "Okay, I deserved that," she said, staring at her fingers. "No comments, please." Pulling a tissue from her purse, she wiped the lipstick from her fingers.

"Wouldn't think of it." Sam moved to the row behind her and started collecting the cups. "Speaking of a puppy following you around, have you had any more puppies of either the human or canine variety tagging at your heels since I've been away?"

"Other than you? No."

"You adopted Hershey right before my family moved to Rockbridge, right?" He'd apparently decided to ignore her insinuation.

Sarah snapped her gaze to Sam's, surprised he'd remembered. "Yes. How. . ."

"I remember more than you might think, Sarah. Are you thinking of getting another dog?"

Shaking her head, she lowered her gaze. "No. My parents are planning to do some traveling, and Tess doesn't have much of an interest in getting a pet. She never did. And"—she reached for Sam's collection of cups—"with nursing school, I won't be able to have a dog." She stopped her work. "I seem to recall a teenager in town who adopted every stray dog and cat and made sure they had good homes. Whatever happened to that guy?"

Sam's gaze zeroed in on her. "He grew up and realized he couldn't save every unwanted pet in the world. Not that he won't one day rediscover that passion, but he's currently pursuing other interests."

Okay, then. They worked in companionable silence before moving to another section together. Sarah greeted a few of the ladies and told them she'd take care of the remaining cups.

"I'm sorry for being so short with you in recent days," she said finally. "You were only being my friend, and I haven't been particularly nice." She heaved a sigh. "You didn't deserve to be on the receiving end of my frustration."

"I'm here, there—wherever—if you need me."

She smiled. "I know. Thanks." They worked again in silence for another minute. Maybe longer. Time could be a funny thing. "So, I take it you're the talented artist who made the drawing?" she said when they were alone in the sanctuary. The aromas from the kitchen down the hall wafted to her, making Sarah ravenous. To think this wasn't even the Father's Day Luncheon—that event was next Sunday and traditionally one of the biggest feasts of the year.

"Yes, I'll take credit for the drawing."

"It was exquisite. A gift. Thank you for that, too." Sarah's gaze locked with his, and she melted a bit more.

"I'm happy you like it."

"I'll treasure it. But I'm not putting it beneath my pillow. And now, my stomach is calling," she said. "I smell Angela Farris's sweet potato casserole. Let's check the other pews and see if all the communion cups have already been collected, and then head over for lunch."

"Sounds like a plan," Sam said. "Mom brought peach pie."

"I wouldn't expect anything else."

"The peach is the best fruit ever. Hands down. No debate."

"Wouldn't debate you on that one, even if I could."

"Meaning you agree?"

Sarah laughed. "When it comes to peaches baked in one of your mother's delicious pies, I do. You'd better get a slice before it's all gone."

"Trying to get rid of me, Sarah Jordan?"

"Never, Captain."

A couple of minutes later, after checking the remaining pews, Sam gave her a charming, irresistible smile. Part of her wished she could see that smile and not melt while another, bigger part of her, could stare at this man all the livelong day. "Ready?"

"Yep. Looks like we got them all." She handed the stack of communion cups to him and then grabbed her purse from the pew. "Let's go eat."

Sarah stole glances at Sam throughout the meal in between small talk with the others seated at her table. Sylvie Foster made sure she occupied the chair next to Sam and his family across the room while Sarah sat with her mother and father. Tess was sitting elsewhere, laughing and chatting with a group of friends. She'd invited Sarah to join them, but she'd declined, preferring to sit and sulk.

"Looks like Captain Lewis found himself a girlfriend." Alice Kindred's remark prompted everyone at their table to stare across the room at Sam.

Sarah slowed her chewing. Cheeks burning, she refused to follow the crowd this time.

"Doesn't mean anything," Alice's husband, Donald, said. "That boy's playing the field. I'd do the same thing in his shoes." Alice looked none too pleased at her husband's remarks, and some of the other wives shot glances at their own husbands.

Wiping her mouth with her napkin, Sarah kept quiet with no intention of joining in their speculation. She attacked the sweet potato casserole with renewed interest, keeping her head down.

In the middle of their meal, everyone stopped talking. Twisting in her chair, Sarah almost collided with Sam as he took the vacant seat beside her. He set a plate with a generous slice of his mother's pie in front of her.

"Aren't you sweet." She lowered her voice as the others resumed their conversations. "I thought I'd missed out."

"You would have, but I had her save an extra slice special for you in the kitchen. I would have brought it over sooner, but—"

"You were otherwise occupied. I understand. This wasn't necessary, but I appreciate your thinking of me." She patted his hand. "Don't let me keep you."

Could I be any more of a snit?

Sam chuckled. "You're not keeping me from anything."

"I'm sure Sylvie would disagree."

"Don't presume anything, Miss Jordan." Propping one elbow on the table, Sam leaned his head against his fist. No fair. The man was giving her his most irresistible smile. Was he purposely toying with her emotions?

This is so confusing, Lord.

Picking up her fork, Sarah poised it above the plate. "You came to see me eat the pie? In that case, pie is always better when shared, don't you think? Thank you for not smothering it in vanilla ice cream. That would have been overkill." Stabbing a warm peach slice in the pie, Sarah offered it to him.

"I know you prefer it *non*-à la mode," Sam said. He remembered something like that? The man did seem to pay attention.

Accepting her challenge, Sam leaned close. She watched as he took the peach from the fork, his eyes never leaving hers. How could he make something as simple as eating a slice of fruit an experience she'd never forget? My, oh my. A quick glance around the table confirmed the amusement of the others. Alice's mouth positively gaped. Sarah avoided direct eye contact with her mother. She felt giddy and silly, and wished she could slip under the table.

Placing the fork on the side of her plate, she cleared her throat. "Well, now, that's a surefire way to get the rumor mill circulating. You see me every day at the diner," she said, keeping her voice low. "I should think you'd be tired of me by now."

"I'll never be tired of you. Give me another bite, and let's really get them going." Sam graced her with another heart-melting smile.

"So not fair." If Sarah knew what was in her best interest, she'd ignore that comment. What had gotten into the man? Without a doubt, he'd taken serious leave of his senses. "This pie is absolutely scrumptious. Your mother's outdone herself this time," she said around another mouthful. "How *does* she do it?" Maybe she should gobble down the pie like a pig and then he'd see how unladylike she was. That should do the trick and then he'd rightfully turn his attention elsewhere.

"You know," Sam said, "Mom tells me she'll only share her peach pie recipe with someone very special. It's one of those old family secrets. Guarded like a precious, rare jewel. But she'll only give it to the girl of my choosing. Once in a lifetime opportunity."

Sarah swallowed another bite without tasting it before chasing it down with her pink lemonade. "Is that so?" She slicked her tongue over her teeth, and then wiped her mouth with her napkin. "That's a mighty tall responsibility. And quite an honor. Sorry to say, you sound a little cocky about that fact, too." Her heart pounding, she pushed the plate across the table to Sam. "Here, you finish it. It's delicious but too much for me."

"Aren't you going to ask?" He polished off the pie and gave her a smile of satisfaction.

"I should think not."

"Chicken?" When he borrowed her napkin to wipe his mouth, she pointed to the corner of his lips. With a wider grin, he wiped the napkin across his mouth. "Did I get it all?"

"Yes, but taunting isn't becoming. Of course, I'm not chicken. You know me better than that. However," she said with an exaggerated sigh, "you might as well tell me since you seem determined. That and embarrassing me with your shameless public flirting or whatever it is you're doing. You really should be ashamed, Captain Lewis. You're a respected military man and in the house of the Lord, need I remind you. Why the teenage boys look to you as their role model is beyond me."

Sam rose to his feet and picked up the plate. Pausing directly behind her, he whispered for her ears only, filling her senses with his wonderful cologne. "Guaranteed, Sylvie won't be getting that recipe." With a parting wink, Sam strode away from the table, empty pie plate in hand. She liked it when Sam winked. No, she didn't. More like she shouldn't. Oh, what a fine mess.

Donald Kindred cleared his throat as Sarah stood and gathered other empty dishes from the table. "Alice, would you care to update your remarks about Captain Lewis?"

Sarah ducked her head and fled to the kitchen. Hopefully, she wouldn't be subjected to a barrage of questions about Sam. As it was, she found it difficult to sort out her feelings for the very handsome, incredibly addictive man.

She almost stopped in her tracks as she spied Sylvie walking out of the fellowship hall with Sam. At least she didn't have her arm hooked with his. Sam paused at the door and glanced across the room. Their gazes locked, and he tipped his head. Was she supposed to be a mind reader and know what that meant? No matter what Sam said, Sam was leaving with Sylvie. Oh, bother.

If others weren't present as she dried the communion cups, Sarah would have slapped her forehead. *My stomach is calling*, she chastised herself, silently mimicking what she'd said to Sam earlier. Girls weren't supposed to talk about food, and they shouldn't have such a healthy appetite. Sylvie was a stick, and yet her figure was cute with enough womanly curves to attract the attention of most men.

Why did she care? Sam knew she had a healthy appetite. That was no secret. *You're leaving Rockbridge*. First and foremost, she'd forever be his Tomboy, the younger friend he teased. Who happened to be female. Like the little sister he'd had—and lost—in Rachel. That thought sobered her as Sarah stored some of the dried communion cups in the pantry. If she could fulfill that role for Sam, then so be it. She'd be thankful she could bring a smile to his face and he could tease her all he wanted.

Is that what you want to be to Sam? Or do you want something more? Why did the man have to flirt with her? Attract her? Spend so much time with her? Didn't he know how difficult he was making her life? That nagging little voice inside her was growing more relentless. Retrieving the dishtowel, Sarah stuffed it inside another communion cup and swirled it vigorously. Was she so naïve she couldn't tell the difference between flirting and teasing? Was he playing with her emotions or trying to turn her head with those eyes, that smile, that handsome face? No, Sam wouldn't knowingly toy with her feelings. Would he? Could he not understand what havoc he was wreaking with her emotions?

You flirt with the man, you silly girl. You enjoy it, and you want to be with him.

"I think that glass is dry enough, Sarah." With a knowing smile, her mother took the communion cup from her.

Chapter 25

~~♥~~

Sunday Afternoon

"Confession time." Sam stretched out beside Sarah on the mossy bank of the creek.

"I'm listening although I'm surprised to see you here in the middle of your naptime."

"Couldn't sleep," he said with a chuckle. "I tried, but it wasn't happening. So"—he shot her a wide grin—"I figured I might as well come to Thornton's Creek and bother my favorite nurse-to-be."

He bothered her all right, but not in a way she'd ever admit out loud. "I must be fairly predictable if you knew I'd be out here on a Sunday afternoon. Predictable is one thing I never want to be."

"If it makes you feel any better, Sarah, you're the least predictable person I've ever known."

She laughed. "One of my many charms, right?" Where did the fine line lie between friendly camaraderie with Sam and flirting? Far be it from her to know.

"Exactly." He held her gaze for a long moment before nodding to her bare feet. "Those shoes you've been wearing in church are really nice. Quite. . .sexy."

"Thanks for noticing. They belong to Tess, of course." Her heart pounded. Did he really use the word sexy? Needing to avoid Sam's scrutiny, Sarah doubled over and splashed water on her face. Immature or not, how was she supposed to handle a comment like that?

He leaned back on his hands. "I'll have to thank Tess sometime for allowing you to borrow them. I have a question for you, and I'd like a straight answer."

"Ask away."

"Did you wear those shoes specifically to get back at me for what I said in the diner that night about your shoes? I didn't mean any of it, you know."

Sarah tossed a pebble into the water. "You already apologized, and you're forgiven. And you definitely meant what you said. Look, I know my work shoes are ugly, but there's no way I could wear the heels to work. I'd be in a podiatrist's office in no time flat. Besides, when I'm a nurse, I'm going to wear ugly orthopedic shoes. I've accepted it as my fate in life, and you should, too."

"Nonsense." Sam's gaze moved again to her feet, dangling over the edge of the creek bank. "You have very pretty feet."

Her pulse raced at the compliment. "Thanks, but you don't have to go that far." She could kiss Tess for painting her toenails a few nights ago, this time a soft, pale pink for the summer.

"Please accept the compliment graciously. I like the nail polish, too. It's nice. Here." Sitting up, he patted his left thigh. "Give me one."

"What? One of my feet?" She eyed him askance. "Why would I do such a silly thing? I'm not that ticklish if that's what you're thinking. You can give up that idea now."

"Humor me." He tapped his thigh again and tilted his head with an irresistible grin.

Wondering if it was a dumb idea, Sarah turned toward him. Scooting back a bit, she lifted her right foot. Taking her leg, Sam positioned her foot over his lap. Then he began to massage her foot, kneading it with his fingers. On the top, on the bottom. Everywhere. *Oh, my, that feels good.* She leaned back on her hands as Sam had done. "Tell me the truth, Sam. You don't have some kind of strange foot fetish, do you?"

"No." He chuckled and continued his efforts without stopping. "And you didn't answer my question."

"Which question was that? I'm not sure this is appropriate," she murmured, gesturing to where he was massaging her foot. "Whether it's something a good Christian boy and girl should do."

"Ah, but I'm no longer a boy, and you're—"

"You know what?" she said. "At the moment, I don't really care whether it's appropriate or not."

His lips curled. "Oh, I think you do, and that's a big part of your problem. Back to my question. Did you wear those shoes to prove a point? Because if you did, it worked."

She closed her eyes for a few seconds before reopening them. "I don't know that I like you calling it my problem." She grinned. "Okay, maybe I did wear them to make a point. I didn't really think about it. But, no, if you want to get technical about it, I did *not* wear them with the specific intent to 'get back' at you, as you put it. Please don't flatter yourself, but I'm glad you appreciate them. I'll have you know that I always kick those babies off the first chance I get once I get home again. There's only so much a girl can take."

Sam chuckled in the way she loved—deep and low. "I kick my shoes off first thing, too," he said. "For now, please sit back, relax and enjoy. If you fall asleep, I'll wake you up."

"Gladly, after you tell me where you learned this absolutely fabulous massage technique."

"Overseas." When Sarah stared at him, silently questioning him, he gave a small shake of his head. "Don't jump to wrong conclusions. I didn't visit any Suzie Wongs while I was there."

"What does *that* mean? If I really shouldn't hear the answer, I respect your right to remain silent and forever hold your peace."

"Comes from *The World of Suzie Wong*. It was a book and a movie a couple of years ago with William Holden. Suzie Wong is military slang for an Asian prostitute."

Her parents never would have allowed her to see such a movie even if she'd wanted. Jerking her foot away from his reach, Sarah sat up and crossed her legs. "I'm aware. You felt the need to tell me this. . .why?"

"Relax and give me your foot again. As you might recall, we've discussed this before."

"What, the fact that you're not *that kind* of man? You don't know how happy that makes me. For the record, I'm not *that kind* of girl, either."

"I know. That was never in question."

"How could you possibly know such a thing? I mean, it's not something that's branded across my forehead." She hesitated. "Is it?" What she couldn't believe was that they were discussing such a thing in the first place.

Sam's eyes softened as his gaze rested on her. "I see it every time I look in your beautiful brown eyes, Sarah. There's purity there, a sweet innocence that reflects your heart, the clarity of your soul."

"As flattered as I am, is innocence something you can actually see? How is that even possible?"

He flashed a grin. "You ask a lot of questions. I don't know how to explain it, but I'll try. You don't use innuendo, dress provocatively, or flirt with guys to get their attention. Plus, I love how strong you are in your faith. You live it. More than any other woman I've ever met."

Sarah lowered back onto the ground again, propped on her elbows, but she couldn't stop her pulse from racing out of control. "Those are some of the nicest things you've ever said to me, Captain. Thank you."

"You're welcome. I meant every word."

"I know," she murmured. "That's why they meant so much."

Without speaking, Sam lifted her foot again and continued his massage using exquisite care, focusing on the bottom of her foot. She watched, fascinated, as he rhythmically moved his hands and fingers, massaging and rubbing every part of her foot, making sure to hit every pulse point. Unable to hold it in any longer, a long, slow moan escaped. Slapping her hand over her mouth, Sarah sensed the quick rise of warmth in her cheeks. Falling onto her back in a pitiful effort to hide her flaming cheeks from view, she tugged down on the hem of her T-shirt. All the while praying Tess wouldn't interrupt them. What Sam was doing, and what she was allowing him to do, would require a mighty careful explanation if they were discovered. In spite of it all, she smiled.

"What did you say? I didn't hear you," Sam teased, continuing his ministrations.

"I, um, said maybe you and Tess should open a shop. You can do this"—she waved her hand at him—"and she can do the pedicures and manicures."

When Sam chuckled once more, it reached a place hidden deep inside her. Talk about sexy.

"Of course, I completely agree with you about waiting until marriage," she said after a full minute passed without either one of them speaking. A comfortable silence that wasn't awkward in the least. "After all, it *is* God's plan. Secondly, my parents would kill me."

Sam paused. "I think there's a third reason coming. Statements like that usually come in threes."

She giggled and avoided looking at him but figured he could see her smile, anyway. "Not really. I know I definitely need a man who can give really great foot massages."

He stopped massaging her foot. "Is that a proposal of marriage?"

"Perhaps, but it certainly wouldn't be proper for the woman to do the asking, would it?"

He shook his head. "You constantly amaze me. Not to change this fascinating subject, but what is TeamWork?" He motioned to her green and white T-shirt. "I've never heard of it. I can't see the slogan without looking like a pervert. What does it say?"

She lifted her upper body, propping herself on her elbows again. "TeamWork's a Christian missions organization." She glanced down at the shirt. "The slogan says, Rebuilding lives worldwide and binding souls for Christ."

"A very worthwhile goal. Tell me more," he said, resuming his fabulous massage.

"TeamWork's a worldwide organization. They send relief workers wherever there's a natural disaster. They also have a lot of local groups that dedicate themselves to helping families in crisis, feeding the homeless, working with inner-city children, counseling women, and they have all kinds of outreach ministries. From what I know, they meet people where their needs are, and they do their best to fulfill those needs. I'm not sure where their head office is, but the main TeamWork office here in Texas is in downtown Houston. They also have a branch office in Austin, and I've been in contact with them. I'd like to get involved."

"Because they gave you a T-shirt?" Sam laughed when she rolled her eyes.

She told him about some of the inner-city projects she'd read about in the literature sent to her by the TeamWork director. "I'm thinking I could volunteer for some local projects in Austin while I'm in nursing school. Probably not until my second semester when I've settled in more. I'd like to do some kind of outreach project, and I might be able to earn school credit at the same time. I'd really like to donate my time and efforts to the free medical clinics they offer on the weekends. Sounds like a great ministry, don't you think?"

Sam nodded, but he didn't smile. "Sure sounds like it." His voice was quiet, thoughtful.

"Then, after I graduate, I might travel overseas with TeamWork. It'd be a great way to see the world and put my medical training to good use at the same time. Suits both my goals, so the way I see it, it's a win-win situation."

He stopped massaging her foot. "You don't plan on staying in Texas long term?" He'd turned serious and avoided looking at her.

"Well, not at first," she said. "Texas is my home, so I might eventually come back." She shrugged. "Only God knows at this point. Maybe I'll meet someone in my travels and settle in some exotic country. I could live in India with my missionary husband and gift him with one of those Nehru jackets for his birthday."

Sam turned his head away from her. Why wasn't he saying anything? She'd expected him to laugh, especially at her last comment. When he didn't respond, she sighed. "Not to sound greedy, but can you massage my foot a little more? Unless you're too tired." He appeared dazed for some odd reason. She waved her hand. "Anyone home?"

"Yeah, I'm here. Sorry." He gently lowered her foot to the ground and motioned to the other.

Sarah plopped back down to the ground when he positioned her left foot across his thigh. "If Tess decides to show up while you're doing this, I think I'll have to kill her."

"I'll take the chance." He started massaging her foot.

"Thanks." She settled on the hard ground, but it was worth it for the privilege of being so pampered. She should probably protest, but never in her life had anyone done anything like this for her, much less a man.

Not that you'd allow just any man to do such a thing, Sarah. Her cheeks warmed again, and she was immensely thankful she was flat on her back.

Sam worked in silence for a couple more minutes before speaking. "I didn't realize you were thinking of doing something like that. Not staying in Texas, although the opportunities sound terrific for you."

"I thought you, of all people, would be thrilled."

"Why me, of all people?" Now he sounded defensive. She'd never understand men.

"Well, because it's a Christian missions organization, first and foremost. You're like the strongest Christian guy I've ever known, Sam. Matter of fact, you put most of the men in this town to shame in that regard. Although"—she gave him a wry grin—"I'm not sure the elders, my dad included, would approve of your massaging a woman's foot."

Sam shook his head and concentrated on what he was doing, rendering her almost unable to speak. This special treatment could definitely get addictive.

"You make it sound like it's some kind of competition. The part about being a strong Christian. I'm only living my life the best way I can, with God's help." He stopped the massage but left his hands on her foot. For a long moment, Sarah couldn't move, so relaxed she was sure she could easily fall asleep.

He resumed the massage, but after a few more minutes, he offered his hand and pulled her to a sitting position.

"That was a very special, relaxing and unexpected treat. Thank you."

"I'm glad you enjoyed it. I needed to make up for my boneheaded comments."

"Don't worry another minute about it, but I appreciate your sensitivity." Sarah quickly removed a stray leaf that had blown on her T-shirt. "I'm sorry I made it sound like a competition. I was only making an observation of the truth as I see it."

His smile was slow and easy, a relief to see. "My turn. May I make an observation?"

She nodded, casting a wary glance his way. "Sure. Lay it on me."

"I can't understand why one of the guys in this town hasn't married you yet."

Her heart thudded so hard in her chest Sarah thought surely he must hear it. With that statement, the comfortable camaraderie she shared with Sam disappeared. "Well, I hope you know if I *was* married, I sure wouldn't allow you to. . .do what you just did."

"I know that, Sarah. I wouldn't be doing it if you were married. But I'm glad you're not."

"Please don't say something like that." Plucking a few stray blades of grass from the ground, she tossed them at him.

"Why not?" The underlying challenge in his question was unmistakable. "I thought you might like it."

"Because. . ." She faltered.

Again, Sam waited.

"It's not like I haven't had opportunities. I've been asked out plenty of times."

"I'm aware of that."

She snapped her gaze to his. "You seem to be aware of a lot of things."

"Come on. I know girls talk about guys. It'd be naïve of you to think guys don't do the same thing."

Sarah frowned. "I can acknowledge I'm naïve as to the ways of the world, but yes, I know guys talk, especially about the Suzie Wong aspects of the world and such. As far as that goes, I'd rather *not* know, thank you very much." She squirmed a bit under his intense scrutiny. "I'm not sure I like knowing you've discussed. . .me. . .with anyone else."

Dipping his head, Sam waited until she met his gaze. "You have the utmost respect from everyone in this town, sweet Sarah. When you go to Austin and beyond—wherever you go in the world—please promise me you'll stay close to the Lord, hold fast to His promises, and allow Him to always hold you in the palm of His hand." His voice held almost a resigned tone. Was he somehow disappointed in her? If that was the case, she couldn't begin to fathom the reason.

"I will. Promise. You don't need to worry about that. And I like the 'sweet Sarah' nickname, although I never minded Tomboy. Coming from you, it wasn't all bad. So," she said, "if you wanted a confession, there it is." Her eyes met his, and she sank headfirst into their depths. Tess's words on the day of the homecoming parade floated into her mind. *Like an ocean inviting me to take the plunge.* Who was being the hopeless romantic now?

Sam jumped to his feet and held out one hand. Accepting his offer, Sarah rose to her feet beside him. From his conflicted expression, she could tell he wrestled with an inner turmoil and struggled with whether to voice his thoughts.

"Speak to me, Sam. I'm a big girl. I can take it, whatever it is."

He opened his mouth and then closed it again, avoiding her gaze. "Another time perhaps. I think we've already said enough today." Squaring his shoulders, he gave her a smile, but it seemed forced. "Race you home?"

With that, Sam took off, leaving Sarah staring after him. What was that all about? Fine. She'd let him win this time.

Chapter 26

~~♥~~

Monday, June 11, 1962

Sam startled as a loud rap sounded on his office door. "Come in."

Gina appeared in the doorway. "I'm sorry to interrupt, Mr. Lewis. Tess Jordan is here to see you. She doesn't have an appointment, but—"

Tess? What could she want? "That's fine. Please send her in." He tamped down the swell of disappointment that it wasn't Sarah. Glancing at his watch, he figured he could spare ten minutes before he needed to head out to the school board meeting at Town Hall. From experience, he knew ten minutes should be more than enough time with Tess.

No sooner had Sam lifted out of his chair than the eldest Jordan sister marched into his office and closed the door behind her. From her determined expression, she reminded him of his mother when she was about to scold him for some childhood prank. He sure hoped Tess wasn't about to wag her finger in his face.

"Hi, Tess. Come in, why don't you?" He ushered her to a chair before crossing the room and opening the door all the way. "What's on your mind?"

"Sarah." She shifted in the chair. "And you. As in the two of you. Together."

"I see." Lowering himself into the other chair, he waited for her to say more.

Tess pinned him down with her blue-eyed gaze. "You're in love with my little sister, aren't you?"

Sam met her gaze. "I've loved her for a long time. As a friend. A very close friend. The best." When he glimpsed Tess's raised brow, he hastened to explain. "All right, I'd like it to be more—a lot more—but in Sarah's eyes, I'm destined to be nothing more than the older neighbor boy." He grunted and lightly thumped his fist on the wooden arm of the chair.

Tess blew out a sigh. "Wow. You really don't get it, do you?"

Get what? "I guess I don't, but I'm sure you'll be more than happy to enlighten me." That last comment was ill-advised, but she didn't seem to mind. Oh yes, the woman had a mission in being here.

"If you like her, you need to let her know, you doofus! Are you blind? Come on, Sam. She's all moony-eyed over you and doesn't even know it because she thinks you're interested in Sylvie. And you! Why, you come to the diner practically every day like a romantic fool, and apparently you've been observing her and drawing her in secret under the guise of working. Nice drawing, by the way."

"Thanks." He waited as Tess drew in a quick breath, knowing she had much more to say.

"Then there's all the time you spend with Sarah out at Thornton's Creek. You two are such creatures of habit with your not-so-secret little meetings." She crossed her arms. "I can tell time by when Sarah leaves our front steps to go to the creek every night. And"—she looked at her watch—"oh, yes, there's Sam bounding down his front steps, not less than a full minute behind her. You could stand to play a little harder to get."

The muscles in his jaws flexed. He'd been found out, and by the one person who could—and might—spread the news around town in record time. But would Tess gossip about her own sister? As long as he'd known her, Sam had never known her to be a gossip. Or vindictive.

He frowned. "What do you want me to say? I'll admit that I make opportunities to run into Sarah, yes, and I genuinely enjoy her company. I'd like to believe the feeling is mutual, but it's kind of hard to play hard to get with someone who's not interested."

She obviously didn't like that answer as she huffed and blew out a sigh of frustration. "It's not a matter of not being interested. Sarah's confused, plain and simple. Until you came home, she had her life plan all figured out. Now that you two have spent all this time together, I can see how conflicted she's become."

"And that's what I don't want to happen. I don't want to hold Sarah back from what she wants."

"So, what? You're going to just sit back and let her go? You need to make your feelings known before you and Sarah both end up miserable wrecks because you can't tell each other how you feel. Tell me something, and answer me honestly. How is spending time with Sarah different than spending time with Sylvie, Debbie, or. . .me, for that matter? In other words, any other woman—young or old, married or single—in Rockbridge?"

Sam sat back in his chair, considering his answer. "Sarah doesn't have a clue how beautiful she is. She's intelligent, funny, and she's one of the most giving people I've ever met." He leveled his gaze on Tess. "She accepts me as I am. She always has, and she's never expected anything from me other than friendship." He relaxed and his smile escaped. "I like her gentleness with Perry Sellers, her patience with the kids at church, the way she interacts with her customers and co-workers at Perry's, the compassion she demonstrates for everyone." He gestured to his neck. "Then there's that cute little mole—"

"Enough already!" Tess held up one hand, the slightest hint of a smile upturning her lips. "Good heavens, man. Are you even listening to yourself?" Leaning forward, she slapped one hand on his knee before withdrawing a few seconds later. "Here's an idea. Why don't you haul Sarah into your arms, kiss the living daylights out of her and tell her how you feel? Tomorrow might be good." She sat back in the chair, shaking her head. "The Lord knows, I think you should. I know it's the same for Sarah. Get out all these pent-up feelings inside you before you spontaneously combust."

"I. . ." Sam stuttered. "Because I can't," he said finally. "As much as I'd love nothing more than to do that very thing."

Based on her deep frown, that was not the response she wanted to hear. Tess quickly rose from the chair, the force of her glare boring through him. "Not acceptable. That's the most unsatisfactory, vague response I've ever heard come out of your mouth. You disappoint me, Sam. And here I thought you'd grown up during your time in the service. Guess I was mistaken."

"Wait, Tess." He had to tell her what he hadn't wanted to admit even to himself. She'd started for the door, but paused as he moved beside her. He needed to state his case and make it count.

"You're right." Taking her hand, Sam pulled her back into the office before releasing her. He fixed Tess with his gaze and lowered his voice. "I'm in love with Sarah. I think I have been ever since I came back home to Rockbridge. But as much as I want to tell her how I feel, it wouldn't be fair to her. Her plans to leave are firmly in place, and I can't say anything to keep her from following that dream. She'll be a great nurse. Just yesterday, at the creek, Sarah told me about a missions group called TeamWork, and how she's hoping to join them in Austin, and then maybe go overseas with them after she graduates."

Walking away a few paces, he rubbed his hand over his forehead. "Especially after hearing Sarah talk about her hopes for the future, if she stayed here in Rockbridge on my account, I'd always blame myself for keeping her from—"

"From finding true love? You know how to fly a plane, for crying out loud. She'll be in Austin the next few years, not across the world." She advanced a step toward him. "Sam Lewis, if you let my sister go to Austin without staking your claim on her heart, then you'll have to accept the fact that she *will* eventually find another man willing to give her what you're apparently too chicken to do. If you ask me, you two are perfect for each other, but you both make me so mad, I want to knock your heads together!"

Sam's shoulders slumped. "This isn't about being afraid, Tess. Like I said, I can't hold her back. There's the other part of the equation: if she stayed here, and things didn't work out between us in the long run, I'd never forgive myself. I wouldn't be able to bear the hurt in her eyes. I need to let her go. It's for the best." Not for one second did he believe things wouldn't work out between them if he was able to win Sarah's heart. Was he deluding himself? Taking the easy way out?

Tess's blue eyes sparked, reminding him of Sarah's when she was mad. "So, you're going to stay behind and play the martyr card, is that it? Go through the motions of living and pretend you're not allowing the girl of your heart to walk away forever? While I can admire your oh-so-proper and selfless intentions, Sam, it sure as anything smacks of a big old lack of faith to me."

He reared back. "How do you figure that? I've prayed about this a lot. Trust me." Why was everyone in his life accusing him of acting like a martyr? Sarah, Charlie and now Tess? Since when did wanting the best for someone indicate a lack of faith? No, more like it was a *sacrifice*.

"Then I suggest you pray a little harder." She huffed again and turned abruptly. As her parting gift, Tess slammed his office door behind her. Hard.

With a groan, Sam lowered his head to his hands.

Chapter 27

~~♥~~

Tuesday, Late Evening

Sarah flipped the light switch and then pulled the keys from her pocket. She stopped short as Sam appeared on the opposite side of the glass door. "May I come in?" he mouthed to her. When she nodded, he stepped inside the door. Tonight he was in his full cowboy mode—jeans, short-sleeved shirt, Stetson and boots. Rugged and masculine. Mercy.

Reaching for the bell, Sarah stilled it as she closed the door behind him and turned the lock. "Hi there."

"Hi, Sarah."

"Have you come to divulge the name of my anonymous benefactor?"

"No." Sam shook his head, but he didn't smile. Matter of fact, he looked as serious as she'd seen him since the night when he'd stopped Merle's car. The night when he'd played the part of the big, strong hero and rescued her. The night he'd managed to dig his way deeper into her heart.

"If you're here to eat, I'm afraid you're too late. We're closed for the night."

The corners of his mouth twitched. "I haven't eaten since lunch, but that's not why I'm here."

"I could fix you an omelet at the house, if you'd like."

"Thanks, but I don't want an omelet." He stepped closer, slow and purposeful. "I'm not hungry for food." Sam's face relaxed, softened. And those eyes. . .full of what sure looked like longing, but what did she really know of such things? The air was charged with tension between them like never before, but it was warm. Wonderful. Filling her with anticipation and a world of possibilities.

Her gaze moved across his handsome features, lingering on his mouth. "What is it that you want, Sam?"

Without answering, he crossed to the jukebox. Digging a few coins from his jeans, Sam inserted them into the machine and then made his selections. A few seconds later, Ray Charles began to croon "You Don't Know Me." Without the usual noise and clatter of the diner, the music was loud, but it faded into the background as he returned to her, swallowing her range of vision. She watched as he removed his Stetson and tossed it on a nearby table. A man rarely tossed a Stetson. His eyes never leaving hers, Sam walked slowly toward her, each step of his boots bringing him deeper into her very *soul.*

Stopping in front of her, Sam offered his hand, waiting. Their gazes locked and held. "May I have this dance, Miss Jordan?" His voice was deep, husky. Oh, that voice did such *things* to her. Sarah's pulse raced uncontrollably, and she couldn't breathe.

She gave him her hand. This was real, this was life. *This* was passion. She'd always wondered if she'd recognize it when it happened. Now, she knew. This night, this moment, would change the course of their lives. Was this really happening? Or was she living a precious dream?

Lacing their fingers together, Sam raised their joined hands and rested them over his heart. After moving his other hand around her waist, he inched her closer and began to move with her. Beneath the thin cotton of his shirt, beneath the warmth of him, the firmness of his chest, the steady rhythm of Sam's heartbeat reassured her.

"I don't know what to do," she murmured. "I've never danced before." The top button of his shirt was undone. Although she'd seen him without his shirt on numerous occasions at the creek, this was different. Her senses heated from the intimacy of the moment. The scent of his cologne made her weak. Dizzy.

"I beg to differ. You were doing a very good job of it here in the diner not so long ago."

"That was different," she said with a small smile. "Not at all like this."

"I'll show you."

She leaned her head on his chest and allowed him to lead. His hold on her tightened. "Sarah, you have to know I don't want Sylvie. I've never wanted Sylvie. Or any other girl but you."

She swallowed, raised her eyes to his and stopped dancing. "You don't?"

"I went to see her today and apologized if I'd somehow led her to believe there could be anything between us other than friendship."

"You did?"

He kissed her forehead, allowing his lips to linger. "Sylvie told me she knew I was interested in someone else. Said she'd invited me to meet her folks mainly because her father wanted to talk with me about UT football and the Air Force." He chuckled and moved his warm, soft lips to her cheek. "No matter where you are—Austin, or anywhere else—I want to be with you as often as possible. If that's what *you* want, nothing will deter me."

"You do?" She shook her head. "I mean, it won't?" Although she felt silly for her questions, she was dazed. Hardly able to breathe much less think coherently.

Sam smiled into her eyes and slowed their steps. "Baby, you could go to school across the country, across the globe, or on the moon, but I'll never stop thinking about you. Because you see," he said, "that's like asking me not to picture your face in my mind every night before I go to sleep, or every morning when I get up."

He traced a path along the side of her face with a gentle hand, his fingers lingering. "It's like asking me not to pray. I've prayed for years, asking God to show me the girl of His choosing. Asked Him to lead me in the direction of the right woman."

Sarah's eyes searched his in the dim light.

"I still pray that prayer," he whispered. "Every night since I've been home. And every single time, without fail, my next thought has always been of you. For you see, you're always with me. In here." With their hands still joined over his heart, Sam tightened his grip. Leaning close to her, he brushed his lips over hers. "I think you've always been with me, even though I didn't even know it."

Removing his hand from hers, Sam cradled her face in one hand, smiling as she leaned into his touch. "I want *you*, Sarah. If I spend the rest of my life trying, with everything I am, with everything I can offer, I hope to win your heart." He slid his fingertips down her arms—sending shivers throughout her entire being—then guided her hands around his neck. "Don't be afraid."

"I'm not afraid." Meeting his eyes again, Sarah swallowed.

"You don't know how much I've wanted to do this. Hold you." Sam smoothed one palm over her hair. "Kiss you." She breathed in the scent of him, the masculinity of him, never wanting to let go of the moment and this man.

"You are so beautiful." Henry Mancini's "Moon River" played in the background. She'd never forget this moment, this song, the perfection of it all.

"Thank you. So are you." Laughing softly, she leaned her forehead against his chest. "Not the time to be inarticulate, Sarah." She'd shared so much of her life with this man since he'd returned to Rockbridge, laid her heart bare before him. Surrendered her heart.

Sam lifted her chin with a gentle hand. "I don't think you understand just how special you are. To me. You've always been special. We both needed the time to grow up and recognize the relationship we share. In all its glorious imperfection, it's absolutely perfect."

"I'm not so sure I'm grown up. Enough for you. I mean. . ." Even in her embarrassment, she treasured his words.

He chuckled, deep and low. "I do believe you're more mature than I am." Although she didn't look at him, Sarah felt that incredible smile everywhere.

"I doubt that." She patted his chest with one hand, and he tangled her fingers with his in a firm hold.

"Why me and not another girl, Sam?"

Sam chuckled under his breath. "Why not you?"

"You have this annoying habit of diverting my questions. I'm sure I don't need to point out the obvious. I'm certainly not the prettiest, skinniest—"

"Shh." When she raised her chin, Sam placed two fingers over her lips. "You want a reason? For one thing, you're taller than most girls. All the better to kiss you. You're funny, you're sensitive and compassionate. You somehow seem to understand me. And you tolerate me when I'm irrational and insufferable." He moved his lips to her cheek, heating her skin, a move which prompted untold sensations in her entire being. Tempting her. Teasing her.

"I never want to hear you suggest that I date another woman.

You're everything I want and need, and more. Sarah Jordan, you have no idea what you do to me."

With her face raised to his, with this man she adored standing so close, the warmth of him made her heady with a powerful awareness. "I do?" She shook her head. "You do?" She needed to stop talking.

"Oh, yeah." Cradling her cheeks, Sam's eyes sought her permission.

"Hold that thought." Stepping back, Sarah removed the pins from her hair, loving the adoration in his expression as she did so. Dropping her hairnet to the floor, Sarah finger-combed her hair so that it tumbled down around her face, over her shoulders. "I'm sure it's a mess," she said.

"It's beautiful." Sam tugged her close again. With one hand around her waist, he lightly ran the fingers of his other hand through her hair.

"I think you're about to break that vow to never kiss a Jordan girl."

The smile lines she loved deepened as he brushed his thumb over her cheek. "You know about that? I don't look at kissing you as breaking a vow so much as making a promise for the future." Sam's blue eyes deepened, visible even in the dim lighting. "*Our* future."

Sam brushed his lips over her cheek, sending her heart soaring. The overwhelming urge to feel his lips on hers overtook her wildly fluctuating nerves. Sarah lifted her chin, inviting him, wanting this man's kiss more than anything in the world.

"Sarah." The whispered word was a precious caress. Lowering his head, Sam met her lips. Tugging her closer, covering her mouth with his, Sam's kiss was sweet, gentle, tender. She knew he wanted more, but it was a testament to his strong character in the way he restrained himself. Knowing how inexperienced she was, he respected her, didn't push her. When his lips left hers, Sam cupped her face and feathered kisses on her cheeks, her temple, before brushing his mouth over hers in a light, sweeping motion.

Sarah increased the pressure of her hand on the back of his neck, pulling him closer. She felt his smile as their lips met again.

"Like I said, you understand me," he whispered.

No longer merely friends, they'd stepped over the line into something fresh and exciting, waiting to be explored. Sam was showing her what he wanted and she was giving him her answer.

She'd never known a kiss could be so wonderful. So much *more* than wonderful.

"Why haven't we ever done this before?" she murmured, pulling away for a moment. "This incredible, amazing thing?"

"All in God's timing. You don't know how long I've wanted to do that."

"How long is that?" She smiled as he gave her his answer with another kiss, this one longer.

Sam leaned his forehead against hers. "Pretty much since I returned to Rockbridge."

"I'm very glad you didn't call me Tomboy just now."

"I wouldn't think of it."

"Did I do it right? Because you know how inexperienced I am—"

"You're doing great." His chuckle sat low in his throat. "Sometimes you can say so much without words. You just need a little more practice. What do you say let's work on that some more?"

And so, they did. Captain Lewis kissed away Sarah's smile in the best possible way.

In the back of her mind, Sarah heard someone knocking on the glass door. Reluctantly easing out of Sam's embrace, she glanced at the door through hazy eyes.

Tess stood outside, wearing an expression of disbelief. As usual, her sister had incredible timing. She suppressed her sigh. What had she been thinking, kissing Sam in full view of the entire town? Sarah glanced at the clock on the wall. Although it had only been a few minutes, she would have been content to continue kissing him. In some ways, perhaps Tess's appearance was providential.

"Better answer the door," Sam said, his voice still husky.

"Promise you won't leave me alone with her?"

"Promise." He slipped one hand behind her back, leaving it there. Sarah smoothed the front of her uniform as she moved toward the door with Sam beside her.

Lord, please hold my tongue if she provokes me. Based on Tess's demeanor, that was pretty much a given. Sarah unlocked the front door and stilled the bell. Although she could hardly believe she'd been kissing Sam a moment before, she needed to push that thought aside and concentrate on appeasing her sister. Or figure out a way to get her to leave.

"Here you are! I was worried." Tess's tone was a hair above chastisement. Why had she felt the overwhelming need to come to Perry's after dark to find her?

"This is getting to be a habit with you." Sarah stood aside as Tess passed by her. Try as she might, she couldn't keep the sarcasm from her tone. "Is something wrong? Are Mom and Dad okay?"

"They're fine." Tess's lips lifted at the corners. "By 'habit,' are you referring to my interrupting a private moment between the two of you?" She eyed Sam up and down. "Captain Lewis, I have to say it's about time you came to your senses. But I have to ask—after that blatant display of affection—what are your intentions toward my little sister?"

When Tess winked at Sam, Sarah gawked. *What?* "Tess, have you been drinking?"

Sam strengthened his hold on her lower back, giving Sarah immeasurable comfort. "Tess, I assure you, my intentions are completely honorable. However, if you think I'm going to thank you for interrupting us, you are grievously mistaken."

Sarah chewed her lower lip and glanced from Sam to Tess and back. Was something going on here to which she wasn't privy? Both of them seemed rather amused, but at least Tess hadn't lit into her as she'd feared.

With one hand on her hip, Tess pivoted and headed for the door. "I'll wait for you outside, but a word of advice? People *will* talk if you stand in front of the window with your lips stuck to one another like I just witnessed. Trust me, that's the polite way of describing it. From what I know, people are already speculating about the two of you. Thrilled as I am, it's a good thing no one else was around to witness your little show tonight. Sarah, we need to head home now."

"Did you drive?" Sam said, retrieving his Stetson and anchoring it on his head.

Tess gave him a pouty glance. "No. It's such a nice night, and I thought Sarah and I could walk together. Get some fresh air and clear our heads, so to speak."

"It's late, it's dark, and I'm driving you both home." Sam's command left no room for argument. "Sarah, do you need to do anything else before you lock up?"

"I'll get my purse and check a couple of things in the kitchen, and then I'm ready." She shot Sam a *sorry to leave you alone with Tess* glance and then darted out of the dining room, determined not to be gone longer than necessary. Although Tess seemed to be in a charitable mood, when she set her mind to it, she could do more damage in sixty seconds than most women in a month.

As Sarah walked back out to where they waited a minute later, Tess leaned over to retrieve something from the floor. Her hairnet. "I believe this belongs to you."

Sarah snatched it from her sister's hand and then stuffed it in the pocket of her uniform. "Thanks."

The short ride to the house was quiet in the front seat of Sam's dad's truck. Sarah sat sandwiched between Sam and Tess. So close Sarah felt Sam's warmth on one side and tried not to breathe in the strong scent of her sister's cologne—something new that reeked like stinkweed—on the other. Thankfully, the passenger window was rolled halfway down, and a warm breeze sifted through the long strands of her hair. Reaching for a lock, Sarah twirled it around her finger, over and over.

"Especially now that you'll be squiring Sarah around town, Sam, don't you think it's about time you got your own vehicle?" Tess drummed her fingers on the window ledge as Sam turned the corner onto their street.

Sarah bit down on her lower lip not to say anything. Sam could handle Tess.

"I have a car on order, as a matter of fact." Sam turned the corner onto their street. "It's coming from England, so I have no idea when it will arrive."

Sarah glanced at him in surprise. The muscles flexed in his jaw as he pulled in front of their house. Why hadn't he said anything?

"Imported from England? Well, now, that's quite exciting," Tess said. "Impressive, actually."

Because having a nice car is what's most important in life, after all. She'd ask forgiveness for that one later. Sarah slumped in the seat but remained silent, knowing that doing so would be in her best interest.

"Any other questions?" Sam turned the key in the ignition, shutting off the engine, and leveled his gaze on Tess.

"No, that'll do it for now. Thanks for the ride." Tess opened the passenger door and slid down from the seat. Without glancing over her shoulder, she started up the front walkway. That was a shock that she'd left without getting in another dig or else grabbing her by the arm and hauling her inside the house.

"Wait, Sarah. I'll come around." Sam slipped out from behind the wheel and closed his door.

When she stepped outside the truck, he closed her door and put his arm behind her back as they walked together.

"I apologize for putting your reputation at risk. I never meant to get you in any kind of trouble with your family or anyone else." Standing across from her on the front step, Sam's expression was full of concern, his tone laced with regret. "The problem is, right now, all I can think about is how much I want to kiss you again."

"I should say good night." Sarah gripped her handbag tighter. "Or I'll let you kiss me again."

A slow smile spread across his handsome face. "I'll see you tomorrow at Perry's."

"I'll look forward to it. Thanks for a great Tuesday, Captain Lewis. The best of my life."

He nodded. "Same here, and it was my honor. Good night, sweet Sarah."

Sam waited until she went into the house. Once inside, on a whim, Sarah splayed the fingers of one hand on the screen door. Walking across the porch, standing on the other side of the door, he positioned his hand on the screen. With another smile, Sam raised his hand in a quick wave and then departed.

"Well, that's a different but very romantic way to say good night." Tess lounged against the wall leading from the kitchen into the living room. Her arms were crossed, and the smug grin on her face was annoying.

"Be quiet, please. Allow me to savor my moment." With her head held high, Sarah walked past her sister, wishing—not for the first time—that she had a separate bedroom. At eighteen, after Tess won her umpteenth beauty queen title, Sarah begged her parents, to no avail, to allow her to move into the spare bedroom. Now, it seemed she wouldn't be afforded the luxury of reliving Sam's kisses tonight without an audience. Did Tess possess the inherent right to lecture her simply by virtue of her birthright? Maybe she should sleep in that spare bedroom tonight. As long as she changed the sheets, Mom wouldn't mind.

After grabbing her things, Sarah escaped into the bathroom. Feeling the strong need to pray, she sat on the edge of the bathtub. *Lord, I haven't done anything wrong with Sam. Have I? I'll admit we could have used more discretion and moved out of sight of the front window. But I'll never regret kissing him. Right or wrong, and whether or not the whole town finds out. That's not anyone else's business, but I want to make it your business, Father. I've never been in love before. You know that. All those years ago, Sam and I began a friendship that's continued and is stronger than ever. I mean, it's not like we started kissing the minute he returned to Rockbridge. I really like kissing him, Lord, and I promise to control myself. He's a beautiful man, though. There's a part of me that still can't believe this is happening. Let's face it—Sam could have his pick of any girl in Rockbridge, but he chose me. Me! I'm feeling pretty blessed right now. Help me to sort out my feelings, and to know whether or not he's the man of your choosing for me. He says he wants to be with me whether I'm in Austin or wherever I go. That, too, I leave in your hands. Direct my thoughts, my actions, and my path, dear Jesus. In your name I pray. Amen.*

As she washed her face and brushed her teeth, Sarah felt better but then stewed a bit more. Praying always helped, but her emotions were still somewhat unsettled. She wanted to drift off to sleep in peace instead of listening to her sister's hypocritical chastisement. Maybe she should approach it from a more positive angle. Tess *had* winked at Sam, after all. Perhaps she wasn't in for a tongue lashing, after all. No matter what, she refused to give Tess the power to taint the beautiful memory of her moment with Sam.

"I'm sorry, sis," Tess said twenty minutes later as Sarah came back into the bedroom. Sarah hesitated only a few seconds before pulling back the lightweight coverlet and climbing into her twin bed. If she slept in the other bedroom, avoidance would only make things worse. Might as well face the music, get this inevitable confrontation over with, and then she could move forward.

"What's that?"

"You were right."

Huh. Not what she expected.

Chapter 28

~~♥~~

Sarah turned on her side. Propping herself on one elbow, facing Tess, she prepared to listen. This should be good. "What do you mean?"

"I'm jealous as anything about you and Sam. Remember when I discovered you together—just talking—at Thornton's Creek? You asked me if I was jealous and assured me nothing was going on between the two of you."

"And that was true. . ."

"I know it was at the time, Sarah. Now, after what I witnessed in the diner tonight, I'm so jealous I can't even see straight."

When a tear slid down Tess's cheek, Sarah tossed aside the sheet and moved across to the other twin bed. "Scoot over, I'm coming in."

Her sister shifted and made room for her, patting the mattress with one hand. "Have a seat."

"Please don't cry, Tess. I didn't plan on anything happening with Sam. I can hardly believe it myself, much less try and explain it. It just. . ."—Sarah shrugged—"happened." What a lame thing to say, but it was honest and all she had to offer.

"I know, and I'd be blind if I didn't see how good you two are together. In a lot of ways, you've always been the older sister." Tess sniffled and smiled a little. "You're a lot more mature than me. You always have been. I mean, look at me. I flit around in silly outfits trying to get attention and putting emphasis on the wrong things."

Sarah inhaled a deep breath. This was the Tess she loved. Her sister who stayed up into the early morning hours and shared her heart. When they were younger, they'd spent many a night doing this very thing. Those happier moments had been pushed aside in the past few years, replaced by tedious quibbles and tension. How she'd longed and prayed for this closeness to be restored.

"I hope it works out for you and Sam. He's a great catch—great *guy*—and you deserve all the happiness in the world."

Reaching for her hand, Sarah pulled Tess into a warm hug. "You don't know how much I've missed you." She leaned her head on her sister's slender shoulder. "Thank you for being here for me."

"I know I owe you a long overdue apology. I haven't been a very good friend, much less your sister, especially since Sam came back home. You're only twenty-one and have your whole life ahead of you. Your future at nursing school is all planned out. You know where you're headed and what you want from life."

When Sarah pulled back, she glimpsed fresh tears in Tess's eyes. "It's my plan, yes, but I'm still here. At least for now."

"I'm an old maid, washed up at almost twenty-eight years old," Tess said, her tone this side of whiny. "I always thought I'd be married for a few years by now, and have at least one or two kids."

"Tess, you're not washed up in any sense of the word." Sarah bit back her criticism, knowing that wouldn't help the situation. "The Lord knows the desires of your heart. We need to trust He'll bring the right people into your life, including your future husband, if it's His will. You have so much to give. May I make a suggestion?"

"Sure. Why not?" Tess plopped backwards on the mattress. When another tear streaked down her cheek, Sarah grabbed the tissue box from the desk.

"Here, take this." She pushed a tissue into her sister's hand. "Maybe if you'd stop acting so obvious around guys, then the *real you* will show up. I happen to think the real you is pretty great."

In the middle of dabbing the moisture from her cheeks, Tess paused. "What do you mean? You don't think I'm being myself?"

Sarah searched for what she could say that would make sense. "Let me give you an example. Remember when you were a candy striper and visited Lorraine Carmichael in the hospital over in Springhaven?"

"Ye-es," Tess said, wiping her eyes with the tissue. "What does that have to do with the fact that I'm destined to be single and childless?"

Sarah handed Tess another tissue and waited while she blew her nose. That was one thing her sister did not do in a dainty way, and she chewed her lower lip in an effort not to smile. "Remember how you prayed with Lorraine and then she accepted Jesus as her Savior?"

"Yes, and sorry to pout, but that's not helping," Tess said. "Lorraine may not have her appendix anymore, but she's got a husband and a baby girl. The perfect family."

With a sigh, Sarah tugged on Tess's hand, pulling her upright again. "Dry those tears and listen to me. After that visit, you were so full of enthusiasm. It practically poured out of you, and you couldn't stop talking about how you'd told Lorraine about Jesus. I want to tell you something. As pretty as you were when you won all those beauty queen titles, when you told me about Lorraine, you positively glowed—from the inside out. I remember how in awe I was of you in that moment, how beautiful you were. It was a radiance that came from something other than physical beauty, although you've always had that."

"I still don't see how that makes any difference now."

"You made a difference in her life. An *eternal* difference. Don't you see? It also made *you* happy. Not because of what you'd done, or earned, or won, but because of how the Lord had worked in Lorraine's heart."

Silent for a long moment, Tess wiped her eyes and then glanced up at her. "I've lost the joy. That's what you're telling me, isn't it?"

"No, I don't think you've lost your joy, but you've lost the enthusiasm you used to have. Your light's just been hidden for a few years."

A fresh tear slipped down Tess's cheek. She lowered her gaze to her hands twisting in her lap. "Why won't a man look at me the way he looks at you, Sarah?"

"Oh, Tess." Sarah understood how much it cost her sister to ask that question. How should she answer?

Tess grabbed her hand. "You're right about one thing. Somewhere along the way, I lost the enthusiasm I used to have for a lot of things in life. I've lost my focus."

"I'm so proud of you," Sarah said. "You put in long hours at the law office. I know you do a wonderful job, and I'm sure your dedication hasn't gone unnoticed."

"They're good to me, but it's just a paycheck." Shoulders slumping, Tess looked so forlorn it made Sarah's heart hurt. "I don't have the passion for my job like you do for nursing. It's not like I want to type, file and answer phones my entire life."

"Well, I certainly don't want to be a waitress at Perry's Diner my whole life, but if that's what God wants for me, I'll deal with it. For now, I'm making the most of it."

"There's a difference with you, though, Sarah. You know it's only temporary. A stepping stone to something much bigger and better."

Sarah laughed. "Right. My job at Perry's has been 'temporary' from the time I was sixteen. But you know what? I wouldn't trade my experiences there for anything. More importantly, I've made some great friends, and I'll carry them with me no matter where the Lord leads in my life."

"I wish I had that assurance, that confidence, like you do. So, do you have any suggestions for me?" Tess mopped her cheeks with the side of her hand.

"For one thing, you can stop being such a pretty crier." Sarah pulled her into another hug. "You put me to shame."

"You're funny," Tess said. "So, tell me. How does a girl go about rediscovering her joy? Any idea?"

"Pray about it, first of all. Secondly, would you consider doing some volunteer work again? Whether it's through the church, the hospital, the school or whatever, it might give you a renewed purpose and help fill the holes of your life."

"Holes of my life?" Tess looked at her as if she held all the answers. "What do you mean?"

"We all have empty places inside us, but we can't expect other people to fill them. That's not to say they can't. More than anything, I want to make a difference in someone else's life. You did that for Lorraine once upon a time, and I'm sure there've been many others. More than you can possibly know."

Tess leaned her head on Sarah's shoulder. Moving one arm around her, Sarah smoothed her sister's dark hair from her face with her free hand and kissed her forehead. "You're a very special person, Tess, and you've made a profound impact on my life."

"Thanks. And you inspire me. People gravitate to you because you're so. . .honest."

Sarah laughed. "Which is a nice way of saying I'm blunt?"

"Maybe," Tess said. "But you do it in such a nice way, with a little twinkle in your eye, it softens the blow."

"I do not have a twinkle in my eye."

"Sure you do. Take a look at Sam sometime when he looks at you. You'll understand what I mean."

"I'll tell you something else." Warmed by her words, Sarah eased out of the hug.

"What's that?" Tess tossed the used tissues in the wastebasket beneath her desk.

"Charlie likes you. I've seen the way he looks at you."

"Really? Charlie? Did Sam say something?"

Sarah shook her head. "No, but I can ask him, if you want."

"No, no. Don't do that." Tess laughed a little. "I'm sure you wouldn't hesitate to ask Sam, would you? That's one of the things I most admire about you. You don't worry about what's right or what's proper, but you speak up and always follow your heart." She blew out a breath and ran one hand over her hair. "I envy you in a lot of ways."

"You envy me?" That admission surprised Sarah. "You're tired, and that's your weariness speaking." She collapsed on Tess's bed, flat on her back, her arm draped over her forehead.

Tess nudged her leg. "What are you doing now?"

"I almost fainted from the shock caused by an overload of compliments." Sarah sat up again. "Tess, you're so pretty, dainty, feminine and every hair is always in place. You can wear anything you want and make it look like a million bucks. And the way you sing makes my voice sound like a duck in heat."

Tess swatted her arm, laughing. "Add sense of humor to the list. You're smarter than I can ever hope to be. Sarah, can't you see it? You're beautiful, and you don't even know it."

Sarah stared. "You think I'm beautiful? As I recall, you called me frumpy the night Sam came to dinner. Not all that long ago, and I haven't done anything differently."

"Not my best moment. Sorry. That was one of those times when I was jealous as all get out. I've already confessed that much. Come with me." Tugging on her hand, Tess pulled Sarah off the bed, marched her over to the dresser, and then positioned her in front of the mirror. "Your hair is naturally this fabulous blonde color. Most women pay a fortune, or get it from a bottle, and it still doesn't look as gorgeous. As if that's not enough, you've perfected the art of scooping it up into that bun that takes all of two seconds yet looks like you just walked out of a Paris salon. How you do it is beyond me. And these cheekbones?" Tess ran the back of her hand down the side of her face. "Honey, they're to die for. And my lips are too thin while yours are. . .well, they're just right. Especially for Sam."

Sarah gasped and warmth rushed into her cheeks. Open-mouthed, she watched as Tess plucked one of her tiaras—Miss Rockbridge Harvest, from her best recollection—and positioned it on her head. Standing behind her, reflected in the mirror on the dresser, Tess smiled. "I hereby crown you the most beautiful sister in the world."

That did it. On emotional overload, Sarah rushed for the tissues. Grabbing one, she dabbed it beneath her eyes.

"There is something different about you since Sam came to dinner, you know."

"What's that?" Sarah asked, moving back over to her bed, still wiping her eyes.

"You're a woman in love. If you two get married, you're going to have very attractive children."

Before she could respond, Tess continued. "I know one thing. I'm going to pay more attention to Charlie from here on out. To think he's been under my radar all this time. He's good looking, has a solid job, and he's the only man we know who owns his own home." She shrugged. "He doesn't date much, so I guess I thought he wasn't interested."

"He's been focused on building his career," Sarah said. "I've gotten to know Charlie even better since Sam's return. He comes and sits in the diner with him sometimes. He's very funny and quite charming. Maybe he doesn't believe he'd ever have a chance with you."

"That's not true." Tess waved her hand. "You don't think Charlie really believes that, do you?"

Sarah smiled. "It's possible he hasn't asked out anyone else because the one he wants. . .is sitting here with me now."

"You're sweet. And, let's face it, he does have a very nice car," Tess said. She started to say more and then stopped herself. "Would you listen to me? That's the kind of thing I need to stop saying."

Sarah smiled. "It'll take time. I wonder why Sam didn't say

anything to me about ordering a car? From England, of all things." As predictable as the man could be in some ways, he was apparently unpredictable in others.

"I'd prefer to call him Charles instead of Charlie," Tess said as they both settled in their beds. "Do you think he'd mind?"

Sarah laughed. "Coming from you, I don't think so. I love you, Tess."

"You, too, sis. Good night and sweet dreams."

Not a problem.

Chapter 29

~~♥~~

Sitting at the kitchen table the next morning, Tess's eyes lit with excitement. She'd been bouncing around all morning, and Sarah suspected her sister was hatching a plan. She adored Happy Tess. Happy Tess was more agreeable and less argumentative, and it was good to have her back. Maybe last night had been a turning point in their relationship. A very good one.

"Sarah, while Mom and Dad are on their trip to visit Aunt Mary in Colorado, I think we should redo the kitchen and living room."

Sarah paused in the middle of chewing her toast slathered with homemade raspberry jam. "Redo? As in redecorate?"

Her sister's nod was emphatic. "I'm mainly talking about paint and wallpaper. Spruce up the rooms, give them a fresh new look. Heaven knows, they could use it, don't you think? I suppose we could also move the furniture around and throw some new slipcovers over the sofa and chairs."

"Except for Dad's chair. Best to leave it alone. You don't mess with a man's favorite chair."

"You're right." Tess took another bite of her oatmeal. "She'd never say anything, but Mom must be tired of staring at this ancient wallpaper for years on end. How could she not?" She glanced around the kitchen with an exaggerated sigh.

True enough. Mom and Dad hadn't had the money, much less the time and inclination, to do anything about it. In the past six years, every spare penny had gone for the care of Mom's parents in the nursing home, and they'd passed away within a month of each other last year.

Sarah finished her toast and pushed her plate aside. "I'm not sure how much we can get done in a week, but I'm all for it." She took a sip of her coffee and smiled. "You're really taking my suggestion to volunteer and running with it, aren't you? In a way I never expected. It's a great idea, and Mom and Dad deserve this. Thanks for thinking of it."

Tess's smile grew wider, clearly pleased by her approval. "Welcome."

Rare were the occasions when Tess asked for her opinion. The living room wasn't too bad with a pale green, vertical stripe wallpaper pattern. The furniture and paintings complemented the walls and vice versa. Sarah glanced around the kitchen, taking in the dingy, brown and white wallpaper. Olive green and golden yellow were the only splashes of color in the cutesy owl pattern. Her parents bought the house from the original owners who'd built it in the mid-1930s. That ugly wallpaper had been in place ever since Sarah could remember. Greasy stains marred the wall behind the range. How many times had Mom scrubbed that wall with no luck in erasing the evidence of splattered food? Sarah heard her refer to it once as the bane of her existence. Anything would be an improvement, especially since their mother spent so much of her time in this kitchen.

"The kitchen needs more help," Sarah said. "I can paint, but I have no idea how to wallpaper. I'm willing to try, but maybe we should hire someone with experience instead of trying to do it ourselves?"

Tess considered her question. "I'm sure we can round up a crew. I say we put some of those big strong guys we know to work. Want to meet at Hartmann's after work? You're off at five, right?"

"Right." Sarah figured she might as well put in a good word on Charlie's behalf. "If Charlie's working at Hartmann's this afternoon, I'm sure he'll be happy to help us pick out paint, wallpaper or whatever else we decide to use. Answer our questions and give us some guidance. That sort of thing. What are you thinking in terms of a color scheme?"

Tess appeared deep in thought, but she nodded to indicate she'd heard. "I think Mom would like a pretty pale yellow on the walls here in the kitchen. You know how she's always complaining about how these owls creep her out. Like they're staring at her. Probably anything to cover them up would be fine."

"Good point," Sarah said. "Yellow would be great in here. Sunny and bright. As far as the living room, I think she'd like to keep the original sage green and ivory colors. It's an elegant combination."

"I should call Hartmann's and see if Charlie's working tonight." Tess's grin was coy.

"Better yet, just walk in and surprise him. He's almost always there during the day on weekdays." Sarah winked. "I'm sure he'd love nothing more than the opportunity to help you."

Tess swatted her arm. "Help *us*. You are so not subtle."

Taking another quick sip of her coffee, Sarah surveyed the kitchen, making mental notes. "Can you imagine Mom's face when she gets home from the trip, walks in here and sees her 'new' kitchen? I can't wait, and I'm sure it'll be worth all the effort."

Tess dropped her spoon into the empty bowl after finishing her oatmeal. "She'll either be royally steamed or else she'll love it."

"Or she'll be jetlagged and believe she's delusional," Sarah said. "I'm willing to take the chance. You and I both know if Mom and Dad weren't going away, they'd never allow us to do such a thing."

Tess rinsed her bowl in the sink. With her back turned, Sarah heard the smile in her sister's voice. "And that's exactly why we're going to do it. You know what they say, sis. When the cat's away, the mice will play. But in the best of ways, in this case."

~~♥~~

That Afternoon

Sarah passed Sam sitting at the counter instead of his usual small booth in the back corner.

"Tell Jimmy he's outdone himself this time." Wiping his mouth with his napkin, Sam smiled in satisfaction. "This burger's the best I've had in a long time. Barbecue sauce on beef is my new favorite ingredient."

"I'll be sure and tell him. Arnie said the same thing, and he liked the onion ring, too." She noted Sam had moved the onion ring to the side of his plate. "Not a fan?"

"Not if I hope to get a kiss at some point today."

"I think raw onions are the greater offender." Sarah shook her head. "I have absolutely no idea why I felt the need to say that."

"Love does strange things to a person. Trust me, I know. Hey, it's a proven fact," he insisted. "It messes with your mind, not just your emotions."

Sarah leaned close, a dangerous move when she detected the scent of his aftershave. "Who said anything about love?"

"I did, last I checked. Never fear," Sam said. "I'll have you spouting the 'L' word soon enough."

"Is that so?" She laughed. "Did you know that eighty-five percent of men are overconfident in their sex appeal to women?"

Sam stared at her. "You just made that up."

"Did not." She burst out laughing. "Okay, I did. Lord, forgive me for telling a falsehood in order to keep a man's ego in check. On that note, if you'll excuse me. I'll be back soon."

After darting into the kitchen and catching Jimmy's smile, Sarah carried Jewell Marcum's vegetable plate out to her. "Hi, Jewell. How are you feeling today?" Maybe that question was pointless. From her deep frown, it appeared the mother-to-be was having a rough day.

"I'm ready to pop this baby out whether he or she wants to come out or not." Jewell rubbed her stomach. "I'm ravenous and can't seem to stop eating, so I guess it's a good thing I have an excuse, huh? It's like I'm making up for lost time—and food—when I suffered all that morning sickness in my first trimester." She picked up her fork and stared at the food on her plate.

"If it helps, you're the prettiest pregnant mama I've ever seen. How much longer until your due date?"

"Another week, according to Doc Meriweather."

"Your baby will be here before you know it." Sarah gave her a smile and squeezed the other woman's shoulder. "I'm praying for a safe delivery. Eat up, and let me know if you need anything."

"Don't you worry. You'll be the first to know," Jewell said as Sarah headed back to the counter. Sam was engaged in a lively conversation with the customers sitting on either side of him. He made new friends easily and kept his old ones. Loyalty was sorely lacking in some people, but not Sam. When she'd walked by Harold Anderson's home last week on the way to a late shift at Perry's, he'd been working in the front yard trimming the hedges.

Why should she be surprised? Look what he'd done for Merle at the bank. Ditto helping Fletcher get his prosthetic leg. He spent quality time with his dad after-hours. Her mother had run into Sam at the nursing home the week before where he'd been delivering fresh homemade pies to the shut-ins. He'd volunteered for several committees at the church, both to help refurbish certain Sunday school rooms and to make decisions concerning the future of their congregation. He was already serving on the town board and the school board, not by election but from unanimous appointments. In some ways, the man was a ridiculous overachiever. But a devastatingly handsome one.

"You know, I'm told I'm a pretty decent painter," Sam said, interrupting her thoughts as she passed by after delivering more platters to customers. "I helped Mom wallpaper the front hallway and the kitchen when I was home on break one year."

Turning to Sam, Sarah slid one hand down to her hip. "Congratulations. I'm happy for you. Tell me, Sam. Is there anything you don't—or *can't*—do?" The man wasn't perfect, but he definitely wasn't one to sit idle.

He chuckled. "I hear you're embarking on a home improvement project and thought I'd put in my bid. A kitchen can be tricky to navigate with those big appliances and outlets to work around." His eyes sparkled as he took another bite of his burger.

Tess must have already contacted Hartmann's. "Word gets around quick. Let me guess. Charlie told you?" Sam nodded.

"I'm happy Charlie can help us," she said. "We're going to try and recruit a few guys and girls from the singles group at church. I'll be sure and mention your offer to the boss."

"Hey, my credentials stand on their own." Sam finished his bite. "Do I really need to prove myself worthy to you?"

Sarah cracked a smile. "I suppose we could take you on for the job. Your previous experience in home beautifying is a much better qualifier than an Air Force Academy education and time spent flying jets, after all."

He raised his hands. "I was going to say I'll work cheap, but whatever works."

After first making sure Myrna wasn't in close proximity, Sarah flicked her dishtowel on his arm. He'd removed his suit coat and draped it on the adjacent counter seat, the outline of his muscled arms visible under his dress shirt. His tan had deepened and offset his eyes and smile to great advantage. The soft-looking, silky dark curls hanging over his collar were a little unruly, tempting her to smooth them into place.

Sam was distracting without even trying, but he seemed oblivious to his sex appeal. How could the man not notice all the women fawning over him wherever he went in town? If he did, he didn't show it. His lack of arrogance made him all the more attractive.

"So? Am I hired for the job?" Sam's blue eyes surveyed her from above the rim from his glass.

Sarah inhaled a quick breath. "I suppose I could hire you for a trial run. Provided your work is satisfactory to the boss, we'll likely keep you on."

He lowered the glass to the counter. "Don't tell me. Tess is the boss?"

"Don't tell her, but yes. She's the one who came up with the brilliant idea. I'd better get back to work, but if you want to stop by tomorrow after work, we're going to get started. Mom and Dad left early this afternoon and they're coming back in a couple of weeks."

When she moved down the counter to the cash register, he followed. Sarah rang the sale and rested her hand on the register drawer after he handed her a twenty dollar bill and told her he didn't need change. "Sam, your meal cost less than five dollars."

"Plus tip. Inflation, you know. If it's not against the rules, add it to your nursing school fund."

"It's not against *my* rules." Myrna moved behind Sarah and angled her head at the register. "Sarah, please close that drawer. But not before you take out the money for that exorbitant tip Daddy Warbucks here is giving you." Giving Sam a wink, Myrna moved on down the counter.

Sarah closed the register, dropped half of the amount into the Benson Fund can and then pocketed the other half. "Happy now?"

Amusement glimmered in his mesmerizing eyes. "Yes. Quite."

"You know, there's something I find fascinating."

"What's that?" After returning his wallet to his back pocket, he crossed his arms on the counter and lowered his voice. "How you can't stop staring at my lips and thinking how much you'd like another kiss?"

"As much as I'd love that, I was reading about a SAM the other day. I had no idea there was such a thing, so imagine my surprise."

"As in surface-to-air missile? So, you're saying my kisses are like a missile launch that disarm you and send your equilibrium fluctuating wildly?"

"Something like that," she said, laughing. Such a flirt. "Now, off with you before your ego inflates even more. I have other customers who need my attention."

"See you later." Sam shrugged into his suit coat, a move which drew Sarah's attention all over again to his broad shoulders. "Do you need me to recruit any more volunteers? It's a proven theory that more hands make light work."

"I think we're all set, thanks."

Stopping outside the big picture window, Sam raised his hand and Sarah returned his wave. She stood in the middle of the diner staring after him like a lovesick fool.

"That man's in love with you." Sarah turned to Perry Sellers, sitting on his usual counter seat, and didn't bother to mask her surprise. Perry rarely spoke, but when he did, it was heartfelt. He gave her a gap-toothed grin and raised his coffee cup in a toast.

"Of course, he is. That man's got excellent taste in women." Jimmy passed by the counter on his way from the kitchen to serve his wife and one of their daughters seated at a window table.

"And our Sarah's got herself a real fine man." Myrna lightly bumped her shoulder as she moved past her and into the kitchen.

"God is good." Sarah couldn't stop smiling as she headed to wait on more customers.

Chapter 30
~~♥~~
Friday, June 15, 1962

Sarah traded glances with Randy Sweet as the Rockbridge Justice of the Peace proclaimed Deborah Marie Harrison and Arnold James Franklin as husband and wife. Randy looked handsome, and he'd told her how pretty she looked as they'd exchanged polite niceties before the ceremony commenced.

"You may now kiss your bride."

"Gladly," Arnie said, lowering his lips to Debbie's. The kiss went on. . .and on. . .and it would have continued even longer if Justice Adams hadn't cleared his throat.

Stealing a glance at Randy, Sarah hid her grin. Poor guy darted glances at the door, the ceiling, and the floor while his cheeks grew pinker. Since she'd kissed Sam—and kissed him a few times since—Sarah no longer felt such embarrassment caused by public displays of affection.

"Sorry." Arnie grinned and accepted the tissue Debbie handed him. "I've waited a long time for this moment, and I got a little carried away." He wiped his lips with the tissue while Debbie reapplied her lipstick. Both actions seemed pointless if not for the waiting photographer.

"Perfectly understandable," Justice Adams said. "Congratulations to you both. I wish you a long, happy and prosperous life together."

"Thank you." Debbie positively glowed, and Sarah had never seen her friend so happy. "We plan on it. Let's get this show on the road, handsome!" Arnie dropped another quick peck on his bride's cheek and then offered his arm. With a blinding smile, Debbie wrapped her hand around her husband's arm and gave Sarah a wink.

Justice Adams shook hands all around and, after the hired photographer snapped a few shots, excused himself from the chambers. Sarah followed the newly-married couple from the room and out into the main corridor while Randy brought up the rear of their small procession.

"I hear you're dating Captain Lewis," Randy whispered to her as they walked down the stairs from the second floor to the main floor together. Their steps echoed on the marble steps. "I'm really happy for you, Sarah. You deserve the best." When they reached the main floor, Randy offered his arm. Hooking her arm through his, she smiled and planted a kiss on his cheek.

"Thank you. So do you, Randy. You're a great guy, and I'm sure the Lord has the right girl for you."

If she wasn't mistaken, the fire captain's cheeks flushed an even deeper pink. "I've, um, actually been seeing Candy Wright for a couple of weeks. Things are going well so far."

Sarah couldn't wait to share this news with Sam. "That's terrific! Candy's a very sweet girl." Belatedly, she realized what she'd said, and she and Randy shared a smile as they walked out into the bright sunshine behind the newlyweds, stopping on the wide front steps for more photos. The day was warm and on the humid side, and Sarah tried not to squint as they posed.

When the photographer finished, Debbie tossed her bouquet of pink roses and gardenias directly into Sarah's hands. Seeing Sarah's raised brow, she shrugged with a sheepish grin. "Why bother with tradition? You're my only attendant, and I have the feeling you're going to be next for the matrimonial march."

With a smile, Sarah buried her nose in the fragrant blooms. Her breath caught as she spied Sam on the sidewalk across the street. What was he doing here in the middle of the afternoon instead of at the bank? Her heart raced at the sight of him. Dressed in his best suit—dark blue, white dress shirt and a deep red tie—he looked very patriotic and more handsome than ever. He leaned against a white sports car, imported from the looks of it. Catching her eye, Sam smiled and waved.

"Dig that car!" Randy said. "That is out of sight." He kissed

Debbie's cheek, and after sharing a few words with Arnie, darted across the street to speak with Sam.

"Is that Sam's car?" Debbie said as Arnie whistled under his breath.

Sarah watched Sam talking with Randy, noting the way Sam ran his hand over the car with what looked like paternal pride. "Must be. He said he had a car on order, so my guess is that it's arrived. Came from England."

"Looks like you'll find out soon enough. Do you have plans with Sam tonight?"

Sarah smiled. "I believe I do, although we hadn't planned anything."

"Seems your Sam is full of wonderful surprises," Debbie said. "That's a great quality in a man. You look gorgeous, sweetie, and you'll knock him out in this beautiful dress. Not that you wouldn't, anyway."

"Thanks." Sarah drew her friend into an embrace and hugged her tight. "I love you, Deb, and I'll be praying for you. God go with you both." She smiled at Arnie standing behind them. "Be safe, and have the best time ever. You both deserve it. Take lots of photos, and when you get back, I can't wait to hear all about the Grand Canyon."

"Will do. I have a new camera and"—Debbie winked at her husband—"if we manage to leave the room, I'll get a few pictures." The adoration in Arnie's eyes, combined with the way he flushed from his collar to his hairline, was sweet.

Sarah smiled and tears filled her eyes as Deb whispered, "Thanks for standing up for me today. I can't imagine this day without you."

After waving and wishing Debbie and Arnie the best—Randy and Sam did the same as the newly married couple pulled away in the car a minute later—Sarah crossed the street. Sam was still speaking with Randy but kept his eyes on her as she made her way to his side.

"Well, I'd better get back to the firehouse now." Randy offered his hand to Sam and the men exchanged a congenial handshake.

"Hello, beautiful," Sam said, turning to her as Randy departed. His gaze skimmed over her with obvious appreciation. "You come bringing your own flowers, I see."

"Hello, handsome. This is a nice surprise. Yes, I caught Debbie's bouquet. No teasing, please. There was no one else to catch it except Randy. He's dating Candy, by the way."

Sam laughed. "That's appropriate. Glad to hear it." Reaching inside the open window of the car, he pulled out a bouquet of a half-dozen pink roses with daisies and baby's breath. "You need to add these to your collection."

"Sam! They're gorgeous. Thank you." Leaning close, Sarah gave him a quick kiss. "You're sporting some fancy wheels. You could have bought a stained glass window in the church with the money it must have taken to buy this baby."

Seeing the quick look of hurt that flitted across Sam's features made her regret those words the minute they left her mouth. Why, oh why, did articulation have to be such a stumbling block for her?

Way to go, Sarah.

"I'm sorry, Sam. It's a beautiful car. I assume this is the one you ordered from England?"

Sarah appeared truly sorry, and after all, she spoke the truth. He needed to suck up his pride and get over it. Sure, the car was an excess, but he'd seen it in a magazine when he was overseas. He wanted Sarah to love it as much as he did.

"That's right. It came in earlier than expected. I begged off at work and drove into Houston this morning to pick it up. Since I had the day off, I figured why not take my girl out for dinner to celebrate?"

After the comment she'd just made about the stained glass window, Sam held his tongue not to say the one thing he shouldn't. Telling Sarah he was her mysterious benefactor wouldn't help his situation. For all he knew, she might resent it, be furious with him, and that would be the end of their relationship before it had a chance to blossom into something more. He'd deal with the situation if and when it arose, but today, he wanted to take her to dinner at Quentin's and hold her in his arms again. He'd thought of little else since they danced at Perry's the other night. Then he'd take her home and kiss her on the front porch. His blood pumped at the thought, and he could hardly wait.

Walking beside the length of the car, Sarah touched it tentatively before withdrawing her hand. She glanced at him as if asking his permission.

"Go ahead. It won't bite." *But I might.* He hid his grin. *Rein it in, man.*

"Tell me about this car." She stooped to peer inside the sleek vehicle, and then ran her hand across the top. He could tell she admired it, and all he could think about was how great she'd look in his new car, all that long blonde hair flowing out the passenger side window. She deserved to ride in a fine car like this. Since he'd decided not to buy a house yet, he could well afford the car, and he'd still had enough funds for the cashier's check for Sarah. She hadn't said another word about it, but neither had she cashed the check.

"It's a Volvo P1800. Four-speed M40 manual transmission with D-type overdrive, and a two-door coupe assembled by Jensen Motors in West Bromwich, England. The engine is a B18 with dual carburetors. Lots of horsepower. You see, Volvo wanted to produce a sports car, but their P1900 had turned into a disaster and sold only sixty-eight cars. Determined to keep going, the designer—a man named Helmer Petterson—drove the first hand-built prototype to the West German headquarters of a manufacturer named Karmann in 1957."

Sam smiled as Sarah leaned against the car and crossed her arms, but he could tell he hadn't lost her interest. "They were ready to build and hit the market by December of 1958. But then," he said, raising one finger, "Karmann's most important customer, Volkswagen, forbade them to take the job."

"Because it would compete with their own sales?"

He nodded, pleasantly surprised she was listening as much as anything else. Most girls would have tuned him out after the first couple of sentences. "Exactly. This is where the plot thickens. Volkswagen threatened to cancel all their contracts with Karmann if they produced the Volvo P1800."

"Poor little Volvo." Sarah gave him a coy grin and tapped the top of the car. "So, don't leave me hanging. What happened then, Mr. Lewis?" She batted her eyes in an exaggerated manner.

Opening the passenger car door, he ushered her inside and then pressed his lips to hers through the open car window. Soft. Tempting. "I couldn't resist."

Sarah's cheeks bloomed with a pretty pink flush, and she ducked her head. "Please finish your story. I'd really like to hear it."

"Okay, since you asked for it." After dropping into the driver's seat a few seconds later, he smiled. "Things appeared hopeless. But then our friend, Helmer Petterson, obtained backing from two financial firms. He planned to buy the components directly from Volvo and market the car himself. By this point, Volvo made no mention of the P1800, and the factory made no comment. But then," Sam said, relishing the smile on Sarah's face and the lively sparkle in her incredible brown eyes, "a press release mysteriously surfaced with a photo of the car. And that pressured Volvo into acknowledging the car's existence."

"A press release, eh?" A slow smile creased Sarah's face. "Sounds like one of those television dramas or a movie where a conniving manipulator does something sneaky and underhanded to coerce a rival." As she listened, Sarah ran her hand over the side of the passenger door, the dashboard, and the interior.

"Perhaps, but I guess we'll never know." Sam snapped his fingers. "Suddenly, the company decided to renew its efforts, the car was presented to the public at the Brussels Motor Show in 1960, Volvo turned to a subcontractor in Scotland to make the body, and then to Jensen Motors in England for assembly of ten thousand cars." He drummed a rhythm on the steering wheel. "And the rest, as they say, is history."

"I love your passion for the history of your car. So, you're telling me this car is still quite rare since only ten thousand were manufactured?"

Sam nodded. "Indeed, it is. At least in this country."

Sarah twisted in the car to face him, fanning the skirt of her pretty blue dress on the seat around her. "That's impressive, but aren't you afraid to drive it? Since it's so rare and valuable?"

"Nope."

Humor sparkled in her gorgeous eyes, and the sunlight brought out the hint of caramel in them. "Here's my challenge to you: tell me in five words or less why you really wanted *this* car."

He didn't have to think about that one. "It's built like a tank."

"Excellent answer. Diplomatic, even." Sarah sat back on the seat with a satisfied smile.

"For the record, I'm not looking to impress another woman when the one I want is beside me."

She stared at him and a smile curved her luscious lips. "It's almost scary how you seem to read my mind sometimes."

What a woman. Sam stole another kiss. "Now, it's time to strap on the seat belt. Time for me to demonstrate how all that dry and boring information is manifested in this car."

"It's not boring since it's obviously so important to you," she said. "I can appreciate your passion, but please don't feel compelled to tell me that story ever again."

He laughed. "Point taken."

"I've never used a belt in a car before." Sarah lifted up slightly in the seat and glanced beneath her, adorable in her confusion. "Where would I find it?"

He should have realized she'd never used a seat belt before. "Here. Allow me." Starting to reach across her, he reconsidered as he angled his body very close to hers in the confines of the small car. So close he caught the sweet scent of her hair. A tantalizing hint of her perfume. So close he wanted to kiss the cute little mole on the left side of her neck. Thinking it best not to give any busybodies passing by on Main Street the wrong idea, he reluctantly pulled back. "It's probably better if you do it."

After a couple of brief instructions, Sarah was safely strapped in and Sam followed suit. Turning the key in the ignition, he relished the purr of the engine.

"That's incredible how smooth it is." Sarah giggled. "Our old Chevy never sounded like that, even when it was new." Just as quickly, her lovely smile faded.

"What's wrong?" Sam paused with his hand on the gear shift.

She looked over at him, her eyes wide and brimming with moisture. "I was thinking how differently things might have been for your family if you'd had seat belts in your car when you lived in San Antonio."

Touched by her compassion, a lump lodged in Sam's throat.

"I'm sorry. I shouldn't have said anything."

"Don't apologize. You're right."

"I never want to hurt you, Sam, but you know how I say the wrong thing sometimes. Just know my intentions are good."

"I know." He glided his hand down the side of her cheek, and she leaned into it. "You don't hurt me by speaking the truth, and you *always* speak the truth, Sarah. I wouldn't want it any other way." He cleared his throat and straightened in the seat. "With all that said, I've been lobbying our state legislators to pass laws making it mandatory for belts to be installed in all consumer and commercial vehicles. They've done research that proves seat belts save lives. Anything to spare another family from having to say good-bye to a loved one way too soon is worth the effort."

"I wish I could have known Rachel. From everything you've told me, she sounds very special. Do you have a picture of her?"

"Matter of fact, I do." Shifting again, he dug in his back pocket for his wallet. Pulling it out, he flipped through the plastic sleeves until he found the one he wanted. "Here she is," he said, holding it up for her to see.

"Oh, she's so pretty! She doesn't look like you at all, though. I'm surprised by the blonde hair." Taking it from him, Sarah ran her finger over the photo. "How old was she in this photo?"

"Seven. It was her birthday, and she'd begged Mom for that dress to go with the party she wanted even more."

Sarah handed over his wallet. "Since she's wearing the dress, I assume she also got the party?"

"Yes." He chuckled at the memory. "Rachel was strong-willed, but she always said things in such a nice way that I never minded doing whatever she wanted. Kind of like someone else I know in this car."

Sarah giggled. "Are you saying I'm demanding?"

"Nope. But you know what you want. There's a difference."

"Is that so?"

"I think so, yes. Rachel was a great kid, and I'm sure the two of you would have been fast friends. But now, it's time to get going."

"Care to share where you're taking me?"

"We have dinner reservations at Quentin's."

"Are you sure?" Sarah glanced at her watch. "It's only four o'clock."

"If you're not hungry, I can move the reservation back a couple of hours. Did you eat lunch?"

"No, as a matter of fact. Mom left a list of things to do at home while she's away, and Tess made sure I was busy since I had the day off." A slow smile creased her lips. "Something tells me my older sister might have been in on your little plan."

"You catch on quick." Sam winked and put the car in gear. "Now, it's time to show you what this baby can really do."

Chapter 31

~~♥~~

Sam was a perfect gentleman—opening the car door for her and then resting his hand beneath her elbow as he escorted her into the restaurant. Not controlling but as a gentle support. Likewise when he moved his arm around her waist as the hostess led them to a quiet corner table. After they were seated and placed their dinner orders, he listened attentively as she told him about Debbie and Arnie's wedding.

Every now and again, his gaze dipped to her lips. Sam was so handsome, and he stirred feelings inside her that she'd never before experienced. Different from the crush she'd had on Sam when she was fourteen. She'd never stared at a man with longing the way she did now, and she tried not to be obvious. Although she understood her feelings were normal, she found it hard to believe Sam found her desirable—a woman he wanted to kiss, hold, and love. When she was with him, he made her *feel* like a woman, and it was so wonderful.

Mrs. Bittenbottom—an ironic name if ever there was one—had drilled it into Sarah and the other teenagers in their coed Sunday school class that being attracted to the opposite sex was normal, not sinful. Even so, she needed to keep her thoughts and. . .urges. . .under control in order to be God-honoring. How was she supposed to stop her thoughts? Recite scripture verses over and over in her mind? Pray out loud?

She knew steering away from physical temptation could be difficult for guys, at least from what Debbie and Tess told her. Maybe a complete hands-off policy was best, but that would be tragic. No hand holding, no sweet taps, no gentle nudges with Sam? No, that wouldn't do. Those private moments were special, and she couldn't believe the Lord wouldn't approve as long as those expressions of affection didn't go too far. Boundaries needed to be established and honored. That had to be the best way.

She might not know much about dating or such matters, but the relationship she shared with Sam was extraordinary, and one she needed to cultivate and cherish. Only the Lord knew what would happen when she went to Austin, but she'd push those thoughts to the back of her mind. For now, the relationship was precious, and it was growing stronger every day.

"I finished *To Kill A Mockingbird* last night," Sam said, stirring Sarah from her daydreaming. "Scout shares a number of qualities and character traits with my favorite tomboy."

Sarah glanced up from her delicious filet mignon in surprise, a thrill of pleasure running through her. To think he'd read the book and actually wanted to discuss it melted her heart a little more. She took a quick drink of her water with lime. "Yes, that's true." She agreed and hoped he'd elaborate.

Sam stabbed another bite of his prime rib. "Great book. I can see why you've read it a few times. You really need to read it more than once to get all the subtleties and subtext."

"Exactly. I'm so happy you read it, Sam."

He grinned. "I'll admit my motives weren't exactly pure."

"What do you mean?" Avoiding his gaze, she took another bite of her delicious mashed potatoes. From its elegant furnishings, soft lighting, and attentive waiters in tuxedos, no wonder Quentin's was the best, most expensive restaurant in Rockbridge.

"I hoped to impress you by reading it."

"Well, you accomplished that goal. No matter your motivation, it's a classic, modern work of literature."

"With age-old truths. Believe it or not, I do read quite a bit, Sarah." Sam chuckled. "I spent more time with books when I was serving in the Air Force than fraternizing, shall we say, with the opposite sex."

She swallowed. "We've already had the Suzie Wong discussion already. Forgive me for once again sticking my big foot in my mouth." *You are so naïve. Get hold of yourself and act like a grownup, not a silly little girl.*

"No, no." Sam reached for her hand where it rested on top of the white linen tablecloth. Clasping it in his, he raised it to his lips.

"So, can you share with me what you enjoyed about it?" she asked after being rendered momentarily speechless by Sam's increasingly tender gestures of affection. "The book, I mean?"

"Scout's intelligent, uncommonly so, as evidenced by the fact she learned to read before she began school. She's confident and she can certainly hold her own with the boys." He chuckled as her smile widened. "Like you, she's a deep thinker. Innocent and good-hearted, she doesn't understand the evils in the world. She's kind and acts with the best of intentions. She might be young, but Scout can see beyond the borders of social niceties and morale. She's baffled by the strong prejudices in others." He hesitated. "Again, like you, Sarah."

Sam's comments quickened her pulse. How she'd wanted to discuss the book with someone else. The ladies in the Rockbridge Book Club—all five of them, including her mother—were planning on reading *To Kill A Mockingbird*. Because they met on bi-weekly Wednesdays at noon, Sarah couldn't join them since she was usually working at that time. Most of the members were middle-aged ladies, and all but one most likely steeped in long-held traditions. Translation: they could be narrow-minded. But perhaps that was another unfair judgment on her part.

Focus.

"Atticus raised his daughter to be an independent thinker," she said after taking another quick sip of her water. "I think Scout is who she is because of his influence, and especially since her mother had died. Atticus encouraged her to climb trees instead of wearing dresses like a proper young southern girl. But, at the same time, he protected her from hypocrisy. I love how, throughout the course of the novel, Scout learns that humanity has a great capacity for evil, but also the *greater* capacity for good."

Sam nodded. "Exactly, and how evil can be mitigated if one approaches people and situations with sympathy and understanding." Sam finished his main course.

"Yes!" she said, excited by his words. "Sam, in your speech the day of your homecoming, you mentioned that very thing—how evil exists from all sides, but how we can never allow it to defeat us. You quoted a verse in Psalm 121, and you talked about how the Lord is continually at work in the world."

He regarded her with appreciation. "Right, and in spite of it all, I know He is. The messages in *To Kill A Mockingbird* have far-reaching implications, and they hit us where we live, so to speak, whether in a city or a small town."

"Agreed." Sarah savored the last bite of her filet mignon. "Rockbridge, like Maycomb in the book, has a slow-paced, good-natured feel. Our citizens band together when needed."

"But also like Maycomb, prejudice still exists as proven by that young couple coming into Perry's. Some, like you, can look past the color of their skin," Sam said. "In their ignorance, others are blinded by presuppositions." He thanked the waiter as he removed their plates. When the man asked if they wanted dessert, Sarah declined but encouraged him to order. "Another time," Sam told the waiter.

"Thank you for this wonderful dinner, Sam. It's been an unexpected treat."

"I'm glad you enjoyed it. Would you like me to take you home now or would you like to go somewhere else?"

"Take me home, but if you're game, let's meet later for a moonlight swim." Sarah hoped he wouldn't construe her suggestion as too forward.

Sam's bright smile gave her the answer. "Sounds like a very good plan."

"You actually remind me of Atticus Finch in a number of ways."

At Thornton's Creek, Sarah treaded water opposite Sam a few hours later. He'd been impatient to spend more time with her. Unable to concentrate on much else, he'd taken a rare nap until his alarm awakened him. Finally. Hurriedly changing out of his clothes, he'd pulled on his swim trunks, all the while wondering if Sarah might wear her swimsuit this time. If she did, he hoped she wouldn't be embarrassed and self-conscious.

While he appreciated her modesty, he couldn't understand why she seemed to think she wasn't pretty, and maybe even overweight. Nothing could be further from the truth on both counts. Sarah was a normal, healthy looking girl, physically fit and not stick-thin like many of the other girls in town, including Tess and Sylvie. In his eyes,

Sarah was beautiful, inside and out. Probably sharing a bedroom with a perpetual beauty queen didn't help her self-esteem.

Sarah's words now pleased him, as did the fact that she'd chosen to wear her swimsuit. With the change in their relationship came a heightened awareness of her womanly curves. When she'd tossed her towel on the creek bank and quickly run into the water, he'd followed her with his gaze every step of the way.

Lord, keep me strong. He'd been thrilled when she suggested meeting him, but the cover of darkness brought its own set of challenges. He needed to be on-guard for both their sakes.

"That's high praise," he said. "Atticus Finch is a complex guy, but he makes a great literary hero." Discussing literature should effectively douse his libido at least temporarily. A good thing.

"For one thing, like you, Atticus is well-respected. He has a strong moral backbone and sees past the faults in people. He admires the good and forgives the bad. Perhaps that's the greatest lesson he passes on to his children—especially Scout—in protecting her innocence. Unlike you," she said, giving him a coy smile and making his pulse race with what she'd say next, "Atticus doesn't fish. He's a hero in a three-piece suit and fights injustice with his words, not his fists. He has a profound impact on his children and many people in the town." She tilted her head to one side, observing him. "Like you."

"I don't have children yet. And don't go thinking I'm perfect, Sarah. If you do, you're bound to be disappointed. I've punched out guys a couple of times." Usually defending a woman's honor overseas, but not any woman he'd dated. Not that Sarah needed to know, but if she asked, he'd tell her.

"Oh, I know that." She laughed and then ducked when he splashed her.

Holding his breath, he swam underwater to her. Grabbing her by the knees, he swept her out of the water and into his arms. "Care to repeat that, Tomboy?"

Wiggling in his arms, Sarah made a big show of trying to escape which only made him strengthen his hold on her. He watched with great amusement as she struggled. When she settled down and stopped resisting him, he dipped his head and kissed her. Moving her arms around his neck, she returned his kiss with a passion that surprised and heated him. Never was he more aware of her curves, the desire she stirred in him.

Way to keep things under control, Lewis.

With reluctance, he released her and gently lowered her back down into the water. He hadn't a clue how much time had passed since they'd been in the creek, but he was relieved no one else was around. "Maybe I shouldn't have done that. You're dangerous to be around."

Sarah ducked beneath the water line again so that only her head and shoulders were visible above the water line. He'd embarrassed her and made her self-conscious all over again. Still, he refused to apologize for admiring her although he'd be making a few confessions to the Lord tonight. Sam smoothed his wet hair away from his face and breathed deeply before giving her a smile. "Let's talk. Talking is good."

"Okay," she said. "It's difficult for a good girl to know how to react sometimes. I know right from wrong, of course." The honesty shining in her eyes, so pure and forthright, floored him all over again.

"The lines can get a little blurry," he said. In that moment, something passed between them. A surge of emotion wrapped around Sam, whispering in his heart, threatening to carry him away.

Sarah is your chosen helpmate. Love her. Cherish her.

"Same for a man who wants to maintain his strong testimony and respect the woman he admires and loves."

Her gaze snapped to his and she stilled her movements in the water. "Did you say love?"

His nod was barely perceptible. "Yes. I've been trying to tell you, and show you, since that night in the diner."

"You said you wanted to win my heart."

"And I do." His voice had grown husky.

Sarah shook her head, her expression difficult to read. "That's not possible."

What?

Moving slowly, she moved closer, her eyes never leaving his. This might prove dangerous. Again. Not sure what to expect, he crossed his arms over his chest. Closer. Closer still. Oh, the things she did to him. Her embarrassment appeared to have dissipated, replaced by a new confidence, an awareness of her sensuality and its powerful effect on him. That could be both good and bad. No longer was this his little neighbor girl, and in no way could he deny this gorgeous creature standing before him now.

This is a new brand of torture, Lord. Keep me strong.

"Retraction." Her voice was barely more than a whisper. She stopped inches away. "Sam, you don't need to earn my heart. You already own it." The corners of her mouth curved. "In fact, you've had it pretty much from the moment you opened the door all those years ago and grabbed the pie out of my hands and nearly burned yours in the process."

"Is that so?" He dropped his arms to his sides.

She nodded with the most enticing smile he'd ever seen. "You can't possibly know this, but I've always considered you my first love."

"I hope your affection for me isn't prompted by guilt for almost burning me."

"No, but you should know I've never thrown spitballs at any other boy. You were the chosen victim."

"I'm not a victim now. I'm incredibly blessed." Unable to resist this woman, Sam moved his hands around Sarah's waist and tugged her close.

She wound her arms around him again, fingering the wet hair on the back of his neck. "I love you, Sam Lewis."

"I love you more than you know, Sarah, and I have a confession."

Her gaze moved upward as she pushed damp hair from his forehead. "What's that?"

"You are my first love. My only love." Moving his hands to her face, he caressed her cheeks with his thumbs, drinking in her features, memorizing them, knowing he'd carry her in his heart forever. "You are the only woman I want to hold in my arms until eternity comes in view."

"Captain," she whispered, lifting her lips to his. "The things you say. Kiss me again, please."

"It's my great honor."

Loving the gleam in her eyes, Sam lowered his head. As he settled into the kiss, he knew something else. He'd be walking her home very soon. He was only a man, after all, and so very human.

Chapter 32

~~♥~~

Saturday Morning, June 16, 1962

The phone rang again for the third time in two minutes, so it must be important. Thoughts of her parents immediately popped into Sarah's mind. What if her father had suffered a second heart attack while he was away from home? The day before Father's Day, no less. That thought sent another pang through her entire body.

Lord, let them be safe.

She was the one who always told her mother and sister to think positively, so she needed to follow her own advice.

Dad's fine. He has to be.

"Do you want me to get the phone?" Sam called from where he was painting the side wall of the kitchen.

"No, I'll get it. Thanks." After wiping her hands on a nearby rag as the phone continued to ring, Sarah lifted the olive green receiver from the wall. She made a mental note to order a new phone in a neutral, non-ugly color.

"Jordan residence. This is Sarah."

"Sarah, this is Danny Marcum." Sarah could hear him panting between words. "Jewell's in labor."

"That's wonderful! Thank you for letting me know. We'll be praying—"

"I can't get hold of Doc Meriweather, and Jewell's contractions are coming fast and furious now. Doc Hastings won't be here until next week, so I was hoping you could come and help us."

Where could Doc be? Fear coursed through Sarah and she hoped he wasn't off on a bender somewhere. No time to find him now. This being Jewell's third child, the baby could come quickly. From what she knew, her other two pregnancies had been routine and resulted in easy, natural deliveries. Sarah prayed that'd be the case this third time around.

"How far apart are the contractions?" She chewed her thumbnail.

"Five or six minutes apart, best as I can tell. I don't want to take the chance of drivin' her over to the hospital in Springhaven. That'd take time I don't think she's got. Jewell's scared. We both are. I don't know who else to ask, and we figured since you're planning to go to nursing school, you might know what to do. Please, Sarah. I'm begging you."

"Of course, Danny." She struggled to stay calm and not sound equally desperate. "Don't worry. Everything will be fine. Jewell's pregnancy has been smooth with no complications, right?"

"Yeah, and she's full-term." She heard the relief in Danny's voice. "Doc Meriweather said the baby's in the right position. Least that's what he said when we saw him last week."

"All very good signs," Sarah said. "Okay, Danny. Sit tight, okay? I'm on my way." She frowned as she hung up the phone. Sit tight? What a ridiculous thing to say. As if they'd be out touring the countryside.

Concern etched Sam's features. "What's up?" He put his paint roller in the drip pan and replaced the lid on the can of yellow paint on the floor beside him.

"Jewell Marcum is about to give birth. Doc's not around and Danny's asked for my help. Can you drive me over to their house?"

"Sure, but shouldn't we change our clothes first?"

At first, his words didn't compute. "What?"

Sam gestured to his paint-splattered shorts and T-shirt. "Fresh paint. Turpentine. Strong fumes."

"You're probably right. We should both change." She eyed him up and down. "Let me grab some of Dad's things for you."

He raised a skeptical brow. "No offense, but your dad's clothes would swim on me. I'll run home and be back to get you in five minutes. Promise," he called to her over one shoulder as he rushed through the living room. The screen door banged behind him.

After telling Tess, Charlie and the others working in the living room what was happening and asking them to pray, Sarah flew into the bedroom. She tugged her shirt over her head in one swift motion and kicked off her shoes. Unzipping her jeans, she wiggled out of them and left them with the shirt in a heap on the floor. She ran to the dresser and pulled out a pair of khaki shorts and a clean pink T-shirt. After retying the laces on her tennis shoes, she tucked her house key into her pocket and ran through the house and out the front door. Behind her, Sarah heard Tess call to her that they'd be praying.

Lord, it's you and me. I need you beside me. Please guide me every step of the way.

True to his word, Sam pulled the truck in front of the house within a few seconds of her darting outside. "Do you know what to do?"

She hopped inside the truck and slammed the door as he drove away from the curb. "Haven't a clue," she muttered. "Thanks for the vote of confidence."

"I didn't mean it that way. I was only asking a question."

Sarah frowned. Why was she being snippy with him? "Sorry. I don't mean to be sarcastic." She chewed on her thumbnail again. "Where's Volvo today? Not up for company?"

"Volvo's in the garage. It was easier to bring the truck since Dad doesn't need it today." Sarah felt his gaze on her but avoided looking at him. "You ask me, I think your sarcasm is your defense mechanism."

"Is that right?" She leaned against the passenger door, crossed her arms and stared at him, unsure whether to laugh or throw something. Unfortunately, she had nothing at her ready disposal to use as a projectile. Joseph Lewis always kept the truck in immaculate condition, which was to his credit.

"If you can get over yourself for a few hours," she said, "the simple fact of the matter is that Danny called me, and—with God's help—I'm going to do everything in my power to make sure this baby is delivered healthy."

With a nod, appearing more serious, Sam gunned the truck around the corner onto Main Street.

"Slow down," she cautioned. "You don't want to get a ticket in front of the bank. Being pulled over in front of your place of business? That'd be real smart."

"Emergency situations sometimes call for it. Tommy would cut me a break."

She sank farther down into the seat. "So you're not above bribing the law? Good to know, I have to say."

"No. More like Tommy's a good guy. He'd do the same for anyone speeding to the aid of a woman in the throes of labor." His brow creased. "That's what it's called, right? The throes of—"

"Yes, that's what it's called." She suppressed a grin.

"God sure knew what He was doing in terms of women being the child-bearers."

"I agree," she said. "Contrary to what some believe, I don't think it's a curse. It's an honor and privilege. For one thing, God certainly knew men couldn't handle the pain."

He chuckled. "How many children do you want?"

"I have you, so my quota's currently full, thank you."

Sam's laugh was hearty. "I guess I deserved that one." He reached for her hand, and she immediately gave it to him. Sarah's pulse raced, wondering what she'd find when they reached Jewell. Shouldn't be long now.

Glancing out the front window, Sarah's eyes widened in horror as she spied a red ball rolling into the street. Usually a running child followed a rolling ball. "Sam," she said, putting her hand on his arm. From the corner of her eye, she caught a flash of blue on the right and fast approaching the street.

"Sam! Stop!" Sarah waved her hand to the front window as the ball rolled in front of the truck. Her heart pounded so hard she felt the blood rush to her head.

Slamming on the brakes, Sam threw his arm across her, preventing her from flying forward. At the same time, Sarah put her foot on the dashboard and pushed against the force. A second later, slumped back against the seat, she breathed heavily. Dazed, she watched as Jeff Arnold's dad yelled for his son to stay put and darted into the street to retrieve the ball.

"Sorry about that, Captain Lewis! Thanks for stopping," he called as he ran back to the sidewalk and grabbed hold of his young son's hand.

"Don't mention it." Sam blew out a sigh and turned to her. "Are you okay?"

"I will be." She was still shaking. "Thanks for protecting me. Again. I might have gone. . ." No need to state the obvious. Especially with Sam, he knew firsthand the potential dangers and consequences. Without Sam's strength and quick move to protect her, she could have flown through the front windshield.

"You were right to tell me to slow down, and I should have listened." Crossing his arms on the steering wheel, Sam lowered his head. "Seems God had the same thought."

She put her hand on his upper arm, giving him a light squeeze. "You had no way of knowing that would happen. Jeff's okay, and that's the main thing. Hopefully, he'll learn a valuable lesson."

"Let's hope so." Someone honked from the vehicle behind them. With a frown, Sam lifted his head and straightened in the seat before continuing down the street at a snail's pace. The muscles in his jaw flexed when the person behind them honked again. "Did that numbskull not see what could have happened back there? Good thing for him I don't recognize him."

Sam didn't know everyone in town since he'd been gone so many years. Sarah refrained from glancing out the back window. Better that way in case she knew the numbskull. She preferred to think the best of people until they proved otherwise.

Leaning her elbow on the open window ledge, she stared at the passing houses and the residents of Rockbridge working in their yards. The day was warm and beads of perspiration dotted her forehead that had as much to do with nerves as the actual temperature. As Sam drove them toward the outskirts of town where Jewell and Danny lived, Sarah told Sam about Doc Meriweather's disappearing act. From the tightness of his jaw, Sam must suspect the same thing she did: Doc had gone off on a drinking binge.

Sam fisted his hand on the steering wheel. "The man's a licensed practitioner of medicine. If he wasn't already retiring, I'd bring him up on charges."

Sarah put her hand on his arm again as he turned onto the street where the Marcums lived. "I feel the same way, but our anger at Doc isn't going to help us right now. We've already had one wake-up call today. I think we should pray, okay?"

"You're right." Although he still sounded disgruntled, Sam

reached for her hand as soon as he pulled to the curb in front of the Marcum house. She held on tight and said a quick prayer.

"Amen. Let's go." Not waiting on formality, Sarah threw open the door and slid down from the truck.

"You couldn't wait five seconds?" Sam called after her.

She rolled her eyes but didn't have time to deal with the man's ego. "I appreciate your gentlemanly ways under normal circumstances," she said over her shoulder, "but time could be of the essence here. You'll get over it." Running to the front door, she knocked lightly. She elevated her voice and spoke through the screen door. "Danny! It's me, Sarah. Sam's with me."

"Come on in. We're in the bedroom!" Danny called to her. "First room on the left."

Entering the house, following Danny's direction, Sarah prayed their two small children weren't in the house. "Where are Nell and Scott?"

"With my mom in Houston," Jewell rasped as she entered the bedroom. "She came and got the kids last week." Sweat dotted the expectant mother's face and she was flushed. Danny sat on the bed beside her, holding his wife's hand. Jewell gave her a wan smile. "My water broke and the contractions are four minutes apart now." Her gaze moved to Sam standing in the doorway.

"Sam's here to help, if that's okay."

"Fine." Rising from the bed, Danny offered his hand to Sam. "Did you learn how to birth babies overseas, Captain Lewis?"

Sam cracked a small smile. "Can't say that I did. This is a first, but Sarah will take good care of you. She's in charge." To Sarah's surprise, his cheeks flushed. "I'll, um, step out in the hall. Let me know what you need."

Jewell's face contorted and she grunted. "I think I'm gonna need to push soon."

"Danny, I'll need a few clean towels," Sarah said, setting the process in motion. "We'll also need scissors and some type of cording. You'll need to sterilize them first."

The poor guy looked petrified. "How do you reckon I do that?"

"We'll boil them in hot water for a few minutes." Sam put one hand on Danny's shoulder and guided him from the room. "Let's get a pot of water on the stove and then go find those things."

"I'll only be gone a couple of minutes," Danny said to Jewell before following Sam into the hallway.

"It's okay, sweetie. Just do what Sarah says."

"I need to scrub my hands and arms." Sarah glanced around the bedroom. "Where's the nearest bathroom?"

"Over there." Jewell angled her head to the right. "It's our private bath."

"Great. Be right back." Turning on the warm water, quietly singing "Trust and Obey" all the while, Sarah lathered the soap, taking extra care to scrub in between her fingers and beneath the fingernails. Finished, she air dried her hands, wringing them as she walked back into the bedroom.

"I heard you singing in there," Jewell said. "It was comforting."

Sarah rearranged the pillows and settled Jewell on them. "Sam would disagree, but thank you."

"He's a good man." Jewell shifted her position on the bed and grimaced. "Another contraction," she managed between breaths.

Sarah helped her breathe through it and then grabbed a damp, cool washcloth from a bowl on the nightstand, pressing it on the other woman's brow. "You're doing great. Take a few more deep breaths."

"I can tell Sam respects you, and he always speaks so highly of you."

"We've been friends a long time." Sarah lowered the washcloth into the bowl, swirling it, and then gently wrung out the excess water.

Jewell managed a small smile. "The best marriages start out that way. That's what happened with me and Danny. He told me in fifth grade he was going to marry me one day. As you can tell, we're following God's command to be fruitful and multiply." She leaned back on the pillows, breathing in deeply and then exhaling. Jewell closed her eyes and then reopened them a few seconds later. "Think you and Sam might get married? If you do, I'll be there with bells on. Everybody's rootin' for you two to get together. You seem made for each other."

"Sam and I haven't been seeing each other long," Sarah said. "Since I'm going to Austin, I'm not sure what's going to happen. Only the Lord knows at this point, but I trust Him to guide us." Although it was true, Sarah hoped she didn't come across as holier-than-thou. Right, like she had all the answers. Needing to do something with her hands, she dipped the washcloth in the bowl of cool water again before pressing it over Jewell's forehead and cheeks.

"That feels good. Thanks. Everyone can see how you and Sam only have eyes for each other, Sarah. You probably don't even realize it, but that man's face lights up the second you walk in a room. I'm sure that's why he parks himself at the diner whenever he's not workin' at the bank." Jewell stopped to breathe through another contraction.

Danny rushed around the corner and into the room with Sam on his heels. "Okay, I got all the stuff you asked for."

"Thanks." Sarah instructed Danny where to put the supplies and then asked him for a clean flat sheet and some more towels.

"I'll get them, Danny." Sam darted out of the room and was back in less than a minute. Handing over the towels and the sheet, he started to back out of the room. "Sarah, do you have a minute?"

She glanced at Jewell.

"Go ahead," Jewell said. "Trust me, you'll hear me if I have a really strong contraction."

"I'll only be a minute," Sarah promised as she followed Sam.

He turned to face her as soon as they'd moved out of the hallway and into the living room. "I'll keep trying to call Doc Meriweather."

"Thanks. That's a good idea. Until then, let's hope all those home births I witnessed in your garage will somehow help me in this situation." Sarah shrugged and hoped the fact she was scared witless didn't show. "Pretty much the same process, I imagine. Right?" Try as she might, her lower lip trembled.

"We did watch a lot of puppies and kittens being born, didn't we?" Sam stepped close and covered her hands with his. "Pretty much the same process. Think of it that way and allow nature—and God—to take the natural course. I want to pray for you."

Tears filled her eyes. "I'd really like that." Sarah bowed her head as Sam offered his prayer to the Lord, asking for His mercy and grace on Jewell and her unborn child. He prayed for Danny to remain calm and guidance for Sarah as she assisted in the home birth.

"We know you know this child, Lord, and we ask that you bless his or her birth and bring this child safely into the world," Sam said. "Wherever Doc is, heavenly Father, please keep him sober and bring him here safely, too. We ask these things in the precious name of your Son, Jesus. Amen."

"Amen," Sarah said, wiping away a tear.

Pulling her into his arms, Sam whispered, "Peace I leave with you; my peace I give to you; not as the world gives do I give to you. Do not let your heart be troubled, nor let it be fearful." He brushed a soft kiss on her forehead.

"Thank you, Sam." Sarah squeezed his hands before releasing them.

His eyes met hers, and he tilted her chin. "You can do this, Tomboy."

Sam's faith in her meant so much. She only prayed Danny and Jewell's trust in her wasn't misplaced. No matter what, the Lord had brought her here. A rush of something—only the Lord knew, but energy, confidence, and a determined spirit—surged through her. As if the Lord whispered in her heart, *You can do this, beloved daughter.*

"Sarah! I think you'd better get in here now!" Her eyes widened at Danny's call, and her pulse raced.

"Go," Sam said. "I hope to hear a baby's cries soon."

Without another word, Sarah darted from the room.

Chapter 33

~~♥~~

What was taking so long? Sam had no point of reference for these things, but he'd thought—being Jewell's third baby—he would have heard a baby's cries by now. Why was he so nervous? Anyone would think *he* was the expectant father by the way he paced the living room floor. He couldn't remember the last time he chewed on his fingernails, and he forced himself to stop. He tried sitting on the couch and reading a fishing magazine. Didn't work. Finding a deck of cards on the coffee table, he played Solitaire. That didn't work either. After pacing the floor some more, he wandered into the kitchen and tried to call Doc. No answer.

Shaking his head, he replaced the receiver, careful not to vent his frustrations on an inanimate object. The new physician, Dr. Hastings, couldn't get to town soon enough. The citizens of Rockbridge didn't have many emergencies, mostly general practitioner stuff and routine checkups. But in times like now, they needed a reliable doctor who'd at least answer his phone.

Leaning against the kitchen wall, Sam wrapped his arms over his middle. "Lord, please be with Sarah. Be with Jewell and Danny. Calm my nerves. Help me get through to Doc. And, if there's a way you can use me in all this, please let me know what it is. I feel useless." He darted a glance at the clock on the wall. A little more than an hour had passed since Sarah had been called back into the bedroom. He could hear Sarah speaking in low tones, and Danny was coaching Jewell. From where he stood, he could take heart that everything seemed to be taking its natural course. Whatever that meant. He had no knowledge of labor and delivery, and he was more than happy not to know. How did men go through the endless waiting? How did women go through nine months carrying a child? And then deliver the baby? Awesome as it was, he considered the entire process one of God's biggest miracles.

Crossing the kitchen, Sam opened an upper cabinet and then pulled out a glass. After filling it with tap water, he slumped into a chair by the table and lowered his head. Not knowing what else to do, he prayed. For now, that was the best thing he could do. And he'd keep on praying. As long as it took.

Sarah bit her lower lip. Sweat trickled a quick path down her forehead. She swiped it away with the back of her hand and pursed her lips.

When I am afraid, I will put my trust in you.

"What is it?" Jewell said, her voice cracking. "What's wrong? Why can't I get my baby out?"

"Honey, relax." Sarah kept her voice steady. "Your baby doesn't want to come out quite yet. Don't you worry about a thing. We're going to get this done, but I need you to take some more deep breaths, okay?"

"Sure. Just tell me what to do." Jewell's face twisted with pain.

From what Sarah could tell, this baby was larger than Jewell's other two children. Above all, she didn't want to worry Jewell or Danny.

Lord, help me. Help this child. She'd lost track of how many times she'd repeated the same prayer, over and over. If ever she needed the Lord by her side, it was now. She hadn't heard anything from Sam in a while, but he must be worried, too.

Danny had been so patient and loving, bless his heart. He'd wiped his wife's brow until Jewell barked at him not to touch her anymore. Irritable and frustrated, she'd swatted his hand. He'd put the washcloth back in the bowl and sat quietly by her side. When Sarah glanced at him, he'd given her a slight nod of his head. He knew best, and his assurance gave her comfort.

"Oh, I feel another contraction. This one's coming a lot harder and faster."

"Okay, then, here we go." Sarah did a quick check, and Jewell's cervix appeared fully dilated. "I can see the baby's head!" *Thank you, Jesus.* A rush of adrenaline ran through her. "It shouldn't be too much longer now." The baby had a lot of hair. Wow. Somewhere in the background, she heard the phone ringing.

"Do you want me to answer it? It might be Doc Meriweather," Sam called.

"Thanks. The phone in the kitchen has the longest cord." Danny rose to his feet and took hold of Jewell's hand again. Although his brow was furrowed, he appeared calm. This time Jewell didn't push her husband away but grabbed on tight. "Come on, honey, you can do this," he said. "Just a few more pushes and you'll get that little one out."

"It's Doc," Sam said from the hallway.

"Tell him the baby's head is crowning," Sarah said. "Ask him if Jewell needs to stop pushing."

"Are you sure about that?" Danny eyed her with a raised brow.

"No," Sarah said through gritted teeth, "but I think she might tear something if she pushes too hard."

"I don't know if I can stop!" Jewell wailed. "Don't make me stop! It's burning, and I think my baby finally wants to come out." She blinked hard, her eyes wide, imploring her for answers.

"Try your best to hold on just a minute." Sarah squeezed Jewell's hand. She couldn't imagine what she was going through now, but hopefully her presence gave the other woman comfort.

"Doc says to stop pushing," Sam said, his voice elevated, "or you might tear. . .something important. Hang on."

Sarah breathed through her anxiety.

"Sorry for doubting you, Sarah." Danny sounded apologetic.

"No worries," she said, wiping her forehead and giving him what she hoped was a reassuring smile. A soft-spoken man, he'd worked at the town's one gas station since he was a kid. She'd hated to ask, but she was thankful Danny had thoroughly scrubbed his hands before she and Sam had arrived at the house.

A few seconds later, Sam spoke again. "Doc wants to know if it's still burning?"

When Jewell shook her head, Danny called out that information to Sam. "What's Doc say we should do next?"

A few seconds later, she heard Sam's response. "Is she feeling a numbness in the, um, general area?"

Sarah darted a quick glance in the direction of the hallway. Although she couldn't see him, she assumed Sam was leaning against the wall with the phone against his ear. How thankful she was that he'd insisted on coming with her.

"Yes," Jewell said, gasping and collapsing against the pillows.

"He says that means the baby's head is stretching the tissue and blocking the nerves."

"Right. It's like a natural anesthetic," Sarah said.

"Doc says to continue to fight the urge to push. Lean back and try to go limp as best you can."

"Got that one covered," Danny said. "What else?"

"Relax the muscles of the perry-knee-all floor or something like that. Sorry, I don't know these words."

Sarah bit her lip to stifle her smile. What an adorable man. "Jewell, just focus on your deep breathing," she said in the most soothing tone she could muster.

"Allow the contractions to do the work for you." Sam's voice suddenly sounded stronger and more confident. "Straight from Doc."

"Sweetie, remember when Scotty was born." Still holding Jewell's hand, Danny wiped her brow and leaned over to kiss her cheek. "You're doing great. This part will probably happen pretty fast."

"I sure hope you're right." Jewell let out a small cry and then squeezed Danny's hand so tight his fingers turned white. "Love you, Sugarbun."

Danny brushed the back of his hand over her cheek. "You, too, Dumpling."

Sarah swallowed another smile.

"Doc's over in Springhaven," Sam said next. "He'll be here in about twenty minutes, barring any bad traffic."

"Guess that means we might be on our own." Danny's words seemed intended more for Jewell than for Sarah.

Thank you, Lord. In case of any complications, at least Doc would arrive soon. She'd keep going and hope for the best.

Rotating her aching neck, Sarah nodded. "We've gotten this far along. We'll be just fine."

"I'm holding down the fort with prayer out here," Sam called.

"Thank you, Captain Lewis!" Jewell elevated her voice and then frowned as another contraction began. "Here we go again."

A sense of calm rushed over Sarah and she breathed through another push with Jewell. Everything would be all right. She *knew* it. "That's it, Jewell, honey. You're doing great, and it won't be long now."

Hearing a loud screech outside and then seeing Doc's truck, Sam ran to the front door and swung it wide open.

"How is she?" Doc hobbled across the front yard with his medical bag.

"Almost there, I think. They're back here." Sam stopped in the hallway while Doc went into the bedroom.

A baby's cry sounded. Healthy, loud and piercing.

Praise God.

Sam slumped against the wall, his heart full. He waited in the hallway, finally shifting from one foot to the other, impatient as anything. It wouldn't be right for him to barge in on their private family moment. Doc spoke in low tones, and he heard Danny and then Sarah. None of them sounded panicked, and everything was apparently under control. The baby's cries quieted and then Sam heard Jewell. When Sarah spoke again, she sounded breathless. After a few moments of silence, he heard something that sounded almost like a small sob. Had something happened?

Dear Lord, let everything be all right. Something squeezed his insides hard. He couldn't take not knowing what was happening. "Sarah?" He moved closer to the doorway of the bedroom. "Everything okay in there?"

"Come on in, Sam." The invitation came from Danny. "She's perfectly fine. Everyone is."

Rounding the corner and heading into the bedroom, Sam stopped short. Sarah sat on the floor, her knees raised and her hands clasped around them. Half laughing, half crying, tears streamed down her face. He moved his gaze to Doc and Danny. The baby was on Jewell's stomach, and the young mother looked happy but exhausted. From what Sam could tell, Danny was preparing to cut the cord.

Sam averted his gaze and focused on Sarah. Falling to his knees on the floor beside her, he gathered her in his arms, rocking her back and forth. Then he noticed blood on Sarah's hands, on her shirt. Everywhere. His head pounded and a wave of nausea washed over him.

"I don't feel so hot. . ."

Slumping forward, Sam reached for the bedpost as the room spun out of control around him.

Chapter 34

~~♥~~

"What happened?" After Sam struggled to rise up on his elbows, he plopped back down on his back. He was lying on the bed in Jewell and Danny's guest bedroom. Sarah sat in a chair beside the bed, her eyes closed. Had he actually fainted?

He groaned. "Don't even tell me."

"Okay, then." Her eyes fluttered open. "I won't."

"First time that's ever happened. You'd think a guy who'd spent time in the service would—"

"I happen to think it's adorable."

"You're going to be a nurse and you think fainting is adorable? That's a great bedside manner." He moaned and scrubbed one hand over his face. "Still think Rockbridge is boring?"

She crossed her arms and surveyed him. "While you were passed out"—she grinned when he grunted—"I was thinking you deserve a reward for being so wonderful in coming. You didn't have to stay, but I'm glad you did."

"Right. Like I would drop you off in front of the house, wish you a nice home birth and take off down the street." He caught her expression and needed to cut the sarcasm. "I don't need any kind of reward. You're the one who did all the work." Sitting up on the bed, Sam swung his legs over the edge. Whoa. Maybe that was a little too fast. Closing his eyes for a second, he deep breathed. When he felt as though he could stand without fainting, he focused on Sarah.

"I was so proud of you today, Sarah. You were absolutely

fantastic. Far out," he said with a grin. "Are Jewell and the baby okay?" He rubbed the back of his neck, chastising himself for not remembering to ask about them first thing.

Oh, that smile of hers was a thing of rare beauty, like a slow-blooming rose.

"Let's go find out." Reaching for his hand, Sarah tugged until he reached a standing position. "You okay there, Captain?"

"Yeah. I think." The room spun a bit, but he'd be fine. "Just need to get my sea legs."

"Is it the Ménière's Disease?"

"No, I don't think so. To be honest, I hadn't even thought about that. How did I get moved to the bed in here, anyway?"

"I picked you up and threw you over my shoulder. How do you think?" When he frowned, Sarah shrugged. "Danny did most of the work, but I picked up the rear. I mean," she said, her cheeks flushed a deep pink, "I held your *legs*. You were out cold. Actually, I've never seen you so peaceful or quiet. It was rather nice for a change."

Sam chuckled. "Don't make me take back those compliments, but you can tuck me in anytime you want, Miss Jordan."

"Flirt."

"Only with you."

Laughing softly, Sarah canvassed the room and picked up a red T-shirt from the top of the bureau. She returned to his side and handed it to him, her eyes skimming over his shirt. "Here. You should put this on." When he hesitated, she practically shoved it in his hands. "Jewell told me to grab it for you."

Glancing down at his shirt, Sam grimaced. Blood stains were smeared over much of his T-shirt. "You're right." He looked back at the bed. "I hope I didn't get blood on the sheets."

"Don't worry about it. I offered to strip the sheets and do the laundry, but Jewell told me her mother's coming in a couple of hours and she'd take care of them."

Sarah had changed out of the T-shirt she'd worn earlier. The way the white cotton blouse hung on her, slipping off one shoulder to reveal her smooth, tanned skin, he figured Jewell had loaned it to her. He silently thanked Jewell. Although it wasn't the best time to think of such things—highly improper, actually—that glimpse of Sarah's slender shoulder was nothing short of alluring. Added to that, her cheeks were still flushed and her lips looked entirely kissable. His focus moved to that tiny mole on her neck.

Stop staring at her like a man who hasn't dined in a month. Forcing his gaze away from Sarah, Sam took the shirt she offered.

"What?" Sarah tilted her head. She honestly hadn't a clue as to the thoughts running through his mind. His very male mind.

"Are you going to watch me change?"

She gaped at him. "Does it matter? I've seen you without your shirt on at the creek a number of times, you realize."

"Considering we're in a bedroom, it seems sort of intimate in an awkward way."

"Oh, good grief." She turned her back to him, shaking her head.

"I just thought in case you're having trouble keeping your hands off me." He couldn't believe he'd voiced that comment. What a dumb thing to say.

Her shoulders moved up and down. At least she found his idiocy amusing. Whipping the soiled shirt over his head, he held it in his hand, not knowing where to put it. He could ask her to hold it, but no. Stuffing it between his legs, he tugged on Danny's shirt. After grabbing the stained shirt, he balled it between his hands.

"All done now. You can turn around." Danny was a beefier guy than he was, and the T-shirt hung on him worse than Jewell's top did on Sarah. He should tuck the shirt in his shorts, but what did it matter?

"You look great in red," she said. "You should wear it more often. The color really brings out your eyes." Gesturing for him to hand over his T-shirt, she retrieved a plastic bag from beside the chair and stuffed the shirt inside. When she started to leave, he stopped her with one hand on her arm.

Turning back toward him, Sarah dropped the bag as he pulled her into his arms. She inched her warm hands around his midsection and her teasing smile filled him with the need to kiss her. "This is getting to be a very nice habit with you."

"I hold those in the medical profession in the highest esteem," he said. "I don't know how you can think about seeing blood on a daily basis."

"Then we're even." Was that a giggle?

He cocked a brow. "I beg your pardon?"

"I don't know how you can work around money all the livelong day."

"Oh, it's not so bad."

"It's dirty and full of germs for one thing."

"Huh." Moving his hands to the middle of her back, clasping his hands together in a tight hold preventing her escape, he leaned in for a kiss. Brushing his lips lightly over hers, he smiled and then settled in more fully.

"We're in a bedroom, remember," she said against his lips.

"All the better." He started to deepen the kiss, but she stopped that soon enough when she pushed against his chest with both hands. Playfully, but with a firmness that told him he'd gotten out of line. She was right. Regrettably so.

"Sam, please. What's gotten into you?" She didn't seem upset.

You. That came out wrong in his own mind, so he'd definitely get his face slapped if he said it out loud. He'd deserve it, too. Still, it was true that this woman had settled in every part of him.

He lightly skimmed his thumb over her cheek and drank his fill of her. If he stared all day long, he would never get enough of her. "I'm sorry, Sarah. You're just. . ." He smiled and ran a hand over her hair. "Completely irresistible."

"Don't be sorry," she said, sounding slightly breathless as she smoothed down the front of his T-shirt. "To be continued another time. But, um, not in a bedroom." When she winked with a grin—saucy and feisty—Sam knew he'd do anything for this girl. Without a doubt, Sarah was his perfect match.

"I'll definitely keep that in mind." He followed Sarah back down the hallway and into the master bedroom. "Sorry about fainting," he said to Danny, Doc and Jewell. Might as well acknowledge his shortcomings before someone else did. "I didn't mean to cause a scene, but I guess I can kiss my macho image good-bye." After he heard Sarah snort, he grunted. He'd pay her back later for that one.

"That's okay." Danny winked at Sarah. "Now we know you're human."

Awed by the sight of the sleeping baby in Jewell's arms, Sam moved closer to the bed. "Boy or girl?"

"Boy," Danny said, sounding proud as a new papa should. Sam couldn't imagine how it must feel to know you'd created a new life. Hopefully, one day he'd experience the joy of bringing children into the world. In his heart, he couldn't imagine anyone other than Sarah being the mother of his kids.

"You can hold him, if you want," Jewell said. She lifted her sleeping son, offering him to Sam.

"Only for a minute." Cradling the baby in his arms, Sam marveled at his perfection. Truly, this child represented God's promise, innocence in its purest manifestation. "He's a treasure." He supported the infant's head with one hand and lightly ran his finger over the child's cheek. From the corner of his eye, he caught Sarah watching him with a look of wonder as he smoothed his palm over the baby's head. "Look at all that dark hair. Have you given him a name?"

Turning her head, Jewell smiled at Sarah. "Jordan. In honor of the one who helped bring him into the world."

Sam snapped his attention to Sarah. Her eyes were full, and she lowered her gaze.

"That's a great name." He'd never heard Jordan as a first name before, but he loved it.

"Danny and I decided that boy or girl, we were going to name our baby Jordan."

"You should have seen Sarah," Danny said. "She caught him. I mean, my boy came flying out like nothin' I've seen before."

Doc Meriweather chuckled. "I'm thankful you could be here, Sarah. All that time on a softball field came in handy, eh?"

Sarah nodded, wiping away a tear. Could any woman ever be more beautiful?

"Well done. He's incredible. Congratulations to you both." With the utmost care, Sam transferred Jordan back into his waiting mother's arms.

As they returned to the truck a short time later, Sam draped his arm around Sarah's shoulders. Both walked slowly, exhausted in the best way imaginable, leaning on each other for support.

After he climbed in behind the wheel and turned the key in the ignition, Sam heard Sarah's quiet laughter. At first, he thought she might be crying, caught up in the emotion of the day. He quirked a brow and sat back, waiting. "Are you okay, baby?"

"Yes." She sniffled and wiped her fingers beneath both eyes. So, she *was* both laughing and crying. "I can't believe they named their son Jordan. That's incredibly precious to me."

"I agree, but why does that make you laugh?"

She leaned her head back against the seat. "I researched the name

'Jordan' for a school project once. It means 'descend' or 'flow down.'" She waved her hand and closed her eyes. "Forget it. I'm just tired and being silly."

"No, you're right," he said as he pulled the truck onto the road. "It's an appropriate name in more ways than one. In my eyes, the fact that Jordan is the name of the river where John the Baptist baptized Jesus also makes it mighty special."

Sarah's eyes fluttered open and she turned her head to look at him. "Thank you again for being with me today, Sam. You're precious to me, too, you know."

"As you are to me." He dared not dwell on those gorgeous brown eyes or he might run them off the road. Faint circles ringed her eyes, but her face was still slightly flushed from the events of the last few hours.

"Welcome. I'm thankful everything turned out so well. God's answer to prayer. I was driving myself nuts when I didn't know what was happening. The only thing that finally settled me down was when I started to pray." He reached for her hand, an action as natural as breathing. As he drove, he caressed the side of her hand with his thumb. Glancing at their joined hands after he pulled into the driveway a short time later, Sam left the engine idling. For a couple of minutes, he sat transfixed, unable to move, simply observing her. Sarah had fallen asleep, and her chest rose and fell with each quiet breath.

Seeing how she'd reacted in a medical emergency only confirmed what he'd known all along: she'd be a great nurse. If he hadn't already known it, he was filled with complete admiration for the woman beside him. She was compassionate and tender yet tough enough to withstand the intense emotions and stress. By not panicking, she'd kept everyone else around her calm. And she'd dealt with the sight, the smell, the everything of blood. Ugh. *Nothing but the blood* took on an entirely new meaning. Sam shuddered again before guilt consumed him. His Savior had died on a cross, beaten to a bloody pulp, had the oxygen drained from his lungs, and all for what? A military man who was so cowardly he fainted at the sight of a little blood?

I'm not worthy, Father. Thank you for loving me enough. Sam bowed his head for a few moments, allowing a peace to flow over him. He prayed once more, thanking the Lord for strong souls like Sarah who embraced the daunting rigors and demands of the medical profession. He'd stick with handling financial matters and endure the teasing from the woman he loved.

The woman I love. He'd loved her almost immediately upon his return to Rockbridge. She'd enchanted him when he'd spied her standing beside Tess at the parade. Tall, statuesque, and composed. Grownup and lovely. She'd impressed him by the way she'd held her own in the face of Kathy Parker's unkind taunts. When he'd talked with her privately at the counter, he'd admired her obvious intelligence and the fire in those gorgeous brown eyes.

Gifting her with the anonymous cashier's check was probably the best thing he could have done. Sure, he'd miss her like crazy when she left for UT, and he'd be putting a lot of miles on Volvo—he'd adopted Sarah's name for his car—traveling the highway between Rockbridge and Austin.

Slipping his hand out from beneath Sarah's, Sam climbed out of the truck. Hoping not to disturb her, he gently scooped her into his arms. The front door was open, and he flung open the screen door before carrying her into the house. He tried to hide his grin at the sight of her head slumped back in complete abandon. Moving one hand behind her neck to give it support, he couldn't resist kissing her forehead.

Tess and Charlie were working in the living room. Seeing him at the front door, Tess put down her brush and hurried over to him. Sam smiled at her paint-splattered overalls and chuckled when he saw Charlie was equally covered with green paint. From all appearances, they'd had as much fun painting together as he and Sarah had earlier in the morning.

"Looks like you two had some fun paint wars in here today." He glanced around at the room, pleased with how it was progressing. "At least the others got some work done." The way Tess blushed was plenty interesting. Charlie gave him a barely imperceptible nod when Sam quirked a brow in his direction. Well, what do you know? Good for Charlie.

"Everything okay with Jewell?" Grabbing a nearby towel, Tess wiped her hands.

"Yes. Everyone's fine. I'm happy to report that Jewell and Danny are the proud parents of a healthy baby boy they've named Jordan in your sister's honor."

"Really? That's so sweet. Glad everyone's doing well." Based on

Tess's change in behavior—from her willingness to wear overalls and get covered in paint to her softer demeanor—Sam figured that must have been one mighty important conversation Sarah had shared with her sister recently. Matter of fact, Sarah told him she felt as though she finally had her sister back.

"You should have seen Sarah today," he told them. "I know she was nervous, but she didn't show it at all. She was brave, confident, and a big comfort for Jewell. Sarah proved all over again what a great nurse she'll be one day soon."

Tess smiled. "I know it means the world to my sister that you support her in that dream, Sam."

"Did Doc ever show up?" Charlie said.

"Yes, but the baby had already been born."

"At least he got there." Charlie nodded to Sarah. "Looks like the experience completely wore her out."

"Let me take her to the bedroom and get her in bed." Tess stepped forward. When Sam made no effort to move, she hesitated. "You'll have to actually put her down."

"Do you mind if I do the honors? That is, if you don't find it too forward."

Tess angled her head as if considering the idea. "Forward or not, she's clearly exhausted. I suppose it'll be okay. But don't get any ideas just because our parents—"

"I won't. Looks like you two are getting enough ideas of your own." Sam started to walk past them but not before catching the look Tess gave Charlie. Yeah, something was up with these two, and he couldn't be happier. With a chuckle, he headed down the hallway leading to the bedrooms. He didn't know which way to go, but he'd figure it out. When he spied the trophies and a couple of sparkly crowns on a bookshelf in the first bedroom on the right, he knew he had the right room since he was aware Sarah shared a bedroom with her older sister.

Sam carefully lowered her onto the twin bed opposite another trophy display he knew must be Tess's side of the bedroom. He noted the copy of *To Kill A Mockingbird* beside her pillow. Sitting on the bed, he untied the laces of her tennis shoes, smiling when he tugged off her shoes and spied the pale pink nail polish on her toes. Should he pull the sheet over her? Nah, might as leave well enough alone since there was only a small fan to cool the room.

Standing beside the bed, Sam watched Sarah sleep for a few moments before turning to go.

"Captain?"

He paused in the doorway. "Yes?"

"Thanks again for helping me today. You were great"—she yawned—"and a great interpreter for Doc Meriweather. Love you."

"I love you, Nurse Sarah. Sleep well."

Almost immediately, she turned on her side. Her heavy breathing told him she'd already fallen asleep within seconds.

Chapter 35

~~♥~~

The Next Saturday

Shelly Jackson, one of the young mothers on the school's carnival committee, stashed her belongings beneath the face painting table and sat in the folding chair beside Sarah. "Beautiful day for the carnival, huh? God's smiling on us today, and we've already made enough to cover the initial costs for the new playground equipment. I can take over now if you want to go."

"Not yet." Miranda, the granddaughter of the school principal, gave an emphatic nod, setting her red curls bobbing. "Miss Sarah's gotta finish my pretty rainbow first."

Sarah held the paint brush and waited until the head bob ended. "I wouldn't think of leaving until you have every color in your rainbow." Concentrating on keeping her hand steady, she swept an arc of purple on the girl's cheek. After dipping the used brush in the jar of water, she pulled out a clean brush from another jar. "I think that's all except yellow. Hold still for another minute and I'll add that one."

When Sarah finished, she carefully smoothed her index finger beneath the yellow arc to even out the line. Perhaps it was silly to be so precise since the paint would be washed off by the morning. Maybe it brought out her perfectionistic tendencies, but she wanted it to be her best effort. "There now. All done."

The girl turned her head so the other woman could see Sarah's handiwork. "Isn't it bee-u-ti-ful, Miss Shelly?"

"It sure is," Shelly said with an approving nod. "Miss Sarah does fabulous work."

"Yep." Another head bob. "Can I touch it now?"

When the girl moved her hand toward her cheek, Sarah stopped her. "Wait a couple of minutes to give it more time to dry." Handing her a hand mirror, she helped angle it so Miranda could see the colorful rainbow, anchored by clouds on both ends.

"Can you add smiley faces to the clouds?"

"I sure can." Dipping a brush into the black paint, Sarah kept a light but firm hold on Miranda's chin while she quickly dabbed on eyes and smile lines.

"I need my face painted, Miss Sarah."

Speaking of smile lines. Squinting in the bright sunshine, Sarah looked up into blue eyes made even more brilliant in the early afternoon sun. "I was just going to take a break. I'm sure Shelly will be happy to do the honors."

Laughing, Shelly raised her hands. "I only paint the faces of kids, not Air Force captains."

"Ah, come on now, ladies. I'm just a big kid at heart. Right, Sarah?"

"No more than I am." She turned back to Miranda, only to find her gone.

"Her older brother, Johnny, came to fetch her and they took off," Shelly told her. "She's fine."

Sam dropped a twenty dollar bill in the donation jar. "I'd like an airplane and clouds, please. Make them real fluffy. Your best effort, but no smiley faces required."

"I'll give you fluffy." With a wink for Shelly, Sarah instructed him to sit in the chair. "But you have to vamoose if a real paying customer comes along since we only have one chair."

"See how she treats me, Shelly?" Sam shook his head. "No respect."

"I'm not very good at airplanes, but I'll try my best." For the next few minutes, Sam cooperated, only injecting comments here and there as she worked. "There," she said, releasing his chin. "That's all the damage I can do."

"Damage?" He quirked a brow and picked up the mirror. "It's, um"—he angled the mirror—"a good effort. The clouds do look very fluffy."

Sarah dropped the brush back into the jar and sniffed. "Do you want your money back?"

"Not necessary. It was worth it for the opportunity to sit so close to you with your hand on my face for a few minutes."

"Shh," Sarah said, aware she was blushing as Sam kissed her cheek. Thankfully, Shelly was talking with another young mother a few feet away.

"What is it teenage girls say when a guy kisses their cheek? 'I'll never wash this cheek again,'" he said in a feigned tone of voice.

"You're silly." She swatted his arm. "Which station are you working?"

"You'll find out soon enough, I'm sure."

She eyed him up and down. Dressed in his shorts and T-shirt, he looked no different than he usually did after hours from the bank. "Are you going to make me guess? The pie eating contest?"

"No. I gave up on that when I was seventeen. If you were there, you'll recall I turned green and ran off. I'm sure I don't need to tell you the reason."

"Too many peaches?"

"Yeah, right. Mike DeRoss added a secret ingredient to his mother's pies without her knowledge. Those pies were legendary, and—"

"How could I forget?" Her lips twisted.

"Don't worry. We got Mike back for that one."

"I don't think I want to know."

Sam laughed. "Let's just say he won't forget the chili cook-off the following year." He checked his watch. "I've got to run to my station now. I'll catch up with you in a little while. Been to the cakewalk yet?"

"No, but why won't you tell me where you'll be?" She'd been trying to get him to tell her for almost a week, but none of her attempts to bribe, cajole or coerce him had been successful.

He tapped her nose. "See you in about an hour if not before."

"Maybe I'll head on home."

He winked. "No, you won't."

"Overconfident, are we?"

"No," he said. "Confident in *you*."

Puzzling over that remark, Sarah headed toward the school gymnasium for the cakewalk. All the whispering was odd as she slowly walked around the circle, waiting for the music to stop. She stared at the numbers taped on the gymnasium floor. A number of the ladies from church darted covert glances at her and then at one another, as if they were conveying secret messages. Since when was a school cakewalk some kind of conspiracy? Strange.

Maybe the afternoon sun is getting to you.

Twenty minutes later, Sarah walked back outside with one of Catherine Lewis's peach pies in her hands. Funny how it'd been the only pie in the cakewalk. The ladies explained that a Rockbridge cakewalk always included Catherine Lewis's pies. Sensing several pairs of eyes on her back, Sarah turned and spied three ladies smiling from the doorway. They waved. "Enjoy Catherine's pie, dear!" Betty Raines said.

Sarah returned their smiles. "Thanks. I'm sure I will."

What was that all about?

Feeling parched, she headed to the nearest drink station. She wasn't the only one with the same idea, and she joined the line behind Gina, Sam's assistant at Rockbridge Savings & Loan. Since her hands were occupied with the peach pie dish, she couldn't tap her on the shoulder. When she opened her mouth to speak, the young woman beside Gina—Sarah recognized her as a teller from the bank—spoke up.

"Can you believe Sam Lewis did that for her? If you ask me, that's either love or suicide."

Sarah glanced around, unsure what to do.

Leave now, Sarah. This is not going to turn out well. Listening to gossip is never a good thing.

Not wanting to be discovered and have them believe she was eavesdropping, Sarah turned to go.

"He was going to put a down payment on a house, but then decided to wait because he wanted to spend the money on Sarah instead," Gina said.

Forgive me, Lord. But maybe—just maybe—you wanted me to hear this conversation. Was it eavesdropping if she was innocently waiting in a line behind two women—unaware of her presence—discussing something over which she had no control?

Maybe that was stretching the lines of propriety or social norms, but Sarah couldn't leave. Not that she could move her feet even if she tried. For better or worse, she was going to stand her ground and listen until she figured out what these two women were discussing. What money? Sam had taken her to dinner at Quentin's, surprised her with flowers a couple of times in the diner, but they made it sound like Sam had spent significant money on her.

"There's something about this whole thing I don't understand," the first girl said. "If Sam's so in love with her, then why is he risking losing her by paying her way to leave town?"

That does it. Walk away now.

"Miss Sarah!" Miranda and Johnny ran up to her a minute later. Thankfully, Sarah had walked far enough away from the drink station. She dared not glance back over her shoulder in case Gina and the teller woke up to the fact she'd been standing close and might have heard what they'd said. Not that any of it was derogatory, but it was revealing, and their comments left her with more questions than answers.

"What's up, kids?" Focusing on the two children would be good to distract her mind from going places where it shouldn't. Left alone, she'd dwell on what she'd just heard and that could lead to nothing good. A feeling of dread pervaded Sarah's senses. One part of her wanted to escape to somewhere quiet where she could reason through it all. Another part of her—the more rational but annoyingly moral part of her—prompted her to dismiss what she'd heard.

"Captain Lewis is in the dunking booth and nobody can dunk him!"

Sarah stared at the ten-year-old boy. "What did you say?"

"Come on!" Miranda tugged on her hand. "Miss Tess said to come and find you."

"We know you used to play softball and went to state finals and everything," Johnny said. Both kids were on either side of her, jumping up and down in their excitement.

"I'm sure some of the men would be more than willing to take a crack at dunking the military man."

"Yeah, but they're all over at the pie eating contest," Johnny said. "Captain Lewis is only in the booth for another ten minutes, and no one can dunk him! You gotta come and try."

"You already said that." Miranda rolled her eyes at her brother before turning a pleading look on Sarah. "Come on. I'll show you where it is." Taking her by the hand, the little girl skipped in front of her, pulling her along behind her.

Like a homing pigeon, Sarah knew she'd be able to find Sam on her own without any trouble. Pushing all other thoughts aside, she hurried beside them. Less than a minute later, she stood with his mother's pie still in her hands, watching with amusement as a succession of young boys tried to dunk Sam. Good natured as always, he egged them on in the politest of ways. Wasn't that what you were supposed to do when sitting on that bench? Say things to provoke or irritate someone in order to get them riled up enough to put some real strength behind the ball thrown at the bulls-eye?

"Ah, look who's finally come to try and dunk me!" Sam's brilliant smile creased his handsome face. Gone were the shorts and T-shirt he'd been wearing earlier, replaced by swim trunks and a blue tank shirt. Her pitiful painted airplane and clouds still adorned his cheek.

"Want to try your hand, Miss Jordan?"

"You bet I do." The small group parted. Feeling a bit like Moses parting the Red Sea, Sarah handed off the pie to one of the young mothers standing nearby.

"You won one of Mom's pies at the cakewalk, I see. Good. You can share it with me later."

"Don't you ever get enough of peach pie?" Sarah teased, stepping up to the marked line and positioning her toes behind it. Dusting her hands together, she shifted back and forth and then blew on her hands.

"Never!" Acting silly, Sam did a little dance from where he sat on the wooden bench in the middle of the dunking booth. "If you fail to dunk me, I get the pie. Deal?"

"Be prepared to go down, loser!" Might as well give the onlookers a good show.

"Now you've done it." Sam's eyes grew wide and he shook his head. "Show me what you've got." He stuck out his tongue and waved his hands behind his head like an overgrown, ridiculously adorable kid. The children all around them loved the show, and they howled at Sam's antics.

After being handed a ball, Sarah wound up—taking her time and making it as dramatic as possible—and the first ball sailed just south of the mark.

"Missed me, missed me, now you've gotta kiss me!" Sam taunted.

Great. Now the kids would probably repeat that one. Just what she needed to break her concentration. That was probably part of the devious man's plan.

"I've got two more chances. Be quiet and hold your breath, Mr. Lewis!"

"I'm so scared." When she narrowed her eyes, he laughed and winked.

Winding up a second time, Sarah aimed for all she was worth, but again, it fell just shy of the bulls-eye, but closer this time.

"A little rusty there, are you, Miss Jordan?"

"It's the target that's a little rusty. Like I said once, you need some new lines old man." Yes, she was definitely rusty.

Sam held his stomach and laughed as if she'd said the funniest thing he'd ever heard. Of course, the kids went nuts over his exaggerations. He'd make such a wonderful daddy one day.

"You missed your calling and should have been an actor." As she accepted the third ball from one of the kids, Sarah shifted from foot to foot, making Sam wait and drawing out the moment. He deserved it.

Make this one count.

"Chicken?" Sam flapped his arms and squawked. Again, the kids howled. In the process of winding up to throw the ball, Sarah laughed. Really, could the man be any cuter? He was such a good sport. And maddening. Tempting. She was going to dunk him if she had to buy the extra balls to do it. Nothing was stopping her.

The conversation she'd heard from Gina and her friend came to mind again. "Go away. Not now," she muttered under her breath. Something was niggling at her brain, but what? Snippets swirled in her mind, refusing to let go of their hold on her. Why now? Time to concentrate.

Sam decided to wait because he wanted to spend the money on Sarah instead.

That's either love or suicide.

Why is he risking losing her by paying her way to leave town?

Shaking her head, Sarah stood her ground, aware Sam and everyone else watched.

"I'm aging up here, Miss Sarah. Come on! Hand over that pie and call it a day already."

Suddenly, the truth hit her with sudden clarity. Of course! Sarah's eyes widened and she stared at him. "It was *you!*" Stumbling back a couple of steps, she nearly dropped the ball. Putting a hand to her head, feeling dizzy, she was vaguely aware when Sam started to scramble down from his perch.

"Baby, are you okay?"

"Baby, baby," a couple of the little girls chanted, giggling. Soon enough, the boys chimed in as Sarah held up one hand to stop Sam.

"No! Climb back up there, Captain Lewis. *Now*." Her hand trembled, her voice shook. Inhaling a deep breath, she blew it out and bore holes into those blue eyes. "This time, you're definitely going to get wet."

Appearing skeptical, Sam obeyed as he climbed back onto the bench. Surprisingly, he didn't taunt, didn't tease. Matter of fact, he looked confused. Good. The man deserved to be confused.

Winding up, saying a prayer under her breath, Sarah drew upon every ounce of her skill and strength and hoped this one would do the job.

"It was you!" The ball flew out of her hand as if in slow motion. She watched, and everyone around her grew quiet. The bell dinged as the ball made contact with the bulls-eye. The bench separated and Sam tumbled into the water. The kids went wild, jumping up and down, laughing and high-fiving each other.

"You did it!" Miranda and Johnny said at the same time, hugging her in turn.

"Thank you," Sarah said to the young mother holding her pie. She had half a mind to leave it, but she'd won it fair and square—at least she thought she had—but that was another thing to ponder later on.

Hearing Sam call to her, Sarah began to walk away, head held high and shoulders straight.

"Sarah, you forgot your prize!" he called from behind her.

She ignored him and kept on walking.

Chapter 36

~~♥~~

Tess came into the bedroom and gestured to where Sarah sat on the bed. "May I?" When she nodded, Tess she sat down beside her. "Want to talk about it?"

Sarah drew up her knees and clasped her hands around them. "Not sure. I just need some time to absorb what happened." Other than the creek, the bedroom was the one place where she could be alone. Tempted to cry, the tears wouldn't come. She didn't know what to feel.

Sam gave me the money for nursing school. It was him, Lord. I know it was.

"You scared Sam the way you yelled whatever it was and then stomped off. I've never seen a man scramble so fast." Tess's lips upturned. "In an odd way, it was rather comical considering the man was in a dunking booth at the time. I mean, there he was, dripping wet and calling for you to wait. It was the best drama we've had in Rockbridge in a while."

Sarah blew out a breath and guilt overwhelmed her. "Glad I could oblige. I hope I didn't scare any of the kids. I should have handled the situation in a more mature way."

"Sweetie, relationships are tough. That's not to say your feelings aren't valid, or wrong in any way, but I hope you and Sam can talk about whatever it is that's bothering you. Give it to the Lord. I'll be around if you need me." Tess rose to her feet and started across the room.

"Tess, wait."

Jumping off the bed, Sarah ran and threw her arms around her sister, resting her head on her shoulder. "I love him, Tess, but Sam was the one who gave me the cashier's check."

Tess stopped patting her back. "Really? Oh, my."

"I know."

Tess disengaged herself long enough to pluck a tissue from the nearby box. She handed it to her, probably assuming she'd burst into tears at any moment.

"Don't ask me how I know, but I was winding up to throw the final ball to try and dunk Sam, and it just hit me"—she slapped her forehead—"bam! Sam was the one with the biggest motivation to help me, and also the means." Balling the tissue in one hand, Sarah crossed her arms over her middle and started to pace.

"If it's any consolation, you dunked the man and got him soaking wet. Have you done anything with the cashier's check yet?"

"No. I've been praying about it," Sarah said. "I have a little more time, but not much, to reapply for the fall semester or I'll lose the scholarship money I've been offered. Wait a minute." She stopped her pacing. "Only a handful of people knew about that letter, and one of them is standing in this room with me right now."

Tess reared back, and Sarah instantly regretted the accusation. "You think I told Sam?"

"I'm sorry, Tess. I know you didn't, but even if you did, it's okay." Shaking her head, she couldn't stem the tears that flowed down her cheeks. So fast she found it difficult to keep up as she dabbed the tissue over her cheek, absorbing the moisture. "I need to think about what all this means."

"Are you going to see Sam? He hasn't shown up here yet, but I have a strong suspicion he might after he changes out of his wet clothes. I know Charlie was with him."

Sarah met her sister's gaze. "Thanks for coming after me, sis." That did it. She couldn't hold back any longer, and she burst into tears, giving into the release.

"Shh. It's okay, honey." Drawing her into another hug, Tess held her for several minutes as she cried.

"You know how much I want to go to nursing school, but I can't have Sam paying my way." She sniffled some more and dabbed the tissue beneath her eyes. "Why didn't he tell me?"

Tess grabbed another tissue and shoved it into her hand. "I can't presume to understand how a man's mind works. Look at Charlie and me. He didn't tell me he liked me for years, apparently, because he didn't think I'd consider going out with him."

Sarah lifted her head and attempted a small smile. "Are you and Charlie dating now?"

Tess ducked her head. Was she actually blushing? "I think we just might be, but it's still new. We're taking it slow, but so far, so good. You're right about him, you know. He's a very good man. Like Sam. Solid and dependable. He wants to volunteer for some community projects with me."

"That's great. I'm so happy for you, and I hope it works out." Sarah straightened her shoulders. She'd had her time to cry and now she needed to act like a grownup.

"You're young and can't be expected to have all the answers."

Sarah stared at her sister. "If it's possible, I believe you read my mind."

"No, but I've been in your shoes before. Trust me, Sarah, no one has all the answers. We fumble along in life, we make mistakes— some big, some not so big—but then we dust ourselves off and get on with the process of living. But the difference is that we look to the Lord to help us. We know we can't do it on our own any more than we can expect God to hand everything to us just because it's what *we* think we want or need."

"When did you get to be so wise?"

"I'm older, remember." They shared a smile. "Was that one of Sam's mom's peach pies on the kitchen counter?"

Sarah nodded. "I won it at the cakewalk, although there was something odd about that, too."

Tess quirked a brow. "What do you mean?"

The ponytail holder in her hair felt too tight. Sarah tugged on it, shaking her head as her hair fell around her shoulders. "I can't explain it except to say it was like the ladies were playing matchmaker. At a school carnival cakewalk, of all places. Several of them kept giving each other winks and nudges. If I had chosen anything other than that peach pie, I think they would have physically barred my way from leaving the gymnasium until I exchanged it. A few of them even followed me to the door." Sarah shook her head. "It was very strange, but in a wonderful way, which I realize makes no sense."

"They hardly need to play matchmaker since you and Sam are already an item. That's still true, isn't it?" The genuine concern in Tess's expression was sweet, and Sarah's heart swelled.

"Yes, of course. I just need a little time. If I were to give up on this relationship at the first hint of trouble, it would only prove I'm not old enough to handle one." She raised her hands in the air. "Let's face it. I should probably call it a day, crawl under the sheet, and not get up until tomorrow."

"Ah, honey. It'll work out, and everything will be okay."

"I can't keep Sam's money." Moisture filled Sarah's eyes again.

"I know, but I want you to remember something." Tess put both hands on Sarah's shoulders. "Look at me." She waited until Sarah did as she asked.

"Try to put yourself in Sam's shoes, as hard as that might be to do. As I recall, you weren't dating him when you received that cashier's check. Maybe you were close, but you hadn't yet crossed over that line from friendship into something more. Right? Sam could have chosen another girl—a girl who wants to stay in Rockbridge her entire life—and it would have made his life a whole lot easier." When Sarah opened her mouth to speak, Tess stopped her by placing two fingers over her lips, stilling them.

"Sam waited on the Lord, and *you* are the girl he knows the Almighty wants for him. Here's the most important thing as I see it, Sarah: when you love someone, you want them to be happy. If that means sacrificing your own happiness for the good of the other person, then that's what you do."

Tess lifted Sarah's head with her hand anchored beneath her chin. "Sam Lewis is an honorable man. I'm sure he wants to give the woman he loves the opportunity to fulfill her dreams. Whether or not you accept his gift is up to you. But pray about it, and ask the Lord for *His* answer."

Giving her one more quick hug, Tess kissed her cheek. Opening the bedroom door, she departed, closing the door quietly behind her.

Until Tess came into the room, Sarah had wished Dad was home. She'd always connected more with him than with Mom, and she'd always been very much her father's daughter. The past few years, she'd dismissed Tess as someone who cared for herself more than others. But now, a new respect for her older sister had been planted in her heart.

Thank you again, Lord.
Miracles do happen.

~~♥~~

"Sarah's not at her house and she's not at the creek." Hands on his hips, Sam chewed on his lower lip as he paced the floor at home. "Where could she have gone, Charlie?" He sounded this side of desperate, but he didn't care. Finding Sarah and making sure she was all right—and didn't hate him—was paramount.

"Think about it, buddy. What would be the other option if you're young and confused about the well-intentioned but misguided guy who says he loves you but also gives you the money to leave town?"

Irritated by Charlie's tone, Sam smirked. "Forget it. I never should have told you." Other than his best friend, he hadn't told anyone but his parents that he'd funded that check for Sarah. Neither was Charlie the type of guy to spill his or anyone else's personal business on Main Street for the entire town's consumption.

"I'm on your side, remember?"

"Yeah, I know. Sorry." Sam stared at his friend. "Have I messed this up with Sarah? I thought I was doing the right thing at the time. She told me she doesn't plan on staying in Texas after nursing school. She wants to go flying off into the wild blue yonder"—he paused, slammed with the irony of that statement—"and wants to marry some guy who'll wear one of those stupid Nehru jackets, live in a foreign country, and do missionary work together. She'll probably only come home to Rockbridge every furlough or whatever with her doctor husband and cute little kids in tow."

"You could do missionary work."

Sam jerked his gaze to Charlie's. "Yes, I suppose I could. That's not my point."

"I know, buddy." Charlie sounded sympathetic although he looked on the verge of laughing. "Maybe it's a good thing Sarah dunked you in that tank today."

"Thanks for the vote of support."

"Hey, I'm only saying it might have forced a confrontation, or whatever you want to call it, that *should* have happened when Sarah first came to the bank and asked you about that big check. You ask me, it wasn't so much professional ethics that stopped you from telling her so much as your own pride."

Sam shook his head. "If she'd known the check came from me, Sarah never would have accepted it in the first place. You know how stubborn she is. At least by making it anonymous, I had half a fighting chance she'd take the money and run."

"Is that what you wanted her to do? Run away from Rockbridge?"

"You know what I mean," Sam snapped. "All I want now—all I've ever wanted—is for Sarah to be happy. To find her dreams."

"You and your dream talk. Enough already." Charlie raised his hands in the air. "Go find her, kiss her senseless, and then talk about your future. I don't know why you can't seem to get it through your thick skull that Sarah going to Austin isn't a death sentence for your relationship. Make it work *for* you, not against you."

Again, Sam faced off with his friend. "How do you propose I do that?"

A slow smile crept across Charlie's face. "I think you hit upon a key word in that question."

Sam opened his mouth but then closed it just as fast. Was Charlie actually suggesting he propose marriage to Sarah? Well, that'd be one way to stake his claim on her heart. Was it too soon?

You've known her for years. Still, he'd need to think about it. The issue wasn't a question of loving Sarah, wanting Sarah. More than anything, the increasing need to be with her was uppermost in his crowded thoughts.

"As far as where Sarah might be now, let me give you another little clue." Crossing his arms over his chest, Charlie planted his feet apart as they faced one another in the living room. "Where's the one place in Rockbridge where Sarah feels most comfortable and where she's among friends? Other than home or church, that is."

"Perry's." Sam didn't even have to think about it. "Of course. How'd you get so smart? I'm suddenly feeling hunger pains. Let's go." He started for the front door.

Charlie followed him out the door. "Sorry, but you're on your own. It's Saturday night, and I'm escorting Tess to the movies over in Springhaven."

Sam laughed under his breath. "Sounds about right, friend. Have a good time."

"One of these days we'll take the Jordan girls on a double date," Charlie said.

"Let me make sure Sarah's still speaking to me first, and then we'll plan something."

"I have a question." Charlie climbed into his car. "Have you broken that vow yet?"

"I take it you mean the one about not kissing a Jordan girl? Yeah, you could say that." A few times over.

"Good man. Proud of you. Do you want a lift over to Perry's? You could put on that impressive Air Force uniform and sit on the back of the car. That'd make quite an entrance."

After debating it for a moment, Sam shook his head. "No, thanks. I need to clear my head." He inhaled the scent of his neighbor's freshly mown lawn and the flowers in his mother's garden. "It's a nice night. Think I'll walk."

"It'll work out, Sam. See you soon. Later!"

Waving to Charlie, hoping his friend was right, Sam headed in the opposite direction.

Lord, be with me.

Chapter 37

~~♥~~

Upon entering Perry's, Sam stopped abruptly. The busboy, Eddie, was singing into a pretend microphone—a stainless steel serving spoon from the looks of it—and pouring out his heart and soul. His eyes were closed as he gyrated and sang along to "Walk On the Wild Side."

Shoving his hands in his pockets, Sam slid onto the seat at the corner table. The diner was fairly quiet with only a couple of other men sitting at the counter. He exchanged nods with them, knowing the diner would get busier when the high school and college age guys brought their dates in later on. Sitting in Perry's was one way to prolong an evening with a girl since it was a respectable, public place. He'd been guilty of that ploy with his own dates in the past.

As Eddie launched into another song, still with his eyes closed, Patti approached him. "Hey, Sam. How are you?"

He returned her smile. "Hi, Patti. Enjoying the floor show. Is this something new?"

She shrugged. "Every time we're not that busy on the weekends, and as long as Eddie's on his break. Myrna and Jimmy don't mind, and the customers find it kind of fun. They even join in sometimes. He's not half-bad. You should hear him sing 'Town Without Pity.' Sounds just like Gene Pitney, the guy who sings it on the record. Or '(Girls Girls Girls Were) Made To Love by Eddie Hodges.'" She glanced over at Eddie. "Something about that skinny kid who's probably never had a date in his life singing a song like that is rather sweet in a weird way."

Sam nodded as another tune began. He'd never listened to the radio much until he'd been in the service and the guys played it incessantly. "Eddie's doing a decent rendition of 'Gravy (For My Mashed Potatoes)' right now. How are your kids?"

"Active as ever. It's a miracle I'm standing on my own two feet." She gave him a tired smile. "On the other hand, it's a relief to be here. Gives my hubby the privilege of watching his spawn for the night. Equal time, right?"

Patti's humor always made him laugh. She had the kind of pleasing personality perfect for a waitress in a small-town diner. The expression about never meeting a stranger applied to this woman.

"What can I get for you?" When he didn't answer immediately, she winked. "If you're thinking about a tall, gorgeous but feisty blonde, she's already come and gone. She offered to work tonight in my place, but Jimmy wouldn't go for it. He's in charge tonight."

"I see." He couldn't help himself. "Was she. . .okay?"

Patti grinned. "Sarah seemed to have some stuff on her mind, but yeah, she was good. Why?"

"No reason." Sam drummed his fingers on the tabletop. "I don't suppose Sarah mentioned where she was headed?" It was possible he'd just missed her. She might have taken off in the opposite direction and disappeared out of sight just as he'd arrived at the diner. Bad timing.

"No. Sorry." Patti's expression was empathetic. "I'm sure you can catch her at home in a while. As long as you're here, do you want something to eat?"

He might not taste anything, but he might as well give the diner his business while he tried to figure out his next move. As much as he hated to do it, maybe he should wait until tomorrow to see her in church. Give her some time and space. He'd eat a meal and then decide.

"I'll take one of those barbecue burgers, no onion ring, and a soda. Thanks, Patti." Might as well shake it up a little since Patti didn't remember the lemons for his iced tea the way Sarah always did. Not that it mattered much, and Patti had enough on her mind.

"Not a problem. Coming right up."

Jimmy came out of the kitchen a short time later as Sam finished his burger. The cook rarely emerged from that kitchen. The way he walked straight toward the table in spite of his bad leg—not to mention the expression on his face—spoke of a man on a mission. "Captain Lewis," he said with a nod, giving him a quick shake of his hand. "Mind if I sit down?"

"Not at all, Jimmy. Have a seat. Please. Your burger was great, as usual. Thanks."

"Welcome. Adding the barbecue sauce has been a real hit. Glad you liked it." Jimmy dropped onto the seat on the opposite side of the booth. "Somethin' tells me you didn't come in here tonight because you had hunger pangs."

Sam smiled. "And something tells me you're not sitting here chewing the fat with me on a Saturday night." He took a long drink. "The truth? It'd be kind of hard to reason with Sarah on an empty stomach. I needed to fortify myself."

Jimmy chuckled, familiar and raspy. "I figured as much. Sarah was in here a little while ago and came pretty close to beggin' me to put her to work. When I told her she'd already put in way too much time this week, she grumbled about how she'd never get out of Rockbridge and then took off." With a small smile, he shook his head, the folds in his face deepening. "That sweet girl can't wait to get out of this town as much as I've always wanted to live and die here."

"I'm trying to help her do that, Jimmy. The getting out of town part, that is." Sam tossed out the line and hoped the older man would nip at the bait he offered.

"You might not want my advice, but I'm going to give it to you, anyway, Sam. I've seen that girl work hard every week since she was sixteen. That's not to mention all the other stuff she does around town, at the church, and at home. She's earned the right to take that money and run to Austin with it. But she's way too stubborn for her own good." Jimmy ran a hand over his shadowed jaw. "She's got this idea in her head that she doesn't want to be beholden to anyone."

"Jimmy, I love her." Sam drained the glass.

"Tell me something I don't know, son. The whole town knows it."

"So, what do you suggest I do if she won't take my money? Or anyone's money, for that matter." Whether or not Jimmy knew about the cashier's check, and whether or not Sarah had told him, Sam figured he might as well lay it all out on the line.

Sliding out of the booth, Jimmy reached into the pocket of his long white apron and pulled out a small plastic bag. He placed it on the table.

Sam glanced at the bag. "Red jelly beans."

"Cherry jelly beans, to be specific," Jimmy said. "I started givin' them to Sarah when she'd come into the diner with her dad for Saturday lunch. I used to tease her about her tongue turnin' red since she ate so many of them."

Did the man have a point? What did cherry jelly beans have to do with anything?

"Sarah got sassy on me once—she was about ten at the time, I think—and told me she had to earn those jelly beans. Imagine that. A dime bag of candy. She was just a kid yet said she wanted to *earn* them. Said the only thing in life that's really free is our salvation, and all we have to do is accept what the Lord Jesus did for us on the cross." Jimmy chuckled and moved his hands to his hips, shaking his head. "What kind of little girl says something like that?"

"For starters, an honorable one. A girl with the love of Christ in her heart who wants to share that grace and mercy." Sitting back in the booth, Sam waited. He knew Jimmy was leading up to something with this conversation.

Jimmy slowly nodded and pointed to himself. "I want you to know that same little girl led this old sailor to Jesus. And then I led my wife to Him. And then our kids. Changed our lives for the better, and I'll always love my little Jelly Bean for that. No matter where she goes in life, she'll always be in here with me." He tapped a fist over his chest. "To tell you the truth, I'm not sure she even remembered it until I reminded her a while back."

Sam's mind was spinning and, if it were possible, his heart expanded even more to let Sarah in. Jimmy's words only confirmed how special her love was to others, not just to him. "Your nickname for Sarah is Jelly Bean?"

"Sure enough." The other man's dark eyes met his. "Find another way to help her, son. Think about what it is that she wants most and find a way to help get her there. Mind you, I'm not talkin' about Sarah working here at Perry's until she's thirty." He put his hand on the table. "As much as I'd love that, I try not to be a selfish man."

"Thanks, Jimmy. I'll find a way." They shared a smile.

"You do that." Jimmy winked. "A tip? Give her cherry jelly beans every now and then." Sam stared after the cook as he crossed the diner and pushed open the swinging door, disappearing behind it and into the kitchen.

"Hey, Sam!" Eddie stood by the jukebox.

Sam cleared his throat. "Yeah, Ed?"

"Got any requests?"

"How about 'I Wish That We Were Married?' That sounds about right."

"Sure. As long as you're not saying that to me, then we're good. Comin' right up."

"Thanks." Sam wanted to pay his bill and take off, but for now, he'd listen to Eddie's song, wishing the sentiment were true for him and a certain gorgeous Jordan girl. She might throw him out on his ear when he stopped by her house in a bit, but he'd take the chance.

His gaze was drawn to something sitting on the table. The small bag of jelly beans. Cherry. With a smile, he pocketed them.

After walking around Oak Park for more than an hour, Sarah headed home. She needed to finish preparing the Sunday school lesson for tomorrow. She didn't much feel like it, but the girls depended on her, and she couldn't let them down.

"Sarah, is that you?" Tess called from the kitchen as Sarah closed the front door.

"No, it's an escaped puppy from the new Beagle litter over at the Barton house. Yes, of course, it's me." Emotionally spent, she'd tried to be quiet as she entered the house. No reason to be so sarcastic with Tess.

Her sister came to stand in the kitchen doorway. "Now that we've finished the remodeling in the kitchen, are you and Sam willing to help Charlie and me finish painting the living room? Mom called. They're doing fine, but—I could kind of read between the lines— they're coming home on Wednesday as planned. We need to get it done."

"Sure. I'll ask Sam tomorrow after church." Sarah covered her mouth with one hand to stifle her yawn. She hoped she could sleep after the events of the day. "The slipcovers for the sofa and side chair, and the pillows, are all on hold over at Tucker's."

Tess nodded. "I'll pick them up on my lunch hour on Monday. Thanks." Her expression softened. "Did you talk with Sam tonight?"

"No. I wasn't up to it. Did he come here?"

"Yes." Tess nodded as Sarah followed her into the kitchen. "I'm sure he went to the creek, too. Where did you go? That's the question."

"Perry's, but Jimmy refused to allow me to work."

"I've always adored Jimmy. He's a great guy. Not to be nosy, but where did you go after that?"

"I thought about going to see Debbie since she and Arnie are back from their honeymoon." Warmth crept into Sarah's neck and moved to her cheeks. "Then I figured a surprise visit to newlyweds wasn't the best idea on a Saturday night."

Tess grinned. "Good thinking."

"I ended up sitting on a bench in Oak Park and watching the world according to Rockbridge go by. Funny how much you can see." Sarah's eyes glazed. "The couples, young and old. The kids, wild and well-behaved. The love, the laughter, the longing and the loss."

Tess tilted her head. "Are you writing another poem again?"

Sarah laughed softly. "No."

"Well, it sure sounded that way to me. Did you eat while you were at Perry's?"

"No, Mom, as a matter of fact. Eating didn't even cross my mind. I'll make myself a turkey sandwich. You run on to bed."

"Is that your way of saying you don't want to talk about it anymore?"

Sarah gave Tess a quick hug. "It's my way of saying I don't *need* to talk about it anymore. Thanks for earlier, sis."

"That's what older sisters are for, sweetie." With a small wave, Tess departed.

Sarah spread out the weekly newspaper on the kitchen table but quickly lost interest in it as she ate her sandwich a few minutes later. Try as she might, she couldn't stay focused and the words blurred. Maybe she should study her Sunday school lesson instead. After darting into the bedroom and grabbing her Bible and leader's guide, she sat down again at the kitchen table.

She stared at the passage in Philippians 2:3-4, the theme verse for the lesson: *Do nothing from selfishness or empty conceit, but with humility of mind regard one another as more important than yourselves; do not merely look out for your own personal interests, but also for the interests of others.*

Oh, the irony. "Lord, you have a great sense of humor, don't you?" Sarah laughed under her breath. Sacrifice. Seemed to be a running theme today. Would this day never end?

As she finished her sandwich and then washed her plate in the sink, Sarah heard a knock. Tess had probably gone to bed, but maybe she'd gotten up and was in the living room. Not moving, Sarah listened.

Another light knock sounded. Wiping her hands on a towel, Sarah braced herself and then headed into the living room. Someone was at the front door, and she had a good idea who it was.

Chapter 38

~~♥~~

"Hi." Sam removed his Stetson and held it between his hands. Tilting his head to one side, he gave Sarah his best puppy dog imitation as he stood on her front porch. "Can we talk?"

After a moment's hesitation, she pushed open the screen door and stepped outside. She still wore her Perry's uniform and her hair was pulled back, as usual. Judging by the tiny dab of mustard in the right corner of her mouth, she'd recently eaten. Was she mad? Hard to tell, but the fact that she was willing to talk with him was encouraging.

"Only for a few minutes, so make it count. I need to finish studying my Sunday school lesson."

The hint of her usual humor amused him as she sat down on the swing and scooted to the opposite end, no doubt wanting to leave a decent space between them. He'd see what he could do to bridge that gap. She stared straight ahead, so he took full advantage of the opportunity to study her profile. Sarah by moonlight was beautiful. Sarah at any time was beautiful. Twisting her hands on her lap, she avoided his gaze.

Lord, give me the right words.

"What's the scripture reference? For your lesson?"

She mumbled something indecipherable.

"What?"

"It's from Philippians." She cleared her throat. "Suffice it to say it's about sacrifice and putting the needs of others before your own wants."

Thank you, Jesus. He loved how God worked. Surveying the expanse of the front yard, Sam inhaled the sweet fragrance of her mother's rose bushes. On a whim, he left the swing and jumped over the three steps to the ground. A gentle rain had started to fall. After grabbing his pocket knife from his back pocket, he quickly cut off three pink blooms from the back of the bush. Bounding back up to the porch, he shook the raindrops from the flowers and then bowed as he offered them to Sarah.

He heard the sweet hitch in her breath as Sarah took them from him. "Thank you, although these roses are technically stolen property."

"Then we're even since you've stolen my heart." Corny, yes, but her brown eyes softened.

"You make it hard for a girl to resist you when you say things like that, Captain."

"The only woman I care about is you."

She held the roses up to her nose and gave him a small smile.

"You have a little mustard." With one finger, he gently removed it from the corner of her mouth. Rubbing his fingers together, he leaned forward, hoping she might meet him halfway. Instead, she reached into the pocket of her uniform. Pulling out a piece of green, rectangular paper, she offered it to him.

His heart heavy, Sam took it from her. He didn't need to look at it to know it was the cashier's check. What it represented. What returning it meant.

"You're my benefactor, aren't you?"

His pulse raced, but Sarah deserved nothing less than the truth. "Yes. At least I tried. I had the best of intentions, and I was only trying to help you. If it's needed, please forgive me."

"No forgiveness is needed. I was more upset than anything. Well, maybe a little mad. When I got home from the school carnival, Tess talked with me and helped me see it more from your perspective. Then when I saw the Bible verse for tomorrow's lesson, that clinched it. You've got to love the way the Lord works." The corners of her mouth lifted.

"I was just thinking the same thing. In ways our finite minds can't fathom," he said. "Remind me to thank Tess later, but are you absolutely positive this is what you want?"

Sarah nodded, but her lower lip trembled. "I understand what you were trying to do, Sam, and I appreciate it, but I can't accept your money. It wouldn't be right. Please understand it's not a *personal* rejection."

"Would it help if my dad was the one who gave it to you? If it was for a lesser amount or if it was an official bank loan?"

She frowned. "No, and in no way would I qualify for a bank loan."

"I disagree. You're twenty-one, you make a decent wage, you've had a solid job for years, and unless you have a gambling addiction of which I'm unaware, you have no debt. Those qualifications would actually make you a very good candidate." He hadn't even thought of that possibility until this moment. Perhaps he was fumbling, but he had to try. Even before he saw her shaking her head, he should have known Sarah wouldn't accept his suggestion as a viable option.

"I can't allow anyone else to give me the money. I need to earn it myself."

Jimmy's words came to mind. Right. A woman who felt the need to earn cherry jelly beans as a kid would never consider a bank loan. That would mean she owed someone something. Heaven forbid. Sam's jaw tightened. Could the woman be any more stubborn? At the moment, he wanted to shake some sense into her and then kiss her. Kiss her long and hard. Never let her go.

"I love you for what you tried to do."

Sam's gaze met hers and held it steady. "I love you, too. So much."

"Give me a reason to stay, Sam." Sarah's eyes glistened in the dim light.

Lowering his head, he prayed for the strength to resist pulling her into his arms, this woman who held his heart. He couldn't bear the thought of letting her go to Austin. Increasingly, it's all he could think about and distracted him at work, at home, and even in church. Lifting his chin, with everything in him, Sam fought what he was about to say. "I can't."

"I see. My mistake. I thought. . ." Her shoulders heaved and, rising from the swing, she walked quickly to the front door.

"Sarah, wait—"

When she turned back to him, the heartbreak in her features shattered him. Crossing the space between them in seconds, cradling her face in his hands, he brought his mouth down on hers. If he couldn't tell her with his words, he wanted her to know with his kiss. The kiss went on and on, but he couldn't stop. Sarah kissed him back with equal passion. The force of emotion surging between them was palpable. Never had he kissed a woman like this. Never did he want to stop kissing her.

The warmth of her fingers seared through the thin cotton of his shirt. He wanted more, but he couldn't compromise her reputation. Devouring Sarah on her front porch would be bad enough if any of their neighbors happened to pass by now. Not that he cared what anyone else thought of him. He wanted the world to know how deeply he cared for Sarah. How he loved her enough to let her go even though everything in him fought against it.

How would he be able to function, not seeing Sarah in the diner every day, not sharing their special times at the creek? Splashing and swimming. The long talks. Sitting together in church and sharing a hymnal. Helping the kids at the school carnival. Sharing their fears and triumphs. Teasing and pretending it meant nothing when it meant everything. Indulging in kisses and caresses that stirred desire and needed to be tempered in order to maintain their sanity.

He'd somehow manage to go through the motions of life, but nothing would be the same.

"You, Sarah Jordan, are the most precious person in my life." Sam felt moisture on her cheeks and tugged her closer into the circle of his arms. "Don't cry," he murmured against lips softer than silk. Brushing strands of her long blonde hair away from her forehead, he softly kissed her temple. "It'll be okay, baby. I promise. We'll figure out something."

Sarah cried into his shoulder. "I don't want to go if it means leaving you behind." Wiping the back of her hand over her eyes, she half laughed, half cried. With the pads of his thumbs, he absorbed the moisture from her cheeks. Her big eyes, so trusting, searched his.

Lord, help me give Sarah the right answers. What she needs to hear for her heart.

"Guys aren't the best at talking about their feelings, but I can tell you one thing: I've never felt so alive since coming back home to Rockbridge and finding you, *rediscovering* you, all over again."

"I've been here all along. Perhaps waiting for you. I don't know," she said, lowering her gaze. "I'm so confused."

"Pray about it, and I will, too. Let the Lord give us the answer. In the meantime," he said, digging in his pocket, "I have something for you."

"My prize?"

He stopped. "Well, no. I gave it to Miranda and her brother. Hope you don't mind."

"Not at all, but what was it?"

"A red plastic cup with the school name on it that says something like, 'I won the dunking challenge!'" He shrugged and gave her a repentant grin.

"That's okay." Sarah's gaze traveled to his hand. "What do you have there?"

He handed her the package of jelly beans. Perhaps it would work to his advantage. "A peace offering?"

She smiled and ran her finger over the package and then looked up at him, love shining in her eyes. "You went to the diner tonight? And spoke with Jimmy?"

Sam nodded. "I did. He loves you as much as I do. He advised me to keep you supplied with jelly beans in the future. Cherry jelly beans, to be specific."

Sarah blew out a sigh. "He's such a dear."

"So are you. Now, turn your head for me. Please." Without question, she did as he asked. Not speaking, Sam gently removed the pins holding her hair in place.

She shook her head and ran her fingers through her hair, tousling it.

"Let me do it." Sam stroked her hair, being careful not to tangle it more. Her beautiful hair, so shiny and soft.

"That feels wonderful," Sarah murmured. "Thank you. Seems foot massage isn't the only thing you know how to do well. If you've ever worked in a hair salon, I don't want to know."

Sam continued his efforts. After a few more minutes, he tucked her hand in his and rested their joined hands over his heart. "Can you feel how hard and fast my heart is beating?"

She splayed her fingers over the fabric of his thin shirt. All over again, the warmth of her touch seared straight through him as much as her smile. "I do that to you?"

"All that and more." Unable to resist her, Sam kissed her again. This time soft and tender. Not as a good-bye, but as a precious promise.

"So, what does this mean?" Sarah said, easing out of his arms and offering him her hand.

"It means I want to be with you. Together, we'll find a way to get you to Austin."

She studied him. "Sam, why is fulfilling my dream so important to you?"

He smiled and lightly skimmed his finger over her bottom lip. "Ah, Sarah." He kissed her again. "In your dreams, I see *my* future."

Chapter 39

~~♥~~

Wednesday Evening

"Girls, I can't ever thank you enough. What a wonderful surprise!" Mom cried after she walked inside the house, and she immediately noticed the results of their redecorating efforts. "You're both so busy, and I don't know how you found the time to do all this. Oh, it looks absolutely beautiful."

She gave them both hugs and then, as if in a daze, Mom put her hands over her mouth and glanced around the living room with big eyes, drinking it all in. Finally, she lowered her hands and managed to speak. "Bill, look what the kids have done for us! Isn't it wonderful?"

"Sure is. As long as my chair's in its same place, I'm fine." Almost as soon as they walked in the door, Dad made a beeline for that favorite chair. Collapsing in it, he sighed with satisfaction.

Pleased to see her mother so happy, Sarah winked at Tess. She opened the screen door for Sam as he came inside the house, weighted down with suitcases and assorted bags.

"Thank you, son." Bill instructed him to take everything to the master bedroom at the back of the house.

"Glad to help." Sam gave Sarah a quick wink as he headed for the hallway leading to the bedrooms. He'd changed out of his suit before coming to the house, and Sarah loved seeing him in his jeans and blue striped cotton shirt. As usual, the black Stetson was perched on his head. He'd told her he missed wearing it while serving in the Air Force. She'd noticed he'd been wearing the hat with his business suits, and he often parked it on the seat beside him at the diner.

"We had help from a couple of handsome guys and a crew from the church singles group," Sarah told her parents.

Dad chuckled as Sam came back into the living room. "Maybe you'd better sit with me, Captain Lewis. Fill me in." He shot a grin at Sarah. "Seems like it's been an eventful couple of weeks." As the ladies departed to the kitchen, Sarah heard Dad telling Sam about places they'd visited in the Denver area, including a tour of the new Air Force Academy in Colorado Springs. Sarah smiled, knowing how much her father must have loved it.

"We've done the living room and the kitchen so far, but we can work on other rooms in the house, if you'd like." Tess worked beside Sarah as they prepared a light supper of soup and sandwiches. When Mom offered to help, Sarah put a hand on her shoulder and made her sit at the table. She kept them laughing with stories of her sister, Mary, and news from the Colorado side of the family. As she listened, Sarah arranged turkey, ham and roast beef sandwiches on a platter and then pulled out the homemade potato salad from the Frigidaire. She'd made the potato salad for a recent church function, and a certain tall cowboy had raved about it to the point of embarrassment. Not that she ever minded Sam's compliments.

As they ate their meal a short time later, Sam squeezed Sarah's hand beneath the table so many times she lost count. She nudged his knee more than once, not caring if it was inappropriate, and they'd exchanged silly glances as often as possible. Mom and Dad watched them, trading smiles of their own. The expression in her mother's eyes was wistful. Could it be she was reliving memories of shared moments like this with Dad from the early days of their own courtship? At one point, she noticed her parents holding hands on top of the table. That was something she hadn't witnessed in forever.

"Looks like Captain Lewis has stolen my daughter's heart." The ladies washed up the dishes and Sam once again kept company with her father. Thankfully, Mom lowered her voice before she made that statement. Tess had left the kitchen to retrieve something out of Mom's suitcase, and Sarah suspected her mother's request was an excuse for them to talk privately.

"He's wonderful, Mom. I never would have believed it possible, but he's in love with me."

Mom walked over to where she stood at the sink, put her arms around her and hugged her from behind. "Honey, why wouldn't he love you? I know what I said before about the difference in your ages, but I can see now that it doesn't matter. You've always been mature for your age."

Moving beside her, they both faced the kitchen window. "Even when you were much younger, I sometimes thought you could teach your old mother a thing or two. You and Sam have been friends for a long time, and you seem to have a lot in common. More importantly," she said with a slight catch in her voice, "you and Sam share a love of the Lord and a desire to serve Him. That's a bond like none other. I can tell how much you love him. It's in your eyes when you look at him. He's a good man, Sarah, and you'll be happy together."

Sarah finished the dishes and they sat down at the table. "It's premature to talk about such things."

"Perhaps, but it'll happen." Her mother sipped from a glass of water. "When Sam comes to ask your father for your hand in marriage, we'll give him our blessing."

Sarah's cheeks felt warm, and she prayed Sam couldn't overhear their conversation. Dad had turned on the television, and based on the familiar newscaster's voice, she assumed the men must be watching the news. Hopefully, the sound would drown out what was being discussed in the kitchen.

"Tess and Charlie Sorrel are dating, too. He's good for her, Mom, and she seems to really like him."

"That's certainly an answer to prayer. Maybe your father and I should go away more often. You're in that early stage of your relationship with Sam. Enjoy it. That euphoria and passion you're feeling right now won't last forever, but love can endure through the years and be very satisfying in many different ways."

Sarah nodded. "I know." For now, she'd enjoy the euphoria. And yes, the passion. In her heart, she looked forward to the kind of passion to be shared in a marriage relationship. *Sorry, Mrs. Bittenbottom. Yes, I think about these things before marriage.*

Tess came back into the kitchen and held up a blue cup emblazoned with the U.S. Air Force Academy logo. "Is this what you wanted me to find, Mom? Seriously? It took long enough."

"That's it. Sarah, honey, that's your souvenir from Colorado."

Sarah's eyes grew wide as Tess handed the cup to her. "How did you. . ."

Mom shrugged. "Oh, I don't know. Maybe I suspected you had an affinity for a handsome fly boy right here in Rockbridge."

Sam sat beside Sarah on the porch swing outside the Jordan home later in the evening. Shortly after they'd gone outside, Nadine turned on the porch light. Although he knew Bill and Nadine trusted him, and even though he was getting older by the minute, they were Sarah's parents. As such, they were asserting the boundaries. He could only respect their wishes, and he fully intended to honor their daughter. Never would he put Sarah in a position to compromise her. He loved her, and he'd be patient.

The only sound to break the quiet of the night was the pesky buzzing of the insects attracted to the outside light.

"I'm glad you could have supper with us tonight," Sarah said. "The invitation's always open. You don't need to ask or let us know in advance. Just stop by after work."

He laughed. "Admit it. You just needed someone with muscles to bring in the luggage."

"Hey, I've got muscles." She raised her arm and flexed for him.

"Not bad," Sam said, squeezing her upper arm. "Have you been working out?"

"Other than swimming at Thornton's Creek, no. And lifting trays at Perry's, of course."

Whatever she was doing, it worked. "Thanks for the perpetual invite," he said, "but I'm not sure your mother would appreciate such a casual 'do drop in' policy."

"She likes you, Sam. So does Dad. They wouldn't mind." She turned to face him on the swing. "Did I ever tell you that Mom was engaged once before?" When he shook his head, she launched into her story. "She was engaged to her high school sweetheart, but she broke the engagement when she caught him kissing another girl. He'd claimed to be a Christian man, and it left her disillusioned for a few years, thinking men were unfaithful liars. Then she moved from Colorado to San Antonio to live with a widowed aunt for a few years, and worked as a legal secretary. Through clients, she met a young civil engineer named William Jordan. After asking her out for over a year, and repeatedly being turned down, he finally told her to let him know if she ever changed her mind. Then one night, Nadine showed up on his doorstep. As rain poured down, Bill opened the door and she said four words to him. Can you guess what they were?"

Sam's mind had wandered a bit during her story. When he didn't answer, Sarah poked him in the ribs. "I have no idea," he said. "What did she say?"

"I changed my mind."

"Aw, come on, Sarah. Cut me a break. I got distracted by your beauty. Tell me what she said."

She laughed and then laughed some more. "That *was* what Mom said. 'I changed my mind.' Oh, never mind. What were you thinking about? Should I even ask?"

He'd started to move his arm around her but stopped, teasing her. With a smile, Sarah took his arm and planted it on the swing behind her. Pushing against the floor of the porch with his cowboy boot, he started them swinging.

"I was thinking how good Charlie and Tess are together. She brings out the best in him, and he does the same for Tess." Sam laughed. "I'll say one thing. You sure are relentless as a landowner, and that sister of yours can be equally conniving." After dinner, they'd all enjoyed a fun evening playing Monopoly.

Sarah laughed and leaned her head on his shoulder. "You're just upset because I bankrupted the vice president of Rockbridge Savings & Loan. I hated to do it, but when you rent my houses and hotels, you've got to pay up, mister." She patted one hand on his chest. "You're a handsome loser, so you're forgiven."

"*I'm* forgiven?" Laughing, he kissed the top of her head. "I'll forgive *you* as long as you promise never to call me loser again, in any sense of the word."

"Promise." She settled more firmly in the curve of his arm, nestled against him.

He loved sitting like this with Sarah. A gentle rain began to fall, filling the air with the scent of blooming roses and damp earth. He kept them swinging, content in the quiet.

"We haven't been to the creek as much lately. Why is that?" she said.

"Probably because I no longer need to follow you to the creek and then pretend I ran into you by accident, or at least without forethought."

"What?" Sitting up on the swing, Sarah gave him an incredulous look. "You planned it?"

He grinned. "Come on, Sarah. You must know I created opportunities to spend time with you. I'm glad you can be such a creature of habit. Once I realized you went to the creek almost every evening, I made sure I sat and read the paper by the front window. As soon as I saw you come out of your house and come down the street, I'd walk about ten minutes behind you."

"You *followed* me?" She sounded surprised but not mad.

"Not always but sometimes. Call me weird stalker guy. Does that bother you?"

Sarah feigned outrage for a few more seconds before her gorgeous smile emerged. "No. I actually like it, but only because it's you. If it were anyone else, then it would bother me." She tugged on the collar of his shirt. "How clueless was I? I thought it was a God thing, like you just happened to find me there. As if the Holy Spirit whispered to you and filled you with a conviction to visit the creek at such and such a time." Her eyes widened. "Is that a bad thing to say? Irreverent, I mean?"

He chuckled. "No, I don't think so. I know what you meant. More like God bellowed and told me to hightail it over there and get to know my neighbor again. For the record, the very first time I found you at the creek, it *was* by accident."

"Oh, I disagree." With her hand still on his collar, she pulled him close. "It was no accident."

"Hmm," he murmured. "If this is the way you disagree, let's do some more of it."

"Dad might be coming out any minute to check on us," she whispered against his lips. That was no idle threat. Bill had a habit of flicking that front porch light on and off in rapid succession as his cue they'd spent enough time together. Made him feel like a teenager stealing kisses with Sarah, but maybe it was for the best.

"All the more reason not to waste time talking." He lowered his head, anticipating the taste of her sweet lips. The way she responded to him made him forget about everything else in the world and turned him into a romantic fool.

Lightly pushing against his chest, Sarah shook her head. She didn't want to kiss him? That was a first. He didn't like it, but maybe it was best since he needed to keep his emotions in check. The more private time they spent together, the deeper he'd fallen in love with her.

He blew out a sigh. "What's on your mind?"

"I have one last question before I head inside the house."

"Should I be afraid?" His chuckle belied his question.

"Not at all. I just wanted to ask if, in some way, your new car is a substitute for your plane."

That statement surprised him. "A substitute?"

"You know, replaced the plane in your affections."

"My affections? Just give it to me straight, Sarah."

Her eyes met his. "Okay, then. Here goes. Why don't you fly anymore?"

His jaw tightened. In the back of his mind, he'd suspected Sarah would get around to asking him that question. "We've already had this discussion. It's not like I have a personal embargo on flying the plane."

"Are you afraid for some reason? Is it the Ménière's Disease?"

"No, it's not." The words came out harsher than he'd intended. They sat in silence for a few minutes. Finally, he said, "I don't know. Maybe it is. I haven't been able to go out to the airstrip and take Caty in the air since I came home."

"Caty?"

"The name of our plane. It's also my father's nickname for my mom. Meaning I could be in serious trouble if Dad ever finds out that I told you."

"My lips are sealed. Your secret is safe with me although I think it's a very cute nickname." Sarah swept one finger over her lips in a zipping motion. "I don't mean to push you, and of course, you need to work through your issues or whatever. It's just that I know how much you love to fly. For years, it's all you talked about. I remember how happy your parents said you were when you got the acceptance letter from the Air Force Academy. Your mom said you didn't stop smiling for a week. For all I know, you carried that letter around in your back pocket for a month."

"You think you know me pretty well, don't you?"

"I do, and please don't change the subject."

Rising from the swing, he walked to the porch railing. He pushed his hands down into his pockets and stared ahead, unseeing. "Like I said, you catch on quick."

"This isn't about me," she said quietly. "It's about you. I hate to see you not doing something I know you love."

He jerked up his head. "That makes us even then, doesn't it? At least I offered you the means to make your dream happen, but you rejected it."

"I explained that. I wasn't rejecting *you*, Sam." Her voice was so quiet, he almost didn't hear her. "There's a difference. Please understand that."

"Is there? I'm not so sure." He turned and looked out over the dark expanse of the Jordan's front lawn, attempting to keep his frustration in check. "I will fly again, but don't push me."

"I'm sure you will. But sometimes the best way to conquer our fear is to face it head-on." Lifting out of the swing, Sarah walked across the short expanse of the porch to reach his side. His arguments faded a little more with each step she took in his direction.

"Tell you one thing," Sam said, swallowing hard. "When I do fly again, I want my favorite, beautiful daredevil beside me in the cockpit."

"Are you still taking your medicine?"

So much for trying to lighten the mood. "Yes." His shoulders fell.

"Then you're afraid. I can't imagine any valid reason otherwise."

"No, I'm not. It's not that. You're pushing me again." Why couldn't she let it go? Sarah couldn't know how he missed flying, how much he wanted to take Caty up in the air again. He missed flying so much he physically ached at times, as crazy as that sounded. She couldn't understand. Then again, maybe she did. While he appreciated her concern, he didn't want to talk about it anymore.

"I think it is. Your turn to promise me one thing." Taking his hand, she turned his palm face up and pressed her soft lips on it. Oh, my, that was good. His knees almost buckled, and Sam gripped the porch railing to steady himself.

Lowering his hand, Sam tugged Sarah into his embrace and leaned his head against hers. "What am I promising?"

"The Lord is the one who goes ahead of you; He will be with you. He will not fail you or forsake you. Do not fear or be dismayed." When he started to speak, she put one finger over his lips. "Pray about it. Promise me."

"Promise." He walked down the front steps, thankful the rain had stopped, but then turned back to face her, seized by a random thought. "Did you enjoy the peach pie you won at the school carnival?"

"From the cakewalk? It's in the extra ice box we keep in the garage. We wanted to save the pie for when Mom and Dad returned from their trip. I probably should have served it tonight. Why do you ask?"

"No reason. Good night." The corners of his mouth twitched. Turning, Sam started down the front walkway.

"Oh no, you don't. You're coming with me."

Ten minutes later, Sam sat obediently at the kitchen table after Sarah ordered him to stay put. The rest of the family had retired to their bedrooms. Coming back in from the garage, she placed the pie on the table in front of him.

"Is it frozen?"

"No, just cool. Hope that's okay."

"It's fine." He drummed out a beat on the table until she stilled his hands. "The point was that you're supposed to cut into the pie when I'm not around."

"Ah, so I foiled your plan? Good." She grinned as she pulled a pie server from a drawer and held it up in the air. "I knew something was up at that cakewalk. Your merry little band of friends—older ladies, bank customers, young mothers—kept nudging each other and winking at me."

"Good for them." Feeling somewhat disgruntled, Sam watched as she cut a generous slice and put it on a plate. She added a fork and then pushed the plate toward him.

"Would you like ice cream with your pie?"

"Not necessary."

"For a man who loves his peach pie—especially one made by his mother with her special secret family recipe—you don't seem especially happy. Matter of fact, you seem rather sulky tonight."

She made a big show of cutting another slice of pie, a smaller one. Why was she drawing this out and making him squirm? Taking the chair across from him, Sarah picked up the daintiest bite in the world with her fork. "Wait. Shouldn't we pray first? It is food, after all."

"Sure." He grabbed her hand. "Lord, thank you for this peach pie which we are about to enjoy. In Jesus's name. Amen."

"Amen," Sarah murmured. "Short and to the point. Nice."

"By the way, Fletcher came into the bank the other day. Guess who was with him?"

She sectioned off another equally ridiculous small bite of the pie and her eyes grew wide. "Sally Barksdale?"

"Yep. Congratulations on your cupid skills. In other Rockbridge financial news, I presented Martin Benson with a check to cover the cost of the headstone for Marty's grave. There was enough left over for a good start on more memorials. So, kudos to you for your amazing fundraising skills."

"Sam, stop it." Sarah's voice was firm. "You're acting like a spoiled little boy. It's great to hear those things. Thanks for telling me, in spite of the sarcasm behind them. Are you still sore because I asked about—"

"Yeah, maybe. I'm sorry." He put his fork on his plate and rubbed his eyes. "It's been a long day. I'm kind of beat." She'd hit too close to the truth as to why he hadn't flown Caty since coming home, and it bothered him, unreasonable or not. Granted, he *was* tired, and when he was tired, he knew himself well enough to know he got grumpy. He needed to go. When he started to rise from the table, Sarah pushed him back down into the chair with one firm hand on his shoulder. Bossy woman.

"Let's find out what's so special about this particular pie, and then you can be on your way. I'll make it quick. You know, before you came along, I didn't even like peaches all that much."

His frown grew deeper. "Nice to—"

"You didn't let me finish." With the pie server, she dug around beneath the pie while he watched. "I was going to say that through the years, I've developed a great fondness for them, especially in your mom's pie. Bingo!" Her eyes lit. "I think I've found something. What could. . ."

Taking his fork, Sam lifted up a part of the pie to reveal another layer of foil. "Dig beneath the bottom layer of foil."

She glanced up at him for a second before lifting the foil with her finger. "Well, would you look here? It's a card of some sort. In an envelope." She flicked it back and forth between her fingers. "What, oh what, could this be?"

"Look at it and find out."

With a curious expression, Sarah pulled out the card and scanned it. Her eyes grew round. "Sam." Her voice had softened. She put the card on the table and moved beside where he sat.

He didn't budge. He could be as stubborn as Sarah when he wanted. For whatever reason, he was going to make her work for this one.

"Stand up, please."

"Make me."

"I'm ordering you, Captain."

Chuckling, he slowly rose to his feet. "Only because you're beautiful even in your bossiness."

Sarah inched her hands around his neck, once more draining his last ounce of resistance to her. What this woman did to him. She was tempting under any circumstances, but never more so than when she'd just eaten a slice of peach pie. Wow. He must be more tired than he'd thought.

"I seem to recall a handsome man at the church luncheon telling me that only someone very special would be given your mother's peach pie recipe."

"That's right. Secret family recipe, mind you. It's a once in a lifetime offer, and you're it, baby. Please just be quiet and kiss me." Sam lowered his head. "And be sure to guard that recipe with your life."

"It will be my honor, Captain."

And then Sarah gave him the absolute best kiss of his life.

Chapter 40

~~♥~~

The Next Week

Sam's steps faltered as he approached Perry's. How could he tell her? He wasn't sure if Sarah was scheduled to work, but she normally worked the early shift on Wednesday mornings. The familiar smells of coffee and frying bacon greeted him as soon as he pushed open the door and entered the diner. The bell signaled his arrival. Sometimes he wanted to yank that bell off and bury it where it'd never be found.

"Hey, Sam! Have a seat, and I'll go get your coffee."

"Thanks, Myrna." He headed toward his usual spot, thankful it was empty. After nodding at a few of his dad's cronies, Sam dropped into the seat. He felt mentally and physically drained and hadn't slept well once he'd finally gotten home in the wee hours of the morning.

The older woman's brows drew together as she approached his table. "What's made you so sour this early on such a beautiful day?"

She must not have heard the news. "Merle wrapped his car around a tree last night on the outskirts of town."

"Oh, mercy!" Myrna moved one hand over her heart and dropped into the opposite side of the booth. "Is he—"

Full of mixed emotions, Sam heaved a deep sigh. "He's hanging on, but he was in surgery most of the night to repair the internal damage. He lost a lot of blood."

"Was he—"

"Merle wasn't drinking, but he was speeding and hit the tree head-

297

on. Doc said he actually died at the scene, but the emergency personnel managed to revive him. They took him to the hospital over in Springhaven. I stayed until the surgery was over, but then I came back home to catch a couple hours of sleep."

"Poor Merle." Myrna shook her graying head and a tear slipped down her cheek. Lifting the corner of her apron, she dabbed it beneath her eyes. "I sure hope he's gonna be okay."

Sam scrubbed one hand over his face, feeling every one of his twenty-seven years. Closer to twenty-eight now, anyway. Every bone in his body ached like he'd been physically slammed. "Tommy called me late last night. Told me he didn't know who else to call since Merle doesn't have any family left and because he works at the bank with me now." He thumped his curled fist on the table. "I guess that qualifies me as the next of kin, not that I mind being there for Merle."

"Merle was mighty lucky you gave him that job. I know he appreciated it. I've always said that boy was the most likely person in this town to kill himself, one way or the other. Not to sound harsh, but that's just the way it is." Myrna shook her head. "Sounds like he almost got the job done last night."

"Merle suffers from a legacy of low expectations," Sam said. A yawn escaped and he covered his mouth with one hand.

"You're gonna tell Sarah, I take it?"

"Yes. I think I need to be the one to tell her. I probably shouldn't have come here while she's working, but I need to head back to the hospital in a bit." From behind the kitchen door, he heard Sarah engaged in lively banter with Jimmy and Patti, and it swelled his heart even as regret seized him. She sounded happy, and he hated to take away her joy. But it had to be done.

"Sarah covered Patti's shift again last night," Myrna said, interrupting his thoughts. "If she needs to leave, tell her not to worry about it. You take good care of our girl, Sam. We'll make do." She squeezed his hand, and in so doing, gave him a small measure of comfort. "You need to tell her before someone else blurts it out. It's only a matter of an hour, give or take, before it's the talk of the diner."

Myrna leaned close. "Especially when something like this happens, it's a wakeup call from God of how important others are in our life. Family"—she quirked a brow—"or otherwise. Before Sarah goes off to nursing school, I sure hope you're gonna stake your claim on her heart."

Before he could respond, Myrna slid out of the seat and hustled behind the swinging kitchen door. Sam leaned back in the seat and braced himself, closing his eyes for a moment as he whispered a quiet prayer.

"Myrna said you have something you need to tell me?"

Opening his eyes, Sam cleared his throat as Sarah seated herself opposite him. She looked so pretty with the morning light coming through the front window.

"I thought I should wait until later, but Myrna said I should go ahead and tell you now."

"Sure. Sounds serious." She took hold of his hand. "Is everything okay with your mom and dad?"

"They're fine. It's nothing like that." Sam's brow creased and he met her concerned gaze. "It's Merle. He, um"—he swallowed the hard lump in his throat—"he was in an accident last night. Bad one. He survived, but barely. They lost him for a few minutes, but they managed to revive him."

"Oh, no!" Moisture quickly filled Sarah's eyes and tears streamed down her cheeks. Seeing her cry twisted him inside, rendering him with a sense of helplessness he'd never before experienced. Moving quickly to the other side of the booth, he slid in by her side and gathered her in his arms. Yanking a napkin from the dispenser on the table, he handed it to her. Sam held her, blocking out everyone and everything else, absorbing her trembling body and soft sobs.

Sarah's tears soaked through the napkin. Tossing it on the tabletop, she then buried her face against his chest. "I'm sorry about your shirt."

"That's what it's for." The other patrons in the diner were quiet. He noted Myrna moving among the tables, no doubt telling them what happened. Perhaps he should escort Sarah outside the diner and take her somewhere more private, but several of the ladies in the diner were now also openly crying. Even some of the men were wiping their eyes.

Sam hung his head. He'd shared about the Lord with Merle and tried to impress upon him the need for a solid anchor in his life. Based on the way he'd shown up to work faithfully every day, even though only for a short time, Merle seemed to be straightening out his life.

Leaning his head against Sarah's, the sweet-smelling scent of her hair giving him its own comfort, Sam began to pray. "Dear Jesus, I pray what I've shared with Merle might have made an impression upon him. We don't have the answers, but you do."

Sarah squeezed his hand. "Father, no man's life should be full of disappointment and regret." The others in the diner remained quiet, and a number of the other customers had also bowed their heads and nodded at her words. "We ask that you bless Merle, and if it's in your will, please heal him. If he's spared, let us all help Merle in whatever way we can, as you've given to each one of us unique talents and abilities."

When she said nothing further, Sam ended the prayer. "We ask these things in the name of your precious Son. Amen."

"Amen," Sarah whispered. She wiped beneath her eyes with the back of her hand. "Thanks for praying."

Leaving his arm around her, he nodded. "Sometimes prayer is all we have. And it's the *best* thing."

"I need to tell you something." Sarah scooted farther down on the seat, giving him more room. "Merle was here in the diner just last night. Probably not long before the accident. It seems he took Pastor McDonald's message from Second Timothy to heart. The one he heard when he was in church. About fighting the good fight and finishing the race. He said it's only the second time he's been in a church in his entire life except for weddings or funerals."

Sam nodded. "He took off right after church that morning. I wish I could have talked with him then, and I should have talked with him since. It's not like I haven't had the opportunity at the bank."

Cupping his jaw with one hand, Sarah's lips were soft as she graced him with a sweet kiss. "You invited him to church, you know."

"I always invite people to come to church, but—"

"He's watched you at the bank. Without giving me any details, Merle said he admires the way you handle situations and especially the way you deal with people. He said he didn't know a numbers man could be so normal and human. You made him. . .curious about God. *His* words."

Sam scratched his chin and allowed a small smile. "Did he now?" His five o'clock shadow felt rough beneath his fingers.

"Merle's perspective was something I never would have thought about on my own," Sarah told him. "He said he's never felt capable or worthy enough to participate in the race, much less to win one. I've been a Christian so long that maybe I can't fully understand how others feel. People who don't understand what being a believer means because they didn't have parents or anyone to take them to church or read a Bible to them. People who go through the motions without hope for anything after this life." Sarah's eyes met his, and she shrugged. Within seconds, as he watched, another tear streaked down her cheek.

"Ah, baby. Don't cry." Sarah rarely cried, but when she did, it socked him right in the gut.

"I tried to tell Merle how important and valued he is to God. The problem is, from what he told me, he's never felt like he mattered. Not once. His dad wasn't there for school programs. His mother cared more about going out and having a good time than cooking dinner for her son. Can you imagine what that's like, Sam? To feel like your own parents don't want you?" Another tear streaked down her face. "And the worst part of it? I've known Merle a long time and not once have I ever cared enough to speak with him about his salvation."

She raised her hands in frustration. "What kind of nurse will I be if I can't even care for the people who are hurting right in my own neighborhood, so to speak? I have no excuses."

"You can't help them if you don't know they're in pain. Merle stuck to himself. He didn't have many friends. Not that it's an excuse. The simple fact, Sarah—as much as we'd like it to be different—is that we can't save the entire world. But, when circumstances present themselves, like with you and Merle, you took that opportunity, and you ran with it."

The slightest hint of a smile pinched the corners of her lips. "I gave him a Bible, too. I always keep an extra one around in case it's needed."

"That's great," Sam said. "We have to believe he'll be okay." He tugged her closer, unbelievably touched by her compassion. More than ever, Sam determined he'd find a way to send Sarah to nursing school. A way she'd accept. It was probably already too late for the fall semester, but as much as anything else, he acknowledged that nothing was impossible when God was involved.

"You shared your heart with Merle, and we need to pray he'll take your words to heart and read that Bible." He felt as though he should say more. Sometimes, like now, the words wouldn't come. "I wish I had all the answers, sweetheart. But I don't."

"I don't expect you to have the answers." She rested her head on his shoulder. "You're here, and that's all I can ask. We'll let the Lord handle the rest."

Chapter 41

~~♥~~

Two Days Later

Sam glanced up as his father walked into his office without knocking, as usual, and took a chair. He appeared tired, and the deep lines on his forehead seemed more pronounced, especially the vertical one between his brows. He'd admired his dad's work ethic through the years, appreciated his diligence even more since he'd worked alongside him in the bank. His father represented integrity and honesty in a world gone morally and financially bankrupt in many ways.

"What's up, Dad? Are you all right?" Sam lowered his pen to the ledger he'd been examining. Rising from his chair behind the desk, he sat opposite his father. With a start, he glanced out the window and realized the sun had already lowered in the sky. He'd been so involved with his work, he'd barely acknowledged the closing of the bank's front doors and Gina's good-bye.

"I'm fine, son. Just wanted to discuss a few things with you."

"Sure. I'm all ears."

"I've noticed your preoccupation lately."

Sam's brows rose in conjunction with his increased heart rate. "I hope my work performance hasn't slipped in some way."

"No, not exactly."

"Dad, I've dedicated myself to my position and worked hard to—"

"I'm not questioning your work or your dedication." With a

frown, Joseph steepled his fingers, the same action he'd employed through the years. "I'm guessing your preoccupation has a lot to do with Sarah."

Sam swallowed. Had he been that obvious to everyone? This was his dad, and he'd never lied or told a fib to this man. "You're right. I have no excuses." He met his father's eyes. "I'm in love with her."

Joseph surprised him when he broke out in a wide grin. "Well, it's about time you admitted it, son. Have you taken her up in Caty yet?"

Shaking his head, Sam sat back in his chair. "No, but I'm working my way up to it. I need to show her I'm not afraid to fly again, Dad."

"I understand that, son." His father drummed his fingers on the top of Sam's desk in a slow march, his brow furrowed. "Sarah still plans on attending nursing school in Austin?"

"Yes, as soon as she can, but as you know, she turned down my offer to help."

"You know, that move only endears her to me more. I wouldn't have thought twice if she had accepted it, but there's a part of me that admires her more for not taking it." He tapped the top of Sam's desk with one hand before meeting his gaze again. "A woman like that is strong. Like your mother, Sarah's loyal and fiercely independent. However, those same qualities can sometimes work against a man." He chuckled under his breath.

"What are you saying, Dad?"

Joseph leaned forward, planting both hands on the arms of his chair. "When Sarah gets the money to go to Austin—and there's no doubt in my mind that she will, sooner rather than later—I have an idea I'd like to propose, son."

~~❤~~

One Week Later

"Young lady, what do you think you're doing with that creature in here?"

Busted. Slowly, Sarah turned to face the nurse barging into Merle's hospital room. Might as well not try to hide the Beagle puppy she'd smuggled in beneath her cardigan sweater. She shot a *help me!* glance at Sam. He shrugged and grinned. Traitor.

"I'm leaving momentarily," she said to the woman, hoping she sounded appropriately contrite.

Merle chuckled from the bed, a wonderful sound considering everything he'd been through in the past ten days. Three surgeries and two blood transfusions later, he was finally on the mend. "Cut her some slack, Nurse Martha. This is Nurse Sarah, and she didn't mean no harm. She's got the biggest heart of anyone I know. Except you," he added, giving Martha a broad smile.

Sarah almost laughed out loud, but she managed to contain it. Sober Merle amused her. He wasn't half-bad looking either with his hair combed and clean shaven. Her gaze moved to the Bible sitting on his nightstand. Sam had thrown a rock at her bedroom window last night at two in the morning. When she'd snuck out onto the front porch to meet him, he'd told her that Merle had accepted the Lord. In an entirely irreverent manner, they'd kissed to celebrate Merle's decision.

Martha wasn't buying it. Her face seemed frozen in a perpetual frown, and she moved her hands to her hips. "If you're a nurse, then you know better than to bring an animal into a hospital. They're dirty and can bring in germs."

"Yes, ma'am. I'll just be leaving now. Merle, be good." Sarah gave him a wink. "Remember, God's got big plans for you."

"Right back at ya. Thanks for watchin' out for Patches for me until I can get back home."

Sam walked beside her as they took the stairs back down to the ground floor and exited the building together. Holding the adorable puppy in her arms, Sarah murmured sweet nothings and kissed his head.

"I never thought I'd be jealous of a puppy." Sam opened the car door for her. "With all those litters we helped bring into the world, I never could have guessed we'd end up together, conspirators in crime no less."

"Yes, but isn't it grand?" She gave him a blinding smile. "Stop pouting, Captain. It's not very becoming, is it, Patches?" To tease him, she made a big show of showering the puppy with kisses.

"You're nutty, and a disgrace to your intended profession. Smuggling an animal into a hospital. For shame." Sam shook his head but laughed when she swatted his arm. "I'm getting ready to drive us home now. Be nice to me and Volvo, especially since I made an exception for you to bring a dog along in the first place."

"You have a no-pet policy for Volvo? In that case, I have serious doubts about whether or not this relationship will work."

"Oh, it'll work, Sarah." Sam gave her a smile and pulled the car out of the parking lot. As he drove, she played with Patches and then began singing the Dickie Lee song by that name.

"Are you making that up?" Sam darted a skeptical glance her way.

Sarah stopped singing. "What? The song?" She stroked the puppy's head and gave him another quick kiss. "It happens to be the title of a popular song called 'Patches.' It's on the jukebox at the diner. You have to agree it's a perfect name for this little guy, especially since he has these adorable patches of color around his eyes and nose." She traced her finger over the spots.

Sam nodded. "The Barton's dog, Ladybelle, timed that litter well for Merle's sake. Great idea, by the way."

"Thanks. Did you see the way Merle perked up as soon as he got a glimpse of Patches? I just felt so bad when he told me that he'd always felt so alone. No one should be alone in the world. Right, Patches?"

"So, the Bartons are keeping Patches until Merle comes home and can take care of him?"

"That's the plan," Sarah said. "You know I'd love to keep him, but with work and. . ."

"You'll have a dog again in the future, Sarah. Probably more than one. For now, you can rest assured that you've done a good deed for Merle."

"I hope so."

Sam pointed to a billboard on the side of the road close to the Rockbridge exit on the highway. "There's the Perry's Diner sign."

Sarah straightened in the seat and Sam slowed down as they passed the sign. "It's very nice even if the waitresses wear the ugliest orthopedic shoes in the world," she said, laughing when he shot her a look.

"I think on Nurse Sarah, they'll look very sexy."

She laughed. "You're crazy. Just drive, please."

~~♥~~

As he listened to one of the elders deliver the Sunday morning message, Sam felt something flit past the back of his head. Thinking it was a large bug, he ran his hand over his hair. A few seconds later, he felt it again. He startled when something flew past him and hit the pew rack. Bouncing off the hymnal, it dropped to the floor.

Sam retrieved it and had to stop himself from bursting out with laughter. He stared at the balled white paper—a classic Sarah Jordan spitball—and rotated it in his hands. He caught his dad's smile and mother's slight frown. Half the congregation must have seen those flying spitballs. Unless they were napping. That was a strong possibility since the sanctuary was stifling hot today. Everywhere he looked, the ladies were fanning themselves and most everyone seemed uncomfortably hot. Unbuttoning the top of his shirt, Sam loosened his collar and tie. Because of the record heat, he hadn't bothered wearing his suit coat.

She'd never written a personal note on a spitball before, but he sensed today might be different. He started to open it, but the paper rustled with his movements, making too much noise. Not wanting to draw undue attention to himself—probably already too late for that, anyway—Sam paused every few seconds and focused on the message.

Poor Gary Sanders looked so nervous. He alternated between wiping his face with his hankie every other minute and gripping the edge of the pulpit. Considering the message was the next passage in Matthew directly following the one Pastor McDonald had given the week before, he figured Gary was reading a prepared sermon.

Not wanting to be disrespectful, Sam waited until the organist began to play the closing hymn and everyone rose to their feet. Opening the balled wad of paper, he didn't bother to hide his smile.

Meet me at the creek at two o'clock. ~sarah j.

The spitball he held in his hands only confirmed his plan to help Sarah find her way to Austin sooner rather than later.

Opening the front door, Sarah found Sam lounging against the porch railing, a leather glove on one hand as he tossed a softball in the air.

"Hey, Sport. Ready to practice?"

"I beg your pardon?" She laughed and ran a hand over her hair. "I thought we were going to meet at the creek at two. That's what my spitball said."

"Change of plans to prove your adaptability and flexibility"—he grinned—"quite literally for that last one. We're going to the ball field. Time to work on your fastball and your swing."

"Why would we do that?"

"Come with me, and I'll explain on the way."

She shot him a *why would I do that?* glance.

"You seem to need me to sweeten the deal." He moved closer and lounged against the doorframe. He gave her a cockeyed, more handsome than sin—as Debbie would say—smile. She hadn't fully understood that description until this moment. "Come with me now and I'll treat you to dinner one night this week at Quentin's."

Her brows rose. "That's a mighty tempting offer, Mr. Lewis. Quentin's, eh? Pretty fancy schmancy, but I suppose a hifalutin' banker like you can afford it."

"So, what do you say?" He batted his eyelashes in an exaggerated manner, making her laugh.

"I say you're on, but make it a picnic in Oak Park or at the creek instead. That's every bit as romantic, and maybe even more so. Just give me a couple of minutes to change and I'll be right out."

"What's wrong with what you're wearing now?" Sam's admiring gaze skimmed over her, making her heated in an entirely different way than the outdoor temperature. "You look mighty fine to me. Plus, you'll probably get dirty, anyway, so what's the point?"

Laughing, Sarah gave her shorts and TeamWork T-shirt a quick once-over glance. "True. I'll grab my key. Hang on a second." She could hear him tossing and catching the ball as she darted into the bedroom. Glancing in the mirror, she groaned. What a sight. Sam must really love her to see her in this disheveled state and not run in the opposite direction. Her hair was messy and—she leaned closer to the mirror—good heavens, was that dirt smudged on her cheek? She'd been doing some laundry and household chores and expected to cool off in the creek, not work up a sweat playing ball. Even so, the thought of playing softball again thrilled her, but what made Sam think of this idea? No matter the reason, she loved it. She loved *him*.

Grabbing her brush, Sarah ran it through her hair before scooping it into a high ponytail. Then she ran into the hallway bathroom and brushed her teeth in record time. Back in her bedroom again, she fished out a baseball cap before tucking her house key in her pocket.

"Wow. You look adorable," Sam said a minute later, tugging on the brim of her cap. When he leaned close, she met his lips. The rough stubble of his beard irritated her skin, but she didn't mind. His voice was low and husky. She was getting used to that, too, and loved that she could bring about that reaction in Sam.

She tweaked his chin. "You didn't shave on a Sunday morning?"

"Nope. I'm thinking of growing a beard."

Her jaw gaped. "That would be a crime. A beard would cover up those addictive smile lines."

He laughed, bringing them very much into evidence. "Are you saying you like them?"

She smirked. "Smile lines do not make the man, but they're very attractive."

"That's one of the nicest compliments you've ever given me." Sam draped his arm around her shoulders. "I'll shave later on. For you. Want to drive or walk?"

"Let's walk. So you can keep your arm around me and tell me what this is all about."

"I have an idea," he said. "Bear with me and let me explain before you slam the idea."

Sarah frowned. "When you put it like that, I'm not sure, but I'm listening."

"What's your number one goal? Other than to love me until the end of time?"

"To go to nursing school," she said without hesitation. "Oh, and that other thing applies, too."

"Exactly." He nodded. "For nursing school, you need extra funds, but you won't accept my money. Already tried that. As you know, my offer met with spectacularly underwhelming results."

"So, what's your new plan?" They turned the corner of their street, headed to the ball field another three blocks away at the high school.

"What's the one thing you do better than anything else, other than charming the socks off me and everyone else and being the best waitress Perry's Diner has ever had?"

Sarah burst out laughing. "Understanding what you mean even when you spout ridiculously long sentences?"

He paused on the sidewalk. "Besides that?" Tossing the ball in the air, he watched as she reached for and caught it.

"Softball?"

"Yeppers. Combining all those factors, I came up with a brilliant idea. Softball tryouts to determine scholarships for the second semester are being held at the university in three weeks."

"Which university? *My* university?"

"None other." Sam's blue eyes lit with enthusiasm, and he placed his large hands on her shoulders. "Think about it. You'll wow them with your talent, Sarah. I know you will. They won't have any choice but to offer you a full scholarship."

She gulped, trying to absorb this latest bit of information. "At the main campus of the University of Texas? In Austin?"

"Yes, baby. The Longhorns. They have a women's softball team."

Sarah raised her eyes to his. Lowering his head, Sam kissed her, leaving no doubt in her mind of this man's deep respect and love for her. Enough to want her see her dreams fulfilled.

"I haven't played in a few years. I'm probably terribly rusty."

Sam's smile downturned. "I'm sure it'll be like riding a bicycle, and it'll come back to you quickly. You're not willing to try?"

"No. It's not that at all." Sarah shook her head, almost overwhelmed by this handsome, completely wonderful, unselfish man who believed in her, who was willing to sacrifice for her, who loved her. She crooked a finger and summoned him closer. "Come here. Please."

He appeared puzzled but silently did as she asked. Moving her hand to the back of his neck, Sarah raised her chin and kissed him, not holding anything back. In the haze of the kiss, she was aware when he dropped the baseball glove and ball to the ground. Tugging her as close as humanly possible, Sam wrapped his arms around her and deepened their kiss. When she stroked his hair and heard a small moan escape his lips, she smiled.

At length, she whispered against his lips, "Thank you for believing in me, sacrificing so much for me. For loving me."

"If I'd known it would get this kind of reaction, I would have come up with this idea a long time ago," he whispered.

"You're a very wise man."

"Thanks, but I can't take the credit. I give God the glory for this one with a bit of help from Jimmy and my dad for their wise counsel."

She smiled. "Really? That sounds like a story I need to hear sometime."

He kissed her nose. "You will. They both got me thinking, and then I made a couple of phone calls. I have the application for the tryouts at the house. Since we don't have church on Sunday nights this month, I can work on my spreadsheets at your house tonight if you want to work on the application. I kind of like having you around."

"I thought you observed the day of rest and always take a nap on Sundays. And, if you're with me now, I'm sure that's going to seriously cramp your naptime."

His brows lifted. "You can join me for a nap when we get back later. On the sofa, of course. Feet on the floor, if you insist. Perfectly respectable. Besides, I'll probably be too worn out to try anything."

"Sounds like a plan." She grinned. "Dad will be home, anyway. He'll keep us in line."

He frowned. "Don't remind me. I'm almost twenty-eight years old, not in high school."

"You'll understand one day when you're a dad with daughters and their suitors come to call. But, for now," she said, tweaking his chin, "let's go practice."

"That's what I thought we were doing." Sam laughed and gave her a wink as he retrieved the mitt and ball from where they'd landed on the ground at his feet.

"Come on, Captain. Stop dawdling!" Sarah called over her shoulder as she sprinted toward the field.

Chapter 42

~~♥~~

Two Weeks Later

"Sarah?" Eddie called to her from across the diner.

"Yes?" She'd just delivered Perry's platter to him and a vanilla shake to her mother, who sat with Betty Raines at another table. Glancing at the clock, she noted it was almost time for Sam's break soon. The door opened and Tess walked in with Debbie. They both waved and smiled as they found a table in Patti's station.

"A messenger guy just came by with a message for you," Eddie said when she approached him. "It wasn't written down or anything, though. He asked me to play something for you on the jukebox but told me not to sing along even though I have a very nice voice."

Sarah's brows arched. "The delivery guy really said all that?"

"Yeah." He shrugged. "I know, it sounds weird, but just go along with me on this, okay? Hang on a minute, let me find it." She watched as Eddie inserted a coin and punched in a selection. "Sealed with a Kiss" began playing in the dining room as she darted into the kitchen to pick up another order.

Spying her, Myrna frowned. "What are you doing in here?"

"My job, last time I checked." Catching Jimmy's smile, Sarah stopped. "What?"

"Get yourself out there, Jelly Bean."

"Let me get the rest of the orders for Table 16 first."

"You're not any better at following orders now than you were at sixteen. Come on, girl." Taking her by the collar, Myrna practically

312

hauled her to the swinging door.

"Okay, okay. I can handle walking out there on my own," Sarah protested, straightening her uniform. "What's with everyone today?"

Pushing the door, Sarah stopped short. Not one person in the entire dining area was talking. They all looked at her and then followed her gaze as she spied Air Force Captain Samuel Joseph Lewis standing in the doorway, wearing his full dress service uniform, holding a bouquet of beautiful pink, blooming roses.

He walked toward her to the strains of the song playing on the jukebox. Placing the bouquet on a nearby table, he removed his uniform hat and laid it beside the flowers. "Hi." A slow smile teased the corners of his mouth, and his incredible blue eyes danced with light and love.

Sarah beckoned him closer and whispered. "Sam, we're kind of making a scene."

"I don't think anyone minds. Do you hear the song playing on the jukebox?"

"Yes." She nodded slowly. "Sealed with a Kiss."

"Exactly. Sarah, when you wrote that poem to me, and you sealed it—"

"With a kiss," she murmured.

"You catch on quick." Stepping closer, he cupped her face between his hands.

"My mother is sitting right over there in the corner."

"Don't care," he said, his voice already growing husky in the way she loved. Sam brushed his lips over hers. "Hold on just a second." He released his hold on her for a moment and motioned to the busboy still standing by the jukebox. "Eddie? Next one, please."

"Sure thing, Captain Lewis. Sorry about that." Eddie's face turned beet red and he bent his head over the jukebox as he deposited a couple of coins. Soon enough, Elvis crooned "Can't Help Falling in Love."

"May I have this dance, Miss Jordan?" Sam held out his hand to her.

Might as well humor the man. "Certainly, Captain Lewis." Trying her best to tune out everyone watching them in the diner, Sarah walked into his arms. Sam the military officer did such wonderful things to her. Stepping forward, she rested her left hand on his shoulder while he moved his arm around her waist and clasped her right hand. He began to dance with her, his eyes never leaving hers.

"This song was playing on the jukebox here in the diner when you walked in after your homecoming parade," she said. "When you walked into my life again after a very long absence. Too long, I'd say. The song was very fitting."

He smiled and kissed her forehead, moving slowly with her. "I'd have to say the same thing. When I saw you behind the counter, I couldn't wait to talk with you. Get to know you again. Grow to love you—not just as my little neighbor girl from down the street, but as the beautiful woman I hold in my arms now. You, Sarah Jordan, are everything I've ever wanted." Easing out of her arms, he slid down to the floor on one knee.

"Sam. . ." Sarah trembled. Tears sprang into her eyes and she quickly brought her hands to her face. Could this be happening? Was Sam proposing marriage to her right here in Perry's Diner? Her head was spinning. When the bell on the door jingled, and her father—followed by Catherine and Joseph Lewis—stepped inside the diner, crowding the doorway, staring at them with wide smiles, that was all the confirmation she needed.

"Sweet Sarah," Sam said, gently taking her left hand in his, "I've liked you from the first moment you showed up on my doorstep when I was sixteen and you were ten. I've admired you since you sent the poem to me when I was overseas. I've been charmed by you from the day I returned to Rockbridge. I've adored you since that first time we met at the creek. And I've *loved* you since that ridiculous fight we had right here in Perry's about miniature orange slices in a can." Sam waited as she laughed quietly and then bit her lower lip. "I adore your spirit, your compassion and sensitivity, the way you challenge me, and how you make me want to be a better man. For *you*. Always, I have respected you, and forever, I will love you."

Reaching into the pocket of his jacket, Sam smiled as he pulled out a small black velvet box. He opened the lid and turned the box around for her to see the sparkling, marquise cut diamond ring inside. "Sarah Jane Jordan, I'd be honored if you'd agree to become my wife."

"Yes, Sam," she said through her tears. "I'd be honored, and I'd love nothing better, than to be your wife." Everyone in the diner erupted, clapping and chanting their names.

They shared a chaste kiss appropriate for their audience, and then he pulled her close and whispered in her ear. "Just so you know, I've got a plan. No matter what happens at that tryout next week, you're still going to nursing school and I'm joining you as soon as we're married."

"You're coming to nursing school with me?"

"Sort of." Sam kissed her again, this time allowing his lips to linger.

Sarah pulled back, her hands on his chest. "You're still determined to buy my love aren't you?" When he stared at her, wide-eyed, she traced the smile line on the right side of his mouth and winked. "Don't worry. I'm only teasing. I'm definitely going to get that scholarship, and you can ride into Austin on my coat tails."

He laughed and kissed her again. "I love you."

"And I love you more than you know."

"Hey! It's 'Twist and Shout' time, everybody!" Eddie called out to the customers.

As their friends and family partied around them, Sam slipped the ring onto her finger. "Come on," he said in the midst of their merriment, offering his hand to her.

"Where are we going?" Sarah put her hand in his, feeling silly, giddy, and hopelessly euphoric. She'd go anywhere with this man.

"First to change and then—"

"The creek?"

"Can't think of anything I'd like better," Sam said as they ventured out into the sunshine, as bright as the joy in Sarah's heart.

Chapter 43

~~♥~~

Late August 1962

Standing in front of his plane, Sam checked his watch. Ten minutes until Sheriff Tommy should arrive at the airstrip with Sarah. She had no idea she'd be going for her first plane ride today. He couldn't wait to see the look on her face, and could only hope she wouldn't be absolutely terrified. No longer was he afraid to fly again, and he needed to prove it to her. If he wasn't confident in his abilities, he'd never risk taking her up in the air with him. He'd been taking short test flights with his dad quite a few times in the past month, enough to get accustomed to, and feel comfortable in, the cockpit. They'd purposely stayed away from the airspace directly above Rockbridge and soared over empty fields and Springhaven instead. He'd loved every minute.

God, you are so good. Always.

Flying had once been as natural to him as breathing. Well, maybe that was stretching it, but it was pretty close. He'd missed flying with the freedom and excitement it offered, and with the Lord's help, a ton of prayer, and encouragement from his parents, he'd conquered the fear. As long as he continued to take his medication on a regular basis, the Ménière's Disease shouldn't affect his ability to fly. He might start to lose some of his hearing in the future, but he'd deal with that if and when it eventually happened.

Over and over, Sam returned to the verse from 2 Corinthians 12:10: *Therefore, I am content with weaknesses, with insults, with distresses, with persecutions, with difficulties, for Christ's sake; for when I am weak, then I am strong.*

Sarah had worked hard to train and condition up until the time of the softball tryouts. He'd coached her most every night, even in the rain unless they were getting pounded by a thunderstorm. They jogged together around the town most mornings. Then he'd meet Sarah on her front porch and they'd walk downtown together. They'd kiss on the steps of City Hall and then part ways until he came into the diner on his lunch hour. Then, on his afternoon break, he'd go back to Perry's, the green folder tucked under his arm. Instead of sketching Sarah, he'd sketched Perry, Merle and Eddie, to name a few. Each time he finished a sketch, he'd present it to his subjects. He'd started a waiting list and been offered payment for his work, which he always refused. He enjoyed sketching as a hobby, but that's all it was.

The world around them was fraying at the seams. Film star Marilyn Monroe died early in the month from an overdose of sleeping pills, and the Cuban and Soviet governments were reportedly building secret missile bases in Cuba. He'd also talked with the Air Force recruiting office in Austin. With tensions ramping up in Vietnam and Cuba, he might be needed to help get guys signed up for the service.

After checking his watch again—five more minutes if Tommy was on time—Sam smiled as he recalled how Sarah had aced her softball tryout. The day she received the official letter from the University of Texas in Austin, which offered her a full-ride tuition scholarship in exchange for playing on their women's softball team, she'd burst into the bank lobby, waving it in the air. "Sam, I'm in! I'm in!" She'd run to him and thrown her arms around his neck, peppering him with kisses. "We're going to Austin!"

He'd never had any doubt. After reading the letter she'd thrust under his nose, he picked Sarah up and whirled her in a slow circle before lowering her to the floor. In front of God, his bank employees and customers, Sam kissed her. "I'm so unbelievably proud of you. Yes, we're going to Austin, baby." With his arm securely tucked around her waist, he'd announced her good news to everyone. Then he'd kissed her again. Most of the bank tellers stared at them, slack-jawed, while his father shook his head with a wide smile. The customers cheered and rushed over to both of them to extend hearty congratulations, including Martin Benson. From where he'd been working by the front door, Merle had given them a salute and a wide grin.

Based on his dad's recommendation, and after a series of interviews, Sam was set to begin work as the vice president of a prestigious Austin bank in January. Once he'd admitted to his dad that he was in love with Sarah, Joseph had encouraged him to apply for the position, knowing he'd be happiest with Sarah. The new position had been part of the plan his dad had proposed, and what a great plan it was.

Most importantly, Sam would marry his beloved Sarah on Christmas Eve and then whisk her off to The Driskill Hotel, an elegant, historic landmark in downtown Austin, for their honeymoon. Even though it was months in advance, they'd located an apartment complex near the campus. The accommodating landlord assured them he'd reserve a furnished unit, and they'd started to pick up dishes and assorted items. He was more than happy for Sarah to handle that part of it. The one thing she'd insisted on was the drawing he'd made of her and Perry Sellers, and he'd had it framed. As long as he could fall asleep with Sarah in his arms each night, and wake up with her by his side every morning, he'd consider himself the most blessed man on the planet.

Sam spent as much time with her as humanly possible. Their families often dined together. He and Sarah also double dated with Tess and Charlie, Debbie and Arnie, Candy and Randy, and a few others. Sam smiled as he recalled how Randy bounded up the stairs of the town gazebo at the Fourth of July ice cream social and announced his intention to date Candy Wright. "She's my Miss Wright, but I'm not going to rush things," he'd announced, prompting everyone to laugh and clap.

He'd taken Sarah to his cousin's ranch across the state the previous weekend. The image of her galloping on a stallion, her long blonde hair flying in the wind behind her, would forever be imprinted in his mind. Was there anything the woman couldn't do? Much to his surprise, she'd gone nuts over the sight of him wearing his Stetson and chaps. Who knew? He'd helped out on the ranch while Sarah helped the other ladies cook dinner. When he'd come back inside the main house, all disgustingly sweaty, dusty and dirty, she'd thrown her arms around him and kissed him with such passionate abandon that he'd wanted to whisk her to the nearest pastor and beg him to do the honors. She'd taken to wearing his Stetson in recent weeks— perching it on her head, prancing, and teasing him. He couldn't wait to make her his bride.

Sam broke out of his musing when he spied the sheriff's official vehicle coming toward him on the dirt road. After pulling the car to a stop, Tommy waited for the dust to settle before coming around to the passenger side of the car and opening the door for his beautiful fiancée. Sarah stepped out of the car, and what a vision she presented. As soon as she spied him, with Caty parked behind him, she broke into a wide smile. With a few parting words to Tommy, Sarah slowly walked toward him.

The woman could walk like none other. Not strutting, not floating, but the personification of perfect posture with her head held high and her shoulders squared. Her brown dress sported white polka dots and—tied at the waist with a brown bow—might appear drab and lifeless on any woman but Sarah. Same as with her Perry's Diner pink uniform. A thin, off-white scarf was draped loosely about her neck, the ends flying in the wind, rendering Sarah the epitome of classic, timeless elegance. In one hand, she carried a cluster of wilted, pitiful-looking daisies.

Standing in front of his plane, Sam was content to simply watch her.

This woman is mine. How did I ever get so blessed?

Her hair was pulled in back in the usual loose bun like she preferred. Setting her hair free from that bun had become one of his favorite things in life. Once they were airborne, Sam hoped she might allow those glorious blonde waves their freedom to tumble about her shoulders.

"Something wrong?" Sarah stopped six feet away. "You're looking at me a little funny."

He gave a slight shake of his head. "Counting my blessings and admiring you."

"Thank you." The slow flush started on her neck and crept up into her already rosy cheeks. "It seems like the perfect day to fly."

He took her hand and assisted her up onto the steel runner and then into the seat. Quite a feat in her pretty dress, but she managed with style and aplomb.

"That was quite an adventure in itself." She laughed, straightening the skirt of her dress and arranging it around her. "I guess pants might have been a better choice."

"The view's much better this way," he said with a wink as he climbed into the pilot's seat beside her. "You're right about the weather. Very little breeze and not many clouds." He made sure she was secure and then pulled his harness across his body, fastening it. "Are you nervous?"

"Not at all." She gave him a tight smile. "Any reason I should be petrified of falling to my death from this plane?" Her face blanched. "Please tell me you're not planning any aeronautical acrobatic stunts. If that's the case, I'll stand on the ground, content to watch, wave and blow you kisses, thank you very much. Soaring through the clouds without leaving the ground."

Sam brushed the back of his hand across her cheek. "No stunts today. Promise." Reaching for the instrument panel, he began the preparations. He needed to stay focused on getting the plane into the air and giving her the ride of a lifetime in his treasured plane. The innate tomboy in Sarah would love it. He couldn't wait to hear the delight in her voice and witness her joy when they lifted into the air for her first plane flight.

Wait a minute. He did a double take. Sarah wasn't wearing her engagement ring. He frowned. "Sarah, baby, where's your ring?"

"It kept slipping around on my finger, so I took it to the jeweler to be resized. I'm sorry. I didn't get a chance to tell you. Rest assured, the ring's fine, and I'll have it back in place in a few days."

He blew out a breath. "Have to say, I'm relieved. Okay, then, what do you say we see what Caty can do? Ready?"

"Sam, wait." Sarah put her hand on his arm.

He paused in his pre-flight check of the controls. "Second thoughts?" A sharp pang of disappointment shot through him. Maybe she wasn't as daring a girl as he'd thought.

"No, but I'd like to pray first."

"Of course." Exhaling a breath of relief, Sam took hold of her hand. "I usually pray before takeoff, as a matter of fact, but present company has me inordinately distracted."

"Why do you keep saying things like that?"

"Because you make me a little crazy, that's why."

A smile teased the corners of her lovely mouth. "Crazy is as crazy does."

"True enough, and that's why we're so good together." He lightly skimmed his finger over her ring finger, knowing the diamond wouldn't be back in place soon enough for him. "Let's pray."

In his prayer, Sam asked that he'd be able to maintain full control of the plane at all times. She squeezed his hand when he prayed to keep her nerves calm and that she might enjoy the flight.

"Here. You'll need to put these on," he said, after ending the prayer. Handing her a pair of goggles, he helped position them over her head and then made the necessary adjustments.

Sarah watched his every movement—every turn, twist and flip of the controls. Her eyes widened even more when the engine rumbled and the propeller started its rotation.

He strapped on his goggles and gave her a grin. "Away we go!" Sam relished the anticipation in her expression as he guided the plane down the runway. Her smile grew wider as the plane picked up speed and then slowly lifted into the air.

"Oh, my." Sarah tentatively peered over the edge of the plane a minute later and then squeezed her eyes shut.

"Everything okay? Take a few deep breaths, in and out."

She appeared to take his advice as her chest rose and fell. "I'm fine." Opening her eyes, her dark lashes fluttered on her flushed cheeks. "Thanks. That helped."

Sam wanted to kiss her as much as he'd ever wanted anything in his life, but he could kill them both if his attention was distracted. Maybe this plane ride wasn't the best idea. Then again, perhaps it was the best idea in the world. Her scarf flew about in the wind, blowing wildly, and she finally unwound it and tucked it beneath her. Sarah's silky blonde hair loosened with the force of the wind, tumbling about her shoulders and whipping around her face. After a few futile attempts to contain it, she laughed and gave up her efforts to smooth it down.

Sam pointed out the aerial view of a few Rockbridge landmarks—notably the bank, City Hall, Tucker's General Store, Hartmann's Hardware, and Perry's Diner. He'd told Myrna and Jimmy he planned on flying above them at about this time, and Sarah's squeal confirmed they stood on the ground, waving as they passed by. "Fletch and Sally are with them, too! And Eddie! And, look, it's"—she leaned a little too far over the edge for his liking—"Perry Sellers. Oh, this is so great!"

Sarah practically jumped up and down with her enthusiasm. In some ways, she was like a small child with her brown eyes bright, smiling and laughing, her voice filled with excitement as she pointed out more familiar sights. How he loved this woman.

"Look, Sam! I see my house!" He smiled after she squealed again. "And yours! Our families are all standing outside, too. Did you tell the entire town about this marvelous surprise?" Not waiting for his answer, Sarah leaned slightly forward again, peering over the edge of the plane. His gaze traveled over her for a few stolen moments before returning to the controls. If only she knew he'd had a difficult time keeping his hands to himself and his thoughts pure the last few times they'd been alone. The next few months until Christmas would prove a challenge, but he would wait.

"It's Thornton's Creek! Oh, it's so pretty from up here!" In that moment, a strong gust of wind hit the plane, forcing him back to reality. Sam fought to keep the plane steady. He needed to show Sarah he was a skilled pilot and that she could trust him.

"Whoa! Everything all right?"

"We're fine. Just stay in your seat. No worries," he said, keeping his voice steady and firm. If only he could rein in his thoughts as easily as his plane. Giving her a smile, he winked.

"Thank you for one of the most thrilling rides of my life." Sam helped her down from the plane a few minutes later and then drew her into his arms.

"You're welcome. I love your enthusiasm, as always."

She appeared somewhat contrite and flattened her palms against his chest. "Sam, I owe you an apology. I had no right to accuse you of being afraid. I'm sorry."

"No, you were right. Maybe afraid isn't the right word, but it was more like I didn't trust in my own abilities. My confidence was shaken, and I doubted myself. I can do all things—"

"Through Him who strengthens you."

Pulling him toward her, Sarah gave him the kind of kiss he'd been thinking of all day. The kind of kiss he'd be dreaming of for a long time. He loved that she took the initiative as often as he did.

"Marry me, Sarah."

She giggled. "You've already asked me that, silly man."

"I don't want the most beautiful girl in the world to forget it, either. I'm going to keep asking you right up until the day." He kissed her cheek. "We have a date to get hitched in Rockbridge Community Church at eleven in the morning on Christmas Eve."

"I don't think you need to be worried." She gave him another long kiss he'd never forget. "It's a date, Captain."

Chapter 44

On December 24, 1962, eight months after his return stateside, U.S. Air Force Captain Samuel Joseph Lewis married Sarah Jane Jordan in Rockbridge Community Church. Pastor McDonald performed the ceremony. Tess and Debbie served as Sarah's attendants, and Charlie and his father stood with Sam. At Sarah's request, Sam wore his Air Force dress uniform. Sarah wore a simple, white silk organza, off-the-shoulder, scooped neck gown with a short veil edged in Belgian lace, and she carried a bouquet of red, white and pink roses.

After a lunch and reception at Quentin's with their close friends and family, Sam and Sarah drove out of Rockbridge—tin cans tied to the bumper and *Austin or Bust—Newlyweds on Board* written on the back window of Volvo.

~~♥~~

After entering The Driskill Hotel a couple of hours later, Sarah twirled in a slow circle. "This is so beautiful!"

Sam moved his arm around her waist and pulled her close. "I've never stayed overnight, but I had a meeting here in the hotel a few years ago, before I went overseas. The plaque on the wall outside said it was built in the 1880s by a cattle baron."

"That's right, Mr. Lewis." A bellman pulled a cart behind them with their bags. "Colonel Jesse Driskill. The hotel has a rich history."

Pride infused the older man's voice.

Sarah stared in wonder at the magnificent, lavishly decorated Christmas tree. Garlands of holiday greenery adorned with red bows draped the elegant grand staircase, and tiny white lights twinkled from the mezzanine balcony and at various points around the perimeter of the massive lobby in the historic downtown building.

A woman played "O Holy Night" on a harp in one corner as Sarah's steps echoed on the beautiful inlaid marble and tile floor. Her gaze traveled upward to a colorful, stained-glass light fixture, quite possibly a Tiffany, hanging from the ceiling near the Christmas tree.

Sam took her hand as they walked together toward the front desk. As the bellman directed them to the bank of elevators a few minutes later, Sarah noticed a group of children lining up on the staircase.

"Are the children going to sing now?" she asked the bellman.

"Yes, Mrs. Lewis. We can wait, if you'd like to hear them."

"I'd like that." *Mrs. Lewis.* She loved the name, loved the man more.

Sam stepped behind her, wrapping her in his arms. "You didn't ask your husband if he could wait," he whispered, his voice teasing as he pressed his warm lips to her temple.

Turning her head and lifting her chin, Sarah met his waiting lips in a kiss. "Not long, my love. Humor me, please."

"Not a problem, but if they sing more than three songs, I'm carrying you upstairs myself. All five flights." Sam chuckled, but then he quieted as the children began to sing "Silent Night."

Allowing the words of the old hymn to flow over her, Sarah closed her eyes and breathed a prayer of thanks. *Thank you, Lord Jesus. For coming to earth as a tiny baby, for living as a man and walking among us, for dying on the cross to save us from our sins, and for life eternal.*

"Amen," Sam said. Scary how often the man could read her mind. In this case, however, it was more than nice. He tightened his hold on her, and Sarah swayed in his arms as they listened to the sweet voices of the youngsters.

~~♥~~

The Next Morning
The Yellow Rose Suite, The Driskill Hotel

After enjoying a sumptuous breakfast in the dining alcove of their fifth floor honeymoon suite, Sam carried his wife back toward the bedroom. This morning, his gaze barely registered the marble entryway, floor-to-ceiling windows, crown moldings, hardwood floors, and inviting décor in rich shades of gold, ivory, brown and yellow. Sarah had taken an excruciating amount of time yesterday, running around and checking out all the antique furniture, tapestries, and the fanciest bathroom he'd ever seen.

He'd enjoyed her enthusiasm, especially when she'd finally moved into the bedroom with the huge poster bed and discovered a single, long-stemmed yellow rose resting on the overstuffed pillows. Dropping into a chair, Sam listened with an amused smile to her chatter, partly due to nerves, he suspected. When she finally seemed to run out of things to say, he'd risen to his feet and pulled her into his arms. The things they'd whispered, the things they'd shared during the rest of the night, he'd treasure in his heart for the rest of his life.

God, you are so good to me. Thank you for the gift of this woman.

Sarah sighed as he lowered her onto the bed. "I'm going to hold you to the promise that I'll finish nursing school, no matter what comes. And lots of foot massages."

"I want that for you, too, and I always keep my promises. I have a Christmas gift for you." She watched as he walked to his suitcase and pulled out a festively wrapped, square package. Crawling onto the bed beside her, Sam held it out to her. "For my beautiful wife."

Her pleasure of seeing the wrapped gift, not knowing what the box held, made Sam smile. He couldn't wait to see her reaction. "Go ahead. Open it."

"Let me open the card first." Carefully sliding her finger along the edge of the envelope, Sarah lifted the flap and pulled it out. She scanned the printed sentiment and then gave him a quick kiss. "Thank you."

Within seconds, Sarah stared at the book in her hands with obvious astonishment. "Sam, is this what I think it is?" Moving one hand over her heart, her gorgeous brown eyes were wide as she stared at him.

"If you think it's a first edition of *To Kill A Mockingbird*, signed by Harper Lee, you're right. The movie's out now, by the way, and I'm going to take you this week. I hear it's pretty good, and from all reports, Gregory Peck does a great job in the role of Atticus."

"I can hardly wait." Sarah reverently thumbed through the book, and then clasped it to her chest. "I'll treasure this gift always, especially because it means so much in terms of our own story." She picked up the elaborate bookmark he'd nestled inside the book. "For my special Tomboy. Love, Captain Lewis."

A tear slipped down Sarah's cheek. "This is the most beautiful gift anyone's ever given me. Thank you. That seems so inadequate, and I feel horrible that I don't even have a gift for you. Forgive me. I promise I'll make it up to you. We can pick out something in the next few days."

Sam absorbed the moisture from her tear with his thumb. "Sarah, don't you know? You've already given me the most precious gift in the world."

"I have?"

"Yes," he said, running his finger down the length of her cheek. "You."

Putting the book on the bedside table, he cradled her close and enjoyed the benefits afforded a married man as he caressed his wife and murmured how beautiful she was. Nuzzling her, he realized the scruff from his morning beard must be rough on her tender skin. "Shall I go shave? Brush my teeth?"

"Later." Smiling, Sarah loosened her robe and then opened her arms to him. "Welcome home, Captain Lewis."

Resting in one another's arms later in the morning, Sam felt her smile, heard her satisfied sigh. "What are you thinking?"

"About our children."

"Tell me."

"Don't ask me why, but I believe our firstborn will be a son. He'll be tall and strong, a man of God, just like his handsome daddy."

"Lord, help him." Sam chuckled and nestled her closer, loving her warmth, her softness.

"Oh, He will. Maybe we'll have more than one son, and at least one daughter." Tracing her finger in a light, circular pattern on his chest, Sarah leaned her head on his shoulder.

"How many children are we talking?" He buried his lips in her sweet-scented hair.

"At least one of each or whatever the Lord decides is best for us." She propped herself on one elbow. "We're going to have a great life together. You can't begin to know how much I love you."

"I have a pretty good idea." He'd found his home in this woman's arms. Drawing her to him, Sam lowered his lips to hers. "Thank you for the honor of loving you, Sarah."

Epilogue

~~♥~~

April 24, 1966

Sarah held her newborn son in her arms, her heart close to overflowing. After laboring for close to twelve hours, she kissed her firstborn's soft, smooth cheek and marveled over his handsome features, so like his father's.

Lord, you are so gracious to us. Thank you. From the bottom of my heart, thank you.

"Behold, children are a gift of the Lord," she whispered. "The fruit of the womb is a reward, like the arrows in the hand of a warrior, so are the children of one's youth. How blessed is the man whose quiver is full of them; they will not be ashamed when they speak with their enemies in the gate." In a world full of unrest—President Kennedy had been assassinated the year after she and Sam married, and now ground troops were being sent to fight the war in Vietnam—Sarah held her son close, cherishing him as a precious promise from a loving heavenly Father.

Her handsome husband walked into the room with a bright smile. "I just talked with Tess. They're planning to come next weekend."

Sarah laughed quietly. "I'm sure Charlie would like Tess to catch the baby bug while she's here."

"Give them time. They've only been married a year." Sam carefully lowered himself to the bed beside her in the Houston hospital where she'd given birth a few hours before. A sister hospital to the one where she'd worked since finishing her nursing degree earlier than expected.

"We have more important things to discuss." When Sam gazed at his son, love filled Sarah's soul for both of them. "What shall we name this little guy?"

"No question in my mind," Sarah said, caressing the side of Sam's jaw with one hand. He looked tired, but it was the best kind of tired. "Samuel Joseph Lewis, *Jr.*"

Slipping off the bed, Sam held out his arms. "May I?"

"Time to go see your daddy." Sarah kissed the baby's head and transferred the sleeping child to him. Sam cradled the child's head with one large hand. Her husband looked so at home and natural in his new role as papa.

"You're going to be a great father, my love."

"Because he'll have the best mother in the world in you, sweet Sarah. Thank you for this gift. I'm sorry the labor was so long for you, baby, but you did great. I'm in awe." Being mindful of his son, Sam planted a kiss on her forehead.

"Already forgotten," Sarah said. Not really, but she'd recover soon enough. Their son was robust and healthy—uncommonly long and with a terrific head of thick, dark hair—and that's all that mattered.

"I'm glad I didn't faint this time. I hope we can do this again a few more times in the future." Catching her look, Sam chuckled. "Not anytime soon."

Sarah shook her head with an amused smile. Leave it to a man to discuss the next child mere hours after delivery. "For now, let's enjoy this time with the three of us. Get used to being parents."

"Agreed. I look forward to the journey." Sam inspected his son's fingers and toes—and everything else—for at least the tenth time.

"He's real, I assure you." She watched as Sam traced his finger over the baby's cheek. "I hope he has your blue eyes and those irresistible smile lines. A dash of your sense of humor, your compassion, and strong faith."

"What a miracle he is." Holding the baby close, Sam smoothed his hand over his son's dark head. His expression was filled with wonder, his sigh full of contentment. "What a handsome boy you are." With a quiet chuckle, he kissed the top of his namesake's head.

"Sam," he said, his gaze drinking in the sight of his child, "I promise to raise you in the grace and love of our heavenly Father. It's my prayer you'll grow to love the Lord as much as your mother and I do, and that one day you'll raise your own family of children who love the Lord to carry on the Lewis legacy of faith. Train up a child in the way he should go, and even when he is old he will not depart from it."

Already missing her son, Sarah reached for him.

"Time to go back to your mama now." With a gentle smile, Sam lowered the baby into her arms.

"Faith, family and love." Opening the top of her hospital gown, Sarah prepared to nurse her son. "We'll be just fine."

Sam sank onto the bed beside her. "I hope those things will define the Lewis family legacy."

"Amen," Sarah echoed.

After a few moments, the baby began to nurse. Sarah laced the fingers of her free hand with Sam's hand. "This is the anniversary of the day you came back home to Rockbridge."

"God's providence." Sam's smile lines charmed her all over again, the same as they had from the moment she first laid eyes on him, the same as they always would.

"I'm so thankful you came home, Captain Lewis," Sarah whispered.

"For a lifetime, Mrs. Lewis."

THE END
~~♥~~

Awakening
The Lewis Legacy Series, Book 1

A God-fearing man. A God-seeking woman. For Sam Lewis and Lexa Clarke, it proves a combustible combination.

Lexa Clarke signs up for a TeamWork Missions summer assignment expecting adventure in a far-off, exotic country. Instead, she's sent to sweltering San Antonio to help rebuild homes destroyed by sudden flooding. She survives the four-hour bus trip from Houston, dust in the lungs, a flat tire, a tool-throwing incident and a spitting goat—not to mention an inquisition from a distractingly handsome cowboy—all before reaching the work camp.

TeamWork director Sam Lewis isn't sure what to think of his newest volunteer. She's feisty, witty, and incredibly pretty, but looks more prepared to board a cruise ship than build houses. Burned by a past betrayal, he's got a job to do, a reputation to uphold. Sam can't afford to be distracted by a woman who attracts animals, defies his rules, finds trouble at every turn and questions God's purpose. But when she tumbles from the top beam of one of the houses into his arms, Sam suspects his life will never be the same. During their weeks together in the TeamWork camp, Sam and Lexa learn the power of forgiveness and healing.

Enduring a chain of incidents which challenge their faith, trust and growing relationship, they look to the Lord for guidance as together they discover a love greater than either could ever imagine. At the end of the eight-week work camp, Sam is committed to a year-long, dangerous overseas mission for TeamWork. Can Lexa trust the Lord enough to let him go? Will Sam safely return and keep his promise to meet her at the Alamo? You'll keep turning the pages of this sweeping romantic adventure.

With great characters, plenty of humor, enough emotion to make you shed a tear or two, and an ending that'll have you cheering, Awakening will leave you breathless. Hold on tight. The adventures of Lewis and Clarke have only just begun!

Second Time Around
The Lewis Legacy Series, Book 2

Marc Thompson is on top of the world—a newlywed with a beautiful wife, the owner of a thriving Boston sports advertising agency, and a century-old home they're renovating in the suburbs. Then the unthinkable happens. Two months after the wedding, Marc sits in a hospital emergency waiting room after Natalie suffers a horrible fall. One shock follows another. Not only does his wife remember nothing of their life together, but now he has a personal timeline to reconnect with her—seven months.

Marc's gold wedding band mocks him, a glaring reminder of a promise broken by a rotting basement stair and his own negligence. His renowned psychologist advises him to court his wife again—a daunting task the first time around. Then Marc's pastor suggests he call Sam and Lexa Lewis of TeamWork Missions, a ministry dear to Natalie's heart. Determined to help her reclaim her life, the young groom makes great strides until a ghost from the past surfaces, opening fresh wounds and threatening to destroy it all.

With Natalie's trust shattered and Marc's faith wavering, they head to Milestone Ranch outside Helena, Montana, with TeamWork for a two-week work camp. But instead of romancing his wife in the freezing November temperatures with warm fires and shared sweet moments, he's out in the cold and back at square one. Even if Natalie recovers her lost memories, will she forgive him? If not, can Marc come to terms with his deepest fear—the failure of his marriage?

You'll root for Marc and Natalie as they fight against the odds and discover that surrendering all at the throne of grace doesn't mean failure. It's simply called faith. And it might be the only way to finding their way back to one another...the second time around.

Twin Hearts
The Lewis Legacy Series, Book 3

Joshua Grant is a man redeemed. He's worked hard to put the past behind him. A mergers and acquisitions attorney in a prestigious Baton Rouge law firm, he pours his energies into his career, hurricane relief efforts, and numerous civic and charitable causes. A near-fatal event in the life of a fellow TeamWork Missions volunteer prompts him to make some apologies, starting with his friend and mentor, Sam Lewis, Domestic Missions Director for TeamWork in Houston. It's been more than four years since the fateful events in San Antonio when Sam threw him out of the missions camp, and he's still haunted by the bittersweet memory of his final meeting with another TeamWork volunteer. When he also seeks her forgiveness, Josh gets the shock of his life. Could turning his deepest sin into his greatest blessing be God's answer for his hurting heart?

Rebekah Grant, Josh's twin sister, is torn between two men. Adam, a dashing British aristocrat, offers her a world of exotic travel, socializing with royalty, fabulous couture and the life of leisure. Then there's sweet Kevin, the strong, intelligent, faithful TeamWork member. Will the shy Louisiana lumber man ever take the step of faith to move their relationship to the next level? What Kevin lacks in terms of Adam's style and panache, he more than makes up for with heart-stirring kisses and soul-searching conversation. When Rebekah suspects Adam is planning to propose a second time, she knows it's time to make her decision. Juggling both suitors is wrong for so many reasons, but what's a girl to do if she wants to marry and have children in her lifetime?

When family tragedy strikes, Josh and Rebekah learn the true meaning and value of love, loyalty and what's most important in life. Leaning on the encouragement and support from Sam and Lexa

Lewis and their TeamWork friends, both twins look to the Lord for His divine guidance. It's up to them to stake their claim on love before it slips beyond their reach, which means it's also time for a road trip from Louisiana to the peace to be found in seeking and finding the sweetest desires of the heart.

Daydreams
The Lewis Legacy Series, Book 4

It's early December 2002, and Amy Jacobsen is living the dream: a job she loves with a trendy New York City magazine, a Manhattan walk-up inherited from her grandfather, and a busy social life *without* the unwanted complication of a steady boyfriend. During dinner one evening with her Wall Street financier brother, Mitch, she spies Landon Warnick at the next table. He's one of the most influential, successful and youngest magazine publishers in the country—not to mention one of New York's most eligible bachelors.

After Mitch wrangles a meeting between the two, Landon wastes little time asking her to dinner. Usually wary of smooth men and romantic entanglements, Amy questions her sanity when they share a cozy carriage ride in Central Park and she comes *this* close to kissing him. Is it the joy and wonder of the Christmas season that's put stars in her eyes or the enigmatic, intelligent, challenging and incredibly handsome man?

The following weekend, she travels to Louisiana to be a bridesmaid in a wedding and a reunion with Sam and Lexa Lewis and some of her dearest friends and fellow volunteers in TeamWork Missions. Headed down the aisle at the wedding, Amy's steps falter. Standing at the front is a groomsman who flew into town only an hour before . . . She does a double take. What's Landon Warnick doing in *her* world, with *her* friends? Perhaps more important, why does he suddenly have a Texas drawl and a crescent-shaped scar on his forehead? Sharing a romantic dance at the wedding reception, she casts aside her better judgment and kisses him. She's lost her mind, and her heart might not be far behind, it seems.

Let the adventure begin! Is the Lord showing her the "right" man for her heart or is Amy in *way* over her head?

Moonbeams
The Lewis Legacy Series, Book 5

Mitch Jacobsen's younger sister, Amy Warnick, has tried to pair him off with her fellow TeamWork Missions volunteer, Cassie, for over a year. Why can't Amy understand that the harder she pushes, the faster he'll run? Dating a woman who lives 1,600 miles away—no matter how gorgeous and compassionate—isn't on his radar.

Cassandra Thorenson wants nothing to do with a man who works with money and contributes to corporate greed. Dating a Wall Street broker—no matter how handsome and funny—is the last thing she needs.

Surely, the Almighty must have a better plan.

When these two meet during a TeamWork mini-reunion in Houston over Valentine's Day weekend, Mitch and Cassie discover they have a lot more in common than they'd ever imagined. Their plan to resist one another quickly derails and then an unexpected event sends them all reeling.

Let the sparks and the tempers fly!

About the Author

~~♥~~

In addition to *Prelude*, JoAnn Durgin is the author of the contemporary Christian romance series, The Lewis Legacy Series: *Awakening, Second Time Around, Twin Hearts, Daydreams* and *Moonbeams*. Her other books include *Catching Serenity, Echoes of Edinburgh*, and the Starlight Christmas Series: *Meet Me Under the Mistletoe, Starlight, Star Bright* and *Sleigh Ride Together with You.*

A former paralegal, JoAnn is now pursuing her passion and is a full-time author. After living all over the country, she lives with her family in her native southern Indiana.

JoAnn loves to hear from her readers! Feel free to contact her:

Website: www.joanndurgin.com

Facebook: www.facebook.com/authorjoanndurgin